THE STARS BETWEEN US

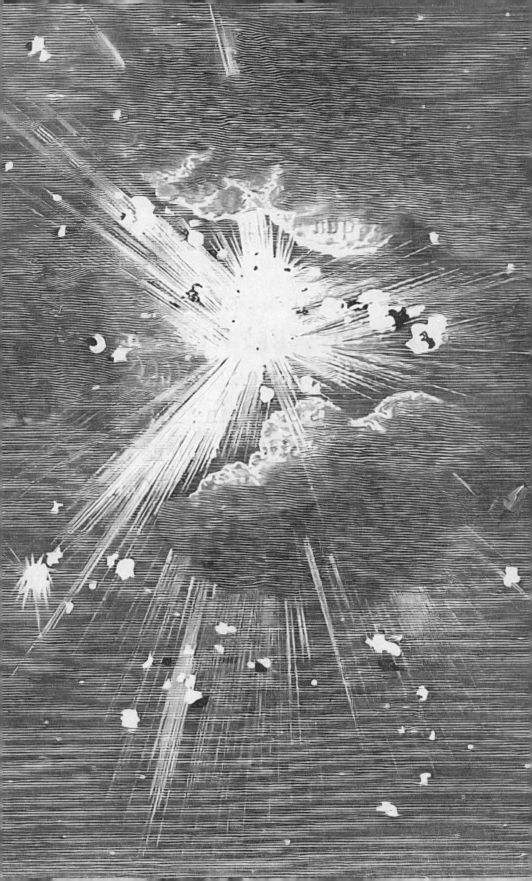

THE STARS BETWEEN US

CRISTIN TERRILL

WEDNESDAY BOOKS
NEW YORK

First published in the United States by Wednesday Books, an imprint of St. Martin's Publishing Group

THE STARS BETWEEN US. Copyright © 2022 by Cristin Terrill. All rights reserved. Printed in the United States of America. For information, address St. Martin's Publishing Group, 120 Broadway, New York, NY 10271.

www.wednesdaybooks.com

Library of Congress Cataloging-in-Publication Data

Names: Terrill, Cristin, author.
Title: The stars between us / Cristin Terrill.
Description: First edition. | New York : Wednesday Books, 2022. | Audience: Ages 14–18.
Identifiers: LCCN 2022005507 | ISBN 9781250783769 (hardcover) | ISBN 9781250783776 (ebook)
Subjects: CYAC: Inheritance and succession—Fiction. | Science fiction. | LCGFT: Science fiction. | Romance fiction.
Classification: LCC PZ7.T27532 St 2022 | DDC [Fic]—dc23
LC record available at https://lccn.loc.gov/2022005507

Our books may be purchased in bulk for promotional, educational, or business use. Please contact your local bookseller or the Macmillan Corporate and Premium Sales Department at 1-800-221-7945, extension 5442, or by email at MacmillanSpecialMarkets@macmillan.com.

First Edition: 2022

10 9 8 7 6 5 4 3 2 1

Always for my mama

THE STARS BETWEEN US

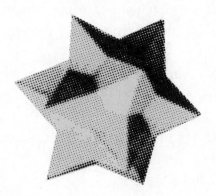

THIS IS IT. The words echoed in his head with every step he took. *This is it. This is it.*

The wind still had a bitter bite to it, but he was sweating as he weaved his way through the bundled-up pedestrians around him. He tugged his high collar away from his neck, letting the cold air move across his throat to get some relief, but it did nothing to bank the fire inside of him.

He touched the small gray box inside his pocket, outlining with the tip of his finger the plastecene safety cover that protected the tiny black button in the center. It seemed to emanate its own heat, like it contained blood pulsing through its veins instead of just a collection of lifeless circuits and wires. Maybe that was what was making him so hot.

As soon as he was inside, door locked behind him, he grabbed the thing out of his pocket and placed it—gingerly—on the table. Minutes passed as he did nothing but stare at it. For something he had sought for so long and had spent every bit to his name to acquire, it was smaller and simpler than he'd expected. Such a flimsy object shouldn't have the ability to alter the course of so many lives.

For months he'd been maneuvering the pieces into place, laying the groundwork. It had been surprisingly easy. Everyone underestimated what he was capable of, so they never suspected he was up to anything, and it had all felt so . . . impermanent. He could always change his mind, let his scheme fall by the wayside, and no one would be the wiser.

But that time was over. Now he had to make a decision he wouldn't be able to unmake.

This is it.

He could smash the little gray box to pieces and let all his plans go swirling down the drain.

Or he could push the button.

CHAPTER ONE

THE BARE BULB ABOVE the sink spluttered and died, and Vika swore, throwing the shirt she was washing into the basin with a heavy thwack. She glanced up at the small window near the ceiling of the building's communal washroom and saw a faint orange glow, so at least the sun hadn't gone down completely yet. But the flow from the faucet slowed to a trickle and then quit altogether, cause no power meant no pump getting water up to the third floor. The juice wasn't supposed to go down for two more hours, but then *supposed to* didn't mean much on this sorry, backwater excuse for a planet.

Course she wasn't unprepared for it. She'd learned from experience to always keep a little bucket in the sink when washing to hold on to some water just in case something went wrong, and something near always did. The water in her bucket was dingy and frothed with soap, but it would do to rinse the shirt she'd been laundering. The rest of the clothes would just have to wait til later.

"About time, duchess," Mrs. Carson said as she exited the washroom. Vika could barely make out the sour old cow in the dimness of the hallway—lit as it was with just the one weak battery light—but she recognized the voice well enough that she didn't need to see Carson's scowl and sloppily buttoned housecoat to know it was her.

"Juice is out," Vika said. The woman cursed with great creativity, and Vika smiled. Ruining Carson's day took some of the sting out of the early outage, at least.

She took the stairs down to the first floor slow and careful. She'd fallen down that poky staircase more than once, and she wasn't about to do it today, not with an armful of clothes she'd spent so long cleaning. The smell of mildew and stale dakha leaf was thick round her, and she skipped the step she knew sagged.

She nudged the door to her flat open with one hip and found that someone had already lit a couple of candles and her family's stinking, smoking gas lamp. Her mum looked up from the cooking and frowned at her.

"You're going to be late," she said, the faint light emphasizing the deep wrinkles in her forehead.

"I know," Vika replied.

"You need a shower."

"I know that, too, Mum, but what would you have me do about it now?"

Her mum muttered something and turned back to the stove. At the other end of the room, Vika's sister, Lavinia, was sprawled out across the bed they shared, her face lit by the blue glow of the screen she held inches from her nose. Once upon a time they'd each had their own bedrooms, and neither of them had had to sleep on a pullout in the middle of the fecking sitting room, but that had been a long time ago. Lavinia was curled under the quilt, cozy as a snail in its shell, watching something on the ancient feed screen they'd bartered for at the little black market behind the Sullivan Street food depot years ago. Lavinia had never been good about pacing herself with the battery, so it was attached to the extension cord that snaked across the room and out the cracked window. There it joined dozens of other cords, like delicate tentacles rippling out from their beast of a building, running down the back alley and into a government transformer someone in the neighborhood had hacked. It was working, for now. When too many people plugged in, it would become as useless as the dead plugs inside, and eventually the mercs would discover them siphoning juice and shut it down. But in the meantime, a steady stream of frigid air came in the window along with the less steady supply of power, and Vika shivered.

"That rich old toser died," Lavinia said as she watched the newsfeed. "Chapin. They're saying he was worth *billions*. Can you even imagine being that rich?"

Vika could hardly care less about some dead Ploutosian fat cat. "You know, you could help Mum with dinner. Or at least let her plug in a light instead of watching your feeds."

Lavinia shrugged. "Mum said she doesn't mind."

"There aren't enough amps in that little line to power anything useful anyway," her mum said, cause why fix a problem now when she could complain about it later.

Vika dropped the basket of washing beside the bed with a bang.

"These better be hung when I get back," she told Lavinia, shucking her shirt and reaching for one of the clean ones pinned to the line strung across the window. There hadn't been much resembling sun for days, so the shirt was clammy and cold where it clung to her skin.

Lavinia didn't look up. "I been working in the office for Da all day."

Vika grabbed her coat off its hook by the door, patting the pockets to check for her sting spray and crank light. "And I'm gonna be working at Nicky's all night, so you'll do your share."

"You an't in charge of me."

"Maybe not, but I'm the one can make your life a living misery if you cross me," Vika said, while across the room their mum said, "Don't say *an't*."

Lavinia rolled her eyes at one or both of them, but Vika didn't have time to get into it with her, so she just kicked the washing basket closer to her sister and left.

Outside it was near dark, the fading light from the setting sun barely penetrating the thick haze—made of natural atmosphere but worsened by coltane pollution—that clung to the entire planet like a skin. There were orange emergency lights all up and down the street that were supposed to stay on even when the juice went out, but, as usual, *supposed to* didn't mean much on Philomenus. All but one had gone dark, either cause someone had ganked the battery or cause the bulb was dead. Luckily there was just enough daylight left for Vika to pick her way over the trash, ice patches, and tangle of extension cords that choked the street as she made her way to work.

Nicky's glowed bright from four blocks away, a beacon through the grayness. It was one of the few places in the THs with its own generator and enough bits coming in the door to keep it fueled. No one dared try to gank juice from Nicky's lest they incur the wrath of the whole neighborhood, not to mention the man himself.

The barracks north of town had been bombed by PLF guerrillas again a few days ago, so there were even more mercs on the street than usual, looking like giant ants in their black uniforms and helmets as they patrolled the pavement. Two of them stopped Vika outside of the bar to search her bag, but she didn't have anything worth stealing, so they let her go on in.

The place was crammed with bodies, stinking of sweat and spilled liquor, the air so humid after being recycled through a hundred pairs of lungs that Vika felt like she was swimming through it. She had to push and elbow her way to the bar, where Stella was pouring with one hand and collecting bits with another. Stella frowned when she spotted her.

"Move!" she barked, and the masses parted to let Vika through. When someone behind the bar spoke, everyone listened, else they didn't drink.

"You're late, Vika," Stella said, although when she said Vika's name, it sounded more like "idiot."

"Juice went out early," Vika replied.

Stella snorted and glanced up at the teeming bar. Dark nights were always their busiest. "Don't I know it."

Vika went to work, pouring glasses of grock and uzso, doing battle with the ancient bit machine, cleaning up after sloppy drunkards. There was just one good thing about a busy night at Nicky's, and it was that it left her with less time to think about how much she hated this fecking job. She knew she was lucky to have it, but she hated every dirty, coarse, lewd patron and every indignity that came with catering to them, like they were somehow better than her just cause she was behind the bar and they were in front of it. She hated being leered at and felt up and spoken down to. Really, the only thing she hated more than working at Nicky's was the memory of not being able to buy enough food to keep her belly quiet, and still some days she'd rather go to sleep hungry.

Tonight was shaping up to be one of those.

"You molly-loving bastard!" a barrel-chested man yelled, slamming his mug to the tabletop as he clambered unsteadily to his feet. "I'll kill you!"

"Shut your fool mouth and sit down, Janus," his friend replied. "You're drunk."

Beside the two arguing men sat one of their regulars, Knox Vega, at his usual spot at the bar, practically folded over his near-empty glass of grock. A blond girl Vika vaguely recognized was trying to wrestle him off the barstool, and he was clinging on so tight his fingers had gone white.

"Come on!" she said. "We're going home."

"An't going nowhere," Knox slurred.

"Yes you fecking well are!" the girl said, heaving him off the stool. Knox's grip failed and he went tumbling against her, which sent her crashing into the back of the barrel-chested man.

"Watch yourself!" he bellowed.

"Leave her alone, Janus," his friend said. "It was an accident."

Janus leapt at his friend, hands outstretched to wrap round his neck, and a cry went up throughout the bar as the fight broke out.

Stella turned to Vika. "It's your turn."

Vika sighed, grabbed the sting spray from her coat, and fought her way through the crowd. Lord she wished she was rich, some fancy Ploutosian lady with the world at her feet, spending her nights drinking champagne with sophisticated people, instead of a barmaid on a crumbling planet breaking up drunken brawls and struggling to keep her head above water.

Knox and the girl had left in a hurry, but the two fighting men were now rolling round on the floor, sweat and punches flying. As she reached them, one knocked into a table filled with glasses and sent it crashing down beside them. They rolled in the glass and booze, and blood joined the mixture. Bystanders whooped and hollered. The mercs outside peered in through the windows but only chuckled at the sight.

"Hey!" Vika yelled, kicking at one of the men's meaty ribs. She knew from experience that she was too young and small to just snarl orders the way Stella did and expect people to listen. "Take it outside!" What a mess this was going to be to clean up. She looked for Jay, the bar's hired muscle, but couldn't see him. He was probably out back grabbing a sneaky smoke. She clicked the safety latch off her sting spray. "Stop!"

When they ignored her, she fogged them with a cloud of the stuff. The crowd backed away, and the fighters broke apart, groaning and grabbing their eyes and noses.

"Now clear out," she said. "Free round to whoever drops them on the pavement."

The two men were carried off and Vika surveyed the damage. Blood and grock and glass everywhere. She dropped to her knees, pushed a dark curl from her eyes, and began mopping up the mess with a towel, hating every second of her miserable life.

Then, over the noise of the band in the corner and the general din of the bar, she thought she heard someone calling her name. She stood and peered at Stella through the sea of heads, but the woman wasn't paying her any mind.

"Vika!" someone said again, the word barely audible over the commotion. Vika hopped, trying to get a clear view over the men who towered round her, and then climbed onto a chair. She spotted a familiar dark-haired figure fighting through the crowd toward the bar.

"Lavinia?" she called.

Lavinia saw her and changed course, like a fish swimming upstream, shoving her way toward her. "Mum and Da says you got to come home right now!" she said.

Vika had never seen her sister so impatient about anything but her supper, but she replied, "Can't. We're short staffed."

"Never mind about that. There's some fecking *toser* in the flat"— Lavinia spat the word as though it tasted bad—"and Da says you got to come now. Hurry up!"

Vika's heart lurched painfully in her chest. She could only think of one reason any toser would want to see her.

She ducked behind the bar, grabbing her coat and fumbling to button it with suddenly numb fingers. Nicky wouldn't fire her for leaving just this once. Her da had given him a good position at the mine when he was down on his luck, which was how Vika had landed the coveted job behind the bar in the first place. People on this planet had nothing, so they made sure to pay back the few things that were handed to them. Nicky would remember that.

Stella stared at her in disbelief as she gathered her things. "What in the hell do you think—"

"I gotta go," she said. "Emergency at home."

"You an't leaving me right now, Vika, or I swear—"

"Sorry!"

Stella yelled after her, but Vika couldn't stop. The last time she'd seen a toser here on this planet, it had been the stuffy old man from across the stream who used to come and tutor her and Lavinia. She hadn't liked it—Mr. Bohr always leaned in too close and smelled of medicine and mothballs—but her mum and da had made the girls take his lessons cause it was good for them and, mostly, cause it was free. Having a real Ploutosian tutor teach them was ten times better than sending them to the overcrowded holding pen masquerading as a neighborhood school. With someone actually teaching her,

Vika had discovered she had a natural ability with maths and numbers, while Lavinia excelled at languages. Not that it really mattered
since neither of them was destined for any kind of higher education. But thanks to the tutor, both girls were able to pass their final
exams and go straight to working several cycles earlier than their
peers. That had made all the difference for the family; there had
been many hungry nights before Vika's paycheck from Nicky's began rolling in.

They'd never known the name of the man who paid the small
fortune it must have cost for the tutor to come every week. Mr. Bohr
was just another part of the big mystery of Vika's life. Ever since that
particular day when an old man had bought her a freeze cream as
a girl, things like this had been happening to her, odd gifts and de-
mands she didn't understand emanating from the nameless benefactor she didn't know. The strangeness had dropped off in the last
few years, and she had begun to think it was gone forever, just an
odd facet of her young life she'd never understand. But a toser coming to see her now with no warning could only mean one thing.

The mystery of Vika's life was rearing its head once again.

CHAPTER TWO

VIKA AND LAVINIA STEPPED out of Nicky's, where it was bright and warm, and into the dark, cold street. The Philomeni Liberation Front had brought out one of their carts and parked it on the corner, distributing cups of coffee and extra gloves and scarves to the rough sleepers who had gathered round to snatch a bit of warmth before they found a place to bed down for the night. The wind was bitter and Vika couldn't see a hand in front of her face, so she grabbed the crank light from her pocket and turned the gear that powered the little bulb inside. The beam it generated was weak, but it was enough to get them home.

Town Housing 76 looked identical to every building round it, just another concrete box thrown up to house the people who came here to work in the coltane mines. The buildings weren't supposed to be permanent, just a way station to hold families while proper housing was built, which was why they were so cramped and falling down now. They were once called *Temporary* Housing, but the folks in charge had just hoped everyone would forget that part when the coltane market cratered and they scrapped the plans for those proper houses they'd promised. Course, no one had.

Vika followed Lavinia to their flat in the back corner of the first floor. A ground-level flat was one of the perks of their da's job managing the building. The atmo-haze got thicker the higher up you went; by the sixth floor, you could barely see out the windows cause the fog was so thick. Not that there was anything much to see.

"She's here," Lavinia said as she opened their front door.

"Yeah, what's—" Vika stopped short. It wasn't a mothballed old man waiting in their tiny sitting room. The toser in question was young, not many cycles older than she was, with blue eyes so bright they were near shocking against his dark hair and sandy skin. Even if Lavinia hadn't told her, she'd have known the second she set her sights on him that he wasn't from Philomenus. His perfectly pressed suit and tailored shirt—pale blue, and she wondered if he chose that color cause he knew what it did to his eyes—instantly marked him as someone from the planet across the stream.

"Good evening," he said, rising from his chair beside her da and giving her a little bow from the waist, the way she'd seen men do on the Ploutosian drama feeds Lavinia liked to watch. "You must be Viktoria."

"That's her," Lavinia said, throwing herself down onto the sofa. Thank the heavens she'd folded their bed away after Vika had left for work. Just the idea of this elegant young man seeing the grubby, thin mattress she shared with her sister—which took up near half of the room—turned her stomach sour. "The queen in the flesh."

Vika ignored her. "Yes, I'm Viktoria."

"Dearest, come in." Her mum was speaking in her best approximation of a proper voice and wheeling her arms like it would draw Vika in faster. "Take off your coat, and have a seat."

Vika shrugged out of her coat, more self-conscious than ever of the faded blouse with the fraying hem she hadn't got round to patching underneath, not to mention the fact that she needed a shower. She was unusually pretty for a Philomeni girl—she knew it and didn't care if it made her sound conceited to say so, cause it was only the truth—but he was unusually handsome *and* from Ploutos. He must spend all his time with rich girls who wore fine clothes and cosmetics and had never had a worry more serious than what party to attend that night; probably she looked to him the way the stray dogs who scavenged the streets late at night looked to her.

But when she glanced at him over her shoulder as she was hanging her coat, there seemed to be a shy little smile lurking round the corner of his mouth, so maybe she didn't look *too* bad.

Vika's mum was gesticulating at the empty seat at their small dining table. Her parents had served tea to the stranger on their good dishes, one of the only possessions left from their old lives, which her mum kept wrapped up in scraps of towel and hidden in a box under her bed. Vika hadn't seen those delicate teacups with their small yellow flowers in years.

"What's going on?" she asked, taking the seat beside her da. He wasn't quite the man he used to be, but he was still the nearest thing she had to a rock in her life. Her mum and Lavinia loved her, she knew, cause biology didn't really give them a choice, but she was pretty sure her da was the only one who actually liked her at all.

He patted her knee. "Darling, this is Mister, um . . ."

"Sheratan," the young man said, saving her da from his poor memory. "Archer Sheratan. I'm very pleased to make your acquaintance, Miss Hale. I do sincerely apologize if my sudden arrival has caused you any inconvenience."

It was that refined Ploutosian way of speaking, never settling for one word when ten would do. "Pleased to meet you," she echoed.

He drew a card out of his briefcase and handed it to her. *Archer Sheratan, Associate Solicitor, Lassiter and Lyons.* It had been some time since she'd seen the name Lassiter and Lyons, and it sent a jolt through her. Her da was holding an identical card, running it between his fingers, the corners already bent from him worrying at them.

"Well, Mr. Sheratan, now that the introductions have all been duly made," her mum said, "perhaps you might illuminate us as to what all of this fuss is in reference to?"

Vika stared at her in horror, but Mr. Sheratan didn't seem to notice how excruciatingly embarrassing she was, or he was too polite to show it. "Of course, madam," he said. "I believe your family is familiar with my employer, Lassiter and Lyons?"

"Naturally," her mum said.

Vika had known Lassiter and Lyons almost as long as she could remember. When she was little—before her da's troubles, so she couldn't have been but seven or eight cycles—she'd pitched a holy fit on the street outside of her da's office, where he helped oversee the running of the planet's largest coltane mine. This wasn't an uncommon occurrence; she often visited her da at work and she was an expert fit-thrower. But that particular time there'd been a man walking out of the building who'd heard her screaming and taken notice.

"You, girl!" the man had said. He'd hobbled toward the two of them, surprisingly fast given his gray hair and the cane he leaned on heavily, and Vika had frozen mid-tantrum. The man looked near ancient to her, much older than her da, whose inky hair, the same shade as her own, was only starting to go gray at the temples. There was something in the man's fierce, ice-colored eyes that put her in mind of the stories kids told about the Shadow Man, who would steal you from your bed when you were sleeping.

"Why are you screaming?" the man had demanded.

"Oh, she's fine, sir," her da had assured him. "She just wants a freeze cream."

"It an't fair," Vika had said, her alarm melting away when the man didn't instantly snatch her up and take her to the Shadow Land. "I helped him at his office all morning, and he won't even do this little thing for me."

"Darling—"

But she was on fire with the injustice by then, and she sensed a kindred spirit in the old man. "He has the bits, I know it!"

The man had laughed and patted her on the head with one knobby hand.

"Good girl. Never settle for less than you know you're worth!" He withdrew a bill from his pocket and handed it to her. "Now go get your freeze cream while I talk to your father."

She'd run off to get a chocolate pop from the street vendor without a second thought, while her da and the man spoke for a few minutes. When they got home, her dad hailed a number the man had written on a piece of paper under the words *Lassiter and Lyons* and discovered it was a fancy law firm on Ploutos. The Shadow Man hadn't looked like a fancy person, but he was, and that was when the mystery of Vika's life had started.

"I'm sure you're aware that my firm has had an interest in Viktoria for some time," Mr. Sheratan said.

"We are," Vika's mum replied, folding her chapped hands primly in her lap.

Vika suppressed a frown; they were aware of it all right. After her da had first made contact with Lassiter and Lyons, months had passed without them hearing a word from the firm. Then one day someone got in touch and said they had, on behalf of an anonymous benefactor, arranged for a gene mapping appointment for Vika. Gene mapping wasn't something her family would ever have been able to afford on their own, so her parents had agreed despite the strangeness of the offer. They were sent to Ploutos to see the doctor, and Vika had fallen instantly in love with that beautiful planet and its clean air and colorful streets. She was so happy to be there that she didn't mind the sick, sharp smell of the hospital or the fat needle the nurse stuck into her neck to extract the DNA sample. She had good strong genes, the doctor had said as he looked at the test results. She should, barring catastrophe, live a long life and give birth to healthy babies. Young Vika had been less interested in that than the lush green park with the carousel across the street that her da had let her ride before they caught the atmospheric ferry back home to Philomenus.

Then the coltane crash happened and her da went through his troubles, and none of the Hales thought of anything so frivolous for a long time. Like so many others, her da had lost his job, and they had to sell their sweet little house outside of town and move to the THs, where he got a position managing 76. Lassiter and Lyons was still a part of their lives, though. They set up the tutor for Vika and Lavinia, sent Vika to more doctors on Ploutos who put her through a battery of psychological and personality tests, and someone came round every year or so to photograph her and ask her questions about her health and schooling. She didn't understand it when she was little and grew to hate it as she got older, but her mum and da wanted the girls to have that tutor, so they cooperated. Vika used to spend a lot of time wondering why he was so interested in her, this Shadow Man or whoever it was he was working for. Was she a candidate for some classified scientific mission? Did they want to harvest her organs to sell to rich people? Was she actually the secret love child of wealthy aristocrats? Her theories became more and more outlandish with every passing year, but eventually Lassiter and Lyons stopped coming round. She realized she'd probably never know why they had cared about her in the first place, so it didn't seem worth wondering about.

Which was now seeming very foolish.

"Did you ever know for whom my firm was working?" Mr. Sheratan asked.

"We think we met the fellow once," her da said, "but we never knew his name. We were told he wished to remain anonymous."

"Which we never should have agreed to," her mum said, her sudden fury barely concealed as she started down the well-worn path of an argument Vika had overheard her parents having for years.

"My dear, this is hardly—"

"—if you hadn't been too cowardly to just insist that—"

"Stop!" Vika said, mortified down to her bones that her mum couldn't hold her tongue in front of this perfect, polished stranger. Mr. Sheratan looked like he was trying to disappear into the peeling wallpaper, and she wished she could, too. "Please, sir, go on."

"At that first meeting, Mr. Hale," Mr. Sheratan said, "our client didn't explain his interest in Viktoria to you?"

"No."

"Well then, I believe I should warn you that this may come as a bit of a shock."

Vika exchanged an alarmed look with her da; her mum was practically on top of the table she was leaning in so close.

"The gentleman tasked my firm with evaluating several young ladies he'd identified over the years," Mr. Sheratan explained. "They all went through a similar process to the one Miss Hale did. Genetic mapping, a full personality profile, regular interviews and monitoring."

Hell's teeth, but it sounded extra creepy when she heard it said all together like that.

"Our client was hoping to find a young lady who would, in his estimation, make a . . ." The solicitor cleared his throat. "Make a suitable wife for his son. He considered nearly a dozen young ladies and recently decided on you, Miss Hale."

Her parents and sister looked at her the way they might look at a bomb they weren't sure was going to explode, the room suspended in stunned silence.

But instead of anger, Vika felt giggles bubbling up her throat. She tried to choke them down cause she knew it wasn't appropriate, but she just couldn't. And once she was laughing, she found she couldn't stop, the laughter pouring out of her. Why did her mum and da look so serious? It was too absurd an idea to even be angry about!

Arranged marriages weren't unheard of on Ploutos, she knew, but had a strange old man she'd spoken to on the street for less than a minute really spent the last decade and heavens only knew how many bits evaluating her suitability to marry his son? Like she was some molly working the street corner or a brood mare he could purchase for his stable? *This* was the great mystery of her life she'd spent so many thousands of hours puzzling over?

"Vika!" her mum scolded. "Please!"

But she couldn't stop. Tears of laughter squeezed out of her eyes, and she covered her face with her hands. "I'm sorry, Mum, but it's just too ridiculous!"

"You must hear the gentleman out!" her mum said, grabbing her arm a shade too hard. Vika knew what she was trying to say through those nails dug into her flesh: someone with money wanted her to marry their son. It wasn't an opportunity to throw away, no matter how ludicrous the situation.

"Please don't be distressed, Mrs. Hale. I'm sure it's a perfectly normal reaction to such unexpected news." Mr. Sheratan set down his teacup gently and looked at Vika with surprising somberness in his pretty blue eyes. "I'm afraid, though, that there's still more I have to tell you."

The rest of Vika's laughter dried up on her tongue at the seriousness of his expression.

"What is it?" she asked.

"Our client was very firm in his belief that his son should marry according to his wishes." He repositioned the cup on its saucer, the soft scrape of porcelain unnaturally loud in the silent room, and Vika had the sense that he was looking for any excuse not to meet her gaze. "So firm, in fact, that he enshrined this belief in his will. His son will only be able to claim his inheritance if he marries you, Miss Hale."

Ah, so she wasn't a brood mare but something more like a house or carpet or *set of fecking spoons* one man felt he could bequeath to another. With the same speed the laughter had overtaken her before, heat began to rise in her blood. She stood, the legs of her chair rasping against the rough concrete floor.

"Vika—" her da said, reaching for her hand. Lavinia snickered from the couch.

She shook him off. "I an't this man's to give away, Mr. Sheratan. I an't *anyone's* to give away."

"Viktoria!" her mum snapped.

"Course not, darling," her da said. "No one is saying—"

"Who does your client think he is to write such a will in the first place?" she demanded.

"I'm afraid that will be another shock for you, Miss Hale," Mr. Sheratan said. "Our client is—excuse me, *was*—Mr. Rigel Chapin."

Vika sank back into the chair as her knees gave way beneath her. As all of the breath left her body, she managed just one word.

"Chapin?"

CHAPTER THREE

VIKA'S FAMILY EXPLODED INTO exclamations and questions and chatter, and she probably would have told them to seal their yaps if she could hear any of it. But the blood was roaring too loudly in her ears, and she was suddenly, strangely transfixed by the way one lock of the young solicitor's hair curled just so under his ear, the brown so dark it was near black against his pale skin. She couldn't stop staring at it, couldn't move her thoughts beyond that square inch of skin. Had he missed that curl when he was combing back his hair in the mirror? Had he shaved that morning or would she feel the scratch of new stubble if she ran her thumb across his jawline? Had he . . .

. . . had he just said "Rigel Chapin"?

Vika flushed hot despite the chill in the flat, like she was burning underneath her skin just the way the coltane fires burned deep underground. Everyone was too close to her and she couldn't breathe. She had to get out of that room.

Without a word, she fled into the dark corridor and took the stairs two at a time up to the roof, huffing with the effort, heart pounding in her chest, but never slowing down. She burst out into the cold, gasping for air. Gooseflesh prickled up her arms but the frigid night cooled a little of the heat inside her head.

Rigel Chapin. The dead old toser who was worth billions. Bloody fecking hell, this couldn't be real.

Once she caught back some of her breath, she walked to the edge of the roof and sat, dangling her legs over the ledge like she'd done ever since she was little. As usual she faced south, where Ploutos was rising on the horizon, huge and gray and indistinct through the haze. The whole planet glowed with the thousands of lights burning across its surface; it wasn't crisscrossed with illegal extension cords trying to wring the last joule of juice from a limping power grid. They had everything they could ever want there.

She looked down at her hands. They were shaking, whether from the chill in the air or . . . something else, she wasn't sure. She tucked them under her thighs, concrete rough against her knuckles.

She'd spent so many hundreds of hours sitting on this damned roof over the years, gazing up at Ploutos, desperately wishing she could be there instead of here, back when she was still young and naive enough to wish for things. She'd have been willing to beg, borrow, or steal her way there if given the chance, anything it took. Lord, she was furious but . . . should she also be happy? Some dark and complicated feeling was taking hold inside of her, like the roots of a plant burrowing deep into the dirt.

Cause what it took to get to Ploutos, it turned out, was selling herself to a stranger. Which was bad enough.

But what was worse was there was a part of her that thought it was a bargain at twice the price.

The door to the roof clanged open behind her, no doubt Lavinia sent to fetch her back or her mum storming up there to tell her off for her rudeness.

"Go away!" she said.

"I'm terribly sorry, Miss Hale," a genteel voice replied. "Please excuse my interruption."

She turned and saw Mr. Sheratan heading back inside the building.

"Wait! I'm sorry," she said. "I thought you were my mother."

"I sensed your parents would appreciate a moment to speak with-out me in the room," he said. Meaning, Vika was sure, that they'd started to argue. "And your father was concerned you'd be cold, so I offered to bring you this."

He held up her worn old coat, which was draped over his arm in a way that made it look like a much nicer garment that it was. He was Ploutos through and through, from the round vowels and more formal vocabulary to the way he stood. Taller, somehow, like he was more willing to take up space. He stepped toward her—a little cau-tiously, as though she were an alley cat who might hiss and swipe at his approach—and when she didn't flinch, he settled the coat over her shoulders. It was only a small kindness, but she was so off balance at that moment that it near knocked her over.

"Would you mind terribly if I were to sit with you for a minute?" he asked. "Given the news I've brought, you'd be well within your rights to pitch me off this roof."

She looked up at him in surprise, and he was giving her a sly little smile. "I think I can restrain myself."

"Your self-control is admirable," he said as he sat beside her on the edge of the roof. "This is a lovely spot."

He wasn't entirely lying. The atmo-haze that blanketed Philo-menus was thick below them, hiding the ugliness of the streets, and there was something oddly peaceful about being surrounded by the gray, wrapped up in its soft, murky cocoon. Or at least there was when her head wasn't spinning so sickly.

She swallowed. "Mr. Sheratan—"

"Miss Hale, may we dispense with the formalities?" He leaned toward her like they were sharing secrets. "I'm not so very much older than you, after all, and I feel a bit foolish keeping up this proper solicitor persona now that it's just the two of us."

"Oh," she said. "Course. You can call me Vika."

He shot her a smile and unfastened the top button of his high collar. "Archer."

The bright flash of teeth suddenly transformed his entire face, from fastidious professional, all good manners and platitudes, into actual person.

"So, now that we're friends," she said, "can I ask you something?"

"Yes, of course."

She thought of how to phrase her question. "Did you know the Chapins?"

"I knew Rigel Chapin. He was . . ." Archer looked down, over the lip of the roof and into the gray. "Well, he was not an easy man, as I think you can imagine. But may I presume that what you really want to know is if I was acquainted with his son?"

She nodded, grateful he understood, cause she hadn't quite been able to get the words past her lips.

"I never met him," he said. "He went away to boarding school on Alastor many years ago and hasn't been back to Ploutos since he was a child. My understanding is that father and son did not get along. Perhaps Leo inherited his father's rather . . . difficult manner. I'm afraid there's little else I can tell you that you won't already know."

What Vika knew was no more than anyone else on Philomenus, and that suddenly seemed like precious little. Rigel Chapin was a brilliant eccentric who'd developed the hydrino fission reactor. He'd been born here on Philomenus but had quickly moved up in the world, and his hydrino reactor, which now powered all of Ploutos and many other planets besides, had made him into one of the wealthiest men in the sector. As he aged, he became a virtual recluse who hardly ever left the penthouse where he lived, at the top of the tallest, grandest, most brightly lit skyscraper on Ploutos.

And then he'd been found dead—curled up on the carpet like a squashed bug, people said—which meant his vast fortune was changing hands. Passing to his only child, a son not much older than she was.

A son she was supposed to marry.

"Did he know about this?" she asked. "The son?"

Archer shook his head. "He only found out about the contents of the will after his father died. He's on his way back from Alastor now."

Vika wondered if his reaction to his father's will had been as horrified as her own. How did he feel when some solicitor he'd never met told him he was expected to marry a poor piece of Philomeni trash, a barmaid his father had taken an inexplicable liking to as a child? She imagined his outrage at hearing about her, his lips curling with disgust as she was described to him til he decided he would give up the fortune owed to him just so he'd never have to endure being married to her, throwing away billions rather than tainting himself with her stink. She smoldered with humiliation and rage just picturing it.

But was it really better if he was willing to marry her just to get his money? To buy her for his own gain?

No matter how he'd felt when they told him about her or what decision he made when the time came, she didn't see how she wouldn't despise him for it. Maybe it wasn't rational or fair, but she suddenly hated Leo Chapin.

She buried her face in her hands, trying to stop the queasy round-and-round of her thoughts. She didn't know if she wanted to marry anyone, certainly not now, but how could she possibly marry someone she already hated?

"I can't imagine what you must be feeling," Archer said. The breeze picked up and she thought she could smell him, a waft of something clean and a little spicy on the wind. "Arranged marriages aren't so very unusual on Ploutos, and though eighteen cycles is a bit young to be married, you are of legal age. But I understand if it's still not an appealing proposition."

"Why me?" Vika asked, wishing she could go back in time and a shake that white-haired old man til the answers came tumbling out of him like coins hitting the pavement. "Why of all the girls on the twin planets would he pick me? There must be a thousand girls who are richer and smarter and prettier—"

"Well, I don't know about *that*," Archer interrupted with a sudden twinkle in his eye.

Even in the midst of everything, Vika felt her cheeks warm.

"I just don't understand," she said softly, "why he'd do this to me."

He considered that for a moment. "I'm afraid I don't know the answer. All I know is that Mr. Chapin was looking for something specific, and he found that thing in you. But Vika . . ." He touched the sleeve of her coat, so softly she could barely feel the pressure of his fingers against her arm beneath the wool. "Nothing has been done to you, not yet. If you want all of this to end, all you have to do is say *no*. Say no right now, and that will be the end of it. Everyone will understand, and I'll take care of everything. Is that what you want?"

She could just say no. One word to Archer right now and all of this would go away, like it had never even happened. It would mean robbing Leo Chapin of his inheritance, which maybe was cruel but which she knew herself to be capable of.

What she didn't know was if she could turn down what was being offered to her. She wanted it so bad. That money. That life. To live in one of those shiny penthouses across the stream, out of the atmo-haze, warm and comfortable and secure. She could actually taste the desire for it bitter in the back of her throat.

She wanted it so bad that she was pretty sure, if Leo Chapin asked her, she'd marry him to get it. Even if she was too young, even if she hated him.

Vika struggled to swallow round the sudden burning pit in her chest.

It was a hard thing, learning the price of her own self-respect.

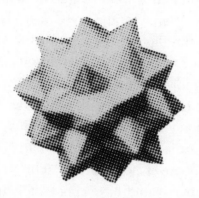

THE PASSENGER LINER *LEANDER* maneuvered slowly into the stream, and Leo stood at the viewport, looking across the miles of empty space to the twin planets. He couldn't sleep. Time after time he'd found himself drawn out of his bed in the passengers' quarters and to this gallery at the bow of the ship, where a window of thick plastecene took up an entire wall. He'd watched the planets slowly growing larger. Glittering Ploutos on his right, where his father's corpse waited. And Philomenus on his left, dark and hazy, where the person waiting was his bride.

Sick laughter lodged itself in his throat, and he nearly choked on it. *Bride.* It was such a romantic word and therefore utterly the wrong term. He'd always known his father was a bastard, but he'd never entertained the notion that he was truly insane until the man was dead and Leo found out about his will and the girl.

He wondered how she'd reacted to the news, Miss Viktoria Hale of Philomenus, whoever she was. Had she been happy, or did she hate him already? Not that the two were mutually exclusive, of course; his mother had been quite happy to marry his father and he was reasonably confident she'd hated him. She had, after all, been a woman of exceptionally discerning taste.

Leo rubbed his chest with his knuckles, trying to soothe the hot ache that kept near-permanent residence there. He wished the voyage from Alastor to Ploutos were longer. In just one day, he would be back on his home planet for the first time since childhood and be expected to make the biggest decision of his life. Unfortunately, decision-making had never been his strongest suit. If only he could stay here—floating through the void in this ship, suspended somewhere between the two very different futures that waited for him— for a little while longer. Maybe his path forward would become clearer with more time. Could he *really* marry someone he didn't even know, let alone love? Leo tried to picture her, to imagine the kind of girl his father would have chosen for him, and hot sweat broke out across the back of his neck.

He rested his forehead against the plastecene window, the coolness of it soothing. Should he feel guilty that he was spending so much more time thinking of this girl rather than his own departed father? They'd never had the best relationship, it was true, but—

The explosion came from somewhere behind him. The concussion of it slammed into his back with the heat and force of a rocket, flattening his lungs and knocking his brain offline. He only registered pain and the sensation of flying. Falling. Surrounded by thousands of tiny twinkles.

Stars, he thought, deliriously. But then understanding filtered its way through his shock. Not stars. Shards of shattered plastecene. And a cold so extreme that it sizzled against his flesh like fire had engulfed his body, which could only mean one thing.

He was in the void. Floating in the vacuum of space, propelled through the ruptured viewport by the force of the explosion.

The *Leander* was just a charred husk in his peripheral vision, growing more distant with each micro-second he drifted away from it. If he'd been in his bed in the passengers' quarters, he'd be dead already, consumed along with all the oxygen inside the ship in the massive fireball that had ripped through it. Instead he was in open space, where his lungs and organs and eyes felt like they were being squeezed in a vise, the pressure so intense he couldn't have gasped for air even if there'd been any to inhale. He tried to scream, but his mouth only opened in a silent wail.

Oh, he thought with the last of his ebbing brainpower, feeling strangely calm. *So this is how I die.*

He saw himself as though he were outside his body: paralyzed, floating, choking on the empty blackness of the stream. No one survived unprotected in the void of space for more than a minute or perhaps two, so at least it would be over soon.

You're going to die.

He thought of his mother, whom he didn't remember, and his dead father he'd tried so long to forget. Would he see them again soon? He thought of that girl waiting below him on Philomenus. Would she be sad when she heard the news of his death, or relieved?

His body was swelling, blood pushing against his skin until he was sure he would burst like an overripe riverberry, the moisture in his eyes and on his tongue beginning to boil.

You're dying . . . Leo Chapin is dying . . .

A white light flooded his cloudy eyes.

. . . Leo Chapin . . . is dead . . .

CHAPTER FOUR

WORK, SADLY, DIDN'T STOP just cause Vika's world had tilted on its axis. But at least the day shift at Nicky's wasn't quite the drunken hellscape that the nights were. It was one of the few places in town with a reliable connection to the feeds and a steady supply of drink, so it was never exactly quiet, but it was calm enough for her to do her work on autopilot. Which was the way she'd done pretty much everything in the three days since she learned about Rigel Chapin's fecking will.

Vika mindlessly wiped down a table, not seeing the crumbs and stains but instead a vision of herself as Mrs. Chapin, dressed in a fine silk dress—red, or maybe green—with her dark curls pulled back with pearl-tipped pins like a girl she'd seen in one of Lavinia's favorite feeds. She was sitting at a table, not like the rickety thing she was cleaning but one that stretched the length of the room and had intricately carved legs and a surface so polished it reflected the glow of the chandeliers. And the fecking thing was *covered* with desserts of all kinds, cakes and truffles and tarts and candies on silver trays spread out before her for the taking, with men in crisp white uniforms standing at the edges of the room, waiting to bring her more whenever she asked.

"Vika," Knox slurred from the bar. "Can I get a refill here?"

The vision—she refused to think of it as a fantasy—popped like a soap bubble. It was just as well since she knew by then how the vision would progress anyway. There she'd be, enjoying her cake and champagne when all of a sudden *he* would enter the daydream. The unwanted husband who was necessary to the whole picture.

For days she'd thought of nothing else besides what she could have as the wife of Leo Chapin and all the things it would cost her in return. There would be the fine home thrumming with more amps of juice than she could ever dream of using, no menial job to work or endless list of chores to complete, the ability to take care of her family and remove the weight from her father's shoulders that was slowly crushing him. But what it would cost . . .

Her independence. Her self-respect. Sharing a house with a stranger she almost certainly wouldn't like, cause how could she ever like a person who would agree to such an arrangement?

And the wedding night. Hell's teeth, the specter of the wedding night had probably intruded on her thoughts more than anything else. The idea of getting all naked and sweaty with anyone was, frankly, a bit repulsive to her, but a stranger? Who'd as good as bought her?

She shuddered as she poured Knox another glass of grock.

"Show me the bits first," she said to him.

He went rummaging in his pockets and finally produced a crumpled bill, waving it in front of her. "You never trust me."

"Should I?" she asked as he slid the bill across the bar in exchange for his drink. "Maybe you ought to be heading home already. An't you got work to be getting to?"

Knox scoffed. "You sound like my girl."

Well then she could worry about him, cause Vika had her hands full with her own problems. Together they watched a report on the newsfeed about a bombing in the stream the night before, but she barely heard a word. She couldn't concentrate on anything cept her own thoughts. Archer had said Leo Chapin would arrive from Alastor in a couple of days on a ship called the *Aquila*, and then she would have to make her decision.

And she still didn't know what that would be.

Another regular, Zeke, and a woman who was definitely not his wife waved at her from their table and gestured for another round. As she poured, Vika imagined the view from the Chapin penthouse, how bright the world must seem from up there. What did sunlight look like without being filtered first through the atmo-haze? She'd seen it on Ploutos during her infrequent visits, but she could barely remember anymore.

"A surprising development in the much-discussed fate of the Chapin fortune," the feed reporter said, her voice cutting through the chatter in the bar like she was speaking straight to Vika, "features an unlikely new character: a young Philomeni barmaid named Viktoria Hale."

The glasses of grock slipped from her fingers, shattering at her feet. Knox grabbed a rag from behind the bar and mopped clumsily at her soaked shoes while she stood there in stunned horror. No one else moved cept for their heads swiveling between her and the feed being projected on the wall behind her.

"The status of energy magnate Rigel Chapin's estimated six-billion-bit fortune has been the subject of much speculation in the days since his death," the reporter continued, "and sources close to the family are now reporting that the estate is set to pass to Chapin's estranged son on the condition that he wed his father's choice of bride . . ."

Vika slowly turned to face the projection. A picture of her face—which, judging from the clothes and sloppy ponytail she was wearing, had been snapped sometime yesterday afternoon as she was leaving work—filled the screen. The caption underneath read "Father Knows Best?"

This was a nightmare. Any second now Lavinia would kick her in her sleep and she would wake up cause she was only dreaming this.

". . . is believed to be Viktoria Hale of the D-4 section of Philomenus. Legal experts say that though the construction of the will is unusual—as might be expected from a famous eccentric like Chapin—it will likely withstand any legal challenge that . . ."

She couldn't breathe. She wanted to run but she was on thin ice with Nicky already and she couldn't lose this job. Her head was spinning and her chest was tight. Her damn shoes were wet and Knox was fumbling with the hem of her trousers, tugging and swiping, trying to dry them and—

"Just leave it, Knox!" she burst.

"Oi, princess!" Zeke said from his table. "That's no way to talk to the help!"

The laughter seemed to come at Vika from all sides. She raised her chin.

"You can head on out of here, Zeke," she said. "I an't serving you anymore today."

"Take a joke, girl." He nodded toward the feed. "Or are you too high and mighty for that now? Eh, Mrs. Chapin?"

She got Jay to throw Zeke and his sidepiece out, but the exchange was only a taste of what was to come during the rest of her shift. News of the Chapin will had rippled through the neighborhood like a power surge and, as much as she'd hated her job before, working the bar while suddenly famous was a new level of torture. She was afraid of reporters lurking everywhere, spying on her, ready to snap another picture, and there was a constant parade of jeers from drunken patrons, whispers behind raised hands, and jealous glares. As though the whole situation was her doing somehow, like she'd taken something away from them by having this mess dropped onto her head like a load of bricks.

It didn't make her any less angry when they seemed to be happy for her, either. Lavinia's friends Astrid and Faye ran up to the bar after they got out of school and demanded fizzy drinks and all the details about Vika's new *fiancé*, a toser word she'd never heard anyone round here use with a straight face. When was the wedding? What was she going to wear? Wasn't she just so lucky and wouldn't they just *kill to be her*?

She still had two hours left in her shift, but their shiny, smiling faces broke her.

"I can't do this," she said, pulling Stella to one side. "I may actually murder someone. Can I take my break now?"

Stella sighed. "Just go home."

"Really?" she breathed. Getting some compassion out of Stella was usually like trying to wring water from a stone.

"It'll be easier with you gone. You're riling everyone up."

Well, that made more sense, at least. Still, Vika was so relieved that if she and Stella had been different sorts of people, she might have hugged her.

"Thank you," she said instead.

Stella frowned. "Make it up to me when you're rich."

Vika fetched her coat and snuck out through the door to the kitchen, which opened into a perpetually dank back alleyway. She walked home fast, head down to hide her face. She didn't want to see her mum, who'd been yammering in her ear nonstop about how she had to marry Chapin for the good of the family, or Lavinia, who now hated her more than she ever had before cause she was so jealous, so she went to her da's office in the basement of their TH. He wasn't there, probably attending to something in one of the units, which was just as well. Solitude was hard to come by on this planet, and she could use some. She hung her coat up by the door, sat down in her da's squeaky office chair, and let her head fall to the desk with a light thump.

Heavens above, why had it not occurred to her that news of the Chapin will could get out? She would never escape it now. If she went to Ploutos and married Chapin, at least she'd have all that lovely money to comfort her when people mocked and judged her. If she refused him, though, how long would she have to live with the ridicule of her neighbors before some fresher gossip made them forget about her again?

Vika sighed, lifted her head, and went to work cleaning up the stacks of paper scattered across her da's desk. Maybe he could get a job in one of the factories and she could take over managing the TH and never have to leave the building ever again. But even managing the building, which was much less taxing than a factory job would be, was near too much for the man her da was now, as the chaos in the room showed. She and Lavinia took turns helping him as often as they could, but it never seemed to be enough.

The comm beeped as she worked, and she hit the button to answer it. "TH 76," she said.

"Good afternoon. I'm looking for Viktoria Hale," a man on the other end replied.

She tensed. "Why?"

"Is she there? I was led to understand that she works there." He paused. "Is this Viktoria?"

"Never heard of her. You want to rent a room?"

"Actually, I'm a reporter from—"

She clicked the comm off. It was only then that she gave a thought to the light on the panel that indicated messages waiting in the system. That light was near always on since there was a constant parade of folks looking for places to live, but now the amber glow seemed menacing. She picked up the comm and began to cycle through each message.

"—and I was hoping to speak to Viktoria Hale—"

"—I'm a producer for—"

"—wondering if she would speak to us about—"

No sooner had she deleted them than the comm began to beep once more with an incoming hail. She pressed the button twice in quick succession to hang it up without answering.

A moment of silence. And then the comm beeped again.

"Fecking hell!" she said, ganking the battery from the back of the thing and shoving it under the desk.

"Hello?" someone said.

"What!" she snapped.

The young man standing in the doorway of the office stared at her in wide-eyed surprise. "I-I apologize. Are you Miss Hale?"

She stood. "Who are you? Are you a reporter?"

He looked bewildered. "Me? N-no. I just wanted to rent a room." He looked away from her, eyes scanning the walls, the overstuffed shelves, anything but her. "I was told to ask here? That someone named Hale could help me?"

"Oh." She frowned at him. He *looked* like a reporter, someone a little too clean and decent-looking to be hunting for a room here. But her da would be upset if he found out she'd turned away an applicant who might actually be able to pay, so she sank back into the chair. "Yes. I can help."

"Are you being pursued by reporters?" he asked, still hovering in the doorway.

That wasn't really any of his business, and if he was the last person on Philomenus who hadn't yet heard about her situation, she wasn't going to enlighten him. "Have a seat. I'll get you an application."

He sank down into the chair opposite her and she started digging through her da's files, looking for the rental application. It was supposed to be filed under *A* but he had misplaced the folder. She finally found it under *G* and shook her head; they had to get him more help somehow.

The young man sitting across the desk was looking at her; she could feel it. She glanced at him, and when her eyes met his, he didn't immediately look away like a normal person would. A cold little prickle itched at the back of her neck as his gaze eventually darted past hers. They didn't keep any cash here in the office, but this guy didn't know that, and there was something about him . . . She was probably being silly, but she looked at her coat hung on a peg by the door and thought of the sting spray in the pocket.

"Is, uh, is that your family?" he asked, nodding at a photograph her da kept on the desk. Vika knew the picture without having to look, and she preferred not to since it only caused her pain. It was the four of them at the summer fair back before her da had lost his job at the mine. She and Lavinia were in their best dresses, each holding a spun sugar. Their mum and da had their arms round each other, and Mum's mouth was open with the big laugh Vika had near forgotten the sound of.

"Technically," she said in a clipped voice.

"It's a nice picture." He was smiling like it was a memory of his and not of hers. "How old were you?"

She narrowed her eyes at him, this non-reporter with all his questions, and slid the rental application across the desk. "You need to fill this out."

He took a pen from the cup on the desk and went to work on the form. Like a decent person, she waited til he was distracted to look at him more closely. He seemed to be a few cycles older than her and he didn't appear dangerous, which already put him a cut above many of those who came to the THs looking for a roof to put over their heads. He actually had sort of a moony, childlike face, or would have if it weren't for the sharp, strong nose that interrupted the softness of his other features. He had dark eyes behind thick-rimmed glasses, the black hair that was in sharp contrast to his milky white skin was freshly trimmed, and his clothes were worn but well taken care of judging by the tiny, even stitches patching a hole near the shoulder. All in all, he looked more respectable than most of their tenants.

Course, appearances could be deceiving. The way the fingers of his free hand drummed irregularly at the desk, like he was trying to hold something inside that had found an outlet in the incessant tapping, made her uneasy.

"So . . . your father is the manager here?" he asked as he filled out the application.

"Yes."

"Do you often help him?"

She didn't want to talk to him, much less make pointless, polite chitchat. But she very much wanted the little bit of extra income her da would get if all the flats in the building were full, so she would make a personal sacrifice to keep him here. "Guess that depends on what you mean by 'often'."

He smiled—she wasn't sure why cause she hadn't said anything funny—and handed the application back to her. Sky Foster, it said at the top. He'd left the employer section blank.

"You don't have a job?" she asked. She'd made fecking small-talk for nothing.

"No, not yet." He looked almost at her, but not quite, his gaze focused somewhere just over her right ear. "I'm new to the area. Do you know anyone who's hiring?"

As though jobs were just round for the asking. She stood, preparing to drop his application in the bin. "I can't rent you a room if you an't got a job, Mr. Foster. If you'll just show yourself out—"

"Wait! Wait, I can pay up-front," he said, reaching into his bag. "A whole month's rent. Will that be enough? It's all I have, but if I . . . if I an't got a job within the next two weeks, you can evict me."

She frowned at him. Who had that many bits to spare and still wanted to live here? There were nicer places on Philomenus. Not a *lot* nicer, but still nicer. Everything about this guy screamed undercover reporter, from the personal questions to the evasions about his work to—

He placed a stack of bits on the desk. A big one.

Vika's breath caught. She couldn't rent him a room til he had a job; those were the rules. But . . .

But she could let him stay in a vacant flat til someone hired him. And in the meantime she could take those bits instead of turning them in to the landlord, who would still think the place was empty. It wasn't exactly legal, but how would anyone know? She could already feel the weight of that money in her pocket, could smell the dinner she would buy her family with it. Meat, and fresh green vegetables. Maybe the guy was a creep, but they had plenty of those round here. If he was a reporter looking for a story, well, there wasn't anything she could do to stop him from sniffing round, and he would get feck-all from her anyway. At least this way, she'd have his money.

She scooped up the bits. "Welcome to Town Housing 76, Mr. Foster."

"HEY, MAN," MERAK GREETED him as he stepped into the dim tavern. "How's it doing?"

"Can't complain," he replied, trying to smile back at the bartender. "Ariel here?"

"Haven't seen her."

He frowned; she should have been waiting for him. But any number of things could have held her up, so there was no need to worry just yet. He ordered a glass of grock and a bowl of the stew he could smell simmering in the back and then took a seat at his usual table in the corner.

His head was pounding. He wasn't cut out for this. When Merak brought him his glass of grock, he downed a third of it in one long draught.

He was starting to worry in earnest by the time Ariel eventually appeared, red-faced and sweating. She dropped into the seat opposite him without a word and drained the rest of his drink.

"Thank the stars," he said. "Where have you been?"

"Sorry," she replied. "Just a little hiccup."

Which, knowing her gift for understatement, probably meant she'd dodged getting arrested or even killed. He imagined her running through the streets, just barely evading capture by mercs on her way here.

"Ratface?" he asked. It was what she called the merc who was her own personal nemesis.

She nodded. "The bastard. Somehow I always seem to cross his path at the exact wrong moment. Thankfully he can't run for shit."

"The cargo make it?" he asked, because she would only roll her eyes if he expressed any concerns about her.

"All safe and sound. So how did it go with Viktoria Hale? Did you see her?"

He nodded and took a bite of his stew. "She was uneasy, but I think she bought it."

"Yeah? And?"

"And what?" he asked innocently, unable to resist.

"You know what I mean!"

"Do I?"

She kicked him under the table. "Tease!"

He laughed, and in retaliation she grabbed his bowl of stew and plucked the spoon from his fingers, tucking in to his dinner.

"I just don't want to rush anything," he said. "We can take our time here. That's why we killed Leo Chapin in the first place, right?"

CHAPTER FIVE

LEO CHAPIN, SOMEWHERE ABOVE her head on a ship called the *Aquila*, was due to arrive on Ploutos the next day. The distant ticking that had started in Vika's ears when Archer told her the date her intended husband would be returning had become a roar. One day left. One day before everything in her life would change forever.

Or nothing would change at all.

But life continued on as normal. There were still drinks to sling and bills to be paid, so she and Lavinia were off to work. As they exited their building, they passed Sky Foster moving in. He tried to hold the door open for them, but he was also clutching a flimsy box of his possessions, and when he fumbled between the two, the heavy wooden door swung back and hit Vika in the face.

"Fecking hell!" she said while Lavinia burst into laughter.

"Oh, I'm so sorry, Miss Hale!" Sky dropped his box, spilling clothes onto the stoop. "Are you all right?"

"I'm fine," Vika said, dodging his hands as he reached for her. Her cheek stung something fierce but she just wanted to get away as quick as she could. "Don't worry yourself."

She dragged Lavinia down the pavement along with her. She

could feel him watching her as she walked away but didn't turn back. "Lord, what an idiot," she said.

"I don't know, he seems kind of sweet," Lavinia said. "And now I'll forever have the memory of that door whacking you in the face."

"Hilarious. Stay away from him, would you?" Vika said. "There's something off about him."

"*Yes, Mum.*"

They reached the end of the road where they would split to head to their individual jobs, and Vika groaned.

"Please don't make me go," she said. Fame, it turned out, was less fun than it looked. At least when you were famous for something so stupid and out of your control. Nicky's was more packed than ever thanks to the rubberneckers who'd come to get a look at her, and between all the questions and taunts and innuendo, she wasn't able to forget about Leo fecking Chapin and his power to change her entire life for a single second. She was exhausted to the bone.

"Want to swap with me?" Lavinia asked. "I think I'd like serving drinks."

Vika shuddered. "Definitely not." Nicky's might be an ordeal, but it was better than Lavinia's job of minding Mrs. Leavitt's three little monsters.

Work wasn't quite as bad as Vika had feared, mostly cause they were so busy that Nicky himself was hustling behind the bar and people didn't dare mess with her when he was within earshot. So she kept her head down and tried to get her tasks done while talking as little as she could to any of the patrons.

They were in the middle of the rush that came after the second shift ended at the one mine still in operation when she saw the woman walk in. She spotted her out of the corner of her eye as she was slicing puckerfruit for drinks, and her knife stilled. This lady wasn't their usual clientele, and more than one head turned to stare at her. Women like that just didn't exist in the THs.

A queasy feeling started to rumble in the pit of Vika's stomach at the sight of the sharp lines of her tailored suit and her freshly styled honey hair. When Archer stepped inside the bar after the woman, Vika's knife slipped and caught the side of her finger, slicing so cleanly through the skin that she didn't even feel the pain til she saw blood.

"Dammit!" she said, reaching for a bar towel that looked reasonably clean. She wrapped it round her finger, which was now pulsing out a deep stinging, the puckerfruit ruined by red droplets across the cutting board.

"Fecking hell, Vika," Nicky said. "Watch what you're doing. That stuff's expensive."

She couldn't answer him cause Archer was pushing his way to the bar while the woman with him waited just behind the scrum.

"Miss Hale," he said, "would you—oh my, are you all right?"

She tried to smile, twisting the rag tightly round her cut. "Occupational hazard. How can I help you, Mr. Sheratan?"

She could feel the people round them straining to hear whatever he'd say next.

"I'm terribly sorry to disturb you at work, but is there somewhere we could possibly speak privately?" he asked.

So not a social call then. Course it wasn't. She turned to Nicky, desperate. He rolled his eyes and chucked her the keys to the back office.

"Five minutes," he said. "Minute six comes out of your pay, got it?"

She nodded and pointed Archer toward the office. He went to retrieve his companion while she fumbled with her apron strings, no doubt bloodying them as she struggled to get the thing off. She ducked out from under the bar and wound her way through the laughs and jeers about "Princess Vika" as she made her way to the office, where Archer and the woman were waiting.

"We can talk in here," she said, unlocking the door.

Nicky's office was even worse than her da's, which she wouldn't have thought possible if she didn't see it day after day. The sight of that perfectly polished woman walking into a cramped room piled with stacks of invoices, dusty tools, and dirty shirts was such a ridiculous contrast that it might have been funny if she weren't wound so tight she could snap.

"Miss Hale, our sincerest apologies for intruding on your time," Archer said once the door was closed behind them, his proper solicitor demeanor firmly in place. "Please allow me to introduce you to Evelyn Lyons."

Hell's teeth, one of the founders of the firm. Vika swallowed. Whatever had happened, it was big, else they wouldn't have called the boss in to take care of it.

"A pleasure to meet you, Miss Hale," the woman said, extending her hand to shake as was the custom on Philomenus. Vika could only lamely gesture to the towel wrapped round her bleeding finger in response. At least she couldn't feel the pain anymore; her entire body had gone numb.

"If you don't mind, Miss Hale, I'd like to summon your parents," Ms. Lyons said. "Will your employer allow you to use his comm?"

She shook her head. "No point. My father won't be in the office at this hour, and we don't have a comm in our flat."

"Then perhaps we could send someone for them."

"You don't need to do that," she said, thinking of how many minutes it would take someone to get to 76 and back and how completely impossible it would be for her to wait that long. "What's happened? Why are you here?"

"I really think your father, at least, should—"

"My father an't any more of an adult than I am," Vika interrupted, "so I'd appreciate it if you'd just tell me what's going on."

Somehow her voice had gotten higher and louder than she'd meant it to. Archer put a steadying hand on her arm, and it made her heart stutter in her chest. Touching was a part of the culture on Philomenus but tosers, she knew, didn't touch each other casually. They hardly touched at all outside of family and formal greetings. But here was Archer with his hand round her arm, softly squeezing it and looking at her so kindly that she knew something was terribly, terribly wrong.

"Have a seat, please, Miss Hale," he said.

Vika lowered herself into Nicky's office chair, which had a hole that bled stuffing and a free spring that stabbed her in the back of the thigh.

"It's about Leo Chapin," Archer said. "I apologize it's taken us so long to bring you this information, but we needed to be sure it was accurate, which took some time to ascertain. Did you hear about the bombing on the passenger liner in the stream yesterday? The *Leander?*"

Her throat went dry. "Yes."

"The Philomeni Liberation Front has taken responsibility for it," Archer said. "They claim the ship was targeted because—"

"Just tell me," she whispered. "Archer, just tell me what's going on."

He gave her that sad, sympathetic smile she recognized. "Vika. Leo Chapin was aboard that ship."

Images from the newsfeeds flashed through her mind. The sudden fireball barely caught by a distant surveillance camera. The halo of shattered plastecene and metal that spread out from the blast. The twisted and charred husk of the ship surrounded by salvage crafts, like insects swarming a carcass.

She shook her head, feeling suddenly slow and foggy. "No. He . . . he isn't supposed to arrive til tomorrow. The *Aquila.*"

Archer's voice was gentle. "He was supposed to be on the *Aquila,* but he changed his plans at the last moment and boarded the *Leander* instead."

"Is he . . ."

"There were no survivors."

Leo Chapin is dead.

At that moment, everything became searingly, blindingly clear. With the spring poking into her thigh, the smell of stale booze in her nose, and the two solicitors in their fine clothes looking down at her, every confused thought that had plagued her since she found out about Rigel Chapin's will evaporated. She realized she'd always known, deep down, what she would do.

She would have said yes.

She'd have married Leo Chapin, left this rotting planet and its nights of waiting on drunkards and walking home in the dark to share a too-small bed with her too-thin sister. She'd have gone to Ploutos with a stranger to start a new life, whether it was demeaning or not, whether she hated him or not, cause that was how desperately she needed out of *this* life.

But now he was dead, and she was trapped here, forever.

Stella took one look at her when she exited the office—after numbly shaking Archer's and Evelyn Lyons's hands with her own still wrapped up in a bloody rag, exchanging platitudes she couldn't remember the instant they'd left her mouth—and poured her a double shot of uzso.

"Her shift's over," she told Nicky, so fiercely he didn't even try to argue with her.

Vika was in a daze. Stella shooed Knox off his customary stool at the end of the bar so Vika could sit and kept her glass filled. Whatever Stella put in front of her, Vika dutifully drank down. She didn't know how much time passed before she heard someone say her name and looked up to see her da suddenly at her side. When had he gotten there? The whole world seemed a little out of focus as he placed her coat over her shoulders and said, "Let's go home."

"He's dead," she told him as they stepped into the chilly afternoon, the low sun turning the atmo-haze a dirty orange. "He was on that ship that blew up, and now he's dead."

"Oh, darling." He put his arm round her shoulders and noticed the dish towel still wrapped round her hand. "You're hurt?"

She looked down at the injury in confusion. He unwrapped the towel to expose the cut.

"That looks deep," he said. "Better get it seen to."

He took her to the clinic a few blocks away. There was a real hospital across town, but hardly anyone could afford to use it. You either used a clinic for the small stuff, like the flu or a broken bone, or you died, cause at least dying was free.

A strange shudder went through Vika as her da ushered her inside. Like most of the clinics on Philomenus, it was run by the Philomeni Liberation Front and everyone knew it, even if they pretended not to. The PLF was near as old as Vika was herself, springing up in the days after the coltane market cratered and Ploutos stepped in to make the planet a protectorate, flooding it with mercenaries to patrol the streets and just enough bits to keep the economy from collapsing entirely. What that really meant was that in exchange for enough bread crumbs to keep them all from starving, Ploutos owned its own planet full of people willing to do menial work for rock-bottom wages. The PLF wanted to break Ploutos's grip on them, whether that was through bombing merc barracks or providing food and medical care to desperate Philomenis. Technically they were criminals, but like most people round here, Vika was glad for them.

Cept . . . now they'd killed the person who was her ticket out of this place. Despite the uzso, she was suddenly feeling very sober.

It took just a few minutes for a doctor to see her and derma-seal her cut. He placed a clean white plaster over the wound and sent them on their way. She could sense her da looking at her as they walked back toward their TH. The concern radiated off of him like heat from their oil lamp, but thankfully he didn't try to get her to talk.

He stopped abruptly at the entrance to the alley behind Sullivan Street. "Do you want a freeze cream?"

She frowned, bewildered by the unexpected question. "What?"

"Come on," he said, tugging her toward the alley. "You've had a tough day, and I've got a couple of spare bits. Let's get you a freeze cream."

"It's 270 degrees out!" she said. "And you do *not* have a couple of spare bits."

"Shush."

The alley was dimly lit with lanterns hung at different heights on the concrete walls of the adjacent buildings. There was a line of folding tables on either side where the black marketers sold their goods, everything from batteries and feed screens to everyday items like clothing and food, most smuggled onto the planet by the PLF to fund their various activities. The Nut Man was there like always, the sweet-sharp smell of his roasting nuts wafting through the cold air. The vendors paid the mercs good money to turn a blind eye to this place. Sometimes the soldiers would come in and threaten to shut the market down to wring a few more bits in bribes from the sellers, but they shopped here as often as everyone else, so they never followed through. Sullivan Street would outlive them all.

Vika's da found a man with a table full of sweets and smoking leaf. He had a whole boxful of freeze cream pops, cause it was cold enough that they wouldn't melt. When it was hot, when you'd most want a freeze cream, you couldn't beg, borrow, or steal one on Philomenus. It required too much precious power to keep them frozen.

Her da bought her a chocolate pop and, when her attention was focused on unwrapping it, quickly got himself a dakha leaf cig he tried to pocket without her seeing.

"Mum'll have your head for that," she said.

He raised an eyebrow at her. "What Mum doesn't know won't hurt her."

"You'd better go ahead and smoke it then."

He lit his cig and she licked her freeze cream as they walked away from the market, the sharp breeze clearing the rest of the uzso fog from her head. They were close to home and didn't want to get caught with their treats, so they sat on the front stoop of a TH round the corner from their own. Vika sighed and leaned her head against her da's shoulder.

"How are you doing?" he finally asked, squeezing her knee with a hand that never seemed quite as big as she remembered it.

"Not sure. I know I should feel bad that a person died, but all I can think about . . ." Her eyes began to sting and water—from the wind or the dakha smoke, surely—and she squeezed them shut. The vision she'd had of herself all happy and worry-free in that green silk dress had dimmed into blackness. "I'm a terrible person."

"No, you're not."

"Don't be so sure." She bit into the last of her chocolate pop and tossed the stick away. "Why did Rigel Chapin do this to me?"

Her da shook his head. "All I remember him saying the day we met was that he admired your spirit. A 'very promising young lady,' he said."

The words made her sound as ancient as she felt sometimes, an old woman trapped in a girl's body. "Maybe I was back then."

"You still are," he said, putting his arm round her shoulder and pulling her close. He took another puff from his cig, the blue smoke curling up and joining the haze. "I'm afraid you're in for a tough time ahead, though, darling. There's nothing people round here enjoy more than seeing the high brought low, and you were almost very high."

There was no tinge of bitterness in his voice, but she'd have understood if there was. Her da knew that lesson better than most. He used to be an important man on Philomenus, someone who had helped oversee one of the biggest mining operations on the planet. They had lived in a pretty house in the nice neighborhood, not much by Ploutosian standards but big enough for Vika and Lavinia to have their own rooms, a yard to run round in, and plenty of food in the cupboards.

But when Ploutos built her hydrino reactor and didn't need coltane anymore, everything changed. Mines started to close. The second power plant they were building up north to handle the growing electrical needs of the planet was abandoned. The pressure of trying to keep the mine open cause of all the families that depended on it was too much for her da. It took him apart, piece by piece. By the time the planet was in chaos and Ploutos stepped in to take it over, he was broken.

Vika tried to smile, for his benefit. "At least I don't have to go through with that first meeting. Can you imagine how awkward it would have been?"

"Terribly awkward. Bullet well dodged. But still, I'm sorry for you." He coughed, but it wasn't from the dakha, and his voice when he spoke again was rough. "You know, it's my greatest regret that I didn't give you a better life. I failed all of you in that. And to see you get so close to having such a life and to watch it be taken away . . ."

"Da!" She hugged him fiercely, hiding her face over his shoulder. They were her mum's words and she couldn't bear to hear them coming out of his mouth. "Don't you say that! You haven't failed us at all."

"It's kind of you to say, darling, but I know it's true," he said. "You know I would give you everything if I could."

There were so many things she could say. That she didn't want anything more than what she had, which was a lie. Or that she didn't blame him for their lot in life, which was mostly true. But the words seemed to be stuck in her throat, and she was afraid of what else might come pouring out if she tried to jar them loose.

"You'd give me everything?" she teased instead, desperate to take the pain off of his face. "All the freeze cream I could eat?"

He smiled, just a little, and cleared his throat. "Oh yes. You'd be wonderfully fat and happy if it were up to me."

"Come on," she said, standing and pulling him to his feet. "Let's go home."

CHAPTER SIX

VIKA WAS LIVING IN a fog as dense as the atmo-haze. Her da had been right about the neighborhood's reaction to her rapid rise and even more rapid fall; apparently there was nothing as fun as mocking someone for having hopes that amounted to nothing. Maybe she'd have joined in, too, if it had been some other girl in her shoes. Nicky's was a gauntlet of whispers and taunts, and the work itself suddenly seemed more tedious and degrading than it had been before since there was no hope of escape from it now.

This was her life, forever.

At the end of another shift of everyone calling her "Princess Vika," she came home to find her da scrubbing away at the stoop of their TH.

"What is it?" she asked.

"Nothing," he said, wiping sweat from his brow with the back of his sleeve and angling his body to try to cover up the mess. "Just a spill. Darling, I need you to go to the store for me and—"

She pushed past him and stared at the words spray-painted across their stoop in lurid orange letters.

Toser sl

She could guess what it had said before her da and his scrub-brush got there.

She fled into the building, past the flat where she could hear her mum and Lavinia arguing through the door, up the poky staircase, and to the roof. All she wanted was to disappear into the quiet of the haze and have one single fecking moment to herself where she didn't have to look at or listen to another human being.

So, naturally, she found Sky Foster already up there.

He was standing near the ledge, hands in his pockets, looking out over the gray. She had to master the impulse to scream or, better, just give him a good shove. Instead she took a deep breath and reminded herself that murder was bad. But she wasn't going to let him run her off her own roof, either; this was *her* spot. She walked to the opposite corner and sat down with her back to him, swinging her legs out over the abyss. He'd only been living there for a few days, but somehow she'd seen him more in that time than she'd seen any other tenant in months. She bumped into him in the corridors. She passed him outside on the street. He came into the office when she happened to be helping out her da to report a broken window latch in his room. But he never tried to talk to her beyond the expected pleasantries and no stories appeared about her in the press, so if he was an undercover reporter, he was at least a very poor one. She didn't care for the way he looked at her or the nervous, bumbling demeanor that seemed like a cover, but otherwise there was nothing to suggest that he was anything more than an odd guy. And heavens knew he wasn't the only one of those round the place.

She lifted her face up to try to catch a bit of the weak sun filtering down through the haze and wondered, for the millionth time, what she'd done to make old Chapin decide to torture her like this. Was it some cosmic punishment for what an ungrateful wretch she'd been when she'd met him outside her da's work? Her life had been as good as it could be that day, and she hadn't appreciated it one bit. She'd been a happy little girl, well taken care of, visiting a father she adored, a man who was still healthy and untroubled . . .

The backs of her eyes stung with sudden tears.

"Miss Hale?" She heard the shuffle of shoes on asphalt behind her.

Vika closed her eyes. "Lord, not now."

"I've just been meaning to tell you . . . that is, as we discussed . . ."

"What is it?" She whipped her head round to look at Foster, wielding the tears in her eyes like weapons.

"Oh, my," he said, taking an unconscious step back. He dropped his head to study the concrete. "I-I apologize. I didn't mean to disturb you."

"Too late," she said under her breath as she looked back out at the gray.

His footsteps moved closer to her instead of away, and then he was bending down beside her, offering her a worn handkerchief. She didn't know anyone actually carried one of those in real life; she thought they were just an affectation from feed dramas.

Still, it was a nice gesture and the universe owed her a nice gesture or two right now, so she took it. "Thank you."

"I hope you feel better," he said softly and turned to leave.

"Dammit," Vika muttered, cause she suddenly felt *worse*. He hadn't done anything wrong cept be on this roof when she wanted to be alone while possessing a face that inexplicably annoyed her. "Wait, I'm sorry. I shouldn't have been so short."

He looked back at her over his shoulder, eyes not quite meeting hers. "I intruded."

"Still."

"It's fine, truly. I imagine this has been a difficult time for you, what with . . . everything going on."

"Ah. Finally heard about that, did you?"

His grimace was apologetic. "I think everyone has."

She groaned and buried her face in her hands. "It's just so ridiculous! And it will never go away." Yesterday the newsfeeds had still been full of the story, flashing pictures of the new inheritors of the estate now that Leo Chapin was dead and commenting on the tragedy of poor Viktoria Hale of Philomenus D-4, practically widowed and robbed of the fortune that was near hers. Surely there were more important things going on somewhere?

"Would you?" Foster asked. "Have married him?"

"I don't know," she said. It was the only answer she could say out loud without sounding like a terrible person, and anyway it was none of his fecking business.

He examined a scuff on his shoe. "Perhaps you're better off this way."

"Oh yes. I'm sure being fabulously wealthy would have been *such* a disappointment. All that fine food to eat and electricity to burn would have made life so boring."

He smiled. "Who really likes being able to turn on the lights after dark anyway?"

"Exactly!" she said. "It's not like there's anything exciting to see here in 76."

"Other than Mrs. Carson's daring fashion sense."

She snorted and furrowed her brow at the same time, surprised he had said something that amused her when ten seconds before she would have declared herself incapable of amusement in her current mood, or with her current companion. "I'm going to tell her you said that," she said.

His expression of genuine alarm made her laugh a second time. "Please don't," he said. "I'd rather not have to move again right away."

"I suppose I'll let you off the hook this once." She sighed. "Well, I may not be rich, but at least I haven't let myself be bought like some piece of livestock, right? As nice as the food and electricity would have been, I don't think I could have lived with myself."

His expression seemed skeptical. "Most people will put up with a lot for the right price."

She stiffened, something like shame burning at the base of her throat as she looked up at him. "Yeah, well, not me, okay?"

"Right. Of course," he said, and his voice told her that he saw through the utterly transparent lie.

"That's not me," she repeated, trying to convince herself as much as him. His eyes dropped and she knew she'd failed.

"I should go," he said, not looking at her. "Leave you to your privacy."

That desire to push him off the roof was back. "You interrupted my privacy in the first place for a reason, didn't you?"

"Oh, yes. I wanted to inform you that I found employment—"

The door to the roof suddenly burst open, her da near tumbling out. "Vika, there you are!" he said between huffs of air. "I need to talk to you."

Vika jumped to her feet and rushed past Foster, whom she'd already forgotten, and to her da's side. He hadn't just run up all those flights of stairs for nothing. "What is it?"

He turned to go back into the stairwell, waving her after him.

"Slow down!" she said, following him into the dimness. "What's going on?

"I've just been on the comm with Ms. Lyons," he said. "She wants us to come to see her as soon as possible."

She felt suddenly as breathless as he was. "On Ploutos? Why?"

"She wouldn't say, but she was very insistent that we hurry."

Vika froze, the stair under her feet squeaking as she came to a stop. "I don't care, Da! I have no desire to speak to Ms. Lyons, and I won't be summoned like some dog to its master."

Her da turned back to look at her. "Darling—"

"I'm serious," she said. "Lassiter and Lyons ruined my life. I don't want anything to do with them."

"I know, but this is not the time for you to dig your heels in, sweetheart. The only person who will suffer from it is you." He put his hands on her face. "So you'll do this, won't you? For me?"

Her lip gave a dangerous wobble, and she bit it hard. She'd do anything for him. But the idea of going to Ploutos right now, of feeling the unfiltered sun on her face for the first time in years, having to immerse herself in a whole world that was lost to her forever . . .

"I don't think I can," she said softly.

"I understand," he said, "but I think you have to."

She sighed and gave an eye roll so dramatic that Lavinia could only aspire to it, which somehow made her feel better. "*Fine*. But I won't be happy about it."

He gave her a knowing smile and patted her cheek. "That's my girl. Now, let's hurry. We need to make the next passage."

They rushed back to the flat, and the reality of the situation began to sink in as Vika grabbed her square of microcloth and the one nice dress she owned from where it was balled up in the laundry basket. She was going to Ploutos, now. The Chapin affair wasn't through with her yet. She sniffed the dress. Other than the wrinkles, it seemed fine. It certainly smelled better than she did, reeking as she did of sweat and stale grock. Maybe a shower would steam some of the wrinkles from the dress.

The ground-floor bathroom was empty, which might have been a first. There was usually a line two or three people deep. Vika cranked the hot tap, hung her dress from the hook on the back of the door, and jumped into the shower stall, yelping when frigid water that smelled strongly of rotten eggs hit her. She banged the pump beside the tap for a handful of gritty gray paste and used it to scrub her body, hair, and teeth. She tried not to think, just move, but in the tiny stall there was nowhere to escape the questions that came crowding in.

Why was she being summoned like this, all rushed and out of the blue? Surely Evelyn Lyons could have no further use for her now that Leo Chapin was dead and his inheritance passed on to the next people in line in his father's will. Or had the firm cooked up some creative new way to wreck what was left of her life?

She wondered briefly if Archer would be there.

The hot water suddenly kicked in, and she gasped. It was near scalding, but she needed her dress to look presentable, so she didn't turn it down.

She stepped out of the shower onto the cold concrete floor, dirt and grit sticking to the bottoms of her feet. Once she pulled on her dress, she rubbed a window into the fogged mirror tacked to the wall to look at herself. Her tawny skin had turned red from the water and scrubbing, but that would soon fade. The dress was mostly un-wrinkled and looked cleaner than she knew it to be. And although she didn't look anything like the elegant Ploutosian women in their fine silk frocks that she saw every day on the feeds, she was still one of the prettiest girls she knew. All in all, it could be worse.

"Is that what you're wearing?" her mum asked the moment she stepped back into the flat. Her mum was decked out in her only fancy dress, one from their old life, which was a yellow thing with satin ruffles at the hem and neckline. It was hopelessly out of date and had permanent creases etched into the fabric from spending so many years carefully packed away.

"It's the best I have," Vika said. It might have been plainer than her mum's, but at least it didn't make a spectacle of her. "You know that."

"Well, it will have to do, I suppose." Her mum reached out and tucked her hair behind her ears. "Don't hide your pretty face. You never know where it will get you."

Vika saw the hunger in her eyes, the desperation. It made for an uncomfortable mirror of what was in her own heart, and she looked away.

Her da—in his best suit, which had fit him better a few missed meals ago—finished scribbling a note to Lavinia to explain their ab-sence and checked his wristwatch. "We'd best be moving, my loves. The ferry leaves in less than an hour."

The three of them caught the tram to the atmospheric dock, where they joined the queue of workers waiting to get on a ferry bound for Ploutos. Even the least fortunate people living in Ploutos weren't poor enough to work as trash collectors or industrial kitchen hands, so the planet imported its menials. No doubt why Ploutos had in-corporated them in the first place, to have a captive labor pool of its very own. Crossing the stream was an expensive business these days and the costs went up every year, so pretty much the only

Philomenis who made the trip were the domestics and grunt laborers who had their commute passes paid for by their Ploutosian employers.

The dockworker scanned their identity cards and for a moment Vika held her breath, hoping the light would blink red. But the scanner flashed green as it registered the passes Ms. Lyons had arranged for them. Vika wished it was a struggle to remember the last time she'd been to Ploutos, but she knew it practically down to the day. Three cycles ago, an unseasonably warm afternoon just a few weeks after her name day, the streets and shops still decorated with twinkling lights and greenery from the holiday season. She'd turned to her da as they walked and said the air smelled like sugar, and he'd laughed. Then another round of doctors and tests she didn't understand, all to determine if she was an item worthy of purchasing.

And now? What could they possibly want with her now? Maybe old Chapin wanted to marry her off to some other relative from beyond the grave. Or maybe Evelyn Lyons felt so guilty that she wanted to hand her a fat stack of bits for her trouble, though Vika wasn't holding her breath on that count.

They filed into the ship and took seats on one of the long benches that filled the belly of the craft. Vika didn't want to go back to Ploutos, not ever, not if she couldn't stay. But it was too late. Her stomach churned as the ferry pulled away from the dock, and she craned her neck to look out of the nearest port window as they glided away from Philomenus and into the sliver of space that separated the twin planets. There wasn't much to see in the blackness, just the light of distant stars and the salvage crafts that trolled the stream, collecting the scraps of debris that inevitably built up in highly trafficked areas of space. Somewhere out there, she thought with a shiver, the burnt-out shell of the *Leander* was being dismantled by salvagers looking for any scrap of metal still worth a couple of bits, like grave robbers picking through bones.

The ferry docked less than an hour later, and everyone inside shuffled like cattle out of its belly and onto the bi-rail cars that ran underground to the heart of Central City. When they emerged onto the sidewalk, Vika was temporarily stunned. The sun was so bright that her eyes contracted painfully and she stood there in a kind of a trance, not caring about the people whose paths she was blocking, just drinking in the light. She'd forgotten how warm the sun could feel on her skin; the version they got through the haze on Philomenus was such a weak, pale imitation of this. Everything round her seemed to glow. From the buildings that sparkled like gems, their mirrored windows glinting silver and blue and gold in the light, to the lush green of the park across the street, the color so vivid it seemed to pulse with life. Even the people walking past looked like little candies, all wrapped in colorful paper, the soft swish and crinkle of the ladies' dresses like pastilles being unwrapped.

It was so much worse than she remembered, cause it was so much more beautiful. She was suddenly, terribly sure she was going to cry.

"Oh, my girl." Her mum sniffed beside her and dabbed at her eyes. "To think this all could have been yours."

Vika's anger was swift and red-hot. "Don't be ridiculous, Mum," she snapped. "I never would have married him."

"I'm sure you would have!" her mum replied, and Vika hated her for how certain she sounded.

"Bella, please, not now," her da said softly.

"I only want what's best for our daughter. What's so wrong with that?"

"It's just that—"

"Where are we going, anyway?" Vika asked, interrupting the argument before it could gain too much momentum.

Her da pulled a crumpled slip of paper with an address scrawled across it from his pocket. "I'm not quite sure. But we're getting close."

Vika realized exactly where they were headed the moment they turned the next corner. The place was hard to miss, after all.

"Hell's teeth, is this supposed to be funny?" she demanded as they approached the building. If she hadn't recognized its dramatic facade from the feeds—intricately carved stone the color of fresh butter juxtaposed with an ultra-modern wall of windows that ran the entire height of the building like one massive, unbroken sheet of glass—then the name emblazoned over the door in silver script would have given it away.

"Oh dear," her da said, checking the address on his paper again.

People in suits and dresses streamed in and out of the bank of automatic doors, somehow never running into each other or the sliding walls of glass as they created a dizzying kaleidoscope of movement. One of the uniformed attendants stationed outside looked over at Vika, taking in and summing her up with one contemptuous glance, and she struggled not to smooth down the wrinkles in her dress.

"I an't going in there," Vika said.

"Don't say 'an't,'" her mum scolded just as Ms. Lyons, in a dress the color of ice, stepped out of the building.

"Good afternoon," she said. "Welcome to Chapin Tower."

CHAPTER SEVEN

"THANK YOU FOR COMING so quickly," Ms. Lyons continued. "Please, follow me."

Vika was trapped. Couldn't run away now or pitch a fit here on the sidewalk without making a fool of herself, so she let her da propel her through the door with a hand at her elbow. Her heart was fluttering in her chest and all she wanted was to demand to know why she was there, what this was all about, but first there were hands to be shaken and pleasantries to be exchanged as Ms. Lyons walked them through the elegant lobby teeming with businesspeople. Were they all well? Did their trip go smoothly? Wasn't the weather very fine today? Vika wanted to scream.

Instead of taking them to the huge bank of glass-enclosed lifts in the center of the building, Ms. Lyons led them past a security station, exchanging a nod with the guard who waved them through, and toward the back of the building. Tucked against a wall was a handful of service lifts, one of which Ms. Lyons summoned with a wave of an access card. They stepped inside the utilitarian carriage that smelled vaguely of bleach and ozone, and when Ms. Lyons pressed a button on the panel, Vika's stomach unexpectedly leapt *up*. It took her a second to figure out that they were traveling down, into the bowels of the building. She'd been expecting the elevator to rise toward the penthouse that took up the top three floors, the one that had belonged to Rigel Chapin and had played a featured role in both her recent fantasies and nightmares.

"Please." Vika couldn't keep the words back any longer, and they tasted sour and stale on her tongue from rolling round her mouth so long. "Ms. Lyons, what are we doing here?"

"You'll see in just a moment, Miss Hale, I assure you."

The lift doors opened into a plain hallway painted a cheerful sky blue that somehow made the small, poorly lit space seem even grimmer. Ms. Lyons led them past a handful of doors with brass numbers affixed to the outside and knocked lightly at number four.

"One moment!" someone called from inside.

Vika exchanged a look with her da, wishing she wasn't too grown-up to take his hand.

The door opened, and Archer Sheratan was standing there, his blue eyes as striking as she remembered, his presence surprisingly reassuring. He was wearing his professional persona but flashed her a wink behind the backs of her parents and Ms. Lyons as she followed them through the door. She then found herself inside someone's dim, shabby sitting room. The shift was so unexpected—from opulent skyscraper to utilitarian hallway to frumpy floral sofa and hand-knitted cushions—that it took Vika a moment to even register the couple sitting on that sofa.

"Miss Hale, I'd like to introduce you to Harold and Mira Gardner," Ms. Lyons said.

She recognized the names before she recognized their faces. They looked different from the picture she'd seen of them on the newsfeeds. In the photograph—some kind of official portrait of a large group the feeds had cropped so that only the Gardners' faces were visible—he'd been dressed in a navy maintenance jumper and she'd been wearing the standard head-to-toe white of a domestic servant. They'd both been smiling. Now they were each dressed in black and, although they looked nothing alike—he was a large, broad bear of a man with pale skin and white hair and she was a tiny lady with ochre skin and dark hair shot through with gray— their pained, anxious expressions were mirror images of each other.

Vika couldn't imagine what they had to feel anxious about. They'd just inherited one of the largest fortunes in the quadrant. She'd have thought that would pretty much eliminate all worries. She was suddenly so blindingly jealous of them that she might have jumped out of the window if there had been one this far underground.

Ms. Lyons made formal introductions all round, although they all knew perfectly well who each other was. Vika was the girl who'd been willed away to a stranger and then pseudo-widowed when he was caught in a terrorist bombing. The Gardners were the loyal Chapin servants—his personal housekeeper and handyman for decades—who had been the next in line to inherit the fortune since old Chapin had been such a tyrant that he had no family or friends left beyond his estranged son.

The only question that remained unanswered was the sole one Vika cared about: what in the fecking hell she was doing there. The careworn couple didn't look like the types to want to rub their good luck in someone's face, but why else could they possibly want to meet her?

Mr. Gardner somberly shook the hands of Vika's stunned parents and then turned to her. "It's good to finally meet you, Miss Hale," he said, extending a hand to her, "despite the unpleasant circumstances."

She was gripped with the childish desire to stick her hands under her arms but managed to overcome it. "Nice to meet you."

His wife was not so composed. When they'd entered, she'd been paging through a stack of old papers, which she now collected and placed back in the wooden box they'd come from. Her hands fluttered about, from the box to the handkerchief tucked in her pocket to her throat, and she looked as though she might flutter herself to pieces at any moment. Her eyes were thick with unshed tears as she stood and leaned in close to Vika, giving her two airy kisses on the cheeks. "Dear girl," she said. "What a time you must have been having."

Vika gave her a tight smile. Bit of an understatement, that.

Her mum sniffed like she smelled something unpleasant. "Now, to what do we owe the honor of being summoned here when your recent good fortune must have you so occupied?" Vika wanted very much to kick her.

"We just wanted to meet your girl here, Mrs. Hale," Mr. Gardner said, "and to tell you face-to-face how sorry we are for what you've been through."

That was it? *That* was why they'd been hustled to this planet in such a rush, just so that these people could lay eyes on her?

Mrs. Gardner sat and gestured for everyone else to sit as well. It was an almost comical invitation since there was hardly space in the small sitting room for all of them to stand comfortably. Mr. Gardner offered Vika his seat, so she sat beside his wife on the uncomfortably cozy sofa. Archer fetched the two small chairs from the dining table for her parents and then went to the kitchen to make tea. Ms. Lyons observed them all from the doorway while Mr. Gardner slowly paced—as much as a man his size could pace in such a small room—from the sofa to the sideboard.

"You know we knew Leo since he was just a baby," Mrs. Gardner said. They had to sit so close together on the tiny sofa that her knee was pressed into Vika's. "He spent lots of time down here with us because Mrs. Chapin died when he was very young, and I like to think there was a part of him that saw me as something of a mother. We never were able to have children ourselves, but we loved little Leo like he was our own." She stopped to press the handkerchief to her mouth, and her voice was thick when she spoke again. "He always called me 'Mimi,' ever since he could talk. A combination of 'Mira' and 'Mummy,' I think."

"He sent her a gift on her name day every year after he went away," Mr. Gardner said. "He was just nine or ten cycles then but still, every year he remembered her."

Mrs. Gardner nodded and stroked the box, filled with aging papers, that sat in front of her on the coffee table. "And he wrote me all these letters. I hadn't seen him in person for years, but we wrote every month at least. He knew how much I loved receiving real post, letters written on real paper that the other person actually held. They seem so much more heartfelt than some lights on a screen, don't they?" The woman looked to her for agreement, and Vika dutifully nodded. Mira reached inside the box, searching under tattered pages and opened envelopes, til she found a photograph, which she handed to Vika. "There he is, just before he went off to school. He must have grown into a handsome young man, but I suppose we'll never know."

Vika looked at the photo, her stomach twisting itself into strange knots as she gazed down at the face of the person she might have married. The newsfeeds had never broadcast his image before, so this was her first time seeing him. He was a sandy-haired boy with pale eyes and a round face that had yet to lose its baby softness. He was sitting on this exact sofa, right where she was, his arm round Mira's waist and his head resting against her shoulder as he smiled into the camera. It was a gentle, almost sad kind of smile, so at odds with the vision of the haughty, superior Leo Chapin she had constructed in her mind.

"He was such a sweet boy," Mrs. Gardner continued. "It's cruel what happened to him, and to you, my dear." Two fat tears rolled down her cheeks and she dabbed them with her handkerchief while her husband rubbed a hand across her shoulders.

The back of Vika's neck prickled with sweat, and the room seemed to be constricting round her. Sitting so close to Mrs. Gardner's grief, she could feel it radiating off the woman. It seemed to sink into her, like the warmth that bled through her dress and into her skin where their knees touched. Vika didn't want this. The last thing in the world she wanted was to hear about how wonderful and kind Leo Chapin had been. She'd rather think of him as the monster from her worst nightmares and imagine she'd had a lucky escape. She handed Mrs. Gardner back the photograph.

Just then Archer appeared at her elbow with a cup of tea, saving her from having to think of something appropriate to say to the crying woman. As he handed her the saucer, his fingers lingered on top of hers a moment longer than they needed to. The touch was like a cool breeze across the back of her neck, and she was able to take a deep breath.

"I'm sorry for your loss," she told Mrs. Gardner. "I'm sure Mr. Chapin would be glad to know that he's so fondly remembered."

Mrs. Gardner took her hand, holding it in her lap. "I hadn't thought of that. I hope you're right."

"I want you to know, Miss Hale, that we intend to put the money that should have been his to good use," Mr. Gardner told her. "We're offering a hefty reward for anyone who helps us catch the monsters who did this. And we'll be starting a charitable foundation in his name, endowed by us, for child welfare. Fifty million bits."

Vika's eyes widened. They must have *really* loved him.

"Mr. Gardner," Ms. Lyons interjected, like she couldn't stop herself. "Please allow me to reiterate my concerns about that number. It is simply too high a figure—"

"I understand your worries, Evelyn, I do," Mr. Gardner said, squeezing his wife's shoulder, "but we feel it's right."

"How have *you* been, my dear?" Mrs. Gardner asked her as Ms. Lyons bit her tongue. "I imagine it hasn't been easy."

Vika swallowed. Maybe the polite thing to do here was to demur and insist that she was fine, but that, frankly, would require more energy than she had left. "It's been the worst thing that's ever happened to me," she said.

Her mum gasped. "Vika!"

"That's quite all right, Mrs. Hale," Mrs. Gardner said. "I asked, and I want to know."

Vika was glad she couldn't see her mum's glare from this angle. "I was just thrown into this," she said, with some satisfaction that Ms. Lyons would be hearing it. "I didn't ask for any of it. I was just . . . given away, from one stranger to another, like I wasn't even a real person. And everyone hated me so much for it—cause they were jealous, I guess, even though it wasn't much to be jealous of— and then somehow they hated me even *more* after it all went away."

Mrs. Gardner patted her hand. "Oh, dear girl. How awful."

"It's very unfair what's happened to you, Miss Hale. And to your parents." Mr. Gardner turned to her da. "It must have been hard to see your daughter offered a life of security and comfort with a good husband, however unusual the arrangement, and then have that all taken away. We could hardly blame you if you despised the very sight of us."

Vika's mum sat a little straighter in her chair, her lips pinched together so tightly they near disappeared. Her da put his hand on her mum's knee, the tips of his fingers going white. "You're kind to think of us at all, sir," he said.

Mrs. Gardner's eyes were big and dewy as she looked at Vika. "I hope you don't harbor any ill feelings for us."

"Course not," Vika said, a little surprised to discover that she meant it. "You had this whole business just dropped on your head same as I did. You, at least, actually deserve to inherit from Mr. Chapin. I only ever met him once when I was little and you worked for him for years."

"You're a very sweet girl," Mrs. Gardner said.

Vika huffed out a little laugh. She didn't think anyone had ever used that word to describe her in her life. "I'm really not. It's only the truth."

The woman turned to look up at her husband. "Hal?"

Mr. Gardner considered Vika for a moment, looking deep into her eyes like he was trying to find something there, and then nodded. "Yes." He turned to Ms. Lyons, who was still watching silently from the doorway. "Yes."

Alarmed, Vika looked at her da, and his expression matched her own confusion. "What is it?" she asked. She didn't know if she could handle another surprise. She inadvertently glanced up at Archer and found him smiling reassuringly at her. A little of her anxiety eased.

"The Gardners have a proposal for you, Miss Hale," Ms. Lyons said from her position in the doorway where she overlooked them all with sharp eyes. "It's why they wanted to see you today."

Mrs. Gardner squeezed her hand, which Vika worried must be growing clammy in the older woman's. "I have a good sense about people, Miss Hale—"

"It's true," her husband said.

"Always have. And I like you. I think we could be good friends."

"I . . . well, thank you," Vika said, at a total loss as to where this conversation was headed.

"I'm very uneasy with the idea of Hal and me inheriting all this money at your expense," Mrs. Gardner said. "We considered little Leo and even Mr. Chapin to be a part of our family. And with you being so nearly a part of theirs, it doesn't seem to right for our lives to change so much and yours to go on as normal."

Vika glanced at her parents. Her da's frown had turned his thick eyebrows into one straight line across his brow, and her mum was perched on the edge of her chair like a bird ready to swoop in on a meal.

Mr. Gardner sat on the arm of the sofa and put an arm round his wife's narrow shoulders. "We've worked hard all our lives, and now that our circumstances are changing, we intend to enjoy ourselves a little. We'd like to invite you to enjoy yourself with us."

Vika just stared at them.

"We'd like you to come stay with us for a while," Mrs. Gardner said gently, like she was explaining something to a simpleton, which Vika suddenly felt she was. "If that's something you think you'd like, of course. It sounds like a break from Philomenus might do you some good right about now. We'll have plenty of room for you once we move, and we've already been invited to lots of parties and interesting events I think you'd enjoy. After all you've been through, it seems only right to include you in our good fortune. I feel sure dear Leo would have wanted you taken care of in his absence, and that's the least we can do for him now."

"Are you serious?" Vika whispered, suddenly sure the flat was experiencing some kind of gas leak and she was hallucinating all of this.

"Absolutely," Mrs. Gardner said. "You'd be doing us a favor, really. It will be so nice to have a young person around to keep us company, and you can stay as long as you'd like. What do you think?"

Vika didn't need to think at all. For the second time, her whole life had changed in an instant.

She launched herself at the woman, wrapping her arms round Mrs. Gardner's neck. "Thank you, thank you!" Mrs. Gardner laughed and gave her a squeeze, and Mr. Gardner patted her shoulder.

Vika's head was spinning; she was going to live on Ploutos. She was going to leave Philomenus behind, its dirt and haze, the grind of her job, sharing a narrow bed with her sister, all of it. She was going to get to stay here on this glittering planet and live a life full of parties and beautiful clothes and banquets and sophisticated people. She was going to get everything she'd never dared to dream of, and all without having to marry some stranger chosen for her by a dead man.

"So you'll come?" Mrs. Gardner asked.

"Course I will!" Vika said.

Details were discussed and timetables hammered out, but she barely took in any of it cause she was already floating away on dreams made of money. Her dad looked stunned and her mum was misty-eyed. As they all said their goodbyes and Ms. Lyons moved to escort them out, Archer sidled up to her.

"I look forward to seeing you again, Miss Hale," he said softly, his hand just grazing the small of her back as he opened the door for her, "in a less professional capacity."

A warmth like stirred embers glowed in her chest. "I look forward to that, too."

She could feel the entire planet shifting under her feet, and she was determined that nothing would ever be the same again. The Gardners' charity might be what was bringing her to Ploutos, but she was going to find some way—no matter what it took—to stay.

CHAPTER EIGHT

AS SOON AS VIKA stepped out of the bright Ploutosian sunlight and into the underground bi-rail station that would take her and her parents back to the atmospheric dock, creeping fingers of doubt started to curl round her heart. Here in the dark, pressed in with dull-eyed workers returning to Philomenus, the scene in the Gardners' basement flat began to seem unreal. Like a particularly vivid dream, one that made her wake up with her arms outstretched, reaching for something that wasn't there.

Ms. Lyons had said it would take a week or more to arrange Vika's transit docs. This wasn't just some day trip across the stream that could be bought at the last minute if you had enough bits for it; an open-ended pass for a Philomeni to live on Ploutos took work to obtain. Til the docs were loaded onto her identity card, Vika wasn't assuming anything. A better life had been promised to her and then snatched out of her hands once already; she didn't think she'd survive a second time.

She tried to put thoughts of Ploutos aside and get on with things, but it wasn't easy. Holding her tongue with bar patrons was harder than ever and keeping her temper in check with a newly sullen Lavinia was impossible. Even her mum's excitement irritated her, so she resorted to just avoiding all human interaction whenever possible. Aside from work, she barely spoke to anyone, running errands and doing chores outside the flat til she knew her family would be asleep, dodging acquaintances at the market, and pretending not to see Sky Foster whenever he tried to approach her for a conversation.

Then, nine days after her meeting with the Gardners, it happened. Lavinia, who was taking her turn helping their da with his work, came into the flat while Vika was enjoying a rare afternoon off with the place to herself.

"Your handyman benefactor's on the comm," she said with an impressively grand roll of her eyes.

Vika tossed aside the feed screen she'd been half-watching and hustled down to her da's office in the basement. Lavinia had left the handset of the comm dangling from its cord off the desk, and it was still swinging slightly, so she must have chucked it. Vika scooped it up.

"Hello?" she said.

"Good afternoon, Miss Hale." Archer's electronic voice was small and tinny but warm. "I have Harold Gardner on the channel as well. I hope you're well?"

"Very well, thank you," she said, a little out of breath.

"I'm pleased to inform you that your transit docs have been successfully processed," Archer said. "They're being loaded onto your ident card as we speak."

"That means you can come join Mira and me as soon as you'd like!" Mr. Gardner added. "We moved into the new flat over the weekend, and your room is all ready for you."

Vika closed her eyes and let her head drop back. A weight she'd been trying to pretend wasn't there was suddenly gone, and she felt like she might float right out of the chair.

"Thank you so much," she said weakly.

"I'll have my new assistant transfer some bits to you to buy a ferry ticket and whatever else you'll need before you get here," Mr. Gardner continued. "Any idea when we should expect you?"

"Tomorrow?" Vika said. She'd go tonight if she could.

He laughed. "Tomorrow it is."

After they'd worked out the particulars, Vika softly returned the comm to its cradle. Then she just sat there for a long moment, staring at it, trying to wrap her mind round what a difference one conversation could make.

It was all really happening. She was going to Ploutos.

Suddenly she needed to move. There was so much to do before she left, and maybe if she moved fast enough she could somehow speed up the time between now and tomorrow. She dashed up the stairs and back into her flat.

"I'm going!" she announced as she flung open the door.

An inscrutable mixture of emotions passed across Lavinia's face, finally settling into something between indifference and annoyance. Vika briefly wondered if she should have asked if Lavinia could come stay at the Gardners with her, but it wasn't her place to impose on their generosity like that. Besides, if she was being honest, she didn't actually want her there. For years they'd shared a bed and clothes and meals and even the tutor that Rigel Chapin had arranged just for her. For once, Vika wanted something for herself.

Besides, someone had to stay behind to help their da.

"So they didn't change their minds about taking you in?" Lavinia asked. "Like a stray dog off the street?"

"Nope!" Vika chirped. She refused to be baited by her sister's bitterness. She fetched a carry-all from the closet and dumped the contents of her drawer in their communal bureau—every possession she owned—onto the bed. She attempted to pack but found herself just staring at her belongings. Mostly black, utilitarian clothes for working behind the bar, shirts and pants that were worn from too much washing and were never quite free of the smell of grock, no matter how much she scrubbed. A couple of novels she and Lavinia had read near to pieces over the years whenever they had to entertain themselves by lamplight for hours or days at a time. A dented silver-backed hairbrush that had once been part of a set she'd gotten on her name day as a child. They'd sold the mirror and comb that came with it when they left their house for the THs, but Vika had cried so hard her da had let her keep the brush.

She set aside her nice gray dress to wear on the ferry the next day and put the brush and some underthings into the bag along with her identification. She didn't care if she saw anything else in the pile ever again.

"Take whatever you want," she said to Lavinia.

"You're going to regret that if they decide they don't like you and send you home in a few days," she said, already riffling through Vika's belongings.

Not even Lavinia's spitefulness could ruin Vika's good mood, but she didn't see the point in swimming in it all afternoon. She grabbed her coat and headed for the door. "Guess I'll have to make sure they like me, then."

She heard Lavinia scoff and mutter, "Good luck with that," under her breath as she closed the door behind her.

Vika decided to check her bit balance. Maybe Mr. Gardner's new assistant was so efficient they'd already loaded the promised credits onto her ident card. This small errand ended up giving her the chance to take one last look round her entire neighborhood and tell it goodbye cause the first two bit stations she visited were nonoperational. As she walked, she said silent farewells to the cramped little grocery store on the corner, the empty lot by TH 82 that was guarded by a pack of yowling feral cats, the Sullivan Street black market and the Nut Man who always stood at its entrance, and all the other fixtures of her Philomeni life she wouldn't miss one iota once she was gone. Starting tomorrow, when she walked the streets, she'd feel the sun on her face.

The third bit machine she tried had a line half a dozen deep, and a couple of mercs stood on the corner nearby, ready to shake down anyone who looked to have heavy pockets as they left. When it was finally Vika's turn to check the balance on her card, she didn't expect to find much there. Just whatever remained from her last paycheck from Nicky's, which was usually precious little once the bills were paid.

But when she waved her ident card in front of the scanner and pressed her thumb against the print plate, the number that popped up on the screen initially defied her understanding. It was so . . . long. So many digits. She read it once, twice, and then once more to be sure. She laughed and hit the button to withdraw. Heavens bless Mr. Gardner and his very capable assistant!

She jammed her pockets full of cash, glad no one was behind her in line cause she'd cleaned out the machine. She tossed a couple of bills at the mercs on the corner to save them the trouble of extorting it from her and headed for the THs. On the way, she passed a bakery, and despite not even being hungry, she went inside and bought a fizzy drink and one of every baked good lined up in the glass display case. The wind seemed less stinging, the sidewalks less dirty, as she walked along drinking her fizzy and eating a flaky pastry filled with chocolate cream. She floated into Nicky's, as weightless as the bubbles crackling softly inside the bottle.

Stella looked up from the bar at the chime above the door. "You're not on til tonight, Vika."

"I know," she said, catching a stray blob of cream at the corner of her mouth with her tongue. "I just came to tell you I quit."

Stella's mouth dropped open; people round here didn't just quit jobs. "What? When?"

"Now," Vika said, the words muffled by pastry. "I'm leaving and I an't coming back. Let Nicky know, would you?"

"Are you serious?" Stella set down the glass she was washing with a bang. "You can't be this dim."

"Sorry!" Vika said, even though she wasn't really, as she turned to leave. "Tell everyone goodbye for me!"

"Vika, come back here!" Stella called after her. "How am I supposed to cover your shift?"

"Don't care, bye!" Vika said and sailed out the door.

She tossed her half-drunk fizzy into the trash and pulled another pastry, this one dotted with some kind of pink fruit she didn't recognize, out of the bag hanging from her wrist. She didn't want to go home to Lavinia's sour mood and a grilling from her mum just yet, so she stopped at the small park near the school instead. It was deserted this time of day, which suited her perfectly. She sat on a bench eating her pastry while she watched a couple of birds chase each other through the branches of a tree, enjoying the quiet and the knowledge that she was leaving this all behind in the morning.

"Miss Hale?" a voice said.

She suppressed a sigh when she saw Sky Foster walking toward her. His smile was a shade too rigid to seem sincere, and she wondered if he thought he was pulling off charming.

"I've hardly seen you in weeks," he said. "Are you well?"

"Just busy," she said.

"I've been going up to the roof often for a bit of fresh air." He hovered near the end of the bench as though he was waiting for an invitation to sit. He'd be waiting a long time, seeing as how the last time they'd talked, he'd as good as accused her of being willing to sell herself for money. "It's quite a peaceful spot. I thought I might see you up there sometime."

She stood and tossed the last bite of her pastry to the pavement for the birds to fight over. "I'd better get going."

"Ah, I did hear a rumor you might be leaving us."

She whirled round on him. "Oh yes, I'm no better than you thought, am I? Selling out to the highest bidder?" Course, she hadn't *sold* herself to the Gardners. She was accepting their charity but only as a stepping stone to something bigger. Something entirely her own.

"That's not . . . Miss Hale—"

She held up a hand to cut him off. Suddenly she wasn't angry anymore. How could she be on today of all days? She was leaving Philomenus, and she would never see Sky Foster, his moony face, or his sly superiority again. She doubted she'd ever think of him again once she turned her back on him and walked away.

So she just smiled. "Goodbye, Mr. Foster," she said, and left him behind in her wake.

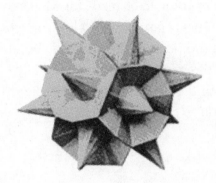

SHE WALKED AWAY FROM HIM, and as soon as she had turned the corner, he kicked a chunk of ice as hard as he could, his toes exploding with pain as the ice went skittering across the pavement.

He dropped onto the bench and rubbed his sore foot. That night on the roof, in the brief moment when he'd made her smile and managed to avoid saying anything catastrophically stupid, he'd felt like he was finally making some progress with her. Like maybe his scheme could actually work. But his strategy was doomed if he couldn't change her mind about him. He had to make her trust him, to *like* him, in order to get what he wanted out of her, and so far he was failing spectacularly.

Well, he might have nothing to show for it, but his job was done for the day. He waited long enough to give Vika a good head start and then headed back to TH 76. He found Ariel sitting on the front stoop waiting for him.

"Tough day at work?" she asked when she saw his face.

He sighed and sat down beside her. "I don't think I can pull this off. Is this the stupidest thing I've ever done?"

"Maybe. I haven't known you long enough to be sure."

He looked up to find her grinning at him. "Has anyone ever told you how terrible you are at encouraging people?"

"It may not be my strongest suit," she said, "but you need to toughen up if you're going to be ready for what's coming next. Cause I'm betting phase two is going to be a lot worse than you think."

He rubbed a hand across his forehead. What came next was a necessary part of the plan, but he wasn't exactly looking forward to it. "I suppose I'll find out."

"Well I hope you're ready," she said, "since your life depends on that girl."

CHAPTER NINE

VIKA'S ENTIRE FAMILY INSISTED on escorting her to the atmospheric docks. She suspected that was her da's doing, cause Lavinia and her mum seemed anxious to see the back of her already, although for very different reasons. Vika wore her gray dress under a fine white shawl she'd bought at the nicest store on Philomenus with some of the money she'd emptied out of the bit machine the day before. She left her ratty winter coat at home. It was warmer on Ploutos anyway, and she'd rather be cold for a few hours than to shame herself or the Gardners any more than necessary.

She bought herself one of the handful of first-class ferry tickets—no riding the bench in the bowels of the craft for her this time—and then pressed the remaining wad of cash into her da's hands. "Here. Take this."

He looked at her in befuddlement. "Darling, I can't—"

"Course you can," she said. "There's plenty more where this came from for me. Have yourselves a nice dinner and buy some new clothes. Replace that fecking oil lamp."

"This isn't necessary, my dear—"

"You want to ruin this for me? By making me worry about you all when I should be enjoying myself?"

That did the trick, and he pocketed the bits. He pulled her close, kissing her temple and resting his cheek against the top of her head like he used to do when she was little. "I'll miss you."

She blinked away the unexpected watering at the back of her eyes. She'd never been away from him before, and now they were going to be on entirely different planets. For the first time it really hit her. The Gardners seemed like nice people, but once she was on Ploutos, she was going to be all alone, with no one she could count on the way she did her da. A tiny part of her suddenly thought she should stay.

Then her mum embraced her. "Do us proud," she said, squeezing Vika a little too tight. "Take advantage of every opportunity you can."

Vika knew what that meant: find a good job or, preferably, a rich husband. The nakedness of her mother's grasping was embarrassing. "Yes, Mum."

Lavinia's face had hardened into a permanent scowl. Vika tried to imagine how she would feel if their roles were reversed but it was too unpleasant to even think about, so she tried to be kind as she kissed her sister goodbye.

"Enjoy having a big bed to yourself again," she said. "You can flail round in your sleep as much as you want."

Lavinia's stony expression cracked just the barest amount into something resembling a smile. "It won't be as satisfying without you to kick."

Vika walked up the gangway to the first-class cabin on the top level of the ferry and waved at them all one last time before disappearing inside. She wondered what they'd do now without her, how her da would cope, how relieved her mum and Lavinia would be to have her gone. She'd never been apart from her whole family at once.

Those thoughts receded as the ferry pulled away from Philomenus, like they were attached to that particular scrap of rock. It helped that she was sitting in what was probably the most comfortable chair

she'd ever experienced, drinking a glass of champagne that had been
brought to her the moment she'd sat down. By the time they were
deep in the stream and she was looking at the stars through the walls
of clear plastecene that made up the first-class cabin, they were gone
entirely.

Once on Ploutos, she was picked up by a driver the Gardners had
arranged for her. Vika had never been in a private car before, and
this one was almost as luxurious as the ferry had been. The driver
took her to Chapin Tower, her heart speeding up as the dramatic
facade with its sheet of windows came into view. But then the driver
turned the corner instead of stopping.

"Where are we going?" she asked.

"Around the back, miss," he said.

He stopped the car in front of a quieter, less grand entrance on the
opposite side of the building. Instead of a bank of doors bustling
with people coming and going, there was a single door flanked
by two massive stone planters spilling over with red-and-purple
blooms that perfumed the air. A uniformed doorman manned the
entrance, and he smiled as she stepped out of the car, her meager
bag of possessions slung over her shoulder.

"Good morning, Miss Hale," he said, opening the door for her.
She wondered how he knew who she was, but she wasn't exactly
surprised that he did. This was Ploutos, after all.

"Good morning," she echoed, stepping inside. She found herself
in a small, elegant lobby. To her right was a lift, and to her left was
a desk where a woman sat behind a holoscreen.

"Hello, Miss Hale," the woman said. "Mr. and Mrs. Gardner are
on their way down to meet you."

"Oh," Vika said. "Thank you."

Moments later, the door to the lift slid open and the Gardners
stepped out.

"You're here!" Mrs. Gardner said, fluttering up to Vika, giving her
a tight hug as though they were lifelong friends. She was wearing
a silk dress with monstrously big pink flowers on it and had her

hair newly styled in a way Vika had seen on many much younger ladies walking down the street. She looked a bit like a child playing dress-up in her mother's wardrobe, but she was beaming. "We're so glad you've joined us at last!"

Mr. Gardner, who was dressed in a fine new suit and had gotten a close shaving that took a decade off his face, said, "Wonderful to see you again, Miss Hale. You received those bits my assistant transferred to your card, I take it?"

"Yes. Thank you so much, Mr. and Mrs. Gardner."

"Oh, please, my dear. Call us Hal and Mira," he said. "We may be rich now—still strange to think that—but we're not all high and mighty."

"Well, you can judge that for yourself when you see the new flat!" Mira said as she waved her hand over the panel by the lift, causing the doors to open with a soft ding.

Vika's throat tightened, making it hard for her to swallow. "You decided to stay in Chapin Tower?" she asked as she followed them into the carriage. She had assumed they were just meeting here, that the Gardners' new flat must be in some other building where they hadn't labored as servants for decades.

Hal pressed one of just a handful of buttons on the inside panel. "We did think about leaving, but this place has been home for nearly thirty years now. Didn't seem right to just pack up and go, especially when we now own a perfectly good flat right here."

"So you've moved into Mr. Chapin's penthouse?" Vika asked. The top floors that made up the penthouse were the only residence in the building; all of the other levels were offices housing some of the planet's biggest companies. She tried not to picture old Rigel Chapin curled up on an antique rug like a giant dead beetle, the way they say he was when he was discovered by his steward. It was supposed to be one of the finest flats in the city, but she couldn't imagine stepping past that spot on the carpet every day.

"In a way," Mira said. "After his wife died, Mr. Chapin closed up the top two floors, and he and little Leo lived on the bottom level only. It seemed a shame to let the place just sit there unused, so we've refreshed the upper levels and moved in there. Perhaps after a respectable amount of time has passed, we'll renovate that lower level as well."

"Oh," Vika said, relieved. That didn't sound so bad.

"Never you worry, my dear, there's plenty of room for the three of us," Hal said. "And our new flat also has access to the roof. Mr. Chapin kept the most beautiful gardens up there. I hear you might particularly enjoy that."

Vika wondered where he'd heard that, but before she could ask, the little lurch in her stomach let her know that the lift had stopped. The doors were sliding open, and every other thought fled as she stepped into her new home.

The lift opened into a grand foyer. It was an entire room, opulently appointed, that had no real function other than to lead to other rooms, while the front door of Vika's flat on Philomenus opened into the room that was her kitchen, sitting room, dining room, and bedroom all at once. The large gilt-framed mirrors hung on the walls reflected the sunlight that streamed in through the floor-to-ceiling windows, and all of that light bounced off the mother-of-pearl floors and massive crystal chandelier. The whole room shimmered and glowed with it, and it felt to Vika like she was stepping directly into a sunbeam. She wanted to spread her arms and just absorb it all directly through her skin; she'd have been happy to live in that foyer forever.

But the foyer was only the beginning. Hal and Mira, as giddy as schoolchildren ready to show off their prized new toy, took her on a tour through the rest of the flat, each room grander than the last. Sitting rooms with fine furnishings upholstered in silk and smelling of the floral arrangements that occupied crystal and china vases, a sleek stainless steel kitchen where a private chef in white was already at work preparing their lunch, vaulted ceilings in every room with intricate crown moldings, bas-reliefs, and colorful frescoes.

And the windows. No matter what finery was in a room, it was always the windows that Vika's eyes went to first. They made up entire walls, letting all that beautiful sunlight flood in and providing spectacular views of the skyscrapers of Central City on one side and the lush greenery and glittering lake of St. Francis Park, the city's natural oasis, on the other. The Chapin Tower penthouse was the highest residence in the entire city, looking down on everything, and it was almost too beautiful to bear.

"She's starting to get that look," Mira said softly to her husband.

"So she is." Hal put an arm round Vika's waist, drawing her away from the window. "Vika, my girl, would you like to rest for a little while? It's a lot to take in all at once, and you've had a busy day already."

"Yes, please," Vika said, dazed, not realizing that so much beauty could wear a person out so much.

"Let's take you to your room," he said. "It's just this way."

Hal and Mira led her back to the foyer, up the grand curving staircase that led to the top level of the flat, and down a corridor.

"Here you are, sweetheart," Mira said, opening a door at the end of the hall. "Your room."

After the rest of the flat, Vika was prepared for luxury. But hearing it called *hers* made it seem all the more lovely. She blinked back tears as she looked round the room. A large bed—one so big she could easily have shared it with Lavinia with no worries about being kicked—dominated the room. It was covered with crisp white linens and an army of pillows embroidered with silver and gold thread. Four wooden posts carved with flowers and vines held up velvet curtains the deep blue color of the evening sky. There was no canopy, though, which seemed a little odd since the ceiling of this room was one of the few totally plain ones she'd seen in the entire flat. The blue velvet of the bed curtains matched the upholstery of the chair at a delicate vanity across the room and contrasted prettily with the pale violet of the tufted sofa and chairs in a sitting area by the expansive windows. There was a grassy balcony outside and a view of the park beyond that.

"Do you like it?" Mira asked, somehow sounding genuinely unsure.

"It's the most beautiful room I've ever seen," Vika breathed.

Mira beamed and gave her shoulder a pat. "I'm so glad. Now why don't you make yourself comfortable, maybe have a little lie-down. Lunch will be ready soon, and then I was thinking we could go do some shopping this afternoon. Lord knows I need some nice new clothes to go with this new flat, and I could use a young person's eye to help me. And you'll be needing some new clothes of your own I'm sure. Does that sound fun?"

Vika laughed. "I'd say so."

Mira clapped. "Excellent!"

"Get yourself settled in," Hal said. "See that sensor beside your bed?"

Vika spotted the small silver plate on the wall.

"That connects to the staff," Hal explained, "so if you need anything at all, just press it and someone will be happy to help you."

Vika's head was swimming. "The staff?"

"Oh, I know!" Mira laughed. "It feels silly to have so many people around to wait on us hand and foot, but we didn't want to let any of Mr. Chapin's employees go."

"We'll let you rest now," Hal said, ushering his wife toward the door. He paused halfway out of the room and turned back to her. "We're so happy you're here, Vika."

Vika smiled. "Me, too."

When Hal and Mira were gone, Vika did a slow turn round the room, taking it all in once more. She hardly knew what to do now that she was here. She was afraid to touch anything, scared of sullying it or watching her hand pass right through it to prove it was all a dream after all. At a loss, she set down the little bag she carried over her shoulder and unpacked its meager contents. She put her change of underthings in the top drawer of the bureau inlaid with gold and laid her dented silver hairbrush—which she'd once thought so fine but which now looked sad and shabby in these surroundings—on the surface of the vanity. Her only other possession, which she had swiped from her da's office on a whim that morning, was the picture of her family at the summer fair. She considered their smiling faces for a moment and then set the frame on the bedside table.

"This is my life now," she whispered to the room. She grabbed the velvet curtains hanging down from the bed and crushed the cool, soft fabric between her fingers, then kicked off her shoes and burrowed her toes deep into the plush carpeting. "This is my life now," she repeated a little more surely.

On impulse, she reached out and touched the silver panel beside the bed.

"Good morning, Miss Hale," a pleasant female voice instantly said. "How may I help you?"

Vika blinked. She hadn't actually considered what she'd ask for. "Oh, um, just a glass of water, please?"

"Certainly, I'll have that right up for you. Would you like anything else?"

"Freeze cream," Vika blurted without thinking.

She half expected laughter in response but the woman only said, "Yes, miss."

Minutes later there was a soft knock at the door, and a servant wheeled in a silver tray and then silently excused himself. On the tray was a chilled glass and a crystal pitcher of sparkling water with slices of puckerfruit and mint leaves floating in it. Beside that was a bowl roughly the size of Vika's head filled with scoops of freeze cream smothered in drizzles of chocolate and caramel sauce and topped with the reddest, plumpest berries she'd ever seen.

Vika threw herself back onto the bed, smothering her laughter and shrieks of delight in the mountain of feather pillows.

CHAPTER TEN

LUNCH FOR VIKA AND the Gardners was served at an intimate dining table on one of the many balconies that wrapped round the flat. Vika caught herself closing her eyes every few minutes so she could better feel the sensation of the sun on her skin. There was a grander dining table inside—a long, shiny one with ornately carved legs, very much like the one from her fantasies—but Vika couldn't imagine anything better than this wrought-iron table in the grass, overlooking the sun-dappled park from the highest point in the city.

She wasn't very hungry on account of all the freeze cream she'd eaten, but she forgot about that as soon as the chef brought out what he'd prepared: fish cooked in wine and herbs, freshly baked bread, and an array of brightly colored vegetables. Very little vegetation grew on Philomenus on account of the haze, so what little produce they ate usually came from cans and had a distinctly gray tinge to it. Vika bit into something purple that was crisp and buttery and felt suddenly starving, like she needed to make up for every meal she'd ever skipped.

"Now, my girl," Hal said as he clumsily skewered a forkful of the delicate fish, "we've had invitations pouring in ever since this whole inheritance business started—"

"Everyone's been so kind," Mira added. "They've really gone out of their way to make us feel welcome."

"—and one of them was from Evelyn Lyons to attend the symphony with her tonight," Hal continued. "Never been to the symphony myself but apparently it's quite the popular thing to do if you've got the bits for it. Ms. Lyons owns an entire box and she said there's a seat for you, too, if you want to come, but of course we understand if you'd rather have a quiet night to get settled in."

Mira sipped a glass of honey-colored wine. "It's entirely up to you, sweetheart."

"I think it sounds like fun," Vika replied. Philomenus had a small concert hall they'd visited sometimes when she was small, and she'd always enjoyed listening to the bands strumming away at their guitars and fiddles.

"Oh, excellent, I was hoping you'd say that!" Mira said. "We'll add that to the list of things we need to shop for this afternoon."

After their lunch was eaten—Vika even managed a small slice of cake for dessert—Hal excused himself to go take care of some business.

"I thought you were a man of leisure now?" Vika teased.

He chuckled and smoothed his shirt over his belly. "So did I! But it turns out that money creates a lot of work. There's managing all the staff and Mr. Chapin's investments, not to mention getting the charitable foundation we're starting in Leo's name up and running. It almost makes me miss the simplicity of fixing a broken toilet. Enjoy your afternoon, ladies."

The moment Vika and Mira stepped out of Chapin Tower, an emerald-green car with its chrome buffed to a brilliant shine pulled up to the curb. The driver, who introduced himself as Grant, came round to open the door for them, and the leather seats of the interior were supple and warm to the touch. Vika felt herself sinking back into them; she'd never realized before today how *comfortable* being rich was. Every surface she came into contact with was clean and soft, like all the sharp edges of the world had been sanded down just for her. The car pulled into traffic, glittering buildings and colorful people passing by in a pleasant blur, and she knew she'd be happy to just be driven round in this car all day.

But then came the succession of shops. They all smelled of perfume and clean linen, and champagne was pressed into her hand the moment she walked in each door. Soon her head was light, and the shop attendants were happy and accommodating, complimenting everything Vika tried on and marveling over her beauty. And the clothes! Vika had never given much thought to clothes but she realized now that it was only cause she'd never been round nice ones. The feel of cashmere and silk and fine wool against her skin made her feel like a different person, one who was more sure of herself, like the world had a space carved into it just for her.

"Are you sure this is okay?" Vika asked as she agreed to one more dress. The shop attendant whisked it away to have it packed up in rose-scented tissue paper and added to the pile Vika was accumulating.

"Of course!" Mira said. "You must have the proper kinds of clothes to wear, after all."

"But the money . . ."

"Never you mind, dear." Mira handed over a bit card. "It's a drop in the bucket!"

At least Mira was buying just as much as she was. By the third store, more than half of the parcels packed into the trunk of the car were hers, and she was having a ball. Vika wondered when the last time this woman, who had labored her whole life as a domestic on this planet, had bought something for herself just cause she wanted it. As Mira twirled in front of a mirror in a dress as sunny as her smile, Vika felt a hard lump develop in her throat as she imagined her mum in Mira's place, how happy she would be, how *relieved*. Maybe she'd go back to being the woman she had been before, who had laughed so loud for the smallest reasons cause she wasn't perpetually on edge, fearing that they'd slip further into poverty, resenting her da for crumbling under the pressure. Maybe her parents' marriage would still be a happy one.

"Oh, Vika," Mira suddenly said, spotting something across the store. "You must try that one on!"

Thoughts of her mum fled her mind as the shop attendant finished buttoning her into the dress. The full skirt and bodice were made of a delicate midnight-blue tulle that was near sheer, and it was covered with an intricate embroidery of crystals in a lacelike pattern that caught the light whenever she moved and made her look like the twinkling of a star in the night sky.

"Oh, Vika." Mira sighed as Vika carefully touched the fabric with her fingertips. "You have to wear this to the symphony tonight."

"I will," Vika said, loving the girl she saw in the mirror, the one she had always wanted to be. "But I think this dress—this life, really—is too grand for Vika the Philomeni barmaid. From now on I want to go by Viktoria."

Mira nodded. "A fresh start. I think that's a lovely idea."

Vika twisted her hips slightly, watching the light pick up the shimmers in the dress. "That name never seemed to fit my old life, but now . . ."

"Yes, it's perfect," Mira said, giving her a squeeze round the shoulders. She quickly turned away, but not before Vika caught a glimpse of her lips trembling in the reflection of the mirror.

"What is it?" she asked. "Are you feeling okay?"

"Oh, I'm fine." Mira waved away her concerns and dabbed at her eyes. "I was just thinking of Leo, imagining him seeing you in that dress. Oh, I'd give it all to have him back."

Vika wouldn't.

As soon as they got home, Vika collapsed onto her bed. Someone had straightened the covers and pillows while she was out, so she had the pleasure of rumpling them all over again as she shucked her old gray dress and climbed under the comforter. Who knew shopping could be so exhausting? The sheets were deliciously silky and cool against her skin, and she fell almost instantly asleep, feeling as though she were floating away on a cloud.

She woke to a soft knocking at her door sometime later.

"Who is it?" she called.

"It's Gemma, miss," came the voice of a maid Vika had briefly met earlier. "I'm here to help you get ready for your evening."

Vika took a shower—marveling at the way the water came out instantly hot and stayed that way—while Gemma unwrapped her new clothes from their tissue paper and stored them in the closet. Vika came out of the bathroom wearing the thick cotton robe that had been hung on the back of the door and sat at the vanity so Gemma could do her hair and face.

"I've never worn cosmetics before," she said, eyes closed, as Gemma used a soft brush to cover her face with a light, sweet-smelling powder. "Never saw much point in saving up for any on Philomenus."

"An't ever worn them myself," Gemma said. "I only learned how to apply them for my last employer cause she had a terror of getting her hands messy and was afraid to do it herself."

"What part of Philomenus are you from?" Vika asked. Most domestics were Philomeni and the girl's accent was unmistakable.

"C-2."

"We're practically neighbors, then."

Gemma smiled. "We *were*."

"Oh." Vika flushed. "I guess you're right."

Gemma finished painting on her eyes and lips and arranged her hair so that it cascaded in curls down her back. Then she helped Vika step into the blue dress and buttoned her into it, finishing up by slipping a diamond collar necklace around her throat and a couple of glittering bangles onto her wrist.

Vika assessed herself in the mirror. Her tawny complexion was smooth and flawless now that her smattering of freckles, the small scar on her chin, and every pore and imperfection had seemingly been erased. Gemma had outlined her eyes in a dark liner and heavy lashes that made her eyes look large and dramatic, and her coral-colored lips combined with the subtle swipe of jade powder over her eyelids made her hazel eyes look almost green. There was no question that she looked more beautiful than she ever had before, but still she worried that there was some invisible mark on her that she couldn't detect. Something underneath the expensive gown and jewels and Gemma's expert work that would broadcast her humble origins to everyone around her.

"Think I'll fool them?" she asked.

Gemma looked her up and down. "You'd fool me."

Vika supposed that would have to do for now. It was time for them to be getting on their way, so she went in search of the Gardners. She found Mira—wearing a deep purple dress with her hair swept back and held in place with a glittering pin—in the sitting room.

"Oh, Viktoria," she said. "You look lovely!"

"So do you!"

"I'll hail down to the concierge and have her summon the car," Mira said. "Would you go get Hal from his office? He wanted to finish up some last-minute business but, honestly, enough is enough."

"Of course," Vika said. She vaguely recalled the location of Hal's office from her tour that morning—Lord, had she really not even been here an entire day yet?—and headed toward it. It was tucked into the back of the lower level, near the kitchen, laundry, and other working parts of the flat. She accidentally knocked at what turned out to be a small powder room and then a cleaning supply closet before she found the right door and heard Hal's voice call her in.

She pushed open the door and stepped inside. Hal, missing his jacket, was sitting at a desk with a holoscreen full of numbers glowing in front of him.

"Sorry to interrupt," Vika said. "Mira sent me to fetch you. She said it's time to go."

"Right, right, coming," Hal said, swiping at the screen to minimize it. He waved vaguely behind Vika. "You haven't met my assistant yet, have you?"

She turned to find another person in the room, a young man standing at a bookshelf, frozen in the act of replacing a book, his eyes burning like a dark sun as they met hers.

Vika's heart stuttered painfully in her chest, and it suddenly felt like her blood was running backward.

Cause Hal's assistant was Sky Foster.

"Sky Foster, this is Miss Hale, the young lady who's staying with us," Hal said, not sensing anything amiss as he rearranged a few papers on his desk. "Sky's helping me get all of my business in order. There's much more to do than I would have thought . . ."

Vika couldn't take in what Hal was saying. She was too busy staring at Sky, who was staring right back at her as though he was just as surprised to see her, which was utterly impossible. Finally he blinked and dropped his gaze to the floor.

"Miss Hale and I are already acquainted, sir," he said. "I rent a room from her father on Philomenus."

"Really?" Hal said. "Extraordinary coincidence."

Vika felt her hands clench into fists at her side. "Isn't it."

"Well, I'd best get moving, don't want to make the old lady mad," Hal said. Sky retrieved his tuxedo jacket and held it out, helping Hal slip it on and then brushing his shoulders and straightening the collar. "Thank you, my boy. Do you mind tidying up the mess I've created in here before heading home?"

"Of course not, sir. Enjoy your evening."

Hal made his way out of the room, and Vika should have followed him, but she found herself rooted to the floor. She and Sky were alone with nothing but the gentle tick of a clock and their held breaths between them. She was so torn between wanting to confront him and wanting to run away that she couldn't do anything but just stand there, staring at him, her stomach roiling. What kind of game was he playing with her?

But then he opened his mouth, and she was suddenly very sure she didn't want to hear whatever sly, stuttering nonsense he was about to speak. She turned and swept out of the office, hoping she

looked haughty and dignified even though she felt like she was fleeing. She heard his footsteps rush after her.

"Miss Hale, wait," he said, his voice low as he caught up with her
in the darkened corridor. "Please. Vika—"

His hand closed around her wrist and she spun on him, yanking
her arm from his grasp. "Don't!"

"I'm sorry, I shouldn't have—" He took a shuffling step back
from her. "Please. Allow me to explain."

"Go ahead then." She raised her chin and tried to master the
tremor in her voice. "Explain what you're doing, following me here."

He frowned at her in bewilderment. "I-I didn't."

"Course you—" She stopped and cleared her throat. "*Of course*
you did."

"I didn't, truly. I told you weeks ago that I'd found employment,
long before the Gardners told me they'd invited someone to live
with them. I had no idea . . ."

"What? No idea that your new employers had inherited my dead
fiancé's fortune?" she demanded. "No idea that the bits you were
transferring to their new houseguest were going into my account?"

For once, he actually held her gaze. "That's right," he said, slowly
and deliberately.

She didn't believe him. Her insides felt hot and smoky, like there
was a smoldering fire burning in her belly.

"I would like it if we could be friendly," he added softly, his dark
eyes behind his dark-framed glasses impenetrable in the dimness.

She didn't trust him, but she wasn't going to let him ruin this for
her, either. Whatever he was after, it wasn't going to stop her from
doing the only thing that mattered now: making this new life her
only one.

"Just stay away from me," she said, and she turned and walked
away, feeling his eyes on her with every step.

CHAPTER ELEVEN

AS GRANT PULLED THE car up to the curb, Vika glanced back at the penthouse of Chapin Tower. Back on Philomenus, the atmo-haze would have been so thick by the fourth or fifth floor that she wouldn't have been able to see beyond that point. But here, on this pristine planet, she was easily able to make out the figure standing at one of the brightened windows. The tower was so tall that Sky Foster was barely more than a dark smudge, and she couldn't tell if he was looking down at her or not, but somehow she was sure he was.

"Viktoria, dear?"

Vika turned at Mira's voice and found the woman beckoning her inside the car while Grant waited, hand outstretched, ready to assist her.

"Everything all right?" Mira asked.

Vika squared her shoulders. She was wearing the most beautiful dress she'd ever seen and she was climbing into a chauffeured car to go to the symphony; she'd deal with Mr. Gardner's underling and whatever his scheme was later. She wasn't going to let thoughts of him ruin this night for her.

"Everything's perfect," she said, taking Grant's gloved hand and letting him help her into the car.

The concert hall was perched on the shores of the lake on the east end of St. Francis Park, a massive construction of chrome and glass stacked up at improbable angles. Vika felt dwarfed by it as she climbed out of the car, struggling with the length and volume of her dress and trying desperately to hide it.

"Oh my," Mira said beside her, gazing up at the strange glass shapes overhead.

Hal took his wife's arm. "Can you imagine what this must have cost? A single pane of that glass must be at least four or five hundred bits . . ."

Vika's cheeks warmed. Luckily no one was close enough to overhear them, but Hal and Mira were both gawking at their surroundings in such an obvious way that they would never be mistaken for people who actually belonged here. Everyone would see how badly out of place they were. Vika took the red-carpeted stairs up into the hall a few steps ahead of them, hoping she wasn't attracting the same scrutiny. Mira had bought her a beautiful pair of silver heels that afternoon, but after practicing walking in them around her bedroom, she'd decided to stick with flats instead until she was able to master them. She couldn't bear the idea of making a fool of herself.

In the lobby, which shone with white marble and gold on every surface, they met Evelyn Lyons and her wife, Beatrix, who greeted them warmly, and then headed to their seats in the auditorium. Vika tried to keep her mouth from falling open as they stepped into their box. The beauty of the lobby paled in comparison to this. A massive crystal chandelier easily the size of her old flat hung in the center of the hall, surrounded by a mural of the heavens, stars and galaxies in vivid pinks and blues chasing each other across the ceiling. The velvet seats below were filled with men in sharp suits and ladies in fine dresses of every shade, reminding her of her mother's old jewel box, back when she still had jewelry to wear. She could almost imagine the ceiling lifting up like the hinged lid of that pretty wooden box she used to rifle through when she was little, touching all of the colored pieces inside, holding them up to her ears or slipping them onto her too-slender fingers. The air was filled with happy chatter and the scent of a thousand different perfumes, and Vika breathed it in as deeply as she could.

"Miss Hale?"

Vika turned and found Evelyn Lyons standing beside a couple who were already greeting the Gardners.

"This is my sister, Leona," Ms. Lyons said, "her husband, Bernard, and their son, Alexander. This is Miss Hale, the Gardners' . . . friend. Oh, there's Richard. I need to speak with him; please excuse me."

"It's a pleasure to meet you," Vika said, extending her hand to the woman who had the same frosty good looks as Ms. Lyons. Her husband was too busy trying to get their boy to put down the feed screen he was attached to in order to pay Vika any mind.

Leona's tight smile didn't touch her eyes. "Likewise." She touched her husband's arm. "We should take our seats, darling."

Stung, Vika let her hand drop as the couple arranged themselves and their son in their seats. She knew clasping the fingers was proper upon introduction in Ploutos; she'd made sure to learn these things before she came here. This greeting was one of the few forms of touching that was accepted and even expected between strangers. Had she done something wrong? Or did they just not want to get her Philomeni stink on them?

She heard a scoff on her other side and turned to find an elegant dark-skinned girl about her age on the arm of a much older man. The girl leaned toward her.

"Don't mind them," she said softly. "Leona and Bernard are both terrible snobs, just because Bernard happens to be his grandfather's favorite and the old man owns a massive trans-sector shipping company. You won't get the time of day from those two unless your family has been worth at least a billion for four generations."

"Oh." Vika blinked. She had never really considered that there might be tiers of wealth and that those in a higher tier would look down on a lower one. She knew there were different kinds of poor, but rich had always just seemed to her to be . . . rich. Apparently that was naive. She wondered where the Gardners ranked; high because theirs was one of the largest fortunes on the planet or low because of when and how they got it?

"Isn't that right, my love?" the girl said, turning to her companion, who was deep in conversation on his other side. The man was more than a little gray and wore thick spectacles that made his eyes look twice their actual size. The girl had to pat him on the arm to get his attention.

"I'm sorry, darling, what?" he asked.

"Leona and Bernard. Aren't they wretched?"

"Oh, the worst!" he agreed sunnily. "If you've been snubbed by them, you're in excellent company."

Vika smiled as a little of the crushing weight on her chest lifted. "Well, that's a relief then."

"I'm Miranda Harkness," the girl said, disengaging her arm from the man's and taking Vika's instead, leading her over to a couple of seats at the rim of the box. "And you're Viktoria Hale, aren't you?"

"I am," she said, wondering how Miranda had known. Had Ms. Lyons told everyone she was bringing Vika and the Gardners along tonight or had the girl recognized her from the newsfeeds? Or was it just that obvious that she didn't actually belong here despite her pricey dress and perfectly applied lipstick?

"How fascinating," Miranda said. "You must tell me everything about yourself."

Vika's laugh was nervous. "Oh, there an't—there's not much to tell, really . . ."

"Nonsense! You're easily the most interesting person here," Miranda said, eyeing her like she was an intriguing new animal at the zoo. The girl waved over a waiter who was standing in the corner of the box with a tray of champagne flutes. "And that dress! Where did you get it?"

That, at least, Vika could talk about. Miranda continued to pepper her with questions until the lights inside the auditorium began to dim and those who were still lingering in the aisles and by the bars moved toward their seats. Vika barely suppressed a sigh of relief. Finally she could stop talking and worrying that she was embarrassing herself with every word. The musicians were taking the stage now, so she expected the crowd to go silent in anticipation of the music.

But it didn't.

"How long have you been on Ploutos?" Miranda asked as the conductor took to his podium and bowed to tepid applause from the audience. Only those sitting nearest the stage seemed to be paying any attention; the rest of the auditorium was continuing to chat just as enthusiastically as they had before.

"I arrived this morning," Vika said, trying to mimic the rounder vowels of Miranda's accent. Her own sounded suddenly harsh in her ears. "Shouldn't we listen to the orchestra?"

Miranda laughed and downed the last of her champagne. "Oh, no one really listens. The symphony is only an excuse for us all to be here. Do you see my husband?"

Vika glanced around the box. "No."

"Nor will you until the night is over," she said. "He'll spend all evening hopping from box to box, chatting with his friends and trying to drum up new business, just like most of the businesspeople. We spouses will sit here and gossip and spy on what everyone else is doing. That's why everyone wants to get an invite to Evelyn's box; she has the absolute best view. It must cost her a small fortune but it's also how she's gotten all the most high-profile clients on the planet."

The view certainly was extraordinary. From this box perched just to the right of the stage, Vika could see practically everyone in the auditorium, and they could all see her. As she looked out, she noticed an uncomfortable number of eyes trained in her direction. Were they looking at her or just this high-profile box? Did they know who she was the same way Miranda had?

"Shall we find you a husband?" Miranda said, scooting to the edge of her seat so she could look out more easily.

Vika swallowed. "I've just gotten rid of a husband, actually."

The girl laughed. "True. Sadly I don't think we'll be able to find you a richer one than the one you lost, at least not on this planet, but maybe we can do better in other ways."

The orchestra played—stringed instruments made of wood that shined like silk, as different from the fiddles and guitars of the bands on Philomenus as this gown was from the blacks she wore to work at Nicky's—and Miranda talked. She pointed out all the people Vika simply had to know and told her the most scandalous bits of gossip about them, and she continued to ask Vika questions about herself and her life that Vika found increasingly difficult to dodge with grace.

"Oh, there's Georgiana Howell, the one in that hideous gown across the way," Miranda said.

Vika followed the point of her chin to a box across the auditorium where a white-haired woman in an aggressively green dress was surveying the audience with a small binoc on a golden handle while two gentlemen stood behind her talking. As Vika watched, the door to the box opened and a young man stepped inside.

"She's a beast but you'll want to get on her good side. She throws the most incredible solstice party every cycle, and you simply can't miss that," Miranda continued. "Do Philomenis even celebrate solstice the way we do? I suppose many of you have to work. Did you have a job?"

Vika leaned forward, wishing for a binoc of her own as the men in the box greeted the newcomer. But no, she was sure, even from this distance. It was Archer Sheratan. Her heart leapt up into her throat at seeing a familiar face on this planet of strangers.

She waited for Archer to visit their box, catching glimpses of him in other boxes around the auditorium as part of the steady stream of networkers and dealmakers filtering in and out. She wondered if he knew she was there, if Ms. Lyons had told him or even if he'd spotted her across the distance like she had him. Maybe he didn't recognize her like this.

After an hour, the orchestra finished their piece and the lights came back up.

"Is it over?" Vika asked.

"Oh no, just the interval," Miranda said as she stood and smoothed the wrinkles from her gown. "Now we go to the lobby and mingle a bit until it starts all over again. I'll introduce you to Howell and get you invited to that party."

Miranda's husband reappeared at her side to escort her out of the box, and Vika hung back to wait for the Gardners, who had been occupied by Evelyn Lyons and her wife all evening.

"There you are, my dear," Hal said, offering her an arm. "How are you enjoying the symphony?"

Vika glanced around to make sure no one was listening. "To be honest, I've barely heard a single note."

"Very strange, isn't it?" Mira said. "Spending all this money to come here only to completely ignore what's happening! I did try to listen to the music when Ms. Lyons wasn't talking our ears off about investment strategies and tax shelters and I don't know what else, and it was quite lovely."

"Maybe that's the point," Vika said, feeling a powerful little shiver race down her spine. "When you're rich, everything is so wonderful that the most beautiful music in the world is only good enough to play in the background."

Hal laughed. "I like the way you think, Viktoria. If I weren't already a happily married man . . ."

Mira slapped his arm. "Don't you dare finish that sentence!"

The interval was another succession of drinks and hors d'oeuvres and people to meet. Maybe she was imagining it, but Vika felt like there were more people crowded around her and the Gardners than anyone else in the entire lobby. Hal seemed to struggle with all the attention, stammering his way through introductions and small talk, while Mira was all smiles and friendly enthusiasm, like a child in a sweet shop. Vika didn't want to be either of those things—uncomfortable *or* excited—because both marked the Gardners as out of place.

She wanted to belong.

She hadn't figured out how she was going to do it yet, but she knew she would. She had a few factors going for her. Her stubborn determination. The Gardners' tremendous fortune, although apparently she didn't yet understand the way the people on this planet saw shades of wealth. And her old standby, which she knew how to use very well: her beauty.

"Oh, Mr. Reave," she said, giving a slow smile and bat of her eyelashes to the elderly gentleman who had replaced her empty glass with a full one. "I see you have anticipated my desires. Does your wife appreciate what a thoughtful husband she has?"

He gave her a little bow. "I may need to remind her."

"Do, or I may just snatch you out from under her nose."

He chuckled, enchanted. Men were so simple.

"Oh, Mrs. Howell!" Miranda said, her voice going up half an octave when she spotted the beast in green. The crowd parted to let the society maven through. "You must meet my new friend, Viktoria Hale."

"Ahh, Hale." The woman looked her up and down. "You're the Chapin girl, aren't you?"

Vika swallowed the burn she felt inside at being referred to as the property of a dead man and instead smiled. "Not anymore."

There was a half second of silence during which Vika's heart stopped, thinking she'd made a grave error, before the group tittered and exchanged pleasantly scandalized looks. Vika was barely able to conceal her grin of triumph.

By the time the lights dimmed, signaling the beginning of the second act, she'd been invited to Mrs. Howell's solstice party and half a dozen other engagements.

As the group made its way back to the box, Vika excused herself to the ladies' room. She took her time, enjoying the jasmine-scented air and the instant flow of warm water from the faucets, and she spent several minutes trying out the variety of perfumed soaps and lotions and breath mints laid out across the countertop. She took the little gold tube of lipstick from her bag and carefully drew over her lips, replacing the color that had been worn away by the rims of champagne flutes. She wasn't as skilled at it as Gemma and struggled to stay within the lines, but after a couple of tries and a couple of tissues to wipe away her mistakes, she was satisfied with the result.

As she was returning to Ms. Lyons's box, she got a behind-the-scenes glimpse of the parade of dealmakers moving from box to box. Young and old, slipping in and out of doors like some choreographed dance, greeting each other in the dim corridor as they passed one another, slipping each other cards and bits of gossip. Vika felt more than one head turn as she passed, eyes following her, and she wondered if the warm sizzle in her veins was from the champagne or if this was what power felt like.

As she rounded the curve that led to the door of Ms. Lyons's box, a figure came into view. He was leaning against the wall, arms crossed over his chest, one corner of his mouth pulled up into a smile she instinctively mimicked.

"You're missing the adagio," Archer said. "The descant in the horns is simply divine."

She raised an eyebrow at him. "You're missing it, too."

He looked her over as though examining her for wounds, but his voice was all warm sincerity when he said, "I wanted to see how you're doing."

"Worried if I'm fitting in?"

He laughed. "Not remotely. All anyone's been talking about is the handyman billionaire and his charming female companion."

"Mira?"

His grin was wicked. "Somehow I think not, particularly now that I've seen you in that dress. You look exquisite."

She hoped the light from the sconces in the corridor was dim enough to hide the heat in her cheeks. "You clean up pretty nicely yourself."

"Well thank you, I do try to look respectable. Are the jackals treating you well?"

Vika thought of the way Leona Lyons had sneered down at her hand. "Most people have been kind so far. There's a girl in my box named Miranda who's been especially—"

"Miranda Harkness?" He dropped his voice as a pair of gentlemen passed them on their parade. "You'll want to be careful of her. I doubt she truly wants you for a friend, just an interesting new pet she can show off. And she'll whisper your secrets into every ear she comes across."

"I suspected as much." Her mum had always told her to believe people when they showed you who they were, and Miranda had done nothing but gossip about everyone around her all night. Vika was glad she'd been so vague in all her answers when Miranda had asked her about herself.

"I don't mean to spread gossip myself, of course. I just . . ." His voice was soft. "I just don't want to see you get hurt. There are people on this planet who will try to use you, and it seems to me you've had enough of that already."

A warm rush went through her and she felt, absurdly, like she might cry, because it was true. She *had* experienced enough of that already, and having someone else acknowledge it made her feel . . . seen. "Thank you," she whispered.

He smiled. "I should go. They'll be sending out a search party for you soon. It was nice seeing you again, *Viktoria*."

Vika floated back into the box and through the rest of the evening.

By the time she and the Gardners arrived home, she was exhausted. It had only been that very morning that she'd woken up on the lumpy pullout next to Lavinia, but it felt like a thousand cycles ago. She bade the Gardners good night and headed for her room.

Beautiful as it was, she couldn't wait to get this dress off, kick off the shoes that had begun to rub a sore into the back of her heel, and slip into something soft and shapeless instead.

She opened the door to her bedroom and gasped. The ceiling had disappeared, revealing the night's sky, stars peeking through the black and wispy clouds passing across the pink moon. She stood staring up at it in open-mouthed wonder for several seconds before her brain was able to make sense of what she was seeing. The roof hadn't been blown away in some freak storm; the ceiling, which had struck her before as exceptionally plain since most of the ceilings in the flat were so ornate, was actually made up of thousands of tiny diodes that perfectly mimicked the sky above. As she watched, a tiny asteroid like the hundreds that burned up in Ploutos's atmosphere every day streaked above her.

"This is my room," she reminded herself. She wished she could whisper in the ear of the little girl she'd once been—lying on the roof of her TH, staring up at the haze, desperate to see the sky—that one day she'd fall asleep looking at the stars.

While she'd been out, a maid had removed the decorative pillows from the bed and turned down the corner of the comforter. The bed looked so inviting that Vika was tempted to just collapse into it to enjoy the view, but instead she stepped into the bathroom and turned on the taps to fill the massive tub. She hadn't had an actual bath as opposed to a rushed shower since her family had been forced to move to the THs. She tossed in some salts and bubbling soap from the crystal decanters provided for her, and as the tub began to fill, she wandered back into the bedroom to order up a snack from the kitchen to enjoy once she was in her pajamas. She couldn't imagine a more perfect way to—

She froze, her hand outstretched to press the panel that would connect her to the servants. She had just noticed the folded sheet of paper on her bedside table, her name written on it in a vaguely familiar handwriting. She picked it up to read the words.

Miss Hale—

I apologize again for the shock I gave you earlier this evening. Please be assured that I intend you no harm, and I will do my best to keep my distance as you've requested. I will give your family your regards.

Most sincerely,

Sky

Vika shuddered, crumpling the note in her fist.

HE COLLAPSED ONTO HIS bed, exhausted from a full day's work. He reached under the corner of his mattress to pull out the small leather-bound notebook where he kept all of his research and plans. At the front was his cast of characters, each with their own page, featuring a photograph and all the notes he'd compiled on them. The first two pages were gone, leaving nothing but the jagged edges where he'd torn them out of the notebook with relish: Rigel Chapin on the night he'd died, apparently of natural causes, and Leo Chapin weeks later, moments after he'd pressed the button that detonated the device hidden aboard the *Leander*.

Now he contemplated the picture he'd snapped of the Philomeni barmaid and pasted into the book before the world had known the name Viktoria Hale.

The girl hadn't figured much into his plans initially. With Leo Chapin out of the picture, she should have been no more than a footnote to the story. But now that Mira had insisted on taking her in, Viktoria Hale presented an interesting opportunity. If only he could get her to fall in love with him. A stretch, he knew, but at least it would be a more pleasant task to work toward than the other items on his agenda, even if she was a sharp, shallow kind of girl.

The key would be not to push her too hard. She was naturally mistrustful and would soon be swarmed by treasure hunters; he had to make sure she didn't see him as someone like them, someone with an agenda. So he would keep his distance and play his hand slowly. That night he'd planted a seed, and with some patience and tending, perhaps he could get it to grow.

CHAPTER TWELVE

AS SOON AS VIKA woke up the next morning, opening her eyes to a deep blue sky unmarred by a single cloud above her, she marched to Hal's office with Sky's crumpled note clutched in her hand and spread it out on his desk.

"He left this beside my bed," she told him, the hours of stewing on it having taken the note from an impertinent annoyance to an assault on her sense of safety. "When I think of him in my room while we were out . . ." It gave her a shiver up her spine, thinking of him there, his fingers brushing the table as he set down the note, maybe touching her pillow or the clothes hanging in her closet. She'd woken up twice in the night, disoriented by the unfamiliar surroundings and sure that there was someone else in the room with her, like he'd left his ghost behind to haunt her.

"Oh, I'm sure he wouldn't have invaded your privacy like that," Hal said. "He's a very polite young man. He probably gave the note to a maid to leave for you."

"Whatever he did, I don't like it!" Vika knew she sounded unreasonable and her voice had gone all high and thin, but she couldn't help it. "You don't think it's strange, him getting a job here with you and renting a room from my father?"

"Oh, Viktoria." A frown etched creases into Hal's forehead and he stood, putting his arm around her shoulders. "What are you worried about, my girl?"

If she closed her eyes, the warm solidness of Hal beside her almost felt like her da. "What if he's . . . I know it sounds ridiculous, but he's always unnerved me, from the very first day I met him. What if he followed me here on purpose? What if he's scheming something?"

"It's very unlikely, my dear." Hal's hand skimmed over and over her shoulder. "He came highly recommended, and I hired him before Mira and I ever met you. He couldn't have known we would invite you to live here with us."

Vika felt herself starting to deflate, but she hung onto the burn of anger that had kept her up for hours after she found the note. "What about that line about my family? That doesn't sound like a veiled threat to you?"

The look Hal gave her was almost sad, and she knew she must sound crazy to him. She sounded a little crazy to herself.

"I'm sure he meant it as a kindness," Hal said. "But if you're that uncomfortable, I suppose I can dismiss him."

Vika took a deep breath, then another. Why was this bothering her so much? After all, Hal was probably right and this was just a coincidence. She certainly had no evidence against Sky, other than her instinctive dislike for him, and that was hardly proof. She would hate to cost *any* innocent person, even him, a good job, knowing what that could mean to someone. Plus she didn't want Hal to start thinking she was irrational.

"No, you're probably right," she said, trying to make herself believe it. "I don't suppose I'll have much contact with him anyway."

"Very little," Hal assured her, giving her a kiss on the top of her head. "He's here for work, and you're here for fun! Shouldn't be much overlap."

Vika did manage to avoid Sky most days with little effort. She often caught glimpses of him around the house as he went about his regular duties of helping Hal manage his business affairs and the household staff, but he was as good as his word and never approached her unless it was for a specific reason. Hal and Mira were such kind people that they often tried to include Sky in things, inviting him to stay for dinner or to go on outings with them. But, with a quick glance at her that she would pretend not to see, he always declined. Often entire days would pass where she would forget all about him, until she'd catch him watching her from across a room or he would relay some greeting to her from her da.

She never approached him. Whenever she accidentally caught his eye, which happened more than it should have since he always seemed to be watching her for some reason, she saw herself through his own gaze. A girl pretending to belong in this cultured, sophisticated world when he'd seen very well who she really was, a barmaid in need of a good shower who lived in a crumbling housing block and had no prospects. She could almost forget that girl until she saw him and his eyes reminded her of what a fraud she was. So she stayed away from him.

Until the day her allowance didn't come through.

Vika crept toward Sky's office—a small room beside Hal's, which she knew the existence of but had never been inside—feeling like some kind of criminal skulking through the house. She could just wait for Hal and Mira to return home from their lunch date, but she was supposed to go shopping with her friends in less than an hour and her bank account was nearly empty. Thank goodness she'd thought to check it before they went out; she imagined a salesgirl whispering in her ear in front of her friends that her account had been declined as insufficient and knew she might very well have died of that humiliation.

Still, she wasn't thrilled about having to go to Sky to ask for money, even if it was coming from the Gardners and not him. She squared her shoulders to at least *look* unbothered and rapped lightly on the door of Sky's office. When there was no answer, she opened it. Well, he certainly wasn't hiding inside. The office was tiny, more like a generous closet than a proper room. It was so meticulously neat that it might have been mistaken for unused, and there were no personal effects except for Sky's coat, which was hung on a hook by the door. It made her think for a moment of her da's office, if only because it was so different. Her da's was no bigger but it was crammed with ten times more *things,* overflowing files and maintenance tools and evidence of who her father was. Two or three cold cups of forgotten tea piled at the corner of the desk, old photos of her and Lavinia in battered frames that had been shuffled from place to place over the years, the fountain pen Vika had saved up to buy him on his name day and which he thought was so nice he refused to ever write with it. Sky Foster, on the other hand, had left no trace of who he was in this room.

The barrenness of the office made Vika's eyes go straight for the one thing that was out of place: a lengthy document, open to a spot in the middle, that was the only thing on the empty desk aside from the holoscreen. She stepped closer and cocked her head to read the words. Somehow she wasn't surprised when she saw the title of the document at the top of the page.

It was the Chapin will.

She'd never read the thing before, only been told what it said. How exactly had Rigel Chapin quantified her worth as a human being in bits and cents? With hesitant fingers, she grabbed one corner of the document and pulled it toward her. Picking it up somehow seemed like too big a step, but if she only slid it . . .

"Miss Hale?" a voice at the door said.

She jumped, snatching her fingers back like a child caught stealing from the sweets jar.

"I do apologize for startling you," Sky said, brushing past her to sit at his desk. He glanced down at the document and then back up at her. "Did you want to have a look?"

"I'm not sure what you mean," she said weakly. After all, she'd been caught red-handed.

"It's a public document, and you have more right than most to see it." He pushed it across the desk toward her.

"No, thank you," she said, examining a glossy red fingernail instead. "Rigel Chapin's wishes couldn't matter less to me."

"I can hardly blame you for that." Sky tapped the papers on the top of the desk to square them and set them aside. Something in the way he wouldn't look her in the eye made her feel sure he was hiding something. It was a familiar sensation and one that disturbed her to feel in her own home, where this person she knew absolutely nothing about always seemed to be.

"Mr. Foster," she said, narrowing her eyes at him. "Where did you say you came from again?"

"I'm not sure that I did," he replied, "but I'm originally from Aerion. Why do you ask?"

"Only because you seem so determined to be a mystery. What brought you to our little corner of the quadrant? I would presume it would have something to do with family since no one moves to Philomenus for the scenery or thriving cultural scene, but I see no photographs or—"

"My sister lives on Philomenus," he said. "Now, how may I help you this morning?"

She'd become so annoyed with him that she'd almost forgotten why she came, but now the queasy feeling in her stomach returned. "It's the fifth," she said.

He blinked. "Yes?"

Hell's teeth, he was dense. She was going to have to actually say the words. "I was supposed to have received a deposit."

"Oh, your allowance!" He gave her a smile that felt decidedly mocking. "We can't overlook that, can we?"

She struggled not to squirm as he reached into one of his desk drawers.

"I do beg your pardon, Miss Hale. I meant to speak with you about this yesterday but it slipped my mind," he said. Actually, he'd tried to speak with her twice and she had successfully dodged him both times. "There was an issue with the bank that made it impossible for me to make the usual electronic transfer. You'll have to make do with cash this fortnight."

He handed her a weighty envelope, and she just barely resisted the urge to stick it immediately in her pocket to hide it away. How did he always make her feel so small? So young?

"The issue is being resolved now," he continued, "so from now on the sum should be deposited directly into your account as usual."

She raised her chin, trying to summon her haughtiest look, like a woman who had been given her due and not a dependent child taking a handout. "Thank you, Mr. Foster. I'll leave you to your work."

His voice stopped her as she reached the door. "Oh, and Miss Hale?"

She turned. "Yes?"

"You do know that I'm happy to distribute your allowance however you'd like?" he said, glancing between her and the holoscreen where he was already at work on something else.

Vika frowned. "What do you mean by that?"

"Only that if you'll provide me with your father's account details, I'm happy to send a portion of your allowance directly to him." He typed away at the light-board, hardly seeming to remember she was there. "I assume you already send some amount home to compensate for your lost salary, which must be an inconvenience for you. It would be no extra trouble for me to do that on your behalf."

Her throat felt suddenly hot and tight, as though she'd inhaled a lungful of smoke. "Thank you," she said, "but I've already made all those arrangements."

"Of course. Good day, Miss Hale."

Vika made herself walk slowly and confidently away from the office because she felt so much like running. She hadn't sent any money home to her family, not a red cent since she'd said goodbye to them at the atmospheric ferry docks. She'd been having so much fun living with the Gardners that the idea hadn't even occurred to her. And for Sky Foster to just assume that she had was like a sharp slap to the face.

Well . . . why *should* she send them money? She wasn't here on
Ploutos to scrimp and economize; she was here to enjoy herself
and to find a way to stay, both of which required bits. Once she had
secured her own future, she would then be in a position to truly
help her family. Each party she went to might be where she met
the person who would give her a lucrative job. Each beautiful dress
she bought might bring her closer to a wealthy husband. Then she
would be able to bring her whole family to Ploutos. Dresses and
parties weren't vanity or frivolousness; they were investments. Who
was Sky Foster to tell her how she should spend her money? What
did he know of her life or her family's?

Besides, her family couldn't want for much with her gone. Her
salary from Nicky's had barely covered the expense of her own food.
They couldn't be more than twenty or thirty bits a week worse off
with her gone. And other than a couple of letters from her da delivered to her by Sky, she hadn't heard from any of them. If they
couldn't be bothered to pretend they missed her, why should she
make sure they lived in comfort on money that wasn't even hers?
The Gardners had given her that allowance to ease her time on
Ploutos, not to subsidize her parents and sister.

Still, the burning in her throat didn't subside for hours, persist-
ing all through her late lunch and shopping trip with Miranda and
her newest friend, Nova. It wasn't until Gemma was helping her
put the final touches on her look for the party the Gardners were
throwing that night that there were enough other concerns in her
head to push thoughts of her family all the way out.

This was the first party the Gardners had hosted themselves in
the penthouse, so Vika was taking extra care in getting ready. The
dress she'd chosen was made of the gauziest, lightest fabric she'd
ever seen, layers and layers of it in different shades of red so that it
seemed to move and breathe around her with even the slightest shift
in the air. After weeks of practice, she'd finally mastered heels and
could perfectly apply lipstick on her own, but she still let Gemma
do her hair, the girl strategically securing dark curls and tiny braids

around her head with diamond-tipped pins until it resembled a crown.

As she combed through her jewel box, which was growing more crowded by the day, it occurred to Vika that she wasn't nervous at all. A few weeks ago, the idea of playing hostess to the cream of Ploutosian society would have terrified her. She would have worried that everyone was watching her, judging her. Thinking of her as just that Philomeni barmaid who was trying to fool the world with a fancy dress. But becoming a high society lady had come surprisingly easily to her, as long as Sky Foster wasn't hovering at the edge of her vision to remind her of the truth. Her mum had always said she was too high and mighty for her own good, but maybe the problem hadn't been her at all. It had only been her surroundings. She'd been too good for her life on Philomenus, and now she was finally where she belonged.

Hal and Mira, it was true, hadn't found their footing as surely as she had. She saw how people looked at them, the open bemusement in their expressions as they took in the billionaire handyman and maid, the jealousy masquerading as contempt in some people's eyes. They were both overly enthusiastic with things, too pleased with their good luck to blend in with the blasé attitudes of the other wealthy people around them. They hadn't learned as Vika had that the trick to fitting in was to act as though nothing pleased you terribly much. So Vika sipped at her wine and nibbled at her canapé rather than inhaling the whole tray the way she wanted to, and she demurred when she was complimented on her dress rather than telling anyone how painstakingly she had chosen it for this evening. It was all a game—flirt a little here, insert a joke there—and she was good at it.

"Quite a turnout," Hal said as he, Mira, and Vika lingered near the entrance of the penthouse, waiting to greet any stragglers.

"Yes, I think our first party should be counted a success!" Mira was beaming, and though it may have been what kept her from fitting in, her delight was infectious.

"I agree," Vika said, scanning the foyer. She wasn't looking for anyone in particular, but when her eyes landed on Archer, they lingered. He was looking even more handsome than usual in his charcoal tails, chatting up two older women Vika knew to be the widowed owners of significant estates.

Then, over Archer's shoulder, she caught sight of a figure standing in a doorway, just beyond the bright light of the chandeliers.

"*What* is Mr. Foster doing here?" she asked.

Hal followed her gaze and sighed when he spotted Sky, standing by himself at the edge of the crowd, sipping a sparkling water and looking distinctly uncomfortable. "Not enjoying himself like I had hoped he would."

"You invited him to stay?" Vika asked.

Hal nodded. "He works so hard, and he always seems so . . ."

"Somber?" Mira suggested at the same time Vika offered, "Creepy?"

Hal laughed. "I think 'somber' is more accurate."

"Really, Viktoria!" Mira patted her arm with a glove-clad hand. "You should give the poor boy a chance. He's a bit quiet, it's true, but he's perfectly pleasant."

"No, thank you," Vika said. "There are too many people around I actually *enjoy* talking to. And speak of the devil."

Archer was striding toward them, a champagne glass in his hand. He gave them a bow.

"Mr. and Mrs. Gardner," he said. "Thank you so much for the invitation. Your new home is magnificent. You must be very proud of it."

"It was more work than we imagined," Hal said.

"Yes, who knew choosing paint colors and furnishings would be so exhausting?" Mira said.

"Quite. Mrs. Gardner, I noticed you were in need of a drink." He handed her the full champagne flute and plucked the empty one from her fingers, placing it on the tray of a passing waiter.

"Well, aren't you attentive," she said. "Please, call me Mira."

"Mira, may I steal away your beautiful young friend?" he asked.

"The quartet has begun to play in the ballroom, and I should like to get my dance in before she's overwhelmed by requests."

Mira laughed. "I believe I can manage without her for a song or two."

Archer turned to her, extending his hand. "Viktoria?"

Vika smiled and took his fingers, and they joined the stream of people heading toward the ballroom. The two outer walls were made entirely of glass that looked out over the city, the lights of the other skyscrapers providing a sparkling backdrop to the musicians assembled on a low dais. The ceiling dripped with purple flowers that made a lush arbor above them, the thousands of blooms having been painstakingly hung for hours that morning by a small army of workers. Dancers were already on the floor, and the movement of the spinning women in their dresses and the honey wine she'd had earlier gave Vika a pleasant, buzzy lightheadedness that Archer's hand under hers was doing nothing to dispel.

"I don't know any of your fancy Ploutosian waltzes yet," she confessed as he led her onto the dance floor.

"Lucky that dress hides your feet so well then," he said, flashing her a grin. "Don't worry. I have to do most of the work anyway. Just follow me."

"Following is not exactly my strong suit."

He curled his fingers around her hand and put his other palm on her waist, and it gave her a warm kind of quiver up her spine. On Ploutos, dancing was one of the few socially acceptable ways that someone like Archer could get so close to her.

"I'm sure you'll manage," he said.

Then he was pushing her, turning her in time with the music. She hadn't realized she'd be moving backward the entire time. Her feet didn't seem to want to keep up with the rest of her body, and she felt like she was constantly on the edge of falling, only Archer's firm grip keeping her upright.

He laughed. "Relax. I'm not going to steer you into anything."

"Easy for you to say. You get to face forward and do this in flat shoes."

But she did try to relax, and once she did it became much easier. Archer was so sure of where he was going and led her there so confidently that she turned control over to him and her feet fell in line. They glided across the floor with surprising speed, and she caught only glimpses of smiling faces as they soared past. Archer's fingers curled more possessively around her waist.

"You're a natural," he said, his voice low as he leaned toward her, lips nearly brushing her ear. "Not to mention the most beautiful girl in the room."

She tried to give him a knowing look but worried the telltale burning she could feel in her cheeks would dampen the effect. "And you are the most shameless flatterer here."

He laughed. "How else would a lowly solicitor get anywhere in this world?"

He said it like it was a joke, but she recognized the hunger in him. She'd seen the way he nurtured his relationship with the Gardners and Evelyn Lyons. How he always seemed to find himself at the side of those who might need legal help, be susceptible to his charms, and have the money to make his time worth it. How else could he have become a solicitor at the top firm on the planet, working on one of its biggest estates, at such a young age? His ambition was like the grasping in her own heart, not satisfied, always wanting better and more. It made her feel as though they understood something fundamental about each other when she looked into his sky-blue eyes.

The whole room seemed to be spinning by the time the music ended, and she gripped Archer's hand a little tighter to keep her balance as he led her off the dance floor. Maybe it was time to switch her drink of choice. She caught the sleeve of a passing waiter who was on his way back to the kitchens with a tray of empty glasses.

"Yes, madam?" he asked, his tone a little more clipped than Vika appreciated.

"A sparkling water," she said. "One that's already chilled, no ice, with mint."

Archer raised an amused eyebrow at her. "You're very specific."

She grinned. "I know what I want."

The waiter nodded and headed off for the kitchen, and Vika's eyes followed him until he passed another person. Sky Foster, who was standing there with a forgotten plate in his hand, just watching her. She swallowed, the tight feeling in her throat back again. He gave her a tiny bow of acknowledgment before turning away, and though his face was as blank as ever, she was sure she knew exactly what he was thinking. Her, a girl from the wrong side of the stream who slung grock for a living, bossing around a waiter just because she could. Poor, plain Vika pretending to be so high and mighty.

"Viktoria?" Archer asked. "Are you all right?"

She shook herself from her thoughts. "Fine. I just . . . think I could use some air."

"Yes, you're flushed." He put a hand on her back with the lightest touch. "Allow me to escort you to the balcony."

"Oh, Viktoria, did I see you dancing with Archer Sheratan before?" Nova asked her later. Nova and Miranda were sitting with her on one of the tufted silk sofas in the reception room as they ate their selection of the desserts the waiters had begun to circulate with. Archer was across the room, chatting with a couple of men she didn't recognize.

Vika dragged her spoon through the fluffy chocolate concoction she'd chosen. "Yes, he's a friend."

Miranda arched an eyebrow at her. "Just a friend?"

Vika wasn't entirely sure of the answer to that herself, so she replied with, "I'm not eager for another fiancé just yet."

"Understandable. Husbands are often more trouble than they're worth." Miranda frowned down at her riverberry tart, no doubt thinking of her own ancient spouse. Mr. Harkness was nice enough and certainly attractively wealthy, but Vika found it difficult to imagine climbing into bed beside him every night, even with all that money to make the bitter pill go down more smoothly. "But you two would have the most gorgeous little babies."

Vika laughed. "He is rather easy on the eyes."

"You know his story, don't you?" Nova asked.

Vika shook her head.

"Oh, Viktoria!" Miranda set her tart aside like it was too much of a distraction to deal with in the face of communicating this vital bit of gossip. "It was such a scandal. His mother was Larissa Beaumont, of *those* Beaumonts, and she was married to Sol Sheratan, who was a very successful businessman from somewhere off-world . . ."

"Demetrios, wasn't it?"

"Yes, that was it." Miranda scooted closer to her. "Anyway, when Larissa became pregnant, Sol was overjoyed. He was bragging to everyone, lining up all the best nannies and schools, even built her a brand-new house outside of the city so the pollution wouldn't affect the baby."

Vika wasn't able to check her eye roll in time. What pollution? Ploutosians wouldn't know pollution if it walked up and introduced itself.

But Miranda was enjoying the story, which she'd obviously told before, and didn't notice. "But then the baby was born. Archer. And there was a problem. Because Sol Sheratan was tall, dark, and handsome, and Larissa was famous for her amber-colored eyes."

Vika glanced across the room to where the fair-skinned, very *blue*-eyed Archer still stood talking. Vika had never excelled at science, but even she understood immediately.

Nova grinned. "Exactly."

"Of course it was obvious to everyone what had happened, although Sol tried to deny it," Miranda continued. "But when his supposed son still had those bright blue eyes on his first name day, he knew he'd been made a fool of. I believe the main suspect was one of the servants."

"The cook."

"Right! So on Archer's name day, Sol packed the cook off back to

Philomenus and left for Demetrios, never to return," Miranda said. "Larissa basically disappeared from polite society after that, and she died a few years later."

Vika looked at Archer again, her heart twisting. His smile was so bright, his whole air so untroubled, like a person who had never known hardship. She would have had no idea the tragedy he carried with him. "Oh, that's terrible."

"Booze," Nova said.

Miranda shook her head. "I heard pills."

Vika was suddenly hit with the memory of her mum putting her to bed when she was young and the silly little song she used to sing as she tucked the covers in tight around her body. She hadn't thought of that song in years, maybe because the mum she had now was so different from the woman she had been before the mines closed and their whole lives had changed. Her parents had been everything to her then, her entire world. She couldn't imagine how she would have coped with losing one of them.

"The Beaumonts had completely disowned Larissa by then, so he was raised by some distant relative or another," Miranda said. "He's done surprisingly well for himself considering where he started, but it's not like anyone who truly matters will ever forget."

Nova laughed. "Certainly not."

Vika put aside her half-eaten dessert; she couldn't stomach the thought of another bite. If no one would ever overlook the circumstances of Archer's birth, what hope was there for her? "So why bother talking about him anymore?" she said, trying to sound as light and careless as they did. "Surely you have some fresher gossip than that ancient story."

"Of course I do!" Miranda said. "Who do you take me for? Did you hear about Charles Wolfe's new mistress?"

It wasn't until the early hours of the morning that the party wound down, long after everyone had had their fill of canapés and cocktails and gossip. Vika and the Gardners finished bidding goodbye to their last guests, and the Gardners excused themselves to bed while

Sky went about paying the staff and overseeing the cleanup effort. Vika felt strangely wired, like there were a hundred amps running through her veins, and couldn't imagine going to sleep herself yet. She swiped one of the few remaining slices of cake off an abandoned tray and went out to the balcony. She kicked off her heels and folded her legs under her as she sat on a divan looking out over the city. Even this late, lights still sparkled below her, and above her the dark sky was perfectly cloudless and clear. She took a deep breath of the cool air, enjoying the feeling of floating through open space on this beautiful gem of a planet instead of being smothered under a blanket of haze.

"Miss Hale?"

She jumped, almost dumping her cake in the process. Sky bloody Foster. He had stepped out onto the balcony behind her, as silent as a wraith.

"What?" she snapped.

"Excuse me," he said. "I just saw you through the window and—"

"Of course you did." She stood, turning to face him, the familiar annoyance bubbling up inside of her. The same today as it had been the first day she met him, when she ignored her gut feeling and rented him a room even though he had no job, because he had money and her family . . . She shook her head. "Mr. Foster, you have to stop this."

He frowned. "Stop what?"

"Stop *watching* me," she said. "Do you think I haven't noticed? The way you're always looking at me? Judging me?"

His expression crumpled into exaggerated confusion. "Miss Hale, I'm afraid we've misunderstood each other. I sincerely apologize if I've given you the impression—"

"I'm not stupid," she said. "You may think I'm a shallow, selfish person who has forgotten her family and only cares about parties and dresses, but you don't know me."

He opened his mouth to argue but then rethought. Instead he stepped to the edge of the balcony, looking out at the buildings below them. When he spoke, his voice was soft. "You're right. I have been watching you, and I apologize for that. All you asked was that I keep my distance, and I have tried, but clearly . . ." He looked back at her, his eyes as dark and deep as the sky above, and there was a low thrum to his voice she'd never heard before. "Miss Hale, if I could just tell you . . ."

That thrum scared her, because she thought she might know what it meant. She suddenly didn't want to hear whatever he was going to say next, in case she was right. "That's enough."

He pressed his knuckles to his chest, as though in pain, and took a step toward her. He was so close now that he could touch her if he chose to. "Miss Hale, you must—"

"Stop!" She threw up a hand. She didn't want to hear what he had to say, didn't want to keep looking at him and seeing the person she didn't want to be anymore reflected in his eyes. "Mr. Foster, I am going to bed, and you should go home. I don't want to repeat this conversation with you. I will live my life as I see fit, and you will remember your place. You are an employee in this household, and this . . ." She didn't dare look directly at him. "Whatever this is, it's not appropriate. Do you understand?"

He swallowed and seemed to shrink before her. "Yes. Of course."

She went to the door and then paused. "I won't tell Mr. and Mrs. Gardner about this conversation."

"Thank you," was his soft reply.

"I'm not . . ." The words escaped her before she could hold them back, and she wanted to bite down on her stupid tongue. "I'm really not a bad person, you know."

"Good night, Miss Hale," was all he said.

CHAPTER THIRTEEN

HE WATCHED HER WALK away. The truth had been on his tongue—not all of it, of course, but some of it—but she hadn't let him say it. Thank the stars. The words burned as he swallowed them back down. He watched her dress ripple around her like flames, the straightness of her spine and haughty tilt to her chin, all of it belied by the occasional wobble as she tried to maneuver in her spindly heels.

Then he realized what he was doing, exactly what he'd just promised her he wouldn't, and turned away.

He checked that the staff had all headed home and then shut down the flat by entering the code into the panel by the door that allowed him access to all of the lights and door locks. When the penthouse was dark and secure, he took the bi-rail to the atmospheric docks, boarded the ferry for Philomenus, and walked to the row of abandoned factories that had been decommissioned after the coltane mines closed, his mind racing the entire time. He didn't want to go back to his little room in the THs just to stare at the ceiling thinking all night.

Not when, after weeks of pained indecision, he finally knew what he had to do.

He entered the old machine-parts factory through a side door that had been crowbarred open years before. People with nowhere else to go had moved in almost as soon as the factories were shuttered, claiming spaces for themselves and their families, erecting makeshift walls and rigging up hoses for water and extension cords for power. Ariel had been lucky. She and her father had been among the first to move in, claiming an office on the second floor of the factory for themselves. Their room had real walls, with windows that overlooked the docks and a door that could be locked, which basically made them the king and queen of Solomon Machine Parts, Limited.

He trudged up the stairs to the second level, careful to keep his footfalls on the exposed metal as light as possible so as not to disturb those sleeping below, and slipped the key Ariel had given him into the office door.

Her father was asleep on a cot in one corner, snoring softly. He wasn't worried about waking him; by sundown the man was always filled with so much grock that an asteroid crashing down beside him wouldn't disturb him.

Ariel's mattress was in the opposite corner, separated from the rest of the room by a sheet she'd tacked up years ago. She was asleep, too, surrounded by the pictures of stars she had drawn or cut out of books and magazines and plastered to the walls around her head. He sat at the foot of her bed, meaning to shake her awake, but he suddenly felt so exhausted that he found himself lying down beside her, resting his head on her calf.

She stirred, rubbing her face. "Is that you?"

"I'm honestly not sure anymore," he said.

"It's you." She yawned. "No one else would dare wake me up just to wax philosophical about identity."

"I'm sorry."

"No, you're not." She propped herself up against her pillows. "What is it?"

He sighed. "I've made a decision."

She waited, and then nudged him with her foot. "Well?"

Leo sat up. "I'm going to stay dead."

CHAPTER FOURTEEN

EARLIER

HE WAS COLD. Not the searing cold that was his last memory before he was enveloped with light but a regular, dull kind of cold. For a while that was all he was. Not a body, not a collection of thoughts, just one simple, persistent sensation.

Then there was pain, and that reminded him that he was a person with arms and legs and a head that could hurt. He didn't know where he was, or maybe even who he was, but he knew that he . . . was.

Then he opened his eyes. He still had eyes to open, so he must be alive. He was lying on a makeshift bed of blankets on a floor of metal grating. The wall in front of him was also metal, and it was curved. It took a moment for his fuzzy brain to parse what he was seeing. He wasn't in a room; he was in a spacecraft.

With a heavy hand, he pulled the blanket laid over him down a few centimeters to look at his body. It all still seemed to be there, thankfully. And he was dressed in the sleep clothes he'd gone to bed in . . . how long ago? Hours, or days? Judging by how thirsty he was, it had been some time.

Some time since the *Leander* had exploded around him, hurtling him out into open space.

Behind him, he heard the door to the craft slide open. A pale-haired girl, several cycles younger than himself, stepped into his line of vision, her eyes trained on a handheld feed screen.

"Hello?" he croaked.

She jumped, the screen nearly flying out of her grasp. "Fecking hell! You're awake."

He tried to sit up, but his head began to swim. "Where am I?"

She reached into the bag slung over her shoulder and pulled out a battered metal canteen. She brought it to him, sitting cross-legged on the floor at his side. He gratefully took it and gulped down the water, trying not to spill it on himself in his hastiness.

"This is my skiff," she said. "We're docked on Philomenus."

Philomenus. It was all rushing back to him now, and his head was throbbing harder than ever as the thoughts crowded in.

His father.

The will.

The girl.

"Do you remember what happened?" she asked.

He emptied the canteen and let his heavy head fall back against the nest of blankets beneath him. "The ship I was on . . . there was some kind of accident."

"Sorry to tell you, but that was no accident," she said.

"It was bombed?"

"So they say."

"How did I get here?" he asked. "I . . . I was in the void."

"My da and I work the stream," she said. "Salvaging scrap. I just happened to be close when your ship blew."

"You rescued me?"

She nodded. "Scooped you right up. Pretty impressive, if I do say so myself. I thought you were dead for sure, and you damn near were. If I'd been even a thousand meters farther off . . ."

He thought of the light that had enveloped him as he was losing consciousness. Not something otherworldly, then, just the spotlight of this girl's spacecraft as she plucked him out of the void, snatching him back from certain death. "How long ago was that?" he asked.

"Just over a full day ago," she said. "Sorry for just leaving you in here. I did try to think of a way to move you somewhere more comfortable, but you're heavier than you look. I've been checking on you every few hours, though."

"There's no need to apologize." He pushed himself up into a sitting position, stifling a groan as pain rippled through his stiff and aching muscles. "I owe you my life."

"And whose life might that be?" she asked. "You didn't have any ident card or anything on you, seeing as how I rescued you in your jammies, so I an't been able to contact your people and let them know you're alive."

"They think I'm dead?"

"Course! The whole fecking ship exploded. They just assumed everyone aboard died." She handed him the feed screen she'd been watching when she came in. It was full of news about the bombing of the *Leander.* A distant security video of the spacecraft erupting into a massive fireball and photos of the charred shell floating in space. Speculation as to who was responsible and what their motive had been. A profile of the captain, who'd been making his final journey before retirement. His dizziness returned. There was nothing about the possibility that anyone had survived, and after seeing the photos of what was left of the *Leander,* he understood why.

"Wait," he said, his thoughts starting to click and whir like an engine powering up. "You didn't tell *anyone* you rescued me? Not the authorities?"

"Oh, well, not exactly." She arched an eyebrow at him. "Guess you're wondering why?"

He was, but it was a distant concern. Because at that moment, all he could focus on was one thing.

Everyone was going to think he was dead.

The information would soon get out that he had been on the *Leander.* He'd been meant to travel back to Ploutos on another spaceliner departing Alastor a couple of days later, but then a spot had opened up on the *Leander* at the last minute and he'd jumped at it. He'd contacted a number of people to tell them about his change of plans: a couple of friends on Alastor, his father's law firm and his own bank, a car service he'd arranged to pick him up at the docks. Not to mention the fact that he'd made the reservation under his own name. It was only a matter of time before the fact that he had been on the *Leander* would be made public.

And then the headlines would change. It would not just be the heinous bombing of a passenger liner that killed eighteen people.

It would be the heinous bombing that killed Leo Chapin, heir to one of the largest fortunes in the quadrant. Of course, one word from him or this girl would change that. But if they kept their mouths shut . . .

Leo Chapin would be dead.

A plan was starting to take shape in his mind, something riskier and less thought-out than anything he'd ever done, but the destruction of the *Leander* had handed him a precious window of opportunity. He rubbed absently at the tightness in his chest as he contemplated his idea. This was a chance to do the one thing he'd always wanted to do but which moving halfway across the universe and cutting off all contact with his father had failed to achieve.

Now, at least for a little while, he could stop being Leo Chapin.

He took a deep breath and looked up at the girl, his decision made. "I'm glad you didn't tell anyone. Promise me you won't."

She hadn't just agreed, of course. She'd wanted to know why, and he hadn't wanted to tell her. She proposed they discuss it over lunch since he needed to make himself scarce anyway; her father was coming soon to take the skiff out for a salvaging run. His stomach growled audibly at the mention of food. She produced a pair of shoes and a worn coat, both at least a size too small for him, and then took him to a tavern in a neighborhood he would have been nervous to walk through on his own.

"So what are you hiding from then?" she asked when they were seated at a table in a corner waiting on the food they'd ordered.

"I'm not hiding, exactly," he said. "I just . . . have some things I'd like to take care of before I let people know I'm all right."

She narrowed her eyes at him. "You're not some kind of criminal, are you, Mr. Whoever You Are?"

He smiled. "Hardly."

"I guess I an't surprised with that fancy accent of yours," she said. "None of the criminals I know, at least, talk like that. Or wear such fine jammies."

His cheeks burned, and she laughed.

"You might as well just tell me what you're up to," she said. "I'm betting I'm a lot more stubborn than you, and I'm *also* betting that you're a toser who's going to need some help to pull off whatever it is you're planning."

"I appreciate your concern, but I'll be fine, thank you."

"Okay, you can buy your own lunch then if you don't need any help," she said. "*And* give me back those shoes."

That brought him up short. Lord, he was a fool. He was in his sleeping clothes, for heaven's sake, without identification or a single bit to his name. He was so used to having everything he needed, being able to navigate the world so effortlessly, that he hadn't realized until this moment how helpless he actually was without the power of his father's name and his father's money. If she walked away from him now, what would he do? He *did* need help, but she was barely more than a child and a total stranger to him.

"You won't tell anyone?" he said.

She shrugged. "No one to tell, really."

"What about your father?"

She smiled but her eyes were sad. "We an't exactly *close.*"

And that, for some reason, was when he decided to trust her.

"My name's Ariel," she said. "And you are?"

He swallowed. Was he going to regret this? "Leo Chapin."

She gaped at him for a moment and then, once she had recovered from the shock, laughed for a solid five minutes.

Once they'd eaten and he'd explained his plan, Ariel had jumped into action. Their first stop was close, an office at the front of the tavern. She ducked under the bar, which none of the employees batted an eyelash at, and grabbed his hand to pull him along when he hesitated. She knocked on the office door, and when a low voice said, "Come in," she pulled him in after her.

"Afternoon, Ariel," the man at the desk inside said. He was whip-lash thin and heavily tattooed, his piercing eyes framed by thick, dark brows. "Who's this?"

Leo tensed, but Ariel said, "Just a friend. He needs some help, Seren."

"What kind?"

"The bit kind."

Seren didn't even blink. "How much?"

"A couple hundred."

The man whistled between his teeth. "That's a lot of help."

Leo frowned at the reaction. Two hundred bits was hardly a princely sum, so he suspected this Seren person just wasn't interested in helping. Perhaps this was a sign that he should call this fool plan off.

"We'll get it back," Ariel promised. "With interest, right?"

Leo nodded. "Of course."

"It's only for a week or two. You know I wouldn't ask if it wasn't important," she added.

The man looked Leo up and down. He must have been satisfied with whatever he saw, because he said, "No interest necessary. Our loans come with just one condition. You repay the favor to someone else in need someday."

Leo wasn't sure what response he'd been expecting, but it surely wasn't that. "I promise."

"It'll take me a little bit of time to get that much scratch together," Seren said. "I'll have someone bring the bits round to yours tonight."

Ariel hugged the man around the neck, pressing a quick kiss to his cheek. "Thanks, boss."

Then it was off to another "friend," one who apparently special-ized in disguises. With no more explanation from Ariel than the vague one she had given Seren, the ginger-haired woman provided Leo with several days' worth of clothes, shoes that actually fit him even if they were worn and broken in all wrong, contacts that turned his blue eyes a dark brown, and thick black glasses with clear frames. She handed Ariel a box of hair dye and sent them on their way, telling them to come back the next day to get Leo's new ident card forged.

"Are *you* a criminal?" he asked Ariel once they were back out on the street.

"Only technically," she said with a grin.

They returned to her home, an abandoned warehouse near the atmospheric docks. Leo tried not to stare as they walked past the other inhabitants, individuals and families who had claimed scraps of space they had erected makeshift walls and curtains around. In-tellectually, of course, he had known that people lived this way, but actually seeing it in the flesh was another matter. His eyes caught the gaze of a boy, no older than he had been when his father sent him away to another planet, who was sitting on a mattress, his bare feet resting on the concrete floor. Leo looked down at his own shoes, which suddenly didn't seem so shabby.

Ariel led him up to the second story of the warehouse, unlocking the door to one of the disused offices. A small salt-and-pepper man with a few days' growth of beard and deep lines in his face was asleep on a mattress in one corner, snoring softly.

"I don't believe this," she said. She kneeled at the man's side and shook him by the shoulder. "Da! Da, get up!"

The man's eyes cracked open. "What is it?"

She recoiled from his breath. Leo could practically smell the booze wafting off him from where he still stood in the doorway. "You promised me you were going on a run! I told you I couldn't cover for you today. We're going to lose our operating license, and then what'll we do?"

"I am going," the man said. "Just give me a minute . . ."

He struggled up into a sitting position and reached for his shoes, jamming his feet inside.

"You an't flying like this," Ariel said. When he fumbled clumsily at the laces, she pushed his hands aside and did them up herself.

"I'm fine! Don't tell me what I can and can't do, girl." He swayed as he climbed to his feet. "I'll be home—"

"After final call, I know," she said, the line of her jaw tense. She reached into a cupboard and pulled out a packet that looked like a sandwich wrapped in paper. "Just go on then, and eat this at some point, would you? I'll take the skiff out myself later."

Her father lumbered out of the door without a backward glance, and the look in Ariel's eyes, which suddenly seemed ancient in her young face, made Leo glad he'd decided to trust her. There was an ache, he was sure, inside of her that was a similar shape and size to the one inside of him. He felt suddenly like he'd known her all his life.

"Sorry about that," she said, closing the office door. Her whole air changed. She seemed to instantly forget what had just happened, like she had closed the door on her father in her mind as well as in reality, although Leo doubted it was as simple as she made it look. "Welcome to my humble home!"

Leo took a look around the repurposed office. He was relieved for her that it was a step up from the makeshift living spaces on the lower floor. The office at least had proper walls, as well as a few pieces of furniture, a shelf of canned foods and a camp stove, and a jar of wildflowers in the window, which Ariel must have collected. She set a pot of water to heat up over the stove and ripped open the box of hair dye that would turn his sandy-colored hair black.

"Sit down," she said, nudging a chair toward him with her foot.

"I really appreciate you helping me," he said, taking a seat. "I know you don't have to."

"Yeah, well, like I said, you wouldn't stand a chance on your own."

"That's becoming clear to me."

"Lucky for you I've got a weakness for lost causes. Besides"—she tossed him a grin over her shoulder—"this is the most fun I've had in ages. And it won't do me any harm to have a rich guy owe me one, will it?"

He laughed. "I believe I owe you more than one by now."

"Even better," she said, handing him a dripping washcloth to wet his hair with. "So, what do you think she's like?"

The girl he was supposed to marry, she meant. His stomach flipped over. "I honestly have no idea."

"You *an't got any* idea, you mean," Ariel said as she went to work mixing up the hair dye. "You can't keep talking like such a toser round here without attracting attention. Now let me hear it."

"I an't got any idea," he repeated, trying to spread his vowels so that they sounded more like Ariel's.

"Not bad! Now just make sure you actually say it when you're talking to her." She glopped a spoonful of the dye onto his head. "So you've never met her? Never even seen a picture or anything?"

He shook his head.

"She *could* be your soul mate," she said, her eyes going surprisingly soft. "You two could fall madly in love and live happily ever after, like you were destined to be together."

"I have just survived being blown up in space," Leo said, "so I suppose anything is possible."

She smiled. "I guess you'll find out soon enough."

It was a simple plan. As far as the world was concerned, Leo Chapin was currently on the *Aquila*, traveling home to claim his inheritance.

In reality, he was standing outside one of dozens of identical blocks of flats, wearing the clothes and glasses he'd been given, his borrowed bits in his pocket, his light eyes and hair now dark. He was ready.

So all that was left for him to do was walk inside.

"What are you waiting for?" Ariel asked him as he continued to stand there, gazing up at the grimy windows and crumbling gray brick of TH 76.

"What if she's not home?" he asked.

"She is," Ariel said. "I watched her go inside not ten minutes ago."

"What . . . what if this is a terrible plan?" He pressed his fingertips against his collarbone. "Maybe I shouldn't do this. There are so many ways it could go wrong."

"You've come too far to start second-guessing now!" Ariel said. "What's the problem?"

He looked back at the building, the empty windows that suddenly felt so much like eyes looking down on him. "I . . . I'm scared," he confessed.

She laughed. "Of a girl?"

"Yes!" He pulled at the shirt that was a little too short on his arms, exposing the bones of his wrist. "I'm not frightened of girls in general—"

She snorted. "Sure."

"—but this one in particular is very scary!" he said. "I'm supposed to *marry* her. And if my sociopath of a father thought she was a suitable bride . . ."

"Well, that's why you're doing this, right?" She put her hands on his shoulders, giving them a reassuring squeeze. "She's not going to know it's you, remember. Even if she's seen a picture, she'll never recognize you like this."

He nodded. This was the plan. Stay dead a little while longer so he could meet the girl, see what she was like before committing to spending his entire life with her. So simple in theory but surprisingly terrifying in execution.

"Now go in there, rent a flat from the father," Ariel told him, "and figure out some way to meet the daughter. Get yourself invited in for tea or pretend you have a mutual friend. Turn on that Chapin charm I'm sure is buried deep . . . *deep* inside of there somewhere."

"You're hilarious," he said.

"I know. Now stop stalling!" She gave him a shove toward the building. "It's time to go meet your wife."

After his first meeting with Viktoria Hale was over, Leo walked to the Thorn and Crown tavern to meet Ariel in a fog, one as thick as the haze above that kept the planet perpetually chilled and damp.

He had known Miss Hale would be beautiful; his father, who was an avid collector of beautiful things, never would have chosen a girl who wasn't. He'd expected her to be young and healthy, able to provide a multitude of heirs for the fortune his father had valued above all else, and to be a worthy ornament for the family like his mother had been. So he wasn't surprised by her beauty, but he hadn't quite been prepared for it, either. For one thing, he had walked into the basement office of the building expecting to find the girl's father. He'd thought he would have to find some way to finagle a meeting with the daughter, which would mean plenty of time to prepare himself to come face-to-face with her, to feel the tension and anticipation build, time slowing to a crawl, as a door opened somewhere and slowly revealed the girl he was supposed to marry.

Instead he'd rounded a corner and she'd been there, indescribably lovely and in a full rage. The unexpectedness of it was almost as much of a shock to his system as being blown through the *Leander*'s viewport into the vacuum of space. He'd never quite recovered his composure, groping and stuttering his way through the whole encounter, hating himself every moment of it.

He'd made it out of the building before the delayed wave of adrenaline hit and made his legs feel wobbly and weak beneath him. He'd stumbled into an alleyway and sat down on the pavement, leaning his head back against the scratchy brick of a building. That was his wife. It was an absurd thought for so many reasons—not the least of which being that neither of them had agreed to his father's psychotic arrangement—but he kept thinking it all the same. That had been his wife.

Her delicate features, tawny gold skin, and bright eyes had made him that much more awkward when he tried to talk to her. But he was sure the thing he wouldn't be able to stop thinking about was her obvious annoyance with him. She'd found him inconvenient and off-putting, and she'd shown it. Leo had never known how to actually show what he was feeling. That was not a highly prized attribute on Ploutos and certainly not within his own family. He'd learned to conceal his feelings so well from such an early age that he rarely even knew what they were anymore. Sometimes he'd only realize weeks after the fact that he was angry about something, and even then he would only silently ruminate on it, dithering over what to actually do about it until so much time had passed that it became ridiculous. But the moment he had set foot in that office, Viktoria Hale had sensed there was something off about him and had treated him accordingly. The way she was able to wear her feelings on her sleeve, so unapologetically, made her seem so much more, well, *alive,* than he had ever felt himself.

And then there'd been the wistfulness, the barely concealed grief, that had passed over her face as she looked at the old photograph of her family. It had rung a kind of bell of recognition inside of himself, only his grief was for something he'd never had, not something he'd lost. For just a second, he'd felt like maybe he was glimpsing something important about her.

He'd been prepared for many things when he'd met Viktoria Hale. But the possibility that he might actually *like* her hadn't been one of them.

Leo reached the Thorn and Crown, passing the line of hungry people waiting for the bowls of free stew the kitchen dished out twice a day for those who couldn't pay.

"Hey, Sky," Merak said as he walked in. Ariel practically lived here when she wasn't on her skiff or sleeping, so Leo had met most of the staff and regulars in the short time he'd been staying with her. "How's it doing?"

"Can't complain," Leo said. "Ariel here?"

"Haven't seen her."

She should have arrived by now, but he wasn't going to worry yet. He wasn't much of a drinker but he ordered a glass of grock, hoping it would help settle his frayed nerves, and a bowl of the stew.

He took a seat at Ariel's customary table in the back corner and gulped down a third of the grock. He'd thought that meeting Viktoria would somehow make his situation clearer, but he could see now how hopelessly naive that had been. If she'd been some kind of monster, casually setting fire to buildings or eating babies, then yes, it would have made his path forward obvious. But she was just a normal girl. Unusually pretty and a bit prickly but still basically normal. He couldn't imagine agreeing to marry her tomorrow, committing to spending the rest of his life with this stranger who'd been chosen for him for reasons he didn't understand by a man who had never seemed to care much for his happiness. But could he just walk away from his father's fortune and the only kind of life he'd ever known? What would he do; how would he support himself? It was an impossible dilemma, but he would have to make his decision soon.

Ariel finally showed up and set herself to work eating his lunch and interrogating him about his meeting with Viktoria Hale. Ariel was one of the toughest people he'd ever met—she was late, after all, because she was running from a mercenary who would happily throw her into detention for the next decade if he caught her—but she was still a teenaged girl and a surprisingly romantic one at that. But before she could wring too many details out of him, Seren sidled up to their table.

"Everything go smooth?" he asked Ariel.

She nodded. "More or less. The cargo's safe."

"Good," he said. "Meeting in five."

"We'll be there," she said, and then hurriedly went about finishing Leo's stew.

Leo glanced at the door tucked into the corner beside the bar. He knew that behind it was a staircase that led into the basement, although he'd never been down there himself. Unnoticed by him, the tavern had been emptying out slowly as men and women, one by one, got up from their chairs and went through that door, not coming back out again.

"Me, too?" he asked.

"Course," she said. "If this is going to be about what I think it is, it involves you as much as anyone."

"I don't want to . . . intrude," he said, not wanting to admit how nervous the idea made him. It hadn't taken him too long to put things together. The no-questions-asked bits that were delivered in the middle of the night, the friend with the stockpile of clothes and appearance-altering accessories, the way Ariel secretly took her father's skiff out on her own and spent all her free time in a tavern that fed the poor for free and had a constant parade of people coming and going from the side office and basement. Ariel was a member of the Philomeni Liberation Front, and it was one thing to have lunch with her here in a PLF haunt, but it was another thing entirely to attend one of their meetings. "I don't imagine anyone else wants me there anyway since I'm . . . not exactly one of you."

"Don't be stupid," she said, standing. "You're with me."

Leo hesitated another moment but then followed her. All morning the newsfeeds had been blasting that the PLF had taken credit for the *Leander* bombing, something Ariel had immediately scoffed at, but if the PLF was involved, he wanted to know. He followed her down the rickety staircase into the basement, which was dimly lit by a couple of bare overhead bulbs and packed with mismatched chairs that had been collected over the years. The chairs were mostly full already, the overflow of people standing around in the back of the room, talking in low voices, but Ariel pushed her way to the front of the crowd, dragging him along after her. He kept his eyes down, not wanting to be noticed. No one knew who he really was, of course—Ariel had told everyone he was her half-brother, newly arrived from Aerion—but he couldn't help feeling like anyone who looked at him too closely would see through that, like there was some invisible mark of Ploutos on him.

A man in the front row of chairs saw Ariel coming and stood, nudging his buddy to get up as well. Ariel thanked them and she and Leo took their seats. She was a PLF pilot, so, despite her youth, she held a special place of status in the organization. Leo could see it in people's eyes when they looked at her.

When Seren stood up in front of the crowd, stepping onto a raised platform constructed out of used pallets so they could all see him, the room fell silent.

"Welcome, brothers and sisters," he said. "Thank you for coming. I an't here to waste anyone's time, so I'll get right to it. As I'm sure you've heard by now, there was a bombing of some fancy spaceliner in the stream a few days ago. Early this morning, the feeds began reporting that the Front had claimed responsibility."

A murmur went through the crowd, and Seren raised his hand to quiet it.

"Thing is, me and the rest of the leadership don't know a thing about a bomb on a passenger liner," he said. "It an't exactly our style, anyway, killing innocents, and it'll only give the tosers an excuse to bring the thumb down even harder on us. So what I want to know is if any of you had anything to do with that bomb or if you took credit for it to the press."

Leo glanced around the room, taking in the members of the Philomeni Liberation Front. He saw every kind of person, old and young, male and female. The only thing they shared, really, was a resolute kind of tilt of the chin, a tired but determined gaze. From his boyhood he'd heard talk of the PLF, even if he hadn't understood most of it, low voices at cocktail parties and receptions discussing those damned Philomeni rebels, animals who robbed supply depots and sabotaged transports. Why couldn't they just accept that

Ploutosian protection was what was best for them? After all, their sad little backwater would descend into chaos without it, so they should be grateful and stop causing trouble.

The picture that had formed in his young mind was of snarling men clad in black, vicious and unreasonable. Not the elderly gentlemen sitting next to him, who was missing a hand that had probably been lost in a mining accident, or the ginger-haired young woman who had outfitted him with his new disguise and was now leaning against a back wall with a baby on one hip and a thumb-sucking toddler holding her hand. He'd learned years ago that the situation on Philomenus was more complicated than his childhood understanding of it, but the reality of living here, even for just a few days, had still come as a shock. Ariel was a respected member of the community and one with a decent job thanks to her skiff, yet she and her father were barely clinging on. The PLF was the only friend most of these people—and he could now count himself among them—had to help them back onto their feet when they tumbled off the high-wire of life on this planet. The PLF fed them when they were hungry and treated their children when they were sick, and they had handed him money, clothes, and a new identity without any questions, just because he needed them. So perhaps the situation wasn't that complicated after all. Perhaps it was actually simple, but the Philomeni Liberation Front were the heroes of the story and not the villains.

Of course, he was going to feel less charitably inclined toward them if it turned out one of them had tried to blow him up.

But the crowd was silent, and eventually Seren nodded. "That's what I thought," he said. "Which means we've got a problem now. Someone put a bomb on that ship, and they want us taking the blame. The leadership is going to have to decide what this means for us, if we need to go quiet for a while til some of the heat is off. In the meantime, be prepared for things to get ugly. Watch out for yourselves, and watch out for each other. Stay safe, friends."

As everyone shuffled out of the basement, Leo went to follow them. But Ariel was still sitting, frowning down at a crack in the concrete floor.

"What is it?" he asked.

She looked up at him. "Why would someone want to blow up that ship?"

"To frame the PLF?" he said. "Make you all look bad, or give the Ploutosian government an excuse to come after you?"

"Maybe," she said, "but why the *Leander* specifically? Bombing that ship wouldn't ever be a realistic PLF operation. We don't mess with civilians, and how would one of us have even gotten all the way to Alastor to plant the bomb? It's practically impossible for a Philomeni to get off-world unless it's to go scrub dishes on Ploutos, let alone reach the other end of the quadrant. If someone wanted to frame us, they couldn't have picked a worse target than the *Leander*."

He sank back into the seat beside her, because her reasoning made a terrible kind of sense. "What are you saying?"

But before Ariel could answer, a cacophony of shrieks and shattering exploded above their heads. Ariel was instantly in motion, like some part of her was always poised for disaster, racing up the stairs toward the noise. Leo ran to catch up to her.

The tavern was full of shouting people crowded around the bar. Ariel went to push her way to the front to see what was happening, but Leo caught her around the wrist, holding her back in case it wasn't safe. He climbed onto a chair and immediately understood what was happening.

The doorway to the kitchen had been ripped off its hinges. Inside, mercs were trashing the place, knocking over pots of stew and smashing the bowls used to serve it with their batons. The hungry people who had been queuing for a free meal had scattered.

Ploutos was turning the heat up on the PLF.

Ariel, who had clambered up onto a chair beside him to watch the destruction, turned to look up at him, her face pale and serious.

"What I was saying before," she said. "What if that bomb had nothing to do with us at all? Maybe we were just a smoke screen."

"For what?" Leo asked, although deep down he already knew what she was going to say.

"What if that bomber was really trying to kill *you?*"

CHAPTER FIFTEEN

AND THAT WAS WHY he'd decided to stay dead a little while longer. It was why he'd gotten the job with the Gardners, to make sure they were okay. He had to know if someone was trying to kill him or them before he could safely come back to life. It wasn't because of Viktoria Hale, and it wasn't supposed to be permanent.

But Vika was the reason he was now collapsed on Ariel's bed in the middle of the night, weary down to his bones, his chest aching as though he were wounded there, ready to give up what was left of his life.

"I'm going to stay dead," he said. "For good."

The words seemed to hang in the air like the scent of something sharp, and Ariel just stared at him, her eyes wide in the dimness of the room. "What are you talking about?" she asked.

"Leo Chapin is dead already and I'm just . . . going to leave him that way," he said. "I'll go back to Alastor and get a job, eventually finish university if I can, just live like a normal person—"

"Are you insane?" She sat up, her voice rising. She froze for a moment, eyes darting to the other end of the room, but when her father's snoring continued, she hissed, "That makes no sense! We haven't found a single scrap of evidence that you were targeted in the *Leander* bombing and you've been all starry-eyed for Vika for weeks now. Why not just come clean? Get the money, get the girl?"

"Because." Leo sighed and repositioned so that he was sitting beside her, his shoulder resting against hers as they both leaned their backs against the rough brick wall. "She can't stand me."

"Oh I'm sure that's not—"

"*Believe* me, it's true. I stayed Sky Foster for this long to make sure the Gardners and I weren't in danger from someone trying to kill Chapin heirs and to maybe try to clear the name of the PLF if I could, but I suppose I also thought . . . well, I was naive enough to believe that if Vika got to know me, she might grow to like me. But she hasn't." He laughed, and the sound seemed to splinter in his chest, lodging shards inside of him. "If anything, the more she gets to know me, the more strongly she *dislikes* me. And that's never going to change. So now that I'm sure the Gardners are safe, it's time for me to go."

"I don't understand," Ariel said, rubbing her face, which was still creased from the wrinkles in her pillow. "This is so stupid. Why can't you just tell her the truth?"

He shook his head. "It was one thing when we were strangers. If we had both agreed to my father's deranged terms and gotten married, it would have been a blind leap for both of us. But now I *know* she doesn't care for me."

From their very first moments together, he'd found her fascinating and she'd found him irritating. He'd thought that perhaps his interest in her would fade when he got to know her better and she was a real person to him instead of just the mysterious bride his father had foisted on him, but it was just the opposite. The more he watched her, the harder it became to look away. She was a bright spark of a person, her every thought and emotion so close to the surface, whether she was beaming with excitement or snapping in anger, like there was always electricity running just under her skin. He felt the thrum of it whenever he was near her, the energy of it waking up parts of him that had long been dull and cold. When she'd still lived at home, he'd found himself contriving ridiculous excuses to be near her just to feel that, hovering in a corridor for half an hour so he could coincidentally be there to open the door for her as she came home from her job or breaking a lightbulb so he could visit her father's office when she was helping out to report the problem. Even when she rolled her eyes at him, he felt admiration, and not a little bit of envy, for her ability to trust her instincts about him and his motives. He had never trusted himself the way she did.

Then she moved to Ploutos and the tough girl he'd met on Philomenus transformed into a frivolous, shallow creature who didn't seem to care about anything but her own pleasure, like so many of the people he'd grown up around. And he'd thought to himself, see, this is the bullet you've dodged, this is the wife he wanted for you. And he'd tried to make himself believe it.

But he couldn't look at her, even in all her new finery, without seeing the girl who had changed his sabotaged lightbulb even after a twelve-hour shift of being demeaned and ridiculed just so that her beloved, broken father could finish his tea in peace and quiet.

"The problem is this," he continued. "I . . . adore her. Heavens help me, she's vain and stubborn and so selfish sometimes, but I still think she's wonderful. And she can't stand to be near me. She thinks I'm judgmental and shifty, and I can hardly blame her because I *am* those things."

"No you're—"

He cut off her protestations. "I concocted an entire false identity precisely so that I could judge her. She's had my number from the very start. But the point is, if I told her who I truly am, I'd be forcing her to choose between a life of poverty and compromising herself by marrying me. I'd be *buying* her. Because I'm rich and she's not and she's a thing I want."

"Oh," Ariel breathed. "Yeah, that's not great."

"It's a thing my father would have done," he said, picking at a stray thread on her quilt, "and I never want to be like him. He and my mother had a loveless marriage, and I grew up in a loveless household. No fortune is worth that. Money . . . it just poisons things. I'd rather do without it."

Ariel climbed out of bed and opened the bottom drawer of her battered bureau. From under a couple of sweaters, she unearthed a round tin and brought it over to him, popping off the lid.

"I think these are called for," she said, grabbing a handful of cookies from inside and passing it to him. He smiled and took a couple himself.

"I was uneasy with the idea of inheriting Rigel's money anyway," Leo said, being careful not to get any crumbs in Ariel's bed, something she didn't seem concerned about herself. "By adding this insane contingency about getting to choose my wife, he's just made the decision easier. He thought he could control me from beyond the grave, but instead he gave me the push I needed to finally break free of him completely."

"Oops," she said around a mouthful of cookie.

"Oops, indeed." He suddenly smiled. "I wish he could see how spectacularly his entire scheme has backfired. And now the fortune he was so obsessed with building his entire life has gone to his servants, because he didn't have anyone else left to leave it to since he was such an insufferable old bastard. The best part is that they're so levelheaded and kind that I'm sure they'll make better use of his money than he ever did, or even than I could. Perhaps it's for the best this way."

"Oh, Leo." Ariel dropped her uneaten cookie back into the tin and put her hands on his cheeks so that she could look him lovingly in the eyes. "You're an idiot."

He blinked. "Excuse me?"

She jabbed a finger into his chest. "This is a plan only someone who has been rich their entire life could come up with, and it's the stupidest thing I've ever heard!"

Leo spluttered. "I know it's not ideal but—"

"No. No, I'm sorry but it's *catastrophically* dumb," she said. "First of all, you don't just give up the security of a fortune without a fight.

I know you're a smart and capable person, but do you know how many smart and capable people stand in PLF food lines every day just so they don't starve? You've been vacationing in our shoes for a few weeks now, but you have no clue what it's *really* like to be poor, and if you did, the idea of giving up everything and just hoping for the best would never have entered your pretty little head. Second, maybe your Gardners will do good things with all that money, but I an't going to believe that they'll do *better* than you could. With six billion bits, you could make real changes. For everyone." Her expression turned fond, and she tucked a strand of dark hair behind his ear. "And . . . you're mad about her. You shouldn't give up yet."

He took his fake glasses off and rubbed the bridge of his nose where they pinched. There had been some relief in his devastation, because at least it had made his decision clear, but now Ariel was rekindling the embers of his hope. "But . . . I told you. She despises me."

"Then she doesn't really know you yet." She nudged him in the ribs. "You're a perfectly lovable person, Leo Chapin. And her entire *world* has changed. Give her a little more time to get her feet back under her. You owe that to yourself, at least, and to her, too."

"Perhaps you're right," he said, any of the certainty he still had left leaching out of him. He wasn't sure if he should thank Ariel or throttle her for making him wonder again if things might work out, sending him back into the half-dead limbo he'd almost resolved to escape.

"I'm always right," she said. "Now go home and let me get some sleep."

CHAPTER SIXTEEN

VIKA HAD COME TO A DECISION. It had been a long time coming, but now her mind was made up. She was sitting on the balcony overlooking the park and drinking her coffee, with heavy cream and four sugars, and trying to figure out how she would say the words aloud when one of the maids approached.

"The concierge just hailed, miss," she said. "Your guest has arrived and is on his way up."

Vika abandoned her coffee, and by the time she'd reached the foyer the lift doors were opening and she was throwing herself into the arms of the stunned man inside.

"Da!" she said. The smell of him, which she had never really noticed before, was so strong and familiar that tears sprang to her eyes. Soap and damp and just a hint of dakha.

"My darling girl." He stepped back, holding her at arm's length so he could take her in. The yellow silk day dress she'd chosen with care that morning in order to impress him, her freshly styled hair that fell in shiny curls over her shoulders, the polish of a light coating of cosmetics. His expression was shock and delight and something that looked a little like pain all in one. "Look at you. You're stunning."

"I'm so happy to see you," she said. "I have the best day planned for us."

"I'm looking forward to it! Will you show me around your new home first?"

Her home. From her da's mouth, the word gave her an odd pang when it hit her. Did he feel she'd abandoned him for something better? Or was it maybe a relief to have her gone, one less mouth to feed?

"Of course," she said, forcing her mouth up into a smile. "Let me give you the grand tour."

As she showed him from room to room, her da's eyes took on a kind of stunned, glossy look. She wondered if this was what she'd looked like when she'd tried to take this place in on her first day. She'd grown so used to the opulence that she hardly even registered it now, so seeing the penthouse through his eyes was like seeing it for the first time again.

They had completed their tour of the main level and were on their way to the stairs when Sky walked into the foyer from the direction of his office, eyes down on his mini-holo.

"Sky!" her da said when he spotted him, his voice so friendly that Vika stopped short. "I wondered if I might see you here today."

Sky smiled warmly and approached them, offering his hand to her da. "Good morning, sir. It's a pleasure as always."

Her da clapped him on the shoulder. "It's just nice to see my girl again. Doesn't she look beautiful?"

Sky's eyes flicked up at her and then down once more. "She seems very well, sir."

"Since you've been too busy lately to hail your old da, we've had to rely on Sky here to tell us how you've been doing," her da explained. "It's lucky for us you two ended up in the same place somehow, else we'd have been worrying."

That unwelcome bit of information straightened her spine. She knew Sky spoke to her father occasionally, but she didn't realize they were talking about her or that they'd gotten to be quite so chummy.

"Yes, well, we'd better get going, Da. Mr. Foster, please have the car pulled around."

Sky seemed to rightly shrink a bit as she reminded him of his proper place, and he gave her a deferential nod. "Of course, Miss Hale. I hope you both enjoy your day."

"Come by the flat sometime," her da told him. "I believe I owe you a drink."

A bit of Sky's smile returned. "Yes, sir, I believe you do."

Vika turned to her da as they rode the lift down to the lobby. "I don't like the idea of him talking to you about me behind my back." Sky could be telling him anything, after all, making up any outrageous lie about what she was up to as he cozied up to her father.

But her da just laughed. "You make it sound much more sinister than it is, darling. We've just become friendly over the last few weeks, and he's been assuring us that you're well and enjoying yourself, that's all."

"It's really none of his business, though, is it?"

"Now, now. Don't get salty with poor Sky just cause you feel guilty about ignoring your old da all these weeks." He reached over and squeezed the ticklish spot on her side.

She tried to squirm away. "That's not what—ahh! Stop it!"

The lift doors slid open with a soft ding and Vika's mouth snapped shut on her laughter when she caught the concierge staring at her. She rearranged her hair over her shoulder and led her da to the waiting car.

She'd reserved them a table at one of the finest restaurants in the city for lunch, wanting to treat her da to something special. Wanting, if she was being honest, to impress him with her fine new life. But his look was so shell-shocked as they were led inside that she wondered if she'd made a mistake. She remembered how overwhelmed she, too, had felt when she'd first entered this place. It felt more like a garden than a restaurant, tables scattered among flowering trees and rosebushes, the glass dome overhead letting the unfiltered light shine down. A waterfall in one corner led to a maze of little streams and ponds, some running exposed through the garden beds and others covered with plastecene that snaked under tables, hundreds of pastel-colored fish swimming through them. She lunched here so often with Miranda and Nova that it had become quite normal to her to dine on fine china and crystal in the middle of a lush indoor garden, which—now that she thought about it—was a little bit insane.

She thought of her da in the days after he lost his job at the mines, pretending not to be hungry so that she and Lavinia could go to bed with full bellies, and she suddenly felt ashamed to have brought him here. How grotesque this place seemed when she remembered how many hungry people there were on her own planet, maybe some of the very ones who would be washing the dishes she was eating from. The queasy feeling eddied and swirled through her all throughout lunch, spiking up in her when her da attempted to order the cheapest thing on the menu and then again when he tried to pay for the meal even though he couldn't possibly have afforded it.

"Come on," she said as they left the restaurant, walking together down the sunny sidewalk with her arm looped in his, pushing down her discomfort. The restaurant might have been a mistake, but she was determined the rest of the afternoon wouldn't be. "It's time for our next activity."

They were only a few blocks away. As they entered the square and heard the tinkling music, Vika saw the recognition light up in his eyes.

"Is that . . . ?"

She nodded. "It's the same one you used to bring me to. The hospital is just round the corner."

The carousel was smaller than she remembered it but just as beautiful, with its golden poles and mirrored sides and intricately painted horses. She paid the vendor and the two of them climbed on with at least as much excitement as the children around them. Vika hunted out the horse that had always been her favorite: a pale violet one with a mane in various shades of minty green. She climbed onto it while her father mounted the bright blue steed beside it, and soon they were beginning to spin.

"Did you ever think we'd be back here?" Vika asked over the delicate strains of music.

Her da laughed. "Can't say I did!"

The guilt that had been festering inside of her all day suddenly burst out. "I'm so sorry, Da. I should have been more in touch. I should have sent more money—"

"Darling." He leaned across the distance between them to take her hand, squeezing her fingers. "Don't be sorry. It's clear being here is a big adjustment, and it's wonderful to see you doing so well. I just miss you, is all."

Vika swallowed down the hot rush of emotion in her throat. "Well, of course you do. I wouldn't want to be stuck with just Mum and Lavinia, either."

In spite of himself, he chuckled. "You're a very nasty child, you know."

"I do."

When the ride was over, she bought them a couple of freeze creams from a nearby vendor and they sat on a bench to enjoy the sunshine. Vika managed only a couple of bites of hers before her stomach turned, and she threw the rest in a rubbish bin.

"Da, there's something I need to tell you," she said.

"Yes?" He caught a melting glob of cream with his tongue before it escaped the cone.

"Please look at me," she said.

He heard the serious note in her voice and turned to her, forgetting the freeze cream.

"I've made a decision," she said. "I'm . . . I'm not going back to Philomenus. And I'm not going to let you all be stuck there, either. I'm going to live here on Ploutos and I'm bringing you all with me."

"Darling." He sighed. "I'm happy you've been enjoying the generosity of the Gardners, but I don't want you to build yourself up for disappointment."

"I'm not. There's an easy solution, and I've made up my mind to do it." She took a deep breath. "I just have to marry someone very rich. I don't even much care who anymore."

"Vika!"

"It's true, Da." She'd rehearsed this speech better in her head, but now the words were just pouring out. "I can't go back to being poor. It was bad before, but now that I know what it's like to really have money? I have to have it. Maybe that makes me a terrible person, but it's true."

Her da was just staring at her, melted freeze cream flowing over his fingers.

"I thought of trying to get a job here," she continued, "but I don't have the education I'd need to do anything that would make me any money. On Philomenus they don't teach us how to do *anything* but low-wage work serving richer people, and even if I could go to university for business or law and get a good job eventually, it would take me years and I might still never make the kind of money I'd need to do all the things I want. It will be so much quicker and easier to simply find myself a rich husband. Once I do, I can bring you and Mum and Lavinia here to Ploutos. Lavinia can go to school to do whatever she wants, Mum can get herself a maid to boss around, and you won't have to work anymore. You'll be able to just lounge in the park reading mystery novels and smoking good cigars like a proper man of leisure." She blinked her eyes rapidly to dispel the tears gathering behind them. "The way you *deserve.*"

"Oh, my dear." He tossed away his melted freeze cream, mopping his sticky fingers with a napkin. "That is a nice picture you paint, but it's not worth your happiness."

"I think it is," she said. "I'll be happy if I'm rich and you're taken care of."

"Not if you have a husband you don't love, you won't."

She sighed. "Can I ask you something, Da?"

"Always."

She paused, unsure if she really wanted to say this, but she needed him to understand. "Did you marry for love?"

"Yes."

"And not for money?"

He almost laughed. "Course not."

"And . . . are you happy?"

His face clouded over. Maybe he was once—Vika could remember those times—but the strain of poverty had broken both of her parents in different ways long ago, and their jagged edges no longer aligned.

"I'm sorry," she whispered. "I don't mean to be cruel. These last few weeks have just made everything seem very clear to me. I'd rather be secure and comfortable and know that the people I love are, too, than try to find some supposed soul mate I would probably tire of in a few years anyway. Money is a safer bet in life than love will ever be."

"Oh, Vika." He pushed the hair away from her eyes and rested his palms on her cheeks. "You're far too young to be such a cynic. It would pain me to see you resign yourself to a life of that."

"Then let's talk about something else," she said, taking his hands in hers and dropping them to her lap, "because my mind's made up."

She pressed several large bills into her da's hand as he got ready to board the bi-rail back to the atmospheric ferry, forbidding him to argue with her about it and telling him that she'd already set up an automatic transfer to send a portion of her allowance into his account every fortnight. He pulled her in for a tight hug, and she swiped away her tears behind his back. Having his arms around her felt like all the best parts of being at home again, and she only realized in that moment just how homesick a part of her was.

But then he was gone, and it was time to get back to work.

Evelyn Lyons was throwing a dinner party for her favorite clients that night, which meant the cream of Ploutosian high society would be in attendance. It was the perfect opportunity for Vika to refine her list of potential husbands and start making some progress toward securing one of them. She'd bought a new dress especially for the occasion, a gold gown that caught the light whenever she moved in such a way that it seemed to be made of molten metal. It had cost her most of her allowance for the week, but it was an investment in her future. She paired it with rubies in her hair and around her neck, and Gemma gave her smoky, mysterious eyes and a bold lip the same color as the jewels. Vika surveyed herself carefully in the mirror when the look was complete. She looked older, sophisticated. If there was a wealthy man who was looking for a trophy to wear on his arm, he could do a lot worse than her.

Vika hurried toward the foyer; they should have left several minutes ago and she was running behind. But she found only Mira perched on the edge of a chair, her fancy shoes discarded, tapping her foot against the marble.

"He's still working?" Vika asked.

"Of course he is!" Mira said. "I swear the man works more hours now than he did when Mr. Chapin had him running around fixing broken sinks and repainting walls."

"Do you want me to go and hurry him along?"

"No need, I'm here!" Hal was striding toward them, Sky at his heels with his jacket. He gave Vika a kiss to her forehead, the smell of dakha faint under his spicy aftershave, and it gave her another pang of homesickness for her da. "Viktoria, my dear, you look ravishing. Apologies for my lateness, ladies. This charity foundation is turning out to be a damnable amount of work. Is the car here?"

"Yes, sweetheart," Mira said with an indulgent smile that didn't quite hide her annoyance. "It's been waiting."

"Ah, that reminds me," Hal said as Sky helped him into his jacket. He held out his arms, and Sky began to fasten platinum cuff links onto his sleeves. "Sky, I need you to gather quotes for a new car service."

"Why?" Mira stood. "I like Grant and Tania."

"Don't worry yourself, love," Hal said, holding her arm to keep her steady as she stepped back into her shoes. "I've just been asking around and I think we're overpaying. It's not right of them to take advantage just because they think we're rubes who don't know the going rate."

Mira frowned. "Well, whatever you think is best, I suppose. But we really must be going or we're going to be late. I don't want Ms. Lyons to think us rude—"

"I understand that, my dear, but I can't just neglect the work that needs to be done because of a party—"

Vika threw her shawl over her shoulders and felt the delicate fabric snag on the back of her earring. She reached up to her ear, trying to untangle the snarl.

"You're right, sweetheart, forget I said anything," Mira said. "Let's just go and have a good time."

"Agreed."

"I'll have those quotes ready for you on Monday, sir," Sky said. He noticed Vika struggling. "Oh. May I—Miss Hale, may I assist you?"

Her instinct was to say no, but she knew that was ridiculous and she might well pull the earring straight out of her ear at the rate she was going. "Yes, thank you, Mr. Foster."

He carefully stepped into her personal space, as though he expected a shove, and his fingertips accidentally grazed her neck as he reached for the shawl, sending an unexpected tingle up her spine. "Pardon me," he said. He gently unhooked the fabric from the back of her earring and smoothed it down across her shoulder. "There you are. I hope you enjoy your evening."

She swallowed. "Thank you."

The Lyonses' home was a stately mansion north of the park. It didn't have quite the splendor of Chapin Tower, floating in the clouds as it was, but it was large and beautifully situated among grand old trees. The heavy boughs were illuminated by hundreds of tiny lights that hovered among the leaves, suspended by some invisible force, making the whole estate sparkle. The circular driveway was full of fine cars and airships; Evelyn's privileged position as the holder of so many secrets of the Ploutosian elite made her parties must-attend functions.

A pretty young woman with flame-red hair and the glint of a communicator in her ear answered the door.

"Do come in," she said. "May I take your coats?"

"Yes, thank you," Hal said, flashing a toothy smile as the girl helped him out of his overcoat.

She looked more closely at his face. "Mr. Gardner?"

"Yes."

"I thought I recognized your voice!" She held her hand out to him. "I'm Carina."

"Oh, Carina! What a pleasure." The two smiled at each other as he gripped her fingers, and after a moment, as if he'd just remembered they were there, Hal turned to Vika and Mira. "My dears, this is Evelyn's assistant. We've spoken on the comm many times."

"Hundreds!" Carina said, laughing. "Well, Mr. Gardner, enjoy your evening. And do please let me know if there's anything I can do for you."

"I certainly will," Hal said.

Inside, Vika found Miranda and soon conversation turned, as it usually did, to the subject of Vika's future husband. This was Miranda's favorite game to play on behalf of other people since she'd already finished her own turn at it. Never forgetting Archer's warning, Vika was careful not to tell Miranda anything she didn't want the whole city to eventually know about, but she figured it could only help her if word got around that she was ready to entertain proposals.

"So who should it be, Viktoria?" Miranda asked in a soft voice as they circulated, sipping their wine and greeting fellow guests.

"Mr. Chason?" Vika nodded at the older man across the room who was holding court with a couple of ladies who looked eager to find a way out.

"Perhaps," Miranda said. "He's terribly full of himself but it could be worse. What about the Rotanevs' oldest son?"

Vika followed Miranda's gaze to Daniel Rotanev, who was laughing with a couple of friends as they swigged—not so subtly—from a bottle of liquor they'd obviously swiped from the bar. She slapped Miranda's arm. "He's practically a child!"

"He's only three or four cycles younger than you."

"And I'm only *just* old enough to be married myself," Vika said, "and far too old to be a babysitter."

Miranda shrugged. "You could have a lengthy engagement."

"No, thank you. Next."

"What about your Mr. Sheratan?" Miranda asked. "You sure seem to have stars in your eyes whenever you're with him."

Vika flagged down a waiter passing hors d'oeuvres and asked for a glass of water. It gave her a moment to think about how she wanted to answer Miranda's question. The truth was the idea of marriage and Archer didn't sit next to each other comfortably in her mind. She liked him very much. He was probably the closest thing she had to a real friend on this planet, and the way he looked at her sometimes, or the memory of his hand curled around her waist as they danced, set off butterflies inside of her. In fact, maybe that was precisely why she didn't want to add Archer to her potential-husband list. It felt . . . a little too real.

"I'm fond of him," she finally said, "but I'm aiming higher than a junior solicitor."

Miranda laughed, so Vika must have managed the airy, unconcerned tone of voice she was going for. "And so you should! Oh, what about Miles Keid? Look, he's talking to your handyman right now."

Vika casually scanned the room until she spotted Hal, who was chatting with Ms. Lyons and a small group of gentlemen by the fireplace. She recognized all of them but one, who must be Mr. Keid. He was perhaps twenty cycles older than her, the barest hint of gray in his hair, and dressed in a plain but well-fitted suit. Everything about him was neat and small, from his glasses to his beard, and he had a nice smile. She didn't hate the look of him, at least.

"I don't know him," Vika said.

"No, you wouldn't," Miranda replied. "He's been away from Ploutos for several years. He's from practically ancient money, not the biggest fortune anymore but a very well-established family. He's recently divorced, so someone will snap him up soon. You'll have to be quick if you want it to be you."

"Well, in that case . . ."

Vika and Miranda approached the group, catching the tail end of the conversation.

"—should be finalized soon," Ms. Lyons was saying, "and then we can address the disposition of your estate."

"Oh yes, you really must, Hal," one of the other men said. "You have to protect yourself."

"Carina!" Ms. Lyons said. The girl, who had been speaking to a waiter, rushed to her boss's side. "Schedule a time for Mr. Gardner to meet with me next week for estate planning. The Greenbriar papers should be ready to sign by then."

"What's this about?" Vika asked.

Hal gave her a sneaky little smile and tapped the side of his nose. "A secret. I'll tell you later."

Vika laughed. "You're very mysterious."

Hal put a hand on the small of Carina's back as she produced a mini-holo and led her to a dim, quiet corner of the room to schedule the meeting, leaving Vika and Miranda with Ms. Lyons and the gentlemen.

"Thank you so much for inviting us to your beautiful home, Ms. Lyons," Vika said.

"It's my pleasure," Ms. Lyons said.

"Mr. Keid," Miranda said. "How are you enjoying being back on Ploutos?"

The man adjusted his glasses on the bridge of his nose. "Very well. Yes, very well."

Then, just as Vika had been hoping, Ms. Lyons stepped in to perform her duties as hostess. "Miles, have you met Viktoria Hale yet?"

Mr. Keid gave her a bow and took the very tips of her fingers in the traditional Ploutosian greeting. "No, I don't believe I've had the pleasure."

They spoke for a few minutes, mostly about the state of the weather. It might not be the most fascinating conversation Vika had ever had, but he seemed a perfectly pleasant sort of man, so she added him to her list.

When a servant came and announced that dinner was served, Mr. Keid offered Vika his arm and escorted her to the dining room.

"May I sit beside you?" he asked. "I would love to continue our conversation."

Vika gave him her brightest smile, as though she couldn't wait to continue discussing how unseasonably warm it had been. "It would be my pleasure, sir."

"So you see it really is quite a complicated business," Mr. Keid said an hour later as they moved out onto the veranda for after-dinner cocktails under the stars. He'd barely drawn breath during the entirety of dinner. Vika had made the terrible mistake of asking him about his family's company and had had the minutiae of the inter-planetary distribution of steel explained to her in excruciating detail over four courses. She tried to pay attention and ask lots questions, because she could tell he enjoyed explaining things to her, and she was sure she'd wake up the next morning with a sore neck from nodding along to his monologue for so long. "It's all about margin, you see. Whatever you can do to eke out an extra percentage or two of profit, when the vast quantities are taken into account—"

"Will make a significant difference to your net earnings since there are so many transactions," she finished. She had always had a mind for maths, after all, and business strategy was much more interesting than the particular applications of different grades of steel.

"A tremendous difference!" Mr. Keid said, apparently delighted by her ability to grasp what seemed like a simple enough concept. "You're a very clever young lady. You should consider a future in business."

Vika smiled demurely and batted her eyes. A future as a businesswoman wasn't exactly what she had in mind. "Perhaps I will. Please excuse me, Mr. Keid. I won't be but a minute."

Vika went back inside the house, headed for the powder room to freshen up her lipstick and get a brief break from smiling at Mr. Keid's conversation before the muscles in her face permanently cramped.

"Viktoria!" a voice said as she crossed the main reception room.

She turned and found Hal hurrying after her.

"Yes?" she asked.

He drew her into a corner. "It's about that secret," he said, keeping his voice low. "I was hoping you would help me with it."

"Of course," she said. "Anything I can do for you."

"I've bought a house," he said, his eyes lighting up like a child's. "The deal will be finalized soon. Mira doesn't know."

Vika's mouth dropped open. "That's a big secret!"

"She's always had this dream of a house in the country where she can have a garden. We've never lived anywhere where she could grow flowers of her own. Old Mr. Chapin used to let her plant some on his rooftop but she never had the time to care for them properly so they always just withered and died. Now that we have the means, I've bought her a lovely little estate called Greenbriar outside of the city where she can grow all the flowers she could ever dream of."

Vika raised a hand to her suddenly aching heart. She could see Mira through one of the lead-paned windows, standing outside in the Lyonses' garden chatting with a few of the other ladies, utterly oblivious to what her husband had in store for her. Had her father once loved her mother like this? "Oh, that's lovely. She's going to be so happy."

"I hope so," he said. "Her name day is in a few weeks, and I was thinking we'd throw her a surprise party at the new house. What do you think?"

Vika smiled. "I think it's a wonderful idea."

"Thing is, there's lots that needs doing to get Greenbriar ready in time," Hal said, "and I've got far too much on my plate already with the charitable foundation and writing our will and everything else. Would you be willing to go and get the house ready? It's only partially furnished, so I need someone who can oversee getting it all set up and looking nice, and you've got such wonderful taste. Plus there are all the party arrangements to be made. Food, decorations, and I don't even know what else."

"Yes, of course!" Vika said, his enthusiasm catching. "It'll be a lot of work to get done so quickly on my own, but I'm sure I can—"

"Oh, you won't be alone. I'm sending Sky as well. You just make the decisions, and he'll make sure everything gets done."

All of Vika's excitement crashed to the floor at her feet. "Oh. You won't need him here? You can't possibly go two weeks without an assistant! I'll manage just fine on my own."

Hal shook his head. "Nonsense, it's far too much work for one person, and I wouldn't feel right you being out there by yourself."

"Well . . ." Vika cast about for any way to change his mind. "Well, what will you tell Mira?"

"We'll say you've gone home to Philomenus to visit your family and that Sky's ill or something," Hal said. "She won't think twice about it."

Vika imagined two weeks of being alone in some house out in the country with no one but Sky Foster for company, working hand in hand with him, and wanted so badly to come up with some excuse for why she couldn't. But this was for Hal and Mira, the sweetest people she knew and the ones who had given her this life. How could she possibly say no?

"Yes, of course," she said. "When do we leave?"

CHAPTER SEVENTEEN

"YOU SURE YOU DON'T MIND?" Ariel asked as Leo packed his clothes into an overnight bag. She was still hovering in the doorway of his little studio flat, her eyes roaming over the room like it was some kind of palace.

"Of course not," he said. "I'm going to be gone anyway. All I care about is that you're safe while I'm away, and you'll be safer here." Since the explosion on the *Leander*, more and more members of the PLF had been arrested on flimsy pretenses in midnight raids or had simply disappeared off the streets with no one the wiser as to where they'd gone. Too many people knew where Ariel lived for him to rest easy with her sleeping on the floor of that warehouse office.

Ariel stepped farther into the room, resting her hand on the back of his chair. Slowly, she curled her fingers into the fabric. "I can pay you. You know, for the rent. I an't got the bits on me but—"

"Don't be ridiculous," he said, although the truth was that he wasn't quite sure how he was going to make his next rent payment. He'd done the figures when Hal hired him and thought his assistant salary, modest though it was, would be more than enough for him. But somehow he was always just scraping by. Expenses he hadn't planned on kept popping up, like new shoes when the ones he'd borrowed from Ariel's friend split at the soles or the shakedown he got from some mercs outside the ferry. Plus buying this bloody overnight bag so he could have the privilege of traveling to his own private version of hell, being alone for two weeks with a girl he was mad about who couldn't stand the sight of his face and had no trouble showing it. If he let Leo Chapin stay dead, he had no idea how he would ever be able to repay the two hundred bits he'd borrowed from Seren and the PLF. It seemed like such a vast sum to him now, when not so long ago he'd have spent that much on a nice lunch with a friend and not thought twice about it. But now that it was taking every ounce of his ingenuity just to stay afloat, it seemed impossible he'd ever be able to get that far ahead.

"I don't know if I should leave my da," Ariel said. "What'll he do without me there to take care of him?"

Leo looked up at her, his heart twisting painfully in his chest. Sometimes it was easy to forget just how young she really was. But when her voice became soft and sad like this, it became possible to see past the tough facade—bad-ass pilot and guerrilla rebel—to the girl she still was. He wanted to tell her to forget her father, that she shouldn't have to be taking care of not only herself but him, too, when he was supposed to be the parent. But it had been easier for Leo. His own toxic father had been considerate enough to forget him first, shipping him off to school on a distant planet where he could be out of sight and out of mind.

He squeezed her arm. "I'm sure he'll be fine. And you'll be no good to him, or to anyone else, if the mercs throw you in detention, right?"

"I guess you're right." She forced a smile. "And I do like the idea of my own room with walls and a door and everything. The shower's hot?"

"If you're quick enough," he said, pulling on his overcoat.

"Okay, you've convinced me," she said. "Thanks, Leo. Really."

"Just be careful, will you?" he said, and she surprised him by pulling him into a tight hug. He rested his chin on the top of her head. "And don't eat *all* of my food."

She laughed. "No promises."

He gave her his key, grabbed his bag, and headed out. He greeted Mr. Hale as they passed each other in the corridor, and on his walk to the tram stop he saw Lavinia across the street, on her way to work.

"Tell my sister I don't miss her!" she cried cheerfully. Leo just raised a hand in response. It was possible he would forget to deliver that particular message.

He took the tram to the ferry and then the bi-rail into the heart of Central City—both expenses he'd failed to budget for when he first began working for Hal, naively assuming his new boss would take care of those costs in addition to his ferry pass—and arrived at the penthouse. It was always strange to walk inside. The levels the Gardners now lived on had been vacant for as long as he could remember, his father shutting them up when he was still just a toddler. When he got older, he would occasionally sneak up there via a back staircase that was never locked, wandering through the silent rooms that felt cold and still, the drop cloths over the furniture and chandeliers like so many ghosts. Sometimes, if he squinted, he could still see those rooms beneath the cheerful, stylish face the penthouse now sported.

He hadn't yet been downstairs, to the place that had once been his home. But he was keenly aware of it, there under his feet, as he headed to Hal's office in the back corner. He knocked and heard Hal call for him to come in.

When he stepped inside, Hal barely acknowledged his presence, his eyes flicking over to him and then back to his holoscreen as he spoke on the comm. For a moment Leo remembered the way Hal's eyes had lit up whenever he came down to the Gardners' flat to escape the suffocating air of his father's home. Hal would often hoist him up onto his shoulder or back, galloping around the tiny flat until Leo was out of breath with shrieking laughter.

"Yes, I do believe we should," Hal was saying to the person on the other end of the comm, his voice unusually low and animated. He laughed. "Careful, you're going to get me in trouble! . . . Thank you, Carina . . . Yes, I'm sure we'll be talking again very soon." Hal clicked off the comm and then steepled his hands together, pressing them to his lips as though deep in thought. "Sky. You're a young man. Have you got a sweetheart?"

It had been, perhaps, the last question Leo had been expecting. "Um, no, sir, I don't."

"Well what are you waiting for, my boy?" he said. "There are so many beautiful young ladies in the world."

"I suppose I just . . . haven't met the right one yet, sir."

Hal nodded thoughtfully. "I never much cared for beauty when I was your age. It was all fine and good—and don't get me wrong, Mira was quite the looker in her day—but I guess beauty felt . . . out of reach. For a simple tradesman like I was. I couldn't just snap my fingers and have the very best of whatever I wanted."

Leo shifted his weight over his feet uncomfortably, not really following what Hal was saying and not entirely sure he wanted to, either.

Hal seemed to shake himself from his thoughts. "In any case, I need you to update my calendar before you go. I have a meeting with Ms. Lyons next week to draw up a will of my own to replace the Chapin will and to finalize the legal framework for this damnable foundation in Leo's name. What a nightmare; I never should have pledged such a ridiculous sum to it."

"I imagine getting everything up and running is a tremendous amount of work," Leo said, "but I'm sure it will also do lots of good. You'll be able to change so many children's lives."

Hal waved a hand. "Yes, I suppose we will, and it'll make the old lady happy, so that's that."

Leo frowned. "As for your will, if you want me to draw up a pre-liminary document—"

"Never you mind about that," Hal said. "Best to leave it to the lawyers. That's what I pay them for, after all. Now to the matter at hand. Viktoria is thrilled to be seeing the new house soon, and there's lots of work to be done. Are you ready to leave?"

Leo gestured to his bag. "Yes, sir."

"Let's get you going, then," Hal said, standing. "Time is money!"

Vika—who was sitting on one of the balconies, soaking up the sun— looked distinctly *un*thrilled when Leo came to tell her that the airship was ready to take them to the country house. He could sympathize. When he'd told Ariel about this disaster, she had punched his arm so hard he could still feel it and told him he was crazy to be dreading this since it was the perfect opportunity to make Vika fall in love with him.

But he, of course, knew better than that.

They took the lift to the roof, which was part garden and part landing pad. A small terrestrial airship was idling there, the low hum of the engines vibrating up through Leo's feet. Unsure if it was the right thing to do or not, he offered Vika his hand to help her make the steep step up into the ship. She hesitated a moment before taking his fingers, her hand cool and soft in his own.

She spent most of the ride with her head turned to the window, looking out over the scenery as it whizzed below them. At first he thought she was just trying to avoid any attempt he might make at conversation, but then he caught a glimpse of her face. Her eyes were as big and unguarded as a child's as she looked out over the landscape, shiny buildings of chrome and glass giving way to grassy hills rolling out in every direction with mountains rising in the distance. Her mouth was opened just a little, and he realized that this girl who had been raised in a crumbling slum city on a planet with no sun had probably never seen so much green before in her entire life. He made himself look down at his mini-holo, studying the tasks he had ahead of him, not wanting to take this moment away from her by reminding her that he was there.

About an hour outside of Central City, the airship began to slow as it approached a house nestled in the trees at the top of a hill.

"Ohh," Vika said. "Is that it?"

Leo looked down at the structure, which was made of pale gray stone and mullioned windows, its roofline a collection of gables and spires. He recognized it from the pictures he'd seen while helping Mr. Gardner complete the paperwork for the sale.

"That's it," he said.

"It's beautiful."

They landed in a clearing at the edge of the trees, and as they climbed out of the ship, a man rushed from the house to meet them.

"Welcome!" the man called as he approached. "Mr. Foster?"

"Yes. Mr. Toliman?" Sky said, offering his hand to the caretaker.

"Good to meet you in person, sir," Toliman said.

"Please, call me Sky," Leo said. "And this is Miss Hale."

Toliman bowed to her. "Allow me to take your bags and I will show you to your rooms."

Leo and Vika followed Toliman toward the house. The entire property was surrounded by a large garden, a stone pathway cutting through the flowering shrubs and beds and around the burbling fountain at the center. Vika held out her hand, brushing petals as they passed, the softness in her face so unlike the tough front she usually presented. Leo wished he could curl his fingers into hers. Instead he shoved his hands into the pockets of his overcoat, frowning when he felt something inside one. He pulled out the object, a folded piece of paper.

Don't be an idiot was scrawled on it in what could only be Ariel's messy handwriting. He grinned and stuck it back in his pocket. An important reminder. Maybe he should have it tattooed onto his forehead so that he'd see it every time he glimpsed his own reflection.

Toliman led them inside. The house, though beautifully built with the finest materials and expert craftsmanship, was little more than a shell. There were a few odd pieces of furniture here and there that were covered by drop cloths, but most of the rooms were empty and had clearly been so for some time. The small crew Leo had arranged for the day before was already hard at work giving the place a thorough scrubbing, raising clouds of dust that hung suspended in the sunbeams that slanted in through the windows.

"It's so lovely," Vika breathed. "Can you imagine someone giving you a *house* for your name day?"

Leo tried to remember the last gift his father had ever given him. He could recall a few presents before he went away to boarding school on Alastor, but though his father's name had been written on the tag, the thoughtfulness of the gifts, not to mention the handwriting, had made it clear they'd actually come from Mira.

"I can't," he said, opting for the shortest answer he could, not sure she actually wanted a response from him at all.

Toliman led them up the stairs, which were wide and highly polished, the dark wood carved with intricate whorls and spirals.

"Here you are," he said, gesturing to two doors side by side. "These are the only bedrooms that are prepared for guests right now. The rest are still in need of furnishing."

Oh, excellent. Leo had been hoping they'd be staying in uncomfortably close quarters.

"Thank you, Toliman," he said. "You can get back to your work now. We appreciate your help."

"Yes, sir."

When Toliman left, it was just the two of them, him standing in front of his door, her standing in front of hers, neither of them sure what to do next. Eventually Leo cleared his throat.

"I believe, uh, I believe I'll take a look around," he said. "Get a better idea of how much work there is to be done. Supper should be soon, so if you'd like to rest or—"

"No, I'll come with you." She opened the door to her room and deposited her bag inside. "Getting this house ready is my responsibility as much as yours, so I've got to do my share."

He gave her a tight smile; perhaps he should just spare them both and jump out the nearby window. "Of course, Miss Hale."

Together they wandered Greenbriar and its grounds, learning the layout, making an inventory of what was already there and starting a list of what still needed to be done. Leo tried to talk to her as little as possible, wanting to respect the wishes she'd made perfectly clear to him. When she marveled at the beauty of the orchard full of trees dripping with heavy fruits at the back of the property, he merely nodded along. When she pointed out a certain repair that would need to be made in the sitting room, he noted it on his mini-holo. When she asked him what he thought about hiring a string quartet for Mira's surprise party, he said he would look into it and nothing more. He'd learned at a young age how to become nearly invisible, and he deployed those skills now for her benefit until he was almost nothing. Barely there. Practically a ghost.

Leo Chapin is dead.

While they were sizing up the master bedroom on the southern end of the house, the local chef Leo had hired came to let them know supper was served. They walked into the dining room, which held nothing except for a hastily wiped-down table and a couple of chairs, and discovered the chef had set their places beside each other, one at the head of the table and the other just to the right. Vika sat, but when Leo hesitated, she threw up her hands.

"Oh, please, just sit!" she snapped.

He did, practically dropping into the chair at her side, unsure what he'd done to annoy her. They ate their suppers in near-silence, only occasionally touching on the tasks ahead of them or commenting on the meal. Leo suppressed his natural instinct to squirm under the heaviness of the air in the room to such a degree that he realized he'd become unnaturally still.

"Well," Vika said, laying her fork down on a plate that was still half-full. "I think I'll head up to my room. It's been a long day."

Leo stood as she pushed back from the table and gave her a bow of the head. "Good night, Miss Hale."

As he lay in bed that night, staring up at the ceiling, he tried not to hear her moving in the room next to him. Certainly tried not to picture what she was doing. There were the faint sounds of her dresser drawers opening and closing, the squeak of the old bed frame as she climbed beneath the covers. He could almost imagine he heard the rise and fall of her breath just centimeters from his own head. The two of them separated by nothing but a layer of plaster and more lies than he could count.

He rolled over and jammed a pillow over his head. *Don't be an idiot,* he reminded himself.

CHAPTER EIGHTEEN

VIKA WOKE UP ON her first morning in Greenbriar House to the sounds of Sky moving in the room next door. She groaned and buried her face in the pillow, pretending she couldn't hear him walking across the floorboards, turning on the shower. Attempting to pretend he wasn't there at all.

But she had to give him credit: he was as good as his word. All day he was careful to keep his distance from her as much as possible given that they were the only two people in the house and were working on the same project. In fact, he was *excessively* careful. He answered her questions with the barest number of words, often nothing more than "Yes, Miss Hale" or "No, Miss Hale." He hardly ever looked at her—even when she was talking to him, instead noting what she was saying on his mini-holo or examining the piece of furniture she was speaking about—and he made himself scarce so well that she'd had to hunt him down multiple times, always finding him in the corner of some far-off room.

"There you are!" she said when she finally found him, hailing a local florist from a dusty room that had once been a library. He was sitting on a wide window ledge that was literally as far away as he could have gotten from where she'd been considering new draperies on the other side of the house. She hadn't seen him in hours, and she hadn't spoken to another soul since she'd asked him to pass the salt at lunch. After a lifetime of living practically on top of so many other people, the solitude combined with the endless, impenetrable expanse of trees she saw out of every window was a little disconcerting.

He stood. "How may I help you, Miss Hale?"

She bit back a sigh of annoyance. Maybe it was unfair of her, but his inordinate courtesy was just bothering her now, especially because she needed his help. She'd been staring at fabric samples for ages, going back and forth, utterly paralyzed when it came to making a decision. She wasn't used to this feeling. She was desperate.

"I need a second opinion," she said and beckoned him to follow her as she headed back toward the ballroom.

"I'm not sure I'm qualified," he said, picking up his pace to catch her.

"And you imagine I received some kind of interior design education on Philomenus?" she said, her tone coming out sharper than she'd intended.

"You're . . ." He hesitated, looking more closely at her face. "You're not worrying, are you?" It was the first time she could remember him voluntarily prolonging a conversation with her.

"Of course I'm worrying!" she said, the words that had been churning inside of her all day tumbling out. "How am I supposed to spend his money, decorating his house for his wife? What if the Gardners hate every decision I make? What kind of way would that be to repay them for all their kindness?" She snapped her mouth shut, forcing an end to the eruption of her anxious thoughts before she revealed too much of herself.

"Miss Hale, you mustn't think that way," he said. "Mr. Gardner trusts you entirely."

They reached the ballroom. In addition to the dozens of furniture catalogs she'd received, a top design firm from Central City had arranged for swatches of their finest fabrics, wallpapers, and paint chips to be waiting for Vika for her to choose from. She had tacked up a couple of the fabric swatches beside one of the ballroom windows that looked out over the rose garden: a warm, golden velvet and some kind of thick green fabric that caught the light whenever it moved. It had taken her the better part of an hour to narrow the decision down to just those two.

"What do you think?" she asked. "I can't make any decisions about the furniture until I've chosen a color scheme. The velvet feels more luxurious, but is it too heavy for a room this size? This green, whatever it is . . ."

"Brocade."

She shot him a look.

His expression didn't change as he added, "Our education on Aerion is obviously more well-rounded." Then he smiled and she realized, as improbable as it seemed, that he was *joking* with her.

She smiled, too, and then caught herself. "Well, whatever you call it, I don't know what I think about it."

He carefully examined both fabrics, as though he were taking her dilemma very seriously. "Normally decision-making is not my strongest suit . . . but I prefer the green," he finally said. "It connects to the garden outside, makes it feel as though the ballroom is just an extension of it."

She looked through the windows at the garden just beyond. "That makes sense."

"Not to mention that brocade is easier to clean, which is important in a room that will be filled with drinking, reveling people. As I'm sure you can imagine."

"Right." Vika shuddered. Nicky's didn't have fancy draperies, of course, but it also didn't have any surface that couldn't be wiped down with a rag soaked in bleach for that exact reason.

It took her another second to wonder if this was some kind of veiled slight, reminding her of her old life and how she used to slave away at cleaning up after drunken bar patrons. She looked sideways at him. A few weeks ago she would have assumed he was deliberately hitting her with that barb, but now for some reason she doubted it.

"Okay." She swallowed. "We'll go with the green, then. Right?"

He nodded. "Excellent choice. I'll put the order in. One decision down."

"Just five or six thousand to go." She rubbed her fingers against one pounding temple. "I'll never make it."

"Of course you will."

"No, I won't. The more I worry, the more I freeze up." The words set off a spiraling kind of momentum inside of her, all of her pent-up fears gaining speed until they came rushing out of her, and this time she was too weak to swallow any back. "And then I worry about falling behind schedule, and that just freezes me up *more*. What if I make a huge mess of this when Hal trusted me? What if I ruin Mira's name day because I can't—I can't—"

"Here, have a seat." He reached a hand toward her, nearly touching her elbow but not quite. With that non-touch, he guided her to the old pink sofa that had been abandoned in the middle of the room. She sat and tried to compose herself while he waved down one of the workmen passing outside the door, asking him to have Toliman bring a cup of tea. "You have no need to worry, Miss Hale. You're a capable person with wonderful taste, and you care for the Gardners very much. Whatever you pick for them will be right, I'm sure. They'll love whatever you do."

"What if they don't?" she asked. "What if I don't even *finish*?"

"We'll get it all finished, I promise. May I offer you some advice?" When she nodded, he motioned at the dozens of furniture catalogs piled on the nearby table. "Choose just one to order from. Fewer options will feel less overwhelming."

"That's smart," she said. "Maybe I can get a discount, too, if I'm ordering so much at once."

Sky smiled. "I doubt Mr. Gardner is too concerned about the expense, but it will make the ordering and delivery process proceed more smoothly if everything is coming from the same place."

"So less chance of Hal and Mira walking into an empty house in two weeks."

"I'm not worried about that," he said. "It's honestly difficult for me to imagine you failing at anything you put your mind to."

She huffed a little laugh. "I am very stubborn."

"Quite right," he said. "And *I'm* the overthinking neurotic, so let's just stick to our lanes, shall we?"

She smiled. "Deal."

It was perhaps the most words he had ever spoken to her at once, and all of them so . . . kind. He soon excused himself to go place the fabric order, and Toliman brought her a cup of mint tea that she sipped while she replayed the conversation in her head. He was right, of course. She wouldn't be defeated by fabric swatches and furniture. It was only shopping, and it might be new to her, but she had a natural talent for it. She would make Greenbriar the most beautiful house the Gardners could imagine, *and* she would get the furniture at a discount.

It helped, too, to feel like the burden wasn't entirely on her own shoulders. Maybe she'd been reading Sky wrong. He didn't seem as off-putting and judgmental as he always had before. Or maybe she was just *that* desperate for company. Either way, she was oddly glad to have him there to help her.

But by the next time she saw him, as they were sitting down to dinner, he had retreated back into his shell. She saw the difference immediately, from how he seemed to take up less space in the room to the way he averted his eyes away from hers when they happened to meet.

"How is your meal?" she asked as they sat side by side in the dining room after many painful minutes of nothing but the sounds of cutlery on china. She wanted him to see that she could be nice, too, not just the demanding and standoffish girl he'd seen so far. Or perhaps she just needed to break up the silence before she lost her mind.

"Very good, thank you," he said, carefully cutting a carrot. "And yours?"

"Wonderful," she said. "Did . . . did you get much work done today?"

He nodded. "I made good progress."

She should just let him eat in peace. Stop bothering him. But she heard herself asking, "You moved to Philomenus because of your sister, right?"

"I did."

"That's sweet." She thought of Lavinia, suddenly missing her caustic cleverness. If she'd been here, she would have been very glad to disturb the tense quiet by ridiculing Vika's new airs and graces. It was likely that Sky, this near stranger, had talked to her sister more recently than she had since Vika had made no effort to reach out to Lavinia all this time she'd been on Ploutos. Hell's teeth, she was a cow. "Would you tell me a little about her?"

He cleared his throat. "She's, well, she's younger than I am. My half-sister, actually."

Vika waited, but that was it; he was finished. She kept trying to offer an open door to him, and he kept slamming it back in her face with his terse answers. She dropped her fork onto her plate with a clank. "Oh, please, Mr. Foster! You can't keep punishing me like this!"

He blinked. "I-I'm sorry?"

"I'm trying so hard to be friendly!" she said. "I know I've been rude to you in the past but you simply have to forgive me, because I can't stand two entire weeks of this excruciating awkwardness. Can you?"

He carefully set down his knife and fork, folding his hands in his lap and contemplating the tablecloth. "I was only trying to give you your space, as you requested."

That's right, a real cow, she heard Lavinia say in her head. "I appreciate that, but I think it's unnecessary now. And with just the two of us here, it's uncomfortable, don't you think?"

He exhaled and nodded. "I do."

"So, can we just . . . be friendly?" she said. "I hereby revoke my request that you leave me alone."

"At least until Mira's name day?"

Slowly, she smiled. "Yes, then I may reconsider."

"I understand," he said. "Just keep me informed."

They chatted a little over dinner, and it was not exactly comfortable yet but it was no longer frosty, either. They kept their conversation largely confined to the job ahead of them until the chef served dessert.

"Have you seen any of my family lately?" she asked, head down as she dug her spoon into the fruit crumble in front of her.

He took a lengthy sip of water, and she wondered if he was stalling for time. She had, after all, historically bitten his head off any time the subject of her family had come up between them.

"Yes," he said. "I see your father around the building most days, and we have tea together every now and then. I spoke briefly with your mother yesterday in the laundry room."

"She must have been in quite a mood. She hates doing the laundry."

"She seemed her usual self to me," Sky said.

Vika laughed at the unintended joke, thinking of her mum's perpetual scowl. But then she saw the sly little smile around Sky's lips and realized it might not have been as unintended as she'd thought.

"Your father misses you, of course, but otherwise he seems well," he continued before she could wrap her head around that possibility, "and your sister has recently taken over your old position at Nicky's."

"Has she?" Vika frowned. "You know more about them than I do."

"Oh, I hardly think that's the case," he assured her. "I just pick up a few incidental details now and then."

She shook her head and put her spoon down. She didn't deserve the last few bites of her crumble. "I've been a bad daughter. I've hardly talked to them at all since I've been here."

"No," he said. "From what I could see, most of your life on Philo-menus was devoted to helping them in one way or another. Working to help support them, helping your father in your off hours, doing chores and errands. You're allowed to take some time for yourself."

She looked up to meet his dark eyes, and he nodded to reinforce his point, like he knew she wouldn't believe him. The fact that he didn't think she'd been acting selfishly—even if she knew better—actually comforted her for some reason. She searched his eyes for the judgment she'd so often seen there before, convinced he was just hiding it, but she found none.

A corner of his lips pulled up into a wobbly smile, and the expression did something strange to her heart.

"Well," she said, suddenly uneasy, the air around her feeling heavy and hard to inhale. "I'm exhausted. I think I'll go up to my room now."

"Right. Of course," he said, leaning back in his chair. She hadn't noticed when he'd leaned forward. "Good night, Miss Hale."

She paused on her way out of the room and looked back at him over her shoulder. "Vika's fine."

CHAPTER NINETEEN

MIRA'S NAME DAY PARTY was in just four days, and it seemed to Leo that there simply weren't enough hours between now and then to get everything done. The house was full of noise as craftsmen and laborers worked, finishing up last-minute repairs to broken banisters and repainting rooms before the furniture was due to be delivered the next day. Leo had spent the entire morning trying to figure out every item of china and cutlery, every cooking implement that needed to be ordered for the kitchen and where they would all go when they arrived, while Vika had been furiously scribbling furniture layouts onto every paper surface that crossed her path.

"We'll never finish," she said for the fourteenth time as they ate their eggs together that morning, drawing a big black X over her plan for the master bedroom furniture placement.

"Yes, we will," he replied, as usual, although he was no more sure than she was.

"How's it going there?" Hal asked him later as they spoke on the comm.

Leo glanced around the library where he was standing, which was only half-painted a warm buttery color and was empty of furniture except for an ancient leather chair in the corner that had been serving as a cozy home for a family of mice. "It's . . . it's coming along."

"Well, do whatever it takes to have it ready," Hal said. "I'm depending on you, Sky."

Leo made himself smile. "Is that a compliment or a threat, sir?"

But Hal didn't laugh the way he'd hoped he would. "Oh, I need you to speak to Evelyn Lyons for me. I sent her the new will Mira and I had drawn up, but I want to make a change to it."

Leo's pulse kicked up. He hadn't expected the Gardners' new will to be ready so quickly. He pulled the small notebook he'd been using to keep notes out of his back pocket. "Yes, of course. What would you like me to tell her?"

"Have her amend Vika's settlement," he said. "One hundred thousand upon the death of myself or Mira, whichever one of us lasts the longest. Once Lyons makes that change, I want the document finalized and made official by the end of the week. I trust you can be discreet about this?"

"Absolutely, sir," he said evenly, despite the complicated tumult inside of him. There was the surge of panic that his father's will was being replaced in the eyes of the law, like it was the lid of a casket being lowered over him, trapping him in this half-dead limbo forever, even though he felt sure the courts would rule in his favor if he came back to life to claim his inheritance. At the same time, there was also happiness for Vika and her family, knowing how much that sum could alter the lives of anyone living on Philomenus, even if it would probably be decades before she'd actually see it. And in the mix was also some confusion that the Gardners weren't leaving her more, considering what a tiny fraction of their fortune one hundred thousand bits was and how much they seemed to love her. "I will make that call right now and have everything taken care of."

"Good," Hal said. "I'm honestly not sure what I was thinking sending you away for two weeks. I'm drowning in work here with no one to help me."

"I-I'm sorry, sir," Leo said. Increasingly conversations with Hal were giving him this unsettled feeling in his stomach that he remembered from his childhood, when he used to tiptoe around his father, unsure of what might set him off. Hal and Mira had always been his safe space then, but working with Hal increasingly felt like trying to traverse a field full of land mines. Of course, being someone's employee was different from being a defenseless child they looked after; he had to keep reminding himself of that. "I *have* been working, but perhaps I could—"

"Yes?" Hal interrupted. His voice was softer and the tone completely different, and Leo realized he must be talking to someone who was in the room with him back in Central City. The sound on the comm went muffled and he could just barely make out a woman speaking on the other end. The words were unintelligible, but the pitch seemed too high to be Mira. Perhaps one of the maids? Hal said something back, laughing as he did. The sound became clear again when he said, "I have to go. Make the call."

"Yes, sir," Leo said. "Would you—"

Hal clicked off. He was busy, Leo reminded himself. He was still acclimating himself to his new world and new responsibilities, and it had to be overwhelming.

As he hailed the Lassiter and Lyons office, Vika stepped into the garden outside the library window. He had said he wouldn't watch her anymore, but he'd been standing here minding his business when she had strolled into his line of sight, so it wasn't as though he was spying on her. She walked amongst the beds, the sunset a deep orange at her back as night began to fall, stopping to examine different flowers, smelling a few. She plucked one bloom off of a bush to study it more closely.

"Lassiter and Lyons, how may I direct you?" a voice said in his ear.

"Evelyn Lyons, please," he replied. "This is Harold Gardner's assistant."

"One moment."

As though feeling his eyes on her, Vika turned to look at the house. Leo wasn't sure if she could see him or if the last of the sun glinting off the windows made him invisible. He raised a hand to her in greeting but she just turned away.

The comm clicked back to life in his ear. "Archer Sheratan."

"Oh," Leo said. "I was trying to reach Ms. Lyons?"

"She's already left for the evening. This is regarding the Chapin/ Gardner estate?"

"Yes."

"Then I can help," he said. Archer Sheratan, the young man Leo had seen Vika laughing and dancing with at the party the Gardners had thrown at the penthouse. All Leo could remember about him was that he'd found him distressingly handsome as the two of them had sailed across the dance floor. "What does Mr. Gardner need?"

Leo explained the amendment Hal wanted made to his will, and Archer sighed.

"Your boss is quite an indecisive man, isn't he?" he said. "Each time we're about to finalize the document, he wants another change made."

"I suppose there's a lot for him to consider," Leo said. "I think he finds such a sum of money . . . quite a burden, in a way."

Archer laughed like they were old friends. "The way only the rich can, eh?"

"Mmm, indeed," Leo replied, just trying to keep the conversation moving.

"He must be a real treat to work for day in and day out. I hope he pays you adequately for your trouble."

Leo wasn't sure how to respond to this, so he decided just to ignore it. "Mr. Gardner would like the document finalized and filed once the amendment is made."

"It's going to take a bit of time," Archer said, "but I'll do my best."

"Will it be possible to wrap this up by the end of the week?" Leo pressed. "Mr. Gardner was very insistent, so I'll have to let him know if it's going to take longer."

"Yes, fine, I can get it done," Archer said. "We wouldn't want Mr. Gardner to have to wait for anything, would we?"

"Sky!" Vika's panicked voice was faint but unmistakable. *"Sky!"*

Leo took off running in the direction of the sound. "I have to go, Mr. Sheratan, thank you for your help!" he said and clicked off the comm. He followed Vika's voice to the master bedroom, where she was standing in the doorway with a vase of freshly picked flowers in a variety of pinks and reds shattered at her feet, glass and water and petals littering the floor.

"What in the bloody hell," she demanded as he entered the room behind her, "is *that?*"

A white-and-gray creature the size of a small dog—with a pointy, whiskered nose, large ears, and thin, clawed little fingers—was blinking up at them from atop an old chair beside an open window. Its eyes flashed in the dim light provided by the single lamp in the corner.

"Oh." Leo laughed, his heart rate returning to something like normal. "Oh, it's just a tree brilby. It must have climbed in here looking for something to eat. You don't have these on Philomenus?"

"I live in a *city*," she said. "So, no, we don't have giant rat creatures emerging from the forests at night to climb through our windows. Just, you know, regular-sized rats."

"Well, they're perfectly harmless," he said, realizing that she had called for him and not for Toliman, wondering if that could possibly mean something.

"You have these things on Aerion?" she asked, keeping a wary eye on the animal.

"Y-yes." Stars, he hoped that was actually true and not an easily demonstrated lie he'd have to explain later.

"It doesn't *look* harmless," she said. "Those teeth!"

Its sharp little fangs were hard to miss, but Leo was sure he remembered that brilbies only ate bugs and other small prey. He was really quite sure. "We just need to coax it back out of the window," he said.

She pushed him farther into the room, stepping behind him. "Well, go ahead then."

"Right." He looked around, spotting a broom one of the laborers had left in the corner. He grabbed it and slowly approached the creature, which watched him, unblinking. He extended the broom toward it, hoping to herd it toward the window. "All right, sir. You know you don't belong here. Out you go, please."

He nudged the brilby with the end of the broom, and all of a sudden it leapt from the chair, skittering across the floor toward the two of them with surprising speed. Leo yelped and leapt back, stepping up onto a laborer's toolbox, while Vika shrieked and ran for the door. She ended up clutching the doorframe, her alarm giving way to hysterical laughter as the brilby hid under the old bed frame.

"What were you saying about perfectly harmless?" she asked.

He stepped down off of the toolbox. "Perhaps that was not my most . . . dignified moment."

She waved a hand. "Dignity is overrated. So *now* what do we do?"

Vika ended up retrieving a long-handled paint roller, and together they tried to persuade the creature back out of the window. It would lumber sedately in the direction they were urging it until it felt cornered. Then it would suddenly bolt, which made it seem much larger, the razor-sharp claws it used to climb trees much more threatening. Intellectually, Leo knew that more people were probably injured climbing out of bed every morning than by brilby attack, but when the thing was hissing and scuttling toward him, the ancient part of his brain told him to get the hell out of there.

When they were both out of breath from trying unsuccessfully to drive the brilby from the room, with not a little bit of shrieking and laughter mixed in, they finally decided just to give up. They'd shut up the master bedroom and hope the thing would be gone in the morning.

"Ignore your problems and they'll go away on their own," Leo said as he closed the door firmly behind him. "That's always been my philosophy in life."

"Or we'll open it tomorrow to find a whole army of brilbies have moved in," Vika said with a shudder. "But I guess that's a problem for tomorrow's us. Now I'm all sweaty from brilby-herding, so I'm going to get some freeze cream. You want some?"

But Leo didn't register the question. He kept hearing her saying the word *us* over and over in his mind.

"Sky?"

He blinked. "Yes?"

"Freeze cream?" she repeated.

He smiled. "Absolutely."

CHAPTER TWENTY

THE NIGHT OF MIRA'S name day party was finally here. Vika had been thrumming with anxiety all day, worried whether things would go as planned, whether Mira and Hal would like what she'd done. Either way, once this party was over, she was going to sleep for a week.

Vika took one last look at herself in her bedroom mirror. She hadn't done as masterful a job with her hair and makeup as Gemma would have, but it would do. Guests would begin arriving any minute. She headed for the foyer. A figure came into view as she descended the stairs: tall and straight-backed, clad in a black tuxedo, just a portion of his face visible as he talked to Toliman, his sharp nose and soft smile. Vika's breath came up unexpectedly short.

He turned at the sound of her heels on the stairs, and his eyes widened as they fixed on her. For a second he looked as exposed as she suddenly felt, as though she'd forgotten to put on her dress or had been caught doing something secret.

But then the look was gone, replaced with a placid smile.

"Toliman says the first airship has landed," Sky said. That meant that soon there would be a steady stream of guests arriving in sleek cars and aircraft for Mira's surprise party.

"Oh, wonderful," Vika said, taking her place at his side. She took another look at his tux, so different from the plain work clothes they'd both been wearing as they rushed to get the house ready. "You clean up nicely."

"Thank you, I do try not to embarrass myself," he said. "I love the gown you've chosen."

She touched the emerald-green satin with its intricate beading. "I'm glad you said that. I changed four times."

"Nervous?"

"No," she said, in what she felt was a convincingly airy tone. "Are you?"

"Very much so." He reached out and brushed a stray thread from her shoulder. "You're a terrible liar, by the way."

Her mouth dropped open. "Excuse you, I'm an excellent liar!"

Vika took one last look around the entrance hall, trying to spot anything in need of a fix before the first guests arrived. It had been a whirlwind two weeks, trying to get the house ready in time for this party. She'd picked out tens of thousands of bits' worth of new furniture to fill out the empty rooms—the sum of money so vast that she had eventually became numb to it—while Sky had directed a small army of painters, movers, and repairmen. As impossible as it had seemed some days, she felt like they'd pulled it off. She might not have been born to beautiful things like the embroidered silk curtains she'd chosen for the windows or the hand-carved chairs upholstered in cream velvet, but she had a natural sense about these things once she was able to relax and trust her instincts. And Sky's flair for the luxurious had surprised her as well. For a poor Aeonian assistant, he'd done a remarkably effective job of choosing just the right cascading centerpieces of lilac and peonies to complement the wallpaper she'd selected and had put together an elegant menu and program of music for a night Mira would never forget.

Or so Vika hoped.

"You have nothing to worry about," Sky told her, seeming to sense her thoughts. Or maybe he'd just noticed her wringing her hands.

"You've done a beautiful job, and Mira will be thrilled. I'll go make myself scarce now that guests are arriving."

"What?" She snagged his sleeve as he turned to walk away. "Why?"

"No one wants to be greeted by the help," he said with a half-smile. "I'm sure your hosting skills are more than up to the challenge."

She didn't let go of him. "Do not even *think* about leaving me alone here."

The smile melted down his face until it was a soft frown. "I . . . If that's what you want?"

She swallowed. "It is."

True to his word, Sky didn't leave her as the guests began to stream in. He did seem to melt into the background somehow, though, still right there but practically invisible to everyone but her. While she complimented ladies' outfits and flirted lightly with their husbands, he quietly directed the waiters who were milling about with canapés and plucked a wilting flower from one of the arrangements in the foyer. His steady presence nearby made her feel less nervous, like they were still a team.

But when Mrs. Howell insisted on a tour, Vika lost track of him in all the bustle. She found herself automatically looking for him in every corner, but he was gone. She was back in the foyer, welcoming the Moravas by asking about their journey and agreeing that the weather was indeed lovely, when she spotted Archer slipping in the front door behind them. He must not have seen her, because he walked right past her without so much as a glance. She caught up with him as he was handing off his coat to one of the staff.

"Archer!" she said. He was as handsome as ever in his impeccably tailored tux, the charcoal color making his blue eyes seem even brighter. "How lovely to see you!"

He turned to look her. "Miss Hale, what a sight you are for sore eyes. Central City has been like a desert without you."

It was the kind of thing he always said to her, but there was no mischievous twinkle in his eye. She laughed a little too hard in response. "And yet you seem well-hydrated enough!"

"I did manage to survive, just barely," he said. "I suppose I should get myself a drink and leave you to your work. You have guests to greet."

"Oh." She blinked. "Yes. Duty calls."

He gave her a small bow and walked away, and with a frown she turned to greet the next couple coming in the door.

When the influx had slowed, Vika went to the bar herself. Small talk made her thirsty, and there was an unsettled feeling in the pit of her stomach that she hoped a drink might ease. She waited in line behind a red-haired young woman who was familiar to her but who she couldn't place, which bothered her. She was sure she knew everyone at this party since she had decided on the invites. But she forgot about the girl as she left with her drink and Vika discovered Sky behind the bar checking on the supply of champagne.

"Sparkling water, please," she told the bartender, no longer feeling the need for a cocktail. She reached over the bar and caught Sky's wrist. "Leave that. The staff will take care of it. You should be enjoying the party."

He looked out over the crowd that had slowly filled up the mansion—jewels glittering with light from the chandeliers above, polite chatter and the clink of crystal glasses creating a pleasant din—and his expression was troubled. "I don't know about that."

"Don't be silly," she said. "You've worked so hard. It's only right you take some time to enjoy yourself." In the corner of the small ballroom the string ensemble began to play a song she loved, and the words tumbled from her lips before she even had time to consider them. "Come and dance with me."

Sky's eyes went wide. "What?"

"Come on," she said, feeling suddenly vulnerable. What if he said no to her? There were half a dozen people within earshot. Why had she asked him something so stupid anyway? "No one's dancing. They need someone to get them started."

One corner of his lips twitched up. "Ahh. Well, I have been tasked with helping this party run smoothly. So if you think it's my *responsibility* . . ."

She bit down on her grin. "Exactly."

She and Sky walked out onto the empty dance floor together, and he extended his hand to her. On Ploutos, touching was rare outside of contact with direct family members. People were forever shaking hands and giving each other kisses on the cheeks on Philomenus, but here on Ploutos, etiquette was more formal. She'd touched Sky once that she could remember, taking his hand as he'd offered it to her to help her step up into the airship on their way here. It had been awkward but necessary thanks to the ridiculously impractical shoes she'd been wearing. But this felt . . . well, she hardly knew how she felt.

She took his hand, his slim fingers warm and gentle as they closed around hers. He drew her closer to him, placing his other palm on her waist. Those who had been mingling on the dance floor began to move to the edges of the room, and other couples slowly joined them. She had a moment's panic as she realized she didn't know if Sky could even dance. Was he about to embarrass her? Make everyone take notice of her dancing with the servant and remember that she herself was just a jumped-up barmaid . . .

But to her surprise, Sky turned her in a sweeping glide across the floor, his movements sure and confident.

"You're good at this," she said. "Where did you learn?"

"Oh, I-I hardly remember."

"We don't dance like this on Philomenus," she said. "It was all I could do not to fall over my own feet the first time."

"You seem to have the hang of it now."

She felt a flush rise in her face. "To tell you the truth, I've been practicing in secret. I got a tutor and have been dancing around my room at night before bed."

He looked delighted. "That's very studious of you."

"I didn't want to embarrass myself in front of these people. I don't like to give them reason to remember I don't belong here."

She hadn't meant to say all of that. It was too . . . true. But she supposed it could be worse, since Sky didn't belong here any more than she did. It would have been far worse to accidentally spill the way she felt to Archer or Miranda or someone else who, well, *mattered*.

He looked at her thoughtfully for a moment, and his eyes were so close and so intent on hers that she had to look down.

"They're not better than you, you know," he said softly. "Only richer."

She looked past him, unable to meet his gaze, at the people who swirled around her. "It's not that simple." Wealth gives a person freedom, while poverty makes them dependent. If she wanted to be her own person and claim back some of the autonomy Rigel Chapin had stolen from her, she had to have money to do it.

"Why not?" His thumb brushed over the skin on the inside of her wrist as he repositioned their handhold. "You're clever and caring and strong. What's wealth to that?"

She felt like the air had been squeezed out of her lungs. He'd said those words so simply, as though they were obvious. She was filled with shame at her own uncharitable thoughts about him and a flood of warmth she couldn't quite name. She opened her mouth to speak, unsure what she was going to say in response.

But a beep forestalled her. Sky dropped her hand to reach for his pocket, where his mini-holo flashed a message.

"They're arriving," he said.

Vika stared at him blankly; it took several seconds for her brain to catch up. "Oh! The Gardners are here."

Sky went to silence the musicians and Vika fetched the small silver bell she'd prearranged for this moment, trying to clear the sudden fog from her brain with a shake of her head. When the song died out, she rang the bell, the peal rising above all the chatter. Faces turned toward her from all corners of the room.

"The name day girl has nearly arrived," she explained. "Please gather in the foyer, and we'll turn out the lights so we can surprise her."

The guests headed for the entrance hall, and Vika skipped ahead of them. She wanted a spot right by the door so that she'd have the best view of Mira's face when she saw the new house full of all her friends. The staff switched off the lights, leaving nothing but the moonlight streaming from the windows to outline the shadows of guests as they crowded into the foyer. Vika stood beside one of the front windows so she could peek around the curtains and see the walkway to the door. She realized Sky was at her back, and she could feel the warmth of him in the close confines of the foyer.

"They just landed," he whispered to her, his breath rustling the hair at the base of her neck. "We should see them any moment."

Seconds later she saw the glow of a lantern coming from the direction of the landing pad. Soon she could make out Hal leading a blindfolded Mira through the garden toward the front door. A flurry of whispering and shushing and a thrill of anticipation went through the guests gathered in the dark. Vika suppressed the ridiculous impulse to grab Sky's hand.

The front doors swung open.

"Here we are, my dear," Hal said as he helped Mira step over the threshold.

"You goose," she said. "Where are we? Can I take this blasted blindfold off yet?"

"If you insist." He stepped behind her and removed the blindfold at the same moment someone hit the lights.

"Surprise!" everyone in the hall shouted.

"Hell's teeth!" Mira clutched her chest in such alarm that for a moment Vika was genuinely concerned that they'd given her a heart attack, but then she began to laugh. "Oh, you all scared me half to death! What a wonderful surprise!"

"It's all yours, my dear," Hal said. "A nice little getaway from the city where you can grow all the flowers you could ever dream of."

Mira's face went slack with shock. "You're joking, surely? This house is *ours*?"

"Happy sixtieth, my love." He kissed her forehead and everyone applauded.

Vika rushed to her side to give her a hug. "Happy name day, Mira! I hope you like it."

"Viktoria and Sky have been here for almost two weeks now getting this all ready," Hal explained. "Didn't they do a wonderful job?"

"Oh, my dear girl." Mira embraced her, her hands shaking. "It's so beautiful. I can't thank you enough."

"Let me show you around," Vika said.

"Oh, yes, please. But first." She crooked her finger at Sky, who was hanging back by the wall, beckoning him toward her. "Come here, sir. You must hug me as well and let me thank you for all your hard work."

Sky smiled. "If you insist, madam."

"I do!" Mira wrapped her arms around his shoulders, giving him a good squeeze. Vika saw Sky briefly close his eyes, the tips of his fingers digging into her as he returned her embrace.

"Happy name day, Mira," he said softly. "You deserve it."

She patted his cheek. "Such a sweet boy. Now, I want the tour!"

Vika led the Gardners through the house, pointing out special features and changes she'd made, the three of them stopping to mingle with party guests along the way. Mira oohed and ahhed over everything, and Vika was so relieved to have her approval that she breathed more easily than she had in weeks.

The final room she showed them was their master bedroom, now brilby-free. Vika had given it special attention once they'd reclaimed it from the creature, filling it with all of Mira's favorite things. She'd chosen a vivid floral paper for the walls and piled the bed with a small mountain of fluffy feather pillows covered in soft pink linen. The ceiling was made of the same implanted diodes that Vika had in her room at the penthouse, showing the night's stars and waxing moon, but Vika had tweaked the display so that the sky was painted in the deep pinks and purples of sunset instead of the inky blackness that was truly above them.

"Ohh," Mira breathed, taking it all in. "Viktoria, it's like a dream."

"I'm so glad you like it," Vika said. "More than anything I wanted to give you a fraction of the happiness you've given me. I'm forever indebted to you both."

Mira took her hand. "Oh, no, darling, please don't think like that. You're our family now. In fact . . . Hal?"

Hal nodded, and the two of them sat Vika down in the small sitting area by the window. They both looked so serious all of a sudden that Vika's heart rate kicked up.

"Is everything okay?" she asked.

Hal patted her knee. "Yes, yes, of course. There's something we've been wanting to tell you, but we needed to get all the pieces put in place first."

"What is it?"

"Hal and I have so enjoyed having you live with us," Mira said. "We've grown to love you almost like you were our very own daughter, and we want you to be well taken care of after we're gone. We feel it's the least we can do for you, and also for our dear Leo."

Vika's heart twisted. "Oh, Mira . . ."

"We've decided to settle some money on you in our will," Hal said. "A hundred thousand bits."

Blood roared through Vika's ears, drowning out the rest of the world. One hundred thousand. She barely noticed the faint frown lines that appeared on Mira's forehead or the complex, indecipherable look they shared.

"Yes, and whenever you're ready to leave us—" Mira said.

"And there's no rush on that score!" Hal said.

"—we want to support you in whatever you decide to do next," Mira finished. "Whether it's to pay for your university fees or to provide you a nice nest egg to get started when you decide to marry."

"Are you serious?" Vika asked, her voice coming out a whisper. She couldn't seem to catch a full breath.

They both smiled and nodded.

"Bloody hell," she said, the room starting to sway before her eyes.

Hal chuckled. "Head between your knees, my girl," he said, patting her hair as she lowered her head to her legs, the delicate beading of her dress pressing against her forehead as she tried to get some circulation back to her brain.

It wasn't that this came as a total surprise. If she was honest, there was a small, somewhat ashamed part of her that always expected they would provide her with something. But harboring those hopes, or even expectations, and having them actually tell her that, yes, she would receive a portion of the Chapin fortune that had once been offered to her and then snatched back straight away again were two very different things.

As soon as she was sure she wasn't going to pass out, she sat up and threw her arms around them. "Thank you, thank you, thank you," she said, pressing kisses to their cheeks.

She was going to be rich. She would have money of her own and the ability to take care of herself and her family. She would never have to go back to slinging glasses of grock ever again and could give up on her husband hunt . . .

Vika shook herself; she couldn't start thinking that way. A hundred thousand bits sounded like a fortune to her, but that was judging by Philomeni standards. It wasn't nearly enough to continue to live the kind of lifestyle she'd become accustomed to here on Ploutos, and it definitely wouldn't be enough to bring her family over and take the burden of providing off of her father's bowed shoulders. It had barely been enough to furnish this house, let alone buy it. Plus she wouldn't receive anything until the Gardners, bless them, had passed away, which would hopefully be a good long time from now. No, she needed to stay the course. But with the Gardners promising her a dowry when she got married, her value on the marriage market had just jumped.

"Well, I think we should get back to the party," Hal said. "It's missing its lady of honor."

"Oh, yes." Vika stood. "The chef has made the most amazing meal, and I'll need to steal your husband here for at least one dance."

Mira laughed. "I hope you're wearing sturdy shoes."

As they made their way back toward the sounds of the party, a thought occurred to Vika. She tried to dismiss it, but it had instantly put down roots inside of her, sending dark shoots into every corner of her being.

"Hal?" she said as they reached the stairway. "Can I ask you a question?"

"Of course, my dear," he said.

"Did you and Mira tell . . . anyone else about your plan for me?"

He frowned. "Only the solicitors. Oh, and Sky. I had him amend the paperwork for me while he was here."

Vika looked out over the foyer below and found Sky looking up at her, a soft smile on his face, and her heart turned to stone in her chest.

CHAPTER TWENTY-ONE

IT WAS EARLY MORNING before all the guests finally left the party, having been poured into their vehicles and airships by patient staff members. Leo, Vika, and the Gardners collapsed in exhaustion in the sitting room while the caterers and cleaners began to whirl around them, stacking dishes and packing away decor.

"I have to congratulate you two," Hal said, swirling the last of his whiskey around a glass, seemingly hypnotized by the movement, "on putting together quite the affair."

"Oh, yes." Mira had long ago kicked off her shoes and was eating the remnants of her name day cake directly off of its giant platter, which she had placed on the coffee table in front of her. "That was the most marvelous party I've ever been to. I can hardly believe it was all for me."

"It was our pleasure," Vika said from where she sat cross-legged on the floor, the pearl-tipped pins that had held her hair in its elaborate style discarded in a pile in front of her. Her curls were pulled up into a simple ponytail that made her look more like her true age.

"Yes, it's the least you deserve, Mrs. Gardner," Leo said. She looked up at him and he gave her a smile despite the ache in his heart. He so badly wanted to take Mira's hand in his own, squeeze those fingers that had tied his tie on his first day of school, smoothed over his forehead when he was sick, and bandaged up a hundred skinned knees. But he knew he couldn't. "*Truly* it is."

Mira sighed, her expression suddenly clouding over. "It's my first name day since he went away to school that I didn't have a letter from him, you know. I'd give up all of this for one more of those."

Hal leaned forward and put a hand on her knee. "Now, my dear. Leo wouldn't want you to be sad."

"He's right, I'm sure," Leo said, battling the sudden urge to blurt out the truth. His guilt at being the cause of her grief pressed down on his chest with the weight of a planet. But he remembered Ariel's note and the reasons he was there, not least of which was to protect Mira, and bit his tongue. Still, as much as it pained him, seeing that someone in the world actually missed Leo Chapin and knowing that his Mimi had loved him as much as he loved her was one of the strange, sweet advantages of being dead.

"I think . . ." Vika downed the dregs of her champagne. "I think that's a beautiful thing. To love someone so much that you would give up a fortune for them. You were lucky to have had that, Mira, and Leo was, too. I don't imagine most people ever love another person enough to sacrifice something like that for them."

"Oh, of course they do," Mira said. "You'll have that one day, my dear."

Maybe he was imagining it in the dim light, but Vika's eyes looked shinier than usual when she shook her head. "I don't think so."

"Well, name day girl." Hal tossed back the rest of his whiskey and, with a mighty effort, heaved himself out of his armchair. "I think it's time we get you to bed."

Mira licked her fork clean of frosting and dropped it with a clang back onto the platter. "I believe you're right."

Mira gave Leo and Vika kisses on the cheek and then she and Hal headed up to their bedroom, giggling tipsily between them.

That left him alone with Vika. He supposed he should be more used to that now, after spending so many days here in this house just the two of them. But any level of comfort he'd achieved with her had been obliterated when she'd taken his hand on the dance floor that evening. In that moment, she had become terrifying to him.

Because in that moment, he'd realized he was completely, stupidly in love with her.

It had been coming on for a long time now, like a train steadily approaching down a track, its lights growing bigger and brighter as it grew nearer. But knowing it was coming hadn't prepared him for the impact. It had hit harder than the concussion of the bomb that killed him. Leo would never be sure why his father had selected Vika for him—and he doubted very much that his son's happiness had ranked highly on his list of priorities—but somehow, as impossible as it seemed, he'd chosen exactly right.

Leo smiled at her. "You've made Mira very happy."

She didn't look at him. "She's a good person. Good people are made happy very easily, I think. Anyway, I should be going to bed myself."

"Me, too." He stood and offered her a hand. "Let me help you up."

"I'm fine," she said, clambering to her feet. Then she spotted the pins that littered the floor and bent down to pick them up. When she straightened, the champagne must have hit her because she swayed in her sky-high heels and began to lose her balance.

"Careful!" Leo stepped in on instinct, catching her around the waist, her arms landing on his shoulders. Suddenly her hazel eyes were so close to his that he could see every lash, every tiny freckle across her nose. He felt her breath, coming a little too fast, against his face. He smelled the perfume she must have dabbed on her skin before the night began, an act he was now picturing in excruciating detail . . .

"Vika . . ." he whispered.

Her eyes flickered down to his lips, and then back up to his gaze. His heart seemed to have become something hot and liquid in the middle of his chest, the churning core of a brand-new planet. He swallowed, shaking and fuzzy-headed, as he leaned down to kiss her.

She pushed him away. "Don't," she said, her voice suddenly acid.

The shock was like a slap across the face. "Why not?"

"You're not being fair," she said, stepping away from him. "Or honest."

"What do you mean?" he breathed.

"Do you think I'm an idiot?" she asked, shoving the pins haphazardly into her hair. "You don't like me. You never have. You think I'm selfish and shallow, and that was fine with me because I didn't like you, either, but this . . . game you've been playing with me, this *scheme* you've enacted—"

Her voice choked and she turned away, heading for the stairs, but he caught her by the wrist. He felt with sudden, terrifying certainty that if he let her walk away now, that would be it.

"Let me explain," he said. How could she have figured it out? How could she know the part he'd been playing?

She shook him off. "Don't bother. I understand exactly what you were after. The Gardners told me you knew."

That brought him up short. "Wait, what are you talking about?"

"Did you think I wouldn't figure it out?" she asked, her eyes blazing in the dimness. "You started being nice to me at the very same time the Gardners decided to share their fortune with me. Tell me, was that why you got a job with them in the first place, in the hopes that this would happen? Did you encourage them to give me the money so I'd be a more valuable prize to win?"

He was so sick to death of money, of his father's blasted fortune. "No, that's how *you* think, not me," he said. Her eyes widened and he realized how sharp his tone had been. Bloody money poisoned everything it touched. He took a deep breath and added more gently, "I don't care about the money. I care about you, Vika."

"Miss Hale," she corrected icily. She backed away from him with small, uncertain steps. "You don't fool me, and even if you did care for me, it wouldn't matter because I don't care for *you*. I've never trusted you, not from the moment we first met, and I was crazy to let the last couple of weeks make me forget that. Besides, I'm . . . I'm too good for you now. I'm aiming my sights higher than some lowly assistant."

Stung, he said, "And you think I'm the one being unfair? I've never treated you with anything but courtesy—"

She scoffed. "Is it courteous to spy on me and shame me for how I choose to spend my money, to try to cash me in like some kind of lottery ticket? It wasn't enough that some stranger felt like he had the right to will me off to his son like I was a piece of property, but now you want to try to profit by me? Fecking hell, can't I ever just be treated like a person and not a *thing*?"

The anguish in her voice was so palpable that it momentarily stunned him. Stars above but his father was a bastard. "I promise you," he said softly. "You have this all *wonderfully* wrong. You are not a thing to me." She turned to go but he put himself between her and the door. Now that he had started, he had to get the words out or they might burn up his insides. "Please, Vika. You have to listen to me. The truth is I . . . I lo—"

He'd hesitated just long enough for her to throw up her hands as though he had brandished a weapon at her.

"Don't!" she said. "Don't you dare lie to me with that word in your mouth."

What could he say to her? Maybe the word cooling on his tongue was true, but every word he'd ever spoken to her had been predicated on a lie. Of course she didn't trust him; she was right not to. Lord, he'd made such a terrible mess of everything.

"But . . . I do," he whispered. It was so inadequate, and he was sure he would be thinking for weeks about what he should have said instead, but they were the only words he had.

"Liar," she whispered back, and this time he let her walk away.

The sound of her receding footsteps was like a hammer driving the final nail into Leo Chapin's coffin. There was a strange kind of peace in the devastation, because at least now he knew. After the best opportunity he could have wished for to win her over, Vika still didn't like him, and she would obviously never be able to love him. There was nothing for Leo to do except to leave his father's fortune in the deserving hands of the Gardners and disappear. He wouldn't have to exist in this strange half-living limbo any longer.

Without Vika, Leo Chapin was well and truly dead at last.

CHAPTER TWENTY-TWO

VIKA WOKE UP WITH her head pounding and her stomach full of acid. She stumbled groggily to the bathroom, hitting a series of buttons on the side of the shower. Instantly water at her preferred temperature and pressure began to pour from the invisible ducts in the ceiling, along with a fog of medicinal steam scented like mint and orange to cure her hangover and help wake up her senses. She shucked off her pajamas and stepped under the stream of water, breathing deeply. The headache quickly disappeared, but her stomach still churned. She realized it wasn't the remnants of champagne and cake that were making her nauseous; it was the memory of Sky Foster trying to kiss her, his eyes so soft as he looked at her. How false it had all been and how incredibly close she had come to believing it.

She supposed she'd better get used to that. Once word got out, as it surely would, that the Gardners were settling money on her, every fortune hunter on the planet would be after her, trying to convince her they were her best friend or soul mate, hoping to cash in on her.

There was only one way she could think of to avoid being a piece in someone else's game, and that was to stay the course. Find a man to marry who was so wealthy he wouldn't care about whatever insignificant bits the Gardners gave her. It was the only way to take care of her family and regain some of the self-respect that had been taken from her when Rigel Chapin turned her into an object.

In this world it was either use or be used, and she was determined to be the user.

She found Hal and Mira in the dining room, a sumptuous spread on the table before them. Her stomach might have been in knots, but she still thought she could choke down a flapcake covered in riverberry compote, or maybe two.

"Good morning, Viktoria, my girl," Hal said. "Sleep well?"

"Fine," Vika said softly, though in truth she had tossed and turned for what felt like hours, painfully aware of the thin wall between her head and Sky's, worrying that he heard her every movement and knew what was keeping her awake. "You?"

"Wonderful!" Mira said. "We woke up to the sound of birds chirping and wind rustling through the trees, and it was just divine. I love the country already."

"I'm afraid we'll need to go back to Central City today, my dear," Hal said. "I thought we'd be able to spend the weekend but I need to have a meeting with Lassiter and Lyons about the foundation."

"Oh." Her face fell. "It can't wait?"

"I'm afraid not," Hal said. "They're trying to back out of their end of the deal, which would cost us *thousands*, and I just won't have it. Not when I'm already paying their exorbitant legal fees. We'll come back next weekend, I promise."

"Darling . . ." Mira said. "Do we even *need* Lassiter and Lyons to contribute to Leo's foundation? Surely we have more than enough to—"

Hal dropped the pair of silver tongs he was using to pick up a sausage link back to the platter with a clang. "I'm weary of this conversation, Mira."

"I know, I know, you're right." Mira toyed with a piece of fruit, pushing it around and around her plate. "Whatever you think is best, of course."

Hal huffed and pasted on a smile. "Anyway, I'm sure Viktoria here is itching to get back to civilization, aren't you? You've been cooped up here so long with no one to keep you company."

"Sky was here, too, my love," Mira reminded him. "Have either of you seen him yet this morning?"

Vika kept her eyes firmly glued on the clotted cream she was spooning over her flapcakes, trying to keep her face absolutely expressionless.

"I did," Hal said. "Wasn't feeling well, said he planned to keep to his room until it was time to leave. Damned inconvenient since it meant I had to coordinate the meeting with Lassiter and Lyons myself. What's the point of even having an assistant?"

"Oh, the poor boy," Mira said, starting to stand. "I should go check on him, see if he needs anything."

Hal waved a hand. "He's fine. Probably just drank too much and doesn't feel like working. Lord knows I pulled that trick a time or two when I was his age. He can always ring a servant if he truly needs something."

Vika frowned; surely Sky wasn't actually ill. Was he just hiding his damaged ego? Or maybe trying to convince her that he truly was heartbroken over her rejection the previous night? Either way, she was glad she wouldn't have to see him sooner than absolutely necessary.

Instead she thought about her own next moves. Of all the men on her list of potential husbands, Mr. Keid was her favorite by far. Suitably rich, not too ancient, a bit boring but not outright unpleasant. She knew he spent most of his nights at the Commodore's Club, smoking cigars and doing whatever else rich men did behind the cloistered walls of their private spaces. Maybe she could contrive to run into him outside, convince him to invite her to dinner where she could work her charms on him more effectively than at a crowded party . . .

Soon it was time to board the airships and head back to Central City. Vika braced herself when she heard Sky's footsteps on the stairs as he emerged from his room and met them in the foyer where the pilots were collecting their luggage. She had to give him credit: he looked the part. There was a gray tinge to his complexion and his eyes looked glassy and dull. He determinedly did not look at her.

Mira rushed to his side, immediately fussing over him.

"Oh, Sky, you look wretched." She pressed the back of her hand to his forehead. "How do you feel?"

"Don't worry, I'm fine." He gave her a wan smile. "I'll be just fine."

Hal looked over at Vika. "I'm sure he will," he said under his breath, "now that he's effectively shirked today's work."

She laughed, more than she felt like, and was gratified to earn both a grin from Hal and a stricken look from Sky that he quickly covered over.

The four of them followed the pilots out to the landing pad, and Vika's heart sank as they approached the crafts. There was the airship she and Sky had come over in two weeks ago and another, just as small, that must have been Hal and Mira's transport. She had hoped the Gardners had traveled in something larger so she could ride back to the city with them, but it was immediately clear that there wasn't room for her. Which meant more than an hour sitting side by side with Sky on the ride back to Chapin Tower, just the two of them.

Well, she supposed she had two options. One was to just live here at Greenbriar House forever, which had some appeal at this moment, or she could ride beside Sky Foster with an air of perfect tranquility and nonchalance, as though he were entirely below her notice, like she hadn't given a single thought to his scheme since she'd exposed him the night before. Yes, that would work. She thought of every haughty, superior woman she'd met while hobnobbing with the elite on Ploutos—and there were many—and she tried to channel them. She was Mrs. Howell. She was Leona Lyons. She would make Sky Foster feel as small as they did her.

Then Hal's mini-holo beeped, and he thumbed it to bring up the message.

"Blast it," he said. "I need to get on the comm. Darling, you and Vika go ahead. Sky and I will follow behind once I take care of this."

Thank the stars, she was saved.

"Are you sure?" Mira asked. "We can wait."

"No, I'm not certain how long this will take," Hal said. "You go on and I'll see you at home."

Vika sighed in relief as she settled into the seat next to Mira in the Gardners' airship. Heavens bless whoever needed to talk to Hal right at this moment. Vibrations traveled up through her body as the engines began to whir somewhere beneath her, and she waved at Hal out of the window as the airship lifted gently off the ground.

Soon they were zipping over the trees, green stretching out in every direction, and Vika had her face practically pressed to the plastecene. She turned to Mira to say something about the trees and how beautiful they were and caught the older woman swiping the side of her finger over her cheek.

"Mira?" she asked. "Are you crying?"

"No."

"You are! What's wrong?"

Mira shook her head. "It's nothing."

"It's not nothing!" Vika took her hand. "You have to tell me."

Mira's eyes were swimming as she dug in her bag for a handker-chief. "I'm probably worrying for nothing. I do that, you know."

"Worrying about what?"

A sudden bang, deafeningly loud, rocked the airship. The craft lurched to its side, sending Vika slamming into the window. She felt herself scream but couldn't hear it over the sudden wailing of alarms from the cockpit and the shriek and shuddering grind of metal.

"We've lost the engine!" The pilot's voice was high and thin over the speaker.

Vika could see they were losing altitude fast, the green rushing up to meet them. Mira's grip on her hand was so tight she could feel her bones bending, and the blood rushing through her veins was like fire.

"Brace!" the pilot commanded.

So this was how she was going to die, she thought, before everything went black.

CHAPTER TWENTY-THREE

LEO MADE HIMSELF BUSY in the house, checking the ongoing cleanup effort, while Hal stayed in the garden, pacing back and forth in front of the windows as he spoke on the comm. Hal hadn't invited him to listen in or take notes as he'd always done in the early days of his employment, so either he was growing in confidence that he could handle his business affairs on his own now or he just didn't want Leo to know the subject of the discussion. Certainly there was one number that had begun to hail often lately that always caused Hal to dismiss him from a room before he answered it.

Leo was relieved, though, not to have to ride back to Central City with Vika. He could hardly bear to look at her without it causing him actual, physical pain. Feeling the heat of her body sitting beside him, hearing the rustle of the fabric of her dress, or smelling the scent of her shampoo would likely have caused him to just open the airship door and jump. He'd been a fool to think she might be feeling the way he was. He couldn't wait to leave these bloody planets and all the misery they'd brought him behind and start fresh somewhere else, not as himself but not as this sad Sky Foster creature, either. Someone new and unencumbered by the past.

"Sky!" Hal barked.

Leo dropped the broom he'd been handling and headed for the front garden. Hal was off the comm and looking impatient.

"There you are," he said. "Let's be off already. I have lots to attend to."

"Yes, sir," Leo said. He picked up Hal's overnight bag as well as his own, and they climbed aboard the airship that had been sitting idle on the landing pad for the two weeks since it had brought Vika and himself here. Was it really such a short time ago? He felt like he'd aged ten cycles since then.

They lifted off and headed for Central City no more than eight or ten minutes behind the ladies. Hal told the pilot to burn hard, so they might even catch up to them. Leo watched the landscape sweeping by beneath them, while Hal fiddled with his mini-holo, laboriously typing out messages with his thick fingers. An air of discontent seemed to waft off of him, and Leo was hesitant to draw his attention, not wanting to be on the receiving end of it . . . but he was dying to know.

"Were you pleased with the house, sir?" he asked over the thrum of the engines.

Hal nodded without looking up. "Yes, Viktoria did an excellent job." He laughed. "And she certainly cost me less than some professional decorator who would have demanded an arm and a leg!"

Leo tried to laugh along with him instead of remembering how many sleepless nights they'd spent trying to get everything ready on time and how distraught Vika had been at the prospect of disappointing Hal. "And the party?"

"The old girl seemed to like it, so I can't complain."

Leo realized he was desperate for a single word of thanks or approval for all the work he'd done, sitting at Hal's proverbial knee now the way he had at his father's for so many years. When he was young and used to feel that way, he would go down to visit the Gardners, and they'd shower him with attention and affection. Mira would pull out the paints she kept just for his visits and they would make pictures together; Hal would ask him to be his helper as he fixed a sink, teaching him how to hand over the right tools and telling him what a good job he'd done. It had made him feel useful and wanted, the man's praise filling him with pride.

But he wasn't a child anymore.

"Well, she was very happy to do it," Leo said. "She cares so much for both of you."

Hal's response was little more than a grunt as he continued to focus on his holo. Leo turned back to look out the window. Ahead, he spotted a plume of black smoke rising from the trees. For a moment he just stared at it, uncomprehending, and then his heart stopped beating.

He fumbled for the toggle that would turn on the comm link to the pilot's cockpit, his fingers suddenly numb and clumsy.

"Smoke!" he croaked. "Smoke ahead!"

"I saw it!" came the pilot's metallic voice over the speakers. "We're heading down!"

"Heavens above," Leo whispered as they drew closer. Hal pressed his face to the window, too, and they looked down at the jagged hole in the trees, the top of the canopy sheared off into naked, splintered branches.

This couldn't be happening. Not again.

"Hurry up, man!" Hal cried, banging on the plastecene barrier that separated them from the pilot.

Just past the trees, a clearing came into view. A black gouge was carved into the earth, and the other airship, smoking and crumpled, lay on its side like a wounded animal, flames flickering at its base.

Leo didn't even wait for the craft to touch down; he threw open the door and jumped the last meter to the ground. His ankle rolled under him and he ended up in the dirt, but he pulled himself up and ran, limping, as fast as he could toward the crashed airship. Vika was inside there. Mimi was inside there.

"Vika!" He scaled the outside of the ship, opposite the fire, trying to get to the door that was now facing up toward the sky. The underbelly of the craft provided multiple handholds, but the metal was hot in places and sharp in others. "Mira!"

Hal and the pilot caught up with him. The pilot began trying to get into the cockpit to help his colleague, while Hal hailed the authorities.

"Are they okay, Sky?" Hal called, his voice thin and reedy.

Leo had reached the window and leaned down to peer inside. Vika and Mira were both lying motionless at the bottom of the craft. Leo shouted their names, banging on the plastecene with his fist.

Vika's eyes cracked open, and Leo's heart beat again for the first time since he'd seen the smoke on the horizon. She was alive. She raised a hand to her head, her fingers coming away bloody. Leo shouted her name, slamming his hands on the window, and she looked up, spotting him above her. He saw the relief flash across her expression.

She turned to an unconscious Mira—Lord, he hoped she was just unconscious—and started shaking her, while Leo wrestled with the door. It was heavy and not meant to open against gravity. He braced his legs on a piece of metal that was used to lash the craft down and used all the strength he had to lever the door open. He scrambled back to the opening, arms and legs quaking from the exertion.

"Mira!" he cried. Vika was still shaking her but she wasn't waking up. She suddenly looked so incredibly small.

Leo clambered down the inside of the airship, lowering himself until he was crouched beside Mira. He grabbed her hand as Vika shook her shoulders, calling her name, and finally her eyes began to open. She rolled them around the craft, her gaze unfocused and hazy with pain, until she spotted him beside her. She beamed, and he had to choke back his sob of relief.

"Dear boy," she said weakly. "What a sight you are for sore eyes."

Leo laughed a shade hysterically. "As are you!"

"Come on, Mira," Vika said. "Let's get you out of here."

Vika took her arm to help her, but Mira winced and cried out as she tried to sit up.

"Wait!" Leo said. His thoughts were ricocheting through his head, mixing with the rush of his pulse in his ears. "Maybe we shouldn't move her. If she injured her back . . . We could make things worse."

"But we have to get out!" Vika said.

Leo was frozen. He couldn't make the wrong decision. If he moved Mira, she might never walk again, or worse. If he didn't . . .

"Come on, Mira," Vika was saying. "We can do this." She was trying to help Mira up, but the older woman was no help and Vika couldn't manage her weight alone.

"Wait, we need to think about this," Leo said. He didn't know what to do. He couldn't let anything happen to Mira. His chest was so tight he couldn't breathe.

"Sky, we're moving her!" Vika snapped. "Help me!"

Her voice, so certain, broke through his agonized paralysis. She was right, of course; Mira was in danger *now*. He would worry about the future when it came. He slung Mira's arm around his shoulders, and together he and Vika got her to her feet. By then their pilot had appeared at the door above them. Mira's leg was too hurt to climb out, but with the pilot grabbing her arms from above while Vika and Leo pushed her from below, they managed to get her out of the craft.

"Your turn," Leo said, looking Vika over. She was bleeding from a cut on her forehead and had a nasty bruise already forming beside it, but otherwise she seemed unhurt. She nodded, and he clasped his hands together to form a makeshift step stool, boosting her up to where she could grab the doorframe and haul herself out. He used the armrests as a ladder to climb up himself, surprised when a hand reached for him as he neared the opening. Vika helped pull him out of the airship, and he had to force himself to let go of her hand so she could climb down the outside of the craft, him following just behind. Mira had sunk to the grass in Hal's arms and he was holding her numbly, his face blank as though in shock, while the pilot was supporting his colleague, who seemed to have a broken arm. The pilot was headed in the direction of the trees, beckoning them all after him, and Vika and Leo grabbed Hal and Mira and led them away from the mangled airship.

They all collapsed to the ground at the edge of the trees, watching the ship belch black smoke from its engine as they waited for rescue. The minor fire that had been isolated on one side of the ship began to spread, flames rapidly engulfing more and more of the craft.

"It's about to reach the fuel tank," one of the pilots said. "It's going to blow."

They all watched in horror, and when the tank detonated like a bomb, momentarily blinding them, Mira sobbed and hid her face in Hal's chest. Leo had to resist the urge to grab Vika and Mira's hands, to feel the warmth of them in order reassure himself that they were really there, safe, and not still inside that ship. If Vika hadn't been there to bring him to his senses in time . . .

"What happened?" their pilot finally asked the other as they watched the charred craft smolder.

The man, cradling his shattered arm, shook his head. "The engine just blew, out of nowhere."

"Good thing you were so close to this clearing when you started going down." Their pilot turned to Hal. "If it weren't for that and some first-rate flying . . ."

"Thank God we're all okay," Mira said. She reached out and laid a hand on Leo's knee. "Thank God you were here."

Leo was hit with a sudden wave of nausea. He lay back in the grass, covering his face with the crook of his elbow and taking deep, shaky breaths. Another aircraft and another Chapin heir narrowly escaping death.

Someone was responsible for this, all right, but he doubted very much that it was any god.

The same person who had killed him had come for Mira, which meant his half-life as Sky Foster wasn't over after all.

HE'D FAILED.

As soon as he could get a moment to himself, he went to an empty room, locked the door behind him, and buried his head in his hands.

He couldn't believe he'd failed.

All of the planning and research, the stress of setting his plan into motion without getting caught, and the pressure of acting like nothing was amiss while he waited for his scheme to finally pay off, had all been for nothing. A fine airship was now a charred and twisted hunk of metal, but otherwise everything was just as it had been before. He was no closer to the freedom he craved so desperately that he was willing to kill to get it.

He'd been holding his feelings in check behind a pleasant mask for too long, and all of a sudden his control snapped. A howl of rage exploded out of him and he grabbed the things nearest to hand—a stack of papers, a small lamp—and hurled them to the ground.

Now what was he going to do?

CHAPTER TWENTY-FOUR

IT COULDN'T BE A coincidence. As the fear and adrenaline from the crash wore off—leaving a bitter, acid taste in the back of her throat—the truth became clearer and clearer to Vika. By the time she was lying in bed that night, staring up at the digital approximation of the night's sky with her head bandaged and pounding, the words were on a loop inside her mind.

It can't be a coincidence.

Leo Chapin had been slated to inherit his father's vast fortune until he died in an explosion on a spaceliner. The Gardners received the fortune instead, only to have the engine of their airship blow up in midair. There was only one reasonable explanation for such an improbable series of events.

Someone was after the Chapin fortune, and they would kill to get it. Which meant Mira and Hal weren't safe, and now that she was due to get a piece of the Chapin pie as well, neither was she.

Vika didn't get much sleep.

Instead she watched, her eyes growing scratchy and sore, as the gold hands of the clock on her bedside table slowly swept around to a decent hour. Then she got out of bed, padded barefoot across the silent penthouse to the master bedroom, and knocked lightly at the door.

"Come in!" Mira called.

Vika found her lying on the made-up bed in silk pajamas and a dressing gown, her broken ankle in its cast propped up on a couple of pillows. Hal was coming out of the bathroom, his hair damp and face freshly shaved.

"Good morning, my dear," Mira said. "You're up early!"

A painful spasm went through Vika's heart at seeing Mira's shining face, thinking about how easily things might have turned out differently yesterday. "How are you feeling?" she asked.

"Oh, I'll manage. I've got a dozen feed dramas to catch up on, and I'm on some truly *marvelous* painkillers." Mira frowned and waved her over. "But you don't look like you've slept a wink! Is your head hurting you? Would you like one of my magic little pills?"

Vika climbed into bed next to Mira, letting the woman stroke her hair, feeling a little of the tension in her shoulders melt away. She felt for a moment like a young girl again, maybe because that was how long it had been since her own mother had comforted her like this.

"My head's fine," Vika said, burrowing a little deeper into Mira's side. "I just can't stop thinking about the crash."

"That's understandable, my dear," Hal said. "You've been through a trauma."

Mira shuddered. "When I think what might have happened if the pilot hadn't been quite so skilled, or if Sky hadn't gotten to us before the fire spread to the fuel tank . . ."

Vika remembered the terror that had seized her as she realized she was going to die, followed by the sickening crunch of impact. Then there had been nothing, until she looked up and saw Sky's stricken face above her, his hands reaching for her as he called her name.

She sat up. "Do you . . . Maybe this is crazy, but do you think someone did it on purpose?"

Mira's hand flew to her chest. "Oh, Viktoria—"

"I'm serious," Vika said. "First the bombing on Leo's ship and now some kind of engine failure on yours? What if someone is coming after the Chapin fortune?"

"Oh, my dear girl, no," Hal said. "You're overwrought. You just need some sleep, and then you'll be able to think more clearly."

Mira took her hand. "The bombing on the *Leander* was tragic, but it had nothing to do with our Leo. And airship accidents happen now and again."

"You think it's just a coincidence? Truly?" Vika asked.

Mira nodded. "I do."

"Absolutely," Hal added. "I know it's uncomfortable to think of the world as a place where these kinds of random, terrible events can take place, but unfortunately that's reality." He gave her shoulder a squeeze. "Don't you worry your pretty head, Viktoria. This isn't a feed drama, and no one is coming for us. We'll just keep our feet firmly on the ground for a little while, eh?"

Vika nodded. They were right, surely. She'd just had a shock, and this was her brain's way of trying to make sense of it. Right? Yes.

It was just a coincidence.

"Now, my love," Hal said to Mira, "it's off to work for me. Can I get you anything?"

Mira gave his face an affectionate stroke. "No, I'm fine. You've taken such good care of me."

He kissed the top of her head. "It's only because you're everything to me."

Hal headed down to his office, and Vika spent the rest of the morning lounging in bed with Mira, watching feed dramas and ordering up snacks from the kitchen. When Mira's ankle began to hurt her, she took another pain pill and ended up with a case of the giggles that lasted until she fell soundly asleep in the middle of a sentence. Vika paused the drama they were watching, tucked a blanket around her, and crept from the room.

As she passed the grand staircase on her way back to her own room, the excellent acoustics of the marble floors brought Hal's voice up to her as clear as a bell. He was standing in the foyer below her, comm held to his ear, waiting for the lift.

"Yes, my darling. I'm on my way now," he said.

On instinct, Vika ducked back behind the wall so he wouldn't be able to see her. *Darling?* Who in the world could he be talking to?

"I can't do it now, not with what's just happened. It will look far too suspicious. You must see that." Hal paused as he listened to the person on the other end, jabbing his meaty thumb into the lift's call button a couple more times. "Of course I will. I just need a little more time."

Vika couldn't draw breath, like all the oxygen had been sucked out of the room. Her vision swam.

She had to be hearing wrong. She had to be misunderstanding. It couldn't be what it sounded like.

"Of course I promise," he said. "Soon we'll be together, my love."

She covered her mouth with one hand, holding back the gasp—or was it a sob?—that threatened to escape her. There was no denying what she'd just heard. Hal was a *liar.* The knowledge seemed to tilt the planet on its axis, reorienting her in relation to the rest of the universe. He wasn't a good man like her da, he wasn't a loving husband, and Mira wasn't everything to him.

And if he'd lied about those things, what else might he have lied about?

Vika hurriedly dressed and had the concierge flag down a car to take her to the Lassiter and Lyons offices downtown. With her understanding of who Hal really was in ruins around her feet, the brief comfort she'd taken in his reassurance that no one was targeting Chapin heirs had evaporated. She couldn't trust Hal anymore to give her the answers she needed, so she needed to look for them elsewhere.

Even if she was afraid of what she might find.

When she arrived at Lassiter and Lyons, she had the receptionist page Archer. Soon he was entering the lobby and rushing to her side.

"Viktoria," he said, and she was surprised at the way his eyes seemed to drink her in. He raised his hand to the bandage on her head, only seeming to realize the moment before he touched her that this was his workplace and that Ploutos had rules about such things. His fingers hovered over her skin, caressing the air instead, and then dropped. "Stars above, it's such a relief to see you looking so well. Before you say anything, you must allow me to apologize. I was in an abominable mood the last time I saw you because of some frustrating work matters, and I fear it might have made me poor company."

"Oh, Archer, you needn't have worried," she said, having forgotten until that moment their awkward interaction when he arrived at Greenbriar.

"I'm sure my rudeness pales in comparison to what happened after. But when I heard the news and imagined how I would have felt if that had been the last time we'd spoken . . ." He looked down at the floor, as though the thought were rushing over him again, and then back up at her with luminous eyes. "Well, I never could have forgiven myself."

"Thankfully it hasn't come to that, then," she said.

"Indeed. How can I help you this morning?"

"I just happened to be nearby," she said, "and I was thinking of you. I thought I might take you to a late breakfast since we saw so little of each other at Mira's party. Can you spare the time?"

His smile was dazzling. "For you, of course I can."

They headed to a small cafe on the corner and got a table away from the other patrons.

"Splendid party the other night," he said after they'd ordered, his lips moving up in a gentle little quirk. "A shame it had such a dramatic ending."

"Oh, yes." Vika tried to laugh. "I could do with a little less excitement at the next one."

For a moment, all of her suspicions were on the tip of her tongue. She wanted so badly for someone to convince her she was wrong, and Archer was the only person on this planet she thought she could count as something like a real friend. The idea of unburdening herself to him, especially when he was looking at her with such warmth and concern, was so tempting that she had to press her lips tightly together to keep the words from spilling out. She didn't want to him to look at her like she was crazy, and the particular suspicion silently growing inside of her at that moment seemed outlandish even to her.

Archer took a sip of his coffee and grimaced, adding more sugar to it. "Have the authorities determined what caused the crash?"

She shook her head. "Not yet. But let's not talk of such unpleasant things."

"Quite right. How shall I amuse you instead?"

He told her all the gossip he had collected at the party and recounted an incident with Mr. Harkness drunkenly mistaking the fearsome Mrs. Howell for his wife. When their meal arrived, they talked about his work and her plans for the weekend, the conversation as light and bubbly as champagne. Then after she paid the bill and they collected their things to leave, she added, as though it were an afterthought, "Oh, Archer, I've been meaning to ask you."

"Yes?"

"Could you give me a copy of Rigel Chapin's will? I imagine you have one."

He laughed. "I could practically recite it to you verbatim by now. But whatever do you want it for?"

She shrugged. "Vanity, I suppose. I'm curious what the old man valued me at."

"Not nearly what you're worth, my dear."

"Well, *obviously*," she said, batting her eyelashes. "Will you get me a copy?"

"Of course."

She walked him back to Lassiter and Lyons, and he ran upstairs, bringing her back a copy of the Chapin will. It was a thin document but felt surprisingly heavy in her hands. Archer left her with a formal kiss to the back of her hand that lingered a moment longer than it should have, and then he headed back up to his office and she hailed a car. While the driver began to navigate the streets back to Chapin Tower, she took a deep breath and opened the document in her lap.

If she was right and someone had tried to kill Mira—and had possibly been responsible for the bombing of the *Leander* that killed her would-be fiancé as well—the most logical suspect was someone who stood to gain financially. Rigel Chapin's will was the most obvious place to discover who that person or persons might be.

She skimmed through the document. It was long and written in dense legalese that made most of it impossible for her to decipher. But the part she was looking for turned out to be surprisingly brief, because Rigel Chapin had not bequeathed portions of his fortune to many people.

He had doled out some thousands here and there to a handful of organizations, which looked to be charities of one kind or another. She only recognized the names of a few, such as the Central City Symphony, where she supposed there would soon be a Chapin wing or auditorium. Others, like the Sagittarius Aid Society and the Ploutosian Defense Fund, were a mystery to her.

Then he had designated a hundred thousand bits go to Mira for her "years of dedicated service and care." Vika frowned and reread that bit to make sure she hadn't missed something, but no, Mr. Chapin had only included Mira in his will. She had always assumed both Mira and Hal had been beneficiaries, but it was Mira alone. Suddenly the conversation she'd overheard in the foyer earlier that day took on an even more sinister tinge in her memory.

It couldn't possibly be.

. . . could it?

She couldn't bear to think of that now, so she pushed those dark thoughts aside for later and continued reading. She finally came to the paragraph, which she had never actually read for herself, that had altered the course of her life.

> *Lastly, the remainder of my estate not heretofore assigned, including the contents of my bank accounts, stocks, patents, properties, and real estate holdings, shall pass to my son Leo Altair Regor Chapin on the condition that he legally and permanently wed, within two years of the date of my death, Miss Viktoria Hale of Philomenus. This I require for his sake and the sake of the Chapin name and legacy, which I have worked my entire life to build. Should he refuse this condition, he shall receive nothing, and the remainder of my estate not already allocated shall pass to the previous recipients enumerated herein in the manner described in Appendix 2b.*

So that was it. Just a single mention of her name and no explanation of why he'd picked her from his many candidates other than that it was for the good of his son and his legacy. What could that possibly mean? Especially coming from a man who, from everything she'd seen and heard, had never seemed to care very much for his son's well-being when he was alive?

"Why me?" she asked the document, but it had nothing more to tell her.

By then the car had arrived back at Chapin Tower, and Vika drifted out in a kind of daze, her mind running in circles. She was in the lift, finger poised over the button, when she realized she couldn't stand to go back to the penthouse, couldn't risk coming face-to-face with Hal after what she'd overheard. So instead she pressed the button that would take her to the roof. She hadn't visited this place as often as she'd expected to, finding herself too busy with shopping and parties and other amusements. The roof of her old TH had been her sanctuary, a quiet place where the haze hid the rest of the planet from her and surrounded her like a comforting blanket instead of bearing down on her like a wave crashing over her head.

But she hadn't needed that kind of escape very often since coming to Ploutos.

Chapin's rooftop garden was beautiful, though, even by her new Ploutosian standards, like a fairy world transplanted to the top of a skyscraper. Towering plastecene walls that were virtually impossible to see until you pressed your fingers up against them protected the garden from the high winds, and heat radiated up through hidden vents that kept the garden warm and encouraged the plants to grow. There were stone paths through the flowering trees and beds of multicolored blooms, and Vika made her way to the carved fountain filled with koi at the center, sitting on the lip of the pool to watch the fish gliding beneath the surface. She dragged the tips of her fingers through the water, watching the waves that rippled out in all directions, trying to get a handle on the thoughts that were rippling through her mind in a similar fashion.

If the airship crash hadn't been an accident and the blast on the *Leander* hadn't been a terrorist attack, then the most likely explanation was that someone was targeting Chapin heirs. With Leo gone, the bulk of the fortune had passed to Mira. If Mira had died in the crash, then the fortune would have passed to one of the other recipients already in the will. Vika just need to scrutinize those remaining recipients, a handful of charities and other organizations, to figure out who was the culprit.

Except . . . the Gardners had told her at the party that they had written their *own* will, which would supersede whatever Rigel Chapin had wanted done with his money after his death if it had been made official. So until she knew which will was in effect, the suspects had to include anyone in the Chapin will *or* in the Gardners' will.

That meant including Hal as a suspect, since Mira no doubt would have willed her fortune to her husband if she were to die before him. And what would have been unthinkable before she overheard that conversation in the foyer now seemed suddenly possible.

Vika closed her eyes and held a hand to the bandage on her forehead; she suddenly had a splitting headache. She thought of her parents and the photo on her night table, her da's arm around her mum's waist, her mum laughing. That photo was proof that they'd been happy once. She remembered the house she'd grown up in as being full of laughter, her mum always making up silly games and songs, the three of them rushing to the door to greet her da when he got home from work. Then he'd lost his job at the mines and gone through his troubles, and Vika didn't hear her mum laugh for months, or maybe years. When they were struggling to keep food on the table and a roof over their heads, nothing much seemed funny.

She'd seen what losing money could do to people who loved each other. Maybe gaining money could do the same thing. She thought of Hal, telling her and Mira to go along in the airship, that he would follow soon behind . . .

She stood, wiping her wet fingers on her dress. The rooftop garden no longer seemed as peaceful as it had been.

She returned to the penthouse, determined to find the answers that would keep her from going crazy. Maybe the constabulary was making progress identifying the bomber responsible for the explosion on the *Leander*. If it really was a terrorist from the Philomeni Liberation Front who had no idea Leo Chapin was aboard the spaceliner, then maybe the crash of the Gardners' airship really was just a freak accident and she was working herself up into a frenzy for nothing.

Vika headed for Hal's office in the back corner of the flat, first peeking her head around the corner to make sure Sky wasn't in his own. He and Hal normally attended meetings outside the penthouse in the mornings, but the last thing she wanted was to come face-to-face with either of them. Sky's sterile room was empty, so she moved on to Hal's door, rapping on it. When there was no sound from within, she pushed open the door and stepped inside.

She went first for the small filing cabinet against the wall, hoping against hope that a printed copy of the Gardners' new will would be there, clearly and prominently labeled, for her to swipe and be out of the room in ten seconds flat. But she wasn't that lucky. There didn't seem to be anything relevant in the physical files, which meant she was going to have to contend with Hal's holoscreen.

She perched on the chair behind his desk, waking the processor with a wave of her hand. Beyond that, she barely knew what to do to make the thing work. Holoscreens were practically nonexistent on Philomenus.

She needn't have worried. The screen immediately prompted her for a fingerprint scan, and her stomach sank. Maybe she could ask Archer for a copy of the Gardners' will as well. He would surely have it, though it would take more than a free breakfast and a bat of her eyelashes to get him to hand it over since it wasn't a public document the way the Chapin will was.

Desperate not to leave empty-handed, Vika began to rifle wildly through the drawers of Hal's desk. Maybe the will was handily placed inside one, or maybe Hal had scribbled some notes about who he wanted to leave money to on a stray pad of paper. The top drawer was nothing but useless office supplies. She pulled on a side drawer but the latch on the inside banged and the drawer stayed closed. She frowned, surprised Hal had locked it. She checked the other drawers but they were locked, too. What could Hal possibly need to lock up inside his own home?

Just then she heard voices coming down the corridor, and her heart rocketed up into her throat.

". . . think I'll be paying for all that, they must have taken leave of their senses," she heard Hal saying. "I won't be taken advantage of that way. And you would do well to remember which one of us is in charge, boy, do you understand?"

Sky's voice was soft. "Of course, sir. My apologies."

Vika scrambled out from behind the desk. There was no way for her to get out of the room without them seeing her.

"Viktoria!" Hal said as he entered the room. "What are you doing in here, my dear?"

"Oh, I-I was looking for Mr. Foster," she said, hoping she didn't sound as guilty as she felt. It was a terrible lie, and she didn't know why her mind had automatically leapt to Sky instead of just saying she was after a pen or something. But she had no choice now but to go with it. "I had a question for him. About the cook he hired for Greenbriar. He wasn't in his office, so I came in here to check for him . . ."

"We were at a meeting for that bloody foundation," Hal said, removing a handkerchief from his pocket to swipe his flushed face. "He's back now. Foster!"

Sky appeared in the doorway moments later, doing a double-take when he saw her. "Sir?"

"Miss Hale has a question for you," Hal said, waving a hand to dismiss them. "See if you can be more help to her than you've been to me this morning."

Vika followed Sky out of the office, the door swinging shut behind them with a bang, and cursed herself for not just saying she needed a pen.

Sky's face was as blank and expressionless as the atmo-haze when he said, "How can I help you, Miss Hale?"

"I . . ." She glanced back at Hal's door. "Is he okay? He seems . . . upset."

Sky abruptly turned to go back into his own office, and she followed him. "He's had a stressful morning," he said as he sat down behind his desk. "What did you need?"

Vika opened her mouth to say that she didn't need anything, that it was just a misunderstanding, but then she stopped. Maybe the solution was sitting right in front of her. True, just looking at Sky and remembering the scheme he'd tried to work on her made her feel as though the blood were boiling in her veins. But Sky had the things she needed. He had access to Hal's files. He had a job that provided him with plenty of cover for asking probing questions. He had a more sophisticated understanding than she did of the law.

And she had power over him.

"I need your help," she said.

CHAPTER TWENTY-FIVE

LEO STARED AT HER—EVEN though it was like looking directly into the sun, since she somehow seemed to have grown more beautiful since moving utterly beyond his reach—because he couldn't quite believe the words that had just come out of her mouth.

"Excuse me?" he said.

"I need your help," she said, her voice low. She glanced behind her to ensure they were alone and then took a deep breath. "I think someone may be targeting Chapin heirs. First Leo Chapin on his voyage back here, then Mira this weekend, and for all I know I may be next. So I'm going to find out who that person is and you're going to help me."

"Why?" he breathed. It was one thing for her to come to the same conclusion he had about the bombings—he thought it was obvious there might be a connection, even if the constabulary didn't seem to agree—but why come to him for help? Why not Hal or her smarmy solicitor friend? After all, she hated him.

"Because if you don't," she said, her voice as brittle as thin glass, "I'll tell Hal about what happened the night of the party, and I don't think he'd appreciate that, do you?"

Ah, so that was why he was her chosen partner, because she could control him. Hal certainly would *not* appreciate Vika's version of events from that evening. It would cost him his job for sure, and Leo couldn't lose this job. He had to stay close to the Gardners right now if he wanted to have any chance of protecting them. And, well, he had no money. He had been subsisting on meager meals of rice and canned produce and whatever the Gardners' cook slipped him that was about to go bad, and his debt to the PLF and the upcoming rent loomed large in his thoughts. Now that he was stuck living as Sky Foster for the foreseeable future, even a week of unemployment could ruin him. He had always thought of his upbringing as one of the young scions of Ploutosian society as being like a gilded cage, but now he knew what being trapped *truly* felt like.

That was a lesson Vika had learned at a much younger age, so she must have understood he couldn't say no to anything she asked of him.

"So will you help me or should I speak to Hal?" she said.

Leo heard the door to Hal's office open next door, and Vika raised an eyebrow at him. At that moment, he hated her just a little bit for putting him into this position. But he also felt he understood her better than he had before.

"Yes, fine," he said softly. "Of course I'll do whatever I can to help."

A moment later Hal poked his head inside. "Sky, I need—oh. My apologies, Viktoria, I didn't realize you were still here. Was Sky helpful?"

She stood. "Yes, very. Thank you, Mr. Foster."

"My pleasure, Miss Hale," he replied weakly.

After that Leo did his work in a kind of daze, one tiny sliver of his mind focused on his actual tasks while the majority of it was trying to adjust to his new reality. He had been so sure of what was coming: abandoning the pretense of "Sky Foster" and returning to Alastor to finish his studies, get a job, and live like a normal person who hadn't been born to one of the richest and most deranged men in the quadrant. As Vika had boarded the airship with Mira, he'd stared at her face, trying to remember every curve and plane of it, convinced it would be the last time he'd see her before he disappeared from the twin planets.

But then her airship had fallen from the sky, and Leo had realized that the attack on him hadn't stopped with him, only paused. Which meant he had no choice but to stay and try to unmask the person behind the bombs before they hurt someone else. And now Vika was his partner in that. He didn't know how he'd bear it, being close to her, talking to her, knowing that there was no hope.

When Hal went out to meet a friend for lunch, Leo retrieved his own lunch from his bag, intending to eat it in the park across the street from Chapin Tower like he did most days. With the sun high in the sky, it was just warm enough, and he needed the occasional break from his manufactured persona and the ghosts that haunted Chapin Tower in order to catch his breath.

He was in the foyer waiting for the lift when he heard labored sounds of movement above him. He looked up just in time to see Mira, leaning heavily on a crutch with her broken foot hovering over the floor, headed for the staircase.

"Mrs. Gardner!" He held out his hands to stop her, terrified she would tumble down the stairs. "Do you need something?"

"Oh, no, I just wanted a break from that room," she said. "I've been cooped up alone there for hours!"

He took the stairs two at a time to meet her at the top, offering her his arm to lean on. "You should be resting. Have you eaten?"

"Not yet," she said, letting him lead her back to her bedroom. "I probably should since these pain pills make me so loopy. Would you care to join me? I don't mean to bother you, but I'm just dying for a chat."

He smiled. "No, that's—I would love to."

He helped her out onto the balcony outside the master bedroom, overlooking the city that seemed to sparkle from this height. He flipped the switch that controlled the hidden heaters that kept the balcony feeling like a perfect spring day at any time of year, helped

Mira arrange herself in a chair with her foot propped up on a cushion, and buzzed the chef to ask him to deliver lunch to them there.

"Thank you for staying with me," Mira said once he had sat down beside her. "You have no obligation to use your personal time to entertain the boss's lonely wife, I hope you know, so you're a sweet boy to keep me company."

"It's no hardship at all," he said. "Truthfully, I . . . I wish we had more opportunities to spend time together."

"I wish that, too." She cocked her head at him. "My husband has you working very hard these days."

Leo tried to smile. "He does, indeed."

"Not too hard, I hope?" she said. "I do worry that Hal has taken the weight of the world onto his shoulders and that he might be . . . shorter . . . than he means to be sometimes because of it. And I don't want you to feel that your work is unappreciated. Even before you saved my life, what you and Viktoria did for me at Greenbriar was so extraordinary."

Lord, he loved her. If his older eyes had removed some of the sheen from his childish idea of Hal, they had only given him greater appreciation for Mira's kindness. "Well, we were very happy to do it," he said.

"Now that's something I've been wondering about, and I'm just a wee bit high on painkillers, as you may have noticed," she said with a mischievous twinkle in her eye, "so I believe I'll finally ask you about it before they wear off and I think better of it. This *we* business. You and our dear Viktoria."

Leo blanched. "I-I'm not sure what you mean."

"Ohh, I think you are." She leaned toward him, like they were whispering secrets. "I've seen the way the two of you look at each other when you think the other can't see you. Hal looked at me that way once. But it felt like something changed after the party, and you've looked miserable ever since. Did something happen between you two?"

He swallowed. Maybe he shouldn't be telling her any of this, but he'd been confiding his hurt feelings to Mimi for as long as he could remember. Plus, given the pinprick size of her pupils, there was a good chance she wouldn't remember this conversation anyway.

"She doesn't like me," he said.

"And you like her?"

His only response was a sad smile, and she put an arm around him. He gave in to the impulse to rest his head on her shoulder, and she leaned her cheek against the crown of his head.

"Oh sweet boy," she said. "There is nothing worse than loving someone who doesn't love you back in the way you deserve. You deserve to be loved, Sky. And someday I promise you will be."

She'd said the exact same words to another boy with another name who she'd also held in her arms, years ago, somewhere below where they sat now. He closed his eyes as she smoothed a hand over his hair the way she had done then.

"Thank you, Mi-Mira," he said.

She put a hand on his chin, lifting his face up so she could look at it. "You know, my Leo would have been just about your age. I often wonder what he was like all grown-up. He was such a kind, unhappy child, but then people can change so much. I hope he was happy, at least." She suddenly smiled. "And I hope he grew into those ears of his! He looked like he might suddenly use them to take flight. Sometimes . . . maybe this is just the painkillers talking, but I swear sometimes when I look at you it's like I'm seeing him." She blinked slowly and then reached up to touch his black hair. "You're very different, course. But I suppose my mental image of him is so old and fuzzy that I use pieces of you to fill in the gaps in my memory of him."

His heart was hammering in his chest; he wanted to tell her so badly. But he couldn't, and anyway she was beginning to fall asleep, her chin sinking down toward her chest.

"Mira?" he said. "How about we get you to bed?"

Her head jerked up. "Oh, what about lunch?"

"Another time," he said, looping her arm around his neck. "Come on."

"Thank you, Sky," she said, letting him help her back into her room and into the bed. "You're such a darling boy."

He leaned down and kissed her forehead. "Get some sleep."

Mira was out before he had even closed the bedroom door behind himself. He grabbed his lunch from the table where he'd left it in the foyer and went to the park across the street to eat like he'd planned.

That was how he saw it. Sitting on a bench across from Chapin Tower where Mira was recuperating from her injuries, trying to make his meager sandwich last as long as he could, Leo watched as Hal climbed out of his chauffeured car with a beautiful young redheaded woman following just behind. He kept watching as Hal pulled her, laughing, into his body, and kissed her like he'd kissed her many times before.

Leo had never been more ready to leave Chapin Tower. His stomach was churning over what he'd seen and everything it meant. It was one thing to suspect what Hal was doing and another thing to know it for sure, to have the man who had once been his hero tumble those final meters down from the pedestal Leo had held him upon for so long.

And then there was Vika. He'd spent the rest of the day braced to see her again, waiting for her to reappear and tell him what she needed him to do. Not that betraying Hal's trust weighed quite so heavily on him now as it had a few hours ago; he would do whatever it took to protect Mira, who was all he cared about now. But Vika didn't come near him. He wasn't even sure if she was still in the penthouse. Perhaps she'd gone out shopping to soothe her anxiety over her suspicions or to try to ensnare a rich husband. Stars above but he felt sick. As soon as the workday was over, he packed up his things, eager to get out of there as soon as possible.

"I'll be heading home now, sir, unless you need anything else?" he asked, sticking his head into Hal's office.

"Yes, wouldn't want to stay a minute over your time, would you?" Hal said without looking up. "Go on, then."

It shouldn't have stung given what he knew now, but it still did. Leo just nodded and backed away, ready to put as much distance between himself and Chapin Tower as he could.

He summoned the lift, but moments before the doors closed Vika appeared around the corner and slid in beside him. He jumped. He'd become so distracted that he'd stopped bracing for her, and so the scent of her perfume and the high color in her cheeks hit him harder than he was prepared for. "Miss Hale!"

Vika hit the emergency stop button and the lift jolted to a halt. Immediately the display panel that showed the progress of the lift through the building transformed into the face of the concierge at the desk downstairs.

"Is everything all right, Miss Hale?" the girl asked. "Do you need me to call for assistance?"

"No, we're quite all right," Vika said. The display returned to numbers, and she turned to him. "I need the Gardners' new will. I assume you have it?"

It took his brain a moment to catch up. "I—no, I'm afraid I don't."

She narrowed her eyes at him. "You have to."

He shook his head. "Mr. Gardner has been working on it directly with the solicitors. He's had me send them a few notes about amendments he wanted made"—including to her own inheritance, which had caused him so many problems—"but I've never seen the full document. He . . . he doesn't trust me with that sort of thing."

"Since when? You're his right hand."

"Not lately," he said, feeling as though she had found a fresh bruise of his and jammed her knuckles into it. "In any case, I don't have access to it."

"Then you'll have to get it."

"I can try, but I don't think I'm likely to be successful. He's very secretive about that sort of thing."

"Well what good are you then!" she said, throwing her hands up in the air.

He heard the words echoed by another voice, gone now, and felt himself shrinking until he was just a little boy again. "I-I'm sorry."

She pressed a hand to her temple and closed her eyes. "That's not what I meant, I just . . . Do you know if the Gardners' will has been made official yet or if they're still working on it?"

"You think the person who sabotaged the Gardners' airship is a beneficiary of their will?"

She looked sideways at him, and he could feel her trying to work out whether she should trust him or not.

"If you want me to help you," he said, "it would be easier if I had some idea what you were thinking."

"Well, the bomber would have to be a beneficiary of *one* of the wills, wouldn't they?" she said. "Why else would anyone want to harm Mira? Leo Chapin, I don't know, maybe he was an awful person with lots of enemies, but not Mira."

"That makes sense."

"But if we don't know who is in the Gardners' will, we don't know who might have had a motive to kill Mira," she said. "The only entities left in the Chapin will are some organizations that look like charities, and I can't see a charity doing in an old woman just to get her money."

Something in Vika's phrasing jumped out at him. He'd read his father's will a dozen times and had always attributed the feeling of unease it gave him to his strained relationship with the man and the insane marriage proviso attached to his own inheritance. But now he realized there was something else that had been bothering him.

"Rigel Chapin wasn't—" He stopped himself. "He doesn't seem to have been a particularly charitable person."

"So?"

"You said he gave to organizations that *look* like charities," he said. "Maybe that was the point. Maybe one, or more, aren't charities at all."

"What do you mean?" she asked. "What could they be?"

He shrugged. "Anyone can form a legal entity and call it whatever they want. The wealthy do it all the time to obscure their identities or hide money away. A charity on this planet is just as likely to be a tax shelter as an organization actually trying to help people."

"Can you find out who's behind the organizations named in the Chapin will?"

"I can try."

For a moment, he thought she was going to smile. But then she seemed to remember who she was talking to and abruptly hit the emergency stop button again, sending the lift moving.

"Do that, then," she said. "I want this over with."

That, at least, was something they could agree on.

CHAPTER TWENTY-SIX

DESPITE HOW DIFFERENT EVERYTHING felt after all that had happened, Vika's everyday life looked very much the same. There were still lunches to be had, parties to attend, and most importantly, a rich husband to nail down.

That night the party was a charity ball to benefit a children's hospital at the Central City Botanical Garden. On Philomenus, whenever there was some kind of need for money—like when the mines first started closing and so many people were out of work, or a couple of cycles ago when a powerful storm had flooded dozens of low-lying housing complexes—the people had always just pooled what bits they could spare and sent it to directly to those who needed it. It seemed to Vika that the Philomeni way made more sense than throwing a party that would eat up most of the donations when the billionaires in attendance could simply give the hospital all the money it needed. But then there would be no party, she supposed, and this was just how rich people did things.

She put on the gown she had chosen strategically for that night. Most of the clothes she was attracted to were in bold colors and dramatic cuts that made her look older and feel powerful for once. She liked thinking people were looking at her because of the clothes she'd chosen instead of the circumstances of her life that she hadn't. But she felt this night, a moonlit party in a garden, was calling for something softer and more traditionally feminine. Mr. Keid was going to be there, and she wanted to be the picture of demure elegance she sensed he would prefer in a wife, someone who would give him and his droning conversation all of her attention, letting him teach her his wisdom like he had ever since he'd discovered she had a mind for business. So Vika had found a gown of pale violet tulle so soft and translucent that it looked more like light than fabric, with pastel flowers embroidered all over the skirt and creeping up the bodice and down the full sleeves. Gemma pinned her dark curls up with pearls and tiny white flowers and gave her a pink flush and soft pink lips, and Vika selected a solitary diamond pendant as her only jewel.

She was descending the stairs into the foyer as Sky entered from the direction of his office, heading home for the day. She was far enough above him that she thought about just freezing in the hopes that he wouldn't notice her, but even as the thought entered her head, he glanced up in her direction and his steps faltered.

"Oh," he said, as though the word had jumped out of his mouth. "Uh, good evening, Miss Hale."

She nodded. "Mr. Foster."

"I was just on my way out." He glanced in the direction from which he'd come and then lowered his voice. "I've started that work you asked me for."

She took the last steps a little quicker. "Anything?"

"Not yet," he said. "I should be going. Do you have any message you'd like me to convey to your family?"

She tensed. She hadn't talked to them since before she left for Greenbriar House, and guilt flared through her. She should have hailed her da after the airship crash, but she hadn't wanted to worry him and hadn't trusted herself not to let all of her worries come tumbling out of her mouth when she heard his voice. So she'd been avoiding talking to him altogether.

Sky must have seen her face change because he quickly added, "I apologize. I always say that to you because I'm trying to be . . . I don't know, helpful somehow. But perhaps it's rude of me."

She sighed. "It *would* be helpful, but it just reminds me of what a bad daughter I am."

"I don't believe that," he said. "I suspect much of what you do here is in service to them in some way."

"Like this dress?" she said. "My family could eat for weeks on what I spent on this dress."

"Even the dress." He then added, straight-faced, "Perhaps not the shoes."

She laughed, surprising them both. He gave her a little bow of his head, bade her good night, and was gone.

"Viktoria!"

She turned to find Hal in his tuxedo with Mira in a wine-red gown on his arm coming down the stairs, both of them beaming at her. Hal took her hand with his free one, spinning her around on the marble floor.

"You look gorgeous, my dear!" he said. "Like some woodland nymph come to steal all the men's hearts."

"Well, thank you," she said, forcing herself to smile as she rearranged the curls on her shoulders. "That's just what I was going for."

"Mission accomplished," he said. "I would marry you tomorrow if I thought the old lady would let me."

The smile died on Vika's lips, but Mira laughed. "I'm standing right here!"

"So you are." Hal pressed a kiss to her forehead, and Vika's stomach turned. "Shall we, ladies?"

They rode the lift down to the ground floor, and Grant had their usual car waiting for them at the curb. Vika slid inside, but as she did a terrible thought occurred to her. Was the car safe? What if there was another bomb hidden under the hood, someone just waiting for the Chapin heirs to climb inside to eliminate them once and for all? Mira climbed in beside her. Vika's heart began to race.

She wanted to throw the door open and fling herself out of the car, and her toes curled in her shoes as she tried to keep her limbs under control. Hal was still outside the vehicle, talking to Grant. Any second now he would get inside and Grant would get behind the wheel. She couldn't just keep sitting here, but she didn't want to reveal her fears to Hal, either. In case.

"Do you smell something?" she asked Mira.

Mira sniffed. "No. What?"

"I'm not sure. Fuel, maybe," Vika said. She opened the door and climbed out, as slowly and calmly as she could, and spoke to Hal over the roof of the car. "Hal, I think I smell fuel back here. Grant, could there be some kind of leak?"

"I don't think so, miss," Grant replied.

Hal's face instantly hardened. "You don't think? Surely part of what I pay you for is to know."

"Well, sir, we did run over some debris in the road as I was going to fuel her up for this evening's trip," Grant said. "I suppose it's possible something was damaged—"

"And you're just now thinking to tell me this?" Hal demanded. Grant's expression went very still, and he seemed to become smaller with every passing second. "What if Miss Hale hadn't mentioned anything? I suppose you would have tried to just get this past me?"

"Hal," Vika said, horrified at what her lie had precipitated. "It's not his fault—"

Mira got out of the back seat. "What's going on?"

"Take this car in for servicing immediately," Hal said. "And find a replacement vehicle to pick us up at the gardens. I'm so sorry, ladies. We'll have to take a hired car to the event."

"Well, that's all right!" Mira said. "No need to be upset, my love, these things happen."

"Not for what I pay for it, it shouldn't," he said, with one more look at Grant. "You can go now and we'll speak later."

Vika burned with guilt, but what could she do? She couldn't admit now that she'd made it all up. And anyway, she was relieved to see Grant driving the car off to be gone over—no doubt with a fine-toothed comb after that dressing down—by a mechanic who would discover if the vehicle had been tampered with. But still she felt like there was a huge weight on her chest, pressing her down into the seat of the hired car they hailed off the street to take them to the botanical gardens. Stella had gone off on her that way more times than she could count back when she worked at Nicky's, sometimes so viciously that she'd had to hide in a bathroom stall during her break and press the heels of her hands against her eyes to stop herself from crying. She could still feel how small and impotent it had made her feel, the sensation burning in her chest for hours afterward. To think she was responsible for that happening to poor Grant . . .

But she had to shake it off. There was nothing she could do about it now, and she had things to accomplish this evening.

A little of the weight lifted from her chest as they stepped into the gardens, and she was moved by the pure beauty of the place. The trees were strung with fairy lights, floating lanterns hovered unassisted in the air, casting off a gentle glow, and the air smelled of flowers and freshly fallen rain. A little more weight evaporated when the first sip of hibiscus champagne hit her tongue. Grant would be fine, and she and the Gardners wouldn't be killed in their car. That was what really mattered, wasn't it? After all, Grant would have been blown to bits right alongside them. She'd actually done the man a favor in the long run.

And now it was time to focus on her mission. If she was going to have safety and comfort in her life, she needed to find a husband as soon as possible.

Illuminated pathways snaked through the gardens, leading to a massive gazebo where a small orchestra was playing for the couples dancing and those chatting at the dining tables. The backdrop was stunning: glittering trees, thousands of flowers in every color, and the moon full and bright above them. But it was just more dinner and dancing, passed hors d'oeuvres and gossip over cocktails. The backgrounds changed, grew more and more elaborate, but parties on Ploutos were all basically the same. The same people having the same conversations over the same caviar-garnished fish in white wine cream sauce. Unbelievable as it might have seemed to her just a few short months ago, it was all becoming rather . . . dull. When she was a society lady with a house and money of her own, she would throw better, more interesting parties.

Speaking of which, she spotted Mr. Keid at the bar and made her way toward him slowly, greeting people she knew along the way. She didn't want it to be obvious that she was heading for him. She sidled up to the bar, turning her body slightly away from his, and ordered herself a sparkling water with puckerfruit. Then she pretended to stumble, falling sideways into him.

"Oh, excuse me, I—" She turned and looked at him, a smile spreading across her face. "Oh, Mr. Keid, I didn't see you there. I do apologize for my clumsiness."

"It's a wonder to me that any of you ladies remain upright in those contraptions you wear on your feet," he replied, bowing his head. "May I say, Miss Hale, you look stunning this evening."

She ducked her eyes shyly. "You're too kind. But really these surroundings put us all to shame. I've never seen such a beautiful place."

He looked around as though just noticing where he was. "Ah. Indeed. Very nice."

"I was thinking of taking a walk through the gardens before dinner is served," she said. He just continued to stare at her. "Mrs. Gardner was going to accompany me, but I seem to have lost her in the crowd."

"Ah! Well, I'm sure you can find her."

Hell's teeth. "Or . . . perhaps you would like to join me?"

"Oh, of course! What a fool I am," he said, offering her his arm. "My brain has been addled by your beauty."

She laughed lightly, although the compliment left her feeling strangely empty. This is what she'd wanted, right? Why she'd chosen this particular dress and hair and jewelry? She would have expected to feel some kind of triumph at having reduced him to such an idiot.

Together they walked down the lighted cobblestone paths that weaved in and out of the gardens. She asked him about his work and feigned great interest as he told her all the details of the latest distribution deal he'd made and its impact on his company's quarterly projections. It felt like a sudden glimpse of her possible future. Years of pretending to care as this man talked at her, never seeming to notice that she was bored down to her bones and never thinking to ask her anything in return. But she supposed there were worse things. She couldn't imagine ever arguing with Keid the way her parents argued; if nothing else, that would require some level of passion that he didn't appear to be capable of. Surely she could stand being bored by a decent man in exchange for a life of comfort for her and her family?

They came to a garden that was surrounded by a wall of hedges with a small stone fountain burbling in its center. The water was lit up from within, teeming with millions of bioluminescent creatures that turned the flow of the fountain into a waterfall of delicate blue sparkles.

"Shall we sit for a minute?" he asked, gesturing at one of the benches that surrounded the fountain.

"What a lovely idea," she said, carefully arranging the delicate fabric of her skirt underneath her.

"You know, Miss Hale," he said, contemplating her face in the moonlight, "I feel as though I've known you for years."

"Really?" she said, trying to look pleased when in truth she was baffled. She knew all his strategies to increase the profit margin in his business and the names of his beloved dogs but little else about him, and she doubted he could name a single fact about her with a knife to his throat.

He nodded. "You're so lovely."

She smiled and dropped her eyes to her lap, trying to look coy.

"I hope soon to know you even better," he said.

"I would like that."

Bloody hell, here it was. She hadn't really expected this to happen tonight and wasn't prepared, even though this was what she'd been working for. His eyes closed and he leaned toward her, and she steeled herself for the impact. She'd never been kissed before, not really, just experimental back-alley pecks with boys from the community school or drunken patrons at Nicky's trying their luck before Jay tossed them out on the street.

His lips were surprisingly cool against hers, and moist. She forced herself not to jerk back. He was gentle, but somehow that made the exploration of his mouth over hers even worse, like some small, uncertain creature was crawling across her lips. And she felt like she couldn't breathe, some part of him always moving in the way each time she tried to inhale, his chilly fingers cradling her jaw.

Was this really what she wanted? A life as a high-class molly? At least the girls on Philomenus who sold it on the streets did it to feed their families, not to buy themselves pretty dresses. But she couldn't be poor again, she just couldn't, and he wasn't so bad, really, she would adjust, she would learn . . .

"Oh, excuse me," a choked voice suddenly said, and Vika pulled away from Keid. Relief flooded through her limbs as she saw Archer standing in a gap in the hedgerow. His expression was stricken, but he quickly hid it behind his most polite mask.

"Mr. Sheratan," she breathed, resisting the impulse to wipe her hand across her lips.

"I'm terribly sorry to interrupt. Please forgive me," Archer said to Mr. Keid with a nod of his head, and turned to leave.

"Is Mira looking for me?" Vika asked, the words bursting out of her.

Archer didn't miss a beat. "Yes, she sent me to find you. But I will tell her you're occupied at present."

"No, no, that's quite all right," Mr. Keid said, standing. "I believe

I've deprived Mrs. Gardner of her companion for long enough this evening, and I should be getting back myself. Thank you for the walk, Miss Hale."

He kissed the back of her hand with his too-cool lips, and as soon as he disappeared through the hedges, she collapsed back against the bench.

"Stars above, Archer, thank goodness you happened upon us!" she said. The memory of those lips crawling across hers came back to her and she shook her whole body to dislodge it.

He smiled and sat beside her. "If I'd realized you were in need of rescuing, I'd have come charging in on my white horse. I was afraid my interruption had been . . . unwelcome."

"Not at all," she said. "He's perfectly nice, but I don't think I've ever been more uncomfortable in my life."

"I'm glad," he said, gazing deeply into her eyes. Then he frowned and shook his head. "That is I'm—I'm not glad you were uncomfortable, of course. Only that . . . well . . ." He ducked his head in embarrassment.

Vika felt her cheeks turn hot. She'd never seen Archer, who was so clever and polished, at a loss for words before. There had always been a certain spark between them from the day they'd met, when she was just a poor barmaid in a fraying shirt in desperate need of a shower, and suddenly the fact that he'd known that old Vika felt important to her.

"I don't think I've ever been more happy to see you," she said.

He smiled and reached his hand toward her. She held her breath as he delicately placed his fingers, which were warm against her skin, on the clasp of her necklace, which had fallen forward. He shifted it to the base of her neck. "Perhaps you should make an effort not to look quite so stunning," he said. "The man hardly had any choice."

"Oh yes, I'm quite the appealing trap," she said, failing to keep the note of bitterness out of her voice. This is what she wanted, after all, to trap herself a husband. So why should it make her feel so sick to the pit of her stomach that using her beauty and the Gardners' money to lure someone in was actually working?

He gave her an understanding look. "Does Mr. Keid not appreciate the finer points of your personality?"

"I haven't been able to get a word in edgewise as long as I've known him, so I doubt it," she said. She was just a shiny, pretty object to be owned by some man or another. Rigel Chapin had seen to that. "Oh! And you'll never believe, but *Hal's assistant* of all people tried to kiss me recently, as though I wouldn't see straight through that."

Archer's eyes widened.

"It's true," she continued, the hurt that had been boiling inside of her for so long finally bubbling over. "Suddenly discovered he was head over heels for me right around the time he found out the Gardners are writing me into their will. Is everyone on this planet just as bad as old Mr. Chapin? I am a *person,* you know, not just a thing to possess."

"Of course you are," he said. "I'm sorry that happened to you. People are beastly. You deserve so much better than that, Viktoria."

He was looking at her so earnestly that the scant centimeters of air between them took on even more electric charge, and she wondered if maybe kissing was only repulsive when it was the wrong person's lips pressed to yours. The thought made her feel happy and confused and unsettled for some reason she couldn't put her finger on. She dropped her eyes so that she wouldn't have to try to understand the look in his.

"How is your evening so far?" she asked, swiftly bringing the subject to safer ground.

He lifted one shoulder. "Oh, the usual. Drinks, dinner, gossip."

There was a faint frown line between his eyes, and she could practically see what he wasn't saying. She nudged him with her elbow. "And?"

He shook his head. "Nothing."

"Come on," she said. "I've told you all of my night's trauma."

"It's nothing new," he finally said. "Just a few snide remarks aimed my way that they think I won't pick up on."

"Are you all right?" she asked, the center of her chest burning with shame as she remembered how eagerly she'd listened to Miranda and Nova's gossip about Archer's parentage. "If you want to talk—"

"Certainly not, that sounds terribly dreary," he said, standing and pulling her to her feet. He twined his fingers into hers, the intimate feel of his warm palm against her own sending a shiver up her spine. "Let's go and dance instead."

She nodded and let him lead her along the garden paths, laughing as he took her on a meandering journey.

"Where are you going?" she said. "The gazebo is that way."

"I thought we'd take the scenic route is all. You must learn to stop and smell the literal roses, Miss Hale."

"I think you're lost and don't want to admit it."

He conceded the point with a grin. "These bloody gardens all the look the same!"

Then he came to a sudden stop. She nearly bumped into him and then spotted the sight that had frozen him in his tracks.

The red-haired girl she now vaguely recognized as Evelyn Lyons's assistant had her back pressed up against a wall covered in creeping ivy, Hal's mouth over hers, his big knobby hands resting on the backs of her thighs, greedily pulling her closer.

Vika felt the air being squeezed from her lungs, like she'd been flung into the vacuum of space. The conversation she had overheard was one thing, but this . . . there was no denying this. There was no chance she was misunderstanding. She wanted to curse or scream or throw herself at Hal, but she couldn't move. Finally Archer drew her away.

"I'm so sorry you saw that," he said.

"Bastard," she whispered as she regained the ability to breathe. Hal and a woman barely older than Vika, not even old enough to be his daughter. It was enough to make Vika sick. "That bloody *bastard.*"

She'd tried to deny her suspicions about who had the opportunity to arrange the air crash and had the most to gain from it, but she couldn't anymore. She needed to talk to Sky. She hoped to heavens he had discovered something incriminating about one of the organizations in the Chapin will.

Because otherwise her prime suspect would have to be Hal.

The party finally started to break up in the wee hours of the morning. Why did these things always last at least an hour too long? Vika was sitting at a table beside Mira, who had her casted foot propped up on a chair and was polishing off the last of her dark chocolate pot de crème, lingering over the spoon. They were waiting for Hal, who was still talking with a couple of his gentleman friends as they sipped the last of their brandies.

"If I weren't already married," Mira said blearily, "I would walk down the aisle with this pudding."

Before tonight, Vika would have laughed, but now hearing those words gave her a fresh wave of anger and hurt. She tried to smile, though, and asked, "How much of that hibiscus champagne did you drink?"

Mira smiled. "It was very tasty, wasn't it?"

Hal turned to them. "Ladies, are you ready to depart?"

"Whenever you are, my love," Mira said. They'd been ready for ages, and it was at least the third time Hal had asked them. Mira turned to Vika. "Think we'll actually get out of here in the next half hour?"

Vika squinted over at the group of men. "He's got at least a finger of brandy left."

Mira sighed and leaned back in her chair. "I suppose we live here now, then."

"Could be worse."

Vika couldn't really hear what the men were talking about, only the general tone of it, but then a few words reached her. Something about "chauffeur" said in an angry tone, and that made her pay attention. She sat up, trying to hear.

"You can't let them take advantage of you," she heard Hal say to a friend as he turned toward her to flag down a waiter.

Vika wanted to scream and shake him. Hell's teeth, even if his servants *were* taking advantage of him, he had more money than one person could ever spend in a lifetime! And he was hardly one to complain about being taken advantage of.

"Mira," she said hesitantly. She'd been bottling up her thoughts for so long and she didn't want them to come exploding out of her. She had to be careful.

"Yes, dear?" Mira was looking up at the floating lanterns above their heads, lazily winding a strand of hair around her finger.

"Is Hal okay? He seems . . . well, he seems to be not quite himself recently," Vika said. She couldn't just come right out and ask, *Do you think your husband might prefer you dead,* so starting with the way Hal was treating his employees seemed like a safer bet.

Mira sat up, the hazy smile gone from her lips. "He just has a lot weighing on his mind these days. It's not easy, you know, suddenly having a fortune dropped in your lap. There's a lot of work and responsibility that comes with it."

"Maybe he needs more help?" Vika said. "Surely someone else could take care of all those responsibilities and you two could just, you know, enjoy yourselves. He's away working such long hours most days. Maybe he could turn more of his work over to Sky or—"

"Oh darling, I've been banging my head against that particular wall for weeks," she said. "There's no point."

"It's just . . ." Vika looked over at Hal, who was waving his hands animatedly as he talked with those men, high color in his cheeks. "Well, have you noticed the way he's been speaking to Grant lately? Or to Sky?"

Mira's spine got even straighter. "I can't say that I have."

"I know how kind and generous Hal is, but lately—"

"Just leave it, Viktoria, please," Mira said sharply.

Vika snapped her mouth closed. She had never seen Mira so close to angry before. She needed to find out what Sky had discovered, and quickly.

CHAPTER TWENTY-SEVEN

LEO SPENT THE NEXT few days digging into his father's will in between his normal tasks for Hal, trying to find out more about the organizations the old man had set aside money for. There were nine altogether, most of which checked out. It was true that the symphony was aggressive in its fundraising efforts, but Leo could hardly imagine them resorting to murder in order to shore up their endowment. There were three, though, that raised more questions than answers when he learned more about them: the Ploutosian Defense Fund, the Sagittarius Aid Society, and Delta Energy Corporation. All three were high up in the chain of the will, meaning that they were due to inherit a significant portion of the estate if both Leo and Mira were unable to for any reason, and all three were highly secretive, with next to no public information available about them. Perhaps Vika was on the right track.

Several days after she'd blackmailed him into helping her, he heard her calling his name as he left Chapin Tower. He stopped on the sidewalk and turned to see her rushing after him.

"Where are you going?" she asked.

He held up the paper bag in his hand. "It's my lunch break. I was going to sit in the park."

"I'll go with you," she said. "You can tell me what you've found out. I'm dying to know."

"Not literally, I trust."

She frowned. "Not yet."

They sat down on his customary bench in the park across the street from Chapin Tower, and he unpacked the lunch he'd brought from home: a cheese sandwich, a tin of mixed fruit, and a couple of precious chocolate squares he doled out sparingly. He'd quickly learned how unrealistic his monthly budget for food was, but now he knew the price of practically every item in the market down to the cent and exactly how long each would keep his stomach quiet. Adjusting from never having to think of money to being hyperaware of every bit he spent was not only exhausting but resulted in quite a lot of unsatisfying meals.

Vika's mouth dropped open and she looked at him in horror. "You cannot be serious," she said.

"What?" he asked, bewildered.

She grabbed his sandwich and tin of fruit—which were both quite sad looking, it was true—and shoved them back into his paper sack. She nodded at the chocolate squares. "Those you can keep. Wait here."

She returned a few minutes later with a bag from a nearby restaurant, and he followed her onto the grass where she set out an impressive spread of fresh salads, thinly sliced meat between buttery rolls, and puckerfruit fizzies.

"You didn't have to do this," he said.

"I did. Just looking at that pathetic little sandwich made me want to cry," she said. "Too many memories. Besides, I was hungry, too."

He sat down next to her under a large tree and they ate in not entirely uncomfortable silence for a few minutes. He was glad for that sliver of peace between them, as well as the food, which was the best meal he'd had since they'd left Greenbriar.

"This is a nice park," she said. "I've never taken much notice of it before."

Leo had played here for thousands of hours when he was little, either with Mimi or the parade of nannies he'd had over the years. He'd even tried to climb this very tree once and sprained his wrist when he came tumbling out of it. He had not been quite the athlete his father had hoped for in a son.

"I've always liked it," he said.

"It's still hard for me to get used to the sun. These people have no idea how good they have it," she said, tilting her head back to receive the beams. Then she seemed to remember what they were here for and shook herself. "Right. What have you been able to find out about the parties in the Chapin will?"

He reached for his mini-holo, where he'd been keeping notes of his investigation, and waved his thumb over the sensor to open it. "Most seem legitimate, but there are a few I have questions about. Delta Energy Corporation is registered on Korybas; I've put in a request for public records but it will take some time. The Sagittarius Aid Society seems to be a shell corporation of some kind. I honestly don't have a clue how to go about trying to find out who or what is behind the shell, but I'll keep researching. The Ploutosian Defense Fund brings up no records at all. I can't even tell if it truly exists. Perhaps Mr. Chapin had the name wrong."

"That's it? You haven't found out anything else?"

He shook his head. "I know it's not much, but it is a start."

"It's not enough!" she said. "If I'm right, Mira's life could be in danger. *My* life could be in danger. I can't just wait for records requests to come through and hope I don't get blown up in the meantime."

"What else can we do?"

She frowned, drumming her fork against the container of pasta salad she had been eating from. He glimpsed a small wobble in her lower lip, which she bit down on.

"Is there . . ." He hesitated. "Is there something else bothering you?"

She looked down at the fork she was rapping against the container, as though just discovering it was connected to her own hand, and tossed it aside. "I just need to find out who's behind this. I need to find out which of these groups it is."

"It may not be any of them," he said.

"It *has* to be," she said, the line of her jaw set tight. Then she added, "I know! We should go to the constabulary. See if we can get any information out of them that might help us move faster."

"But they don't believe the explosions are linked."

She began to pack up the remains of their lunch. "That's why we may catch something they've missed. Besides, I . . . I can't just keep sitting in that penthouse *waiting* and letting my mind run wild. I'll go crazy."

He didn't have much time left on his lunch break, but she sounded so genuinely distressed that he heard himself saying, "All right, but what makes you think they'll tell you anything?"

She shrugged. "I taught myself how to cry when I was eight cycles old."

Leo flagged down a hired car while Vika hurriedly ran upstairs to change her dress. A few minutes later, as he leaned against the idling cab, she emerged from the building. She had washed the cosmetics from her face and swapped the cheerful red silk she'd been wearing before for a modest, long-sleeved dress in charcoal gray. He held the door to the car open for her, and the two of them slid inside and headed for the headquarters of the Ploutosian constabulary, sketching out a rough game plan as they flew through the streets. When they arrived, Vika led the way inside, and sometime while her back was turned to him, she transformed from a calm and deliberate girl into one who was on the verge of a hysterical breakdown.

"Please," she said, her voice cracking with emotion as she rushed up to the reception desk. "Please, I must speak to the chief constable at once."

"I apologize, miss," the officer said, "but you can't just—"

"I have to talk with him!" Vika said, loudly enough that heads turned toward them and took in the tears rolling down her cheeks.

Leo handed her his handkerchief, and she made a show of trying to collect herself while he leaned toward the officer manning the desk.

"Sergeant, isn't there something you can do?" He dropped his voice. "This is Miss Viktoria Hale, ward of Harold and Mira Gardner. The former fiancé of . . ."

The woman's eyes widened.

"Indeed," Leo said.

"My fiancé was murdered and no one can give me any answers!" Vika said. She collapsed, sobbing, against Leo's shoulder. He tried to hide his surprise and put a careful arm around her waist, while the sergeant's eyes darted around the public lobby. Everyone was staring now, and people were beginning to recognize who she was.

"All she wants is to talk to the chief constable," Leo said to the nervous officer, exquisitely aware of Vika's warm breath against his neck as she cried. "I can't imagine he would want her turned out onto the streets, can you?" He looked meaningfully at their rapt audience and saw the horror in the woman's eyes as she imagined the scene and the gossip it would cause.

Minutes later they were being ushered into the chief constable's office on the top floor of the building. The chief, dressed in a smart blue suit with a gold insignia embroidered over the heart, rose to meet Vika as they were let inside.

"Miss Hale," he said. "I'm so glad to finally meet you. How may I help you today?"

Vika drew in a shaky breath, her eyes brimming with tears. "You can help me by telling me when you are finally going to catch the monster who killed my fiancé."

"I assure you that we are doing everything in our power to find out who or what caused the explosion aboard the *Leander*," the chief said as he led her to the chair across from his desk. He practically lowered Vika down into the chair as though he were afraid she couldn't manage it on her own. He didn't seem to notice or care what Leo did.

Vika daintily dabbed at the corners of her eyes. "And what have you discovered so far?"

The chief settled into his desk chair. "Well, of course I can't discuss the particulars of an ongoing investigation—"

Vika's face turned to stone in a transformation Leo was personally familiar with. "Do you suspect me of bombing my fiancé's spaceliner, Chief Lich?" she asked in a chilly voice. Leo had been on the receiving end of that tone and that look more times than he cared to remember, and he knew how unsettling it was.

The chief was aghast. "Of course not, miss."

"And do you have any reason to believe that anyone I know was involved?"

"No, not the slightest."

"Then what harm can there be in telling me what you know?" she asked. "My guardians have provided a substantial reward for information, and we *had* intended to make a sizable donation to your department in order to aid in finding this murderer. But it seems to me as though you're either incompetent or uninterested in our case, so there's no point in wasting a single bit on—"

The man sat forward as he pictured all that money slipping away. "Miss Hale, I can assure you that we're working on the case night and day—"

Vika's stern face suddenly crumpled. "Then why haven't you found who killed my Leo yet?"

It was a strange thing, watching the girl he loved pretend to grieve for him.

The chief pressed a button on his desk. "Shaw, bring me a copy of the Chapin file, immediately." He came around the front of the desk and touched a hand to Vika's shaking shoulder. "There, there, my dear. I promise we're going to find the person who did this."

Soon someone appeared with a file they handed over to the chief.

It looked suspiciously light to Leo, and he had to suppress an irritated frown.

"Here is everything we have so far," he said. "Every piece of evidence and lead we've pursued. Obviously I can't divulge the details but—"

"Isn't there anything you can tell me?" Vika asked, her lip trembling. "My mind is plagued with thoughts of what happened to my fiancé day in and day out, and I think if only I knew something, I could find some sliver of peace."

The chief sighed and leaned back against his desk. "We believe the bombing was done by the Philomeni Liberation Front, as a way to bring attention to their cause and sow fear in the Ploutosian population. Most likely they didn't even know Mr. Chapin was aboard."

"I'm not sure if that makes it easier or more painful," she said. "What makes you think it was them?"

"Well, we received an anonymous communiqué the day after the bombing claiming responsibility."

"Couldn't anyone have sent that, though?" she asked with doe-eyed confusion. "You must have other evidence."

The man considered for a second and then nodded. "A Philomeni man who worked as a janitor in an office building here on Ploutos was on an earlier voyage of the *Leander*. We believe the PLF paid his passage so that he would be able to plant the bomb aboard the spaceliner. We're scouring Alastor for the man as we speak."

Leo frowned. He knew very well that no Philomeni janitor would be able to afford passage on the *Leander* on his own. Was there a chance the PLF was responsible for the bombing after all?

"May I?" Vika asked, gesturing to the file.

The chief hesitated.

"You know, I'm sure, that I was born just a poor Philomeni girl. I can barely even read except to recognize my own name," she said. Leo wasn't sure how she said it with a straight face. Every Philomeni he'd met knew how to read perfectly well, and Vika had been educated better than most. But Ploutosian beliefs about the backwardness of the Philomeni people had the chief constable swallowing her every word. "My Leo was going to save me from all of that, but in the end he needed someone to save him . . ."

Vika teared up again and the man, overcome with the tragedy of this beautiful girl, handed over the file. She didn't open it, just clutched it to her chest.

"To feel this in my hands," Vika said, "and to know that you are going to find justice for him has given me the first moment's peace I've known since he died. I'm sure you won't mind if I keep it?"

"Oh." The chief looked pained. "I'm afraid the contents of that file are confidential, Miss Hale."

"Chief Lich," she said. "Do you see this man with me?"

The chief glanced at Leo for the first time since he'd entered the room. "Of course, miss."

"He works for the private investigator—the very best, you understand, a most discreet and effective man—that the Gardners have hired to look into my fiancé's murder because of the faith they have lost in *your* department," Vika said. "The Gardners are most anxious to discover who killed Leo, as the substantial reward they're offering shows. If their investigator were to solve the case with the help of information you provided him, well then of course you would be entitled to some of that reward. Not that anyone would have to know the information came from you."

The chief seemed almost frozen as he grappled with the dilemma Vika had so expertly laid at his feet. Leo glanced down at his silent mini-holo.

"Miss Hale, the car is here," he said.

Vika rose and squeezed the chief's fingers. "Thank you so much, sir. You are a wonderful man, and I won't forget how helpful you've been."

She swept toward the door, still holding the file in her arms.

The chief stood. "Miss Hale!"

"Yes?"

For a moment he looked as though he would protest, demand the file back, and Leo held his breath. But then he saw the man's eyes clear as he made his decision.

"I'll be in touch with any further developments," he said. "I want to be as much help to you as possible."

The smile Vika gave him was bright enough to power the planet. "Thank you, Chief."

Leo had to struggle not to break into a run as the two of them walked toward the lift, and he could sense Vika's trembling beside him. They stepped into the elevator and the doors slid shut.

"Did that just happen?" she whispered, without turning toward him or even opening her mouth all the way, like she was afraid that any moment might break the spell and send the chief rushing after them.

"I think so," Leo said. "I can't believe you just did that."

She shook her head sadly. "Never underestimate the power of money, Sky."

CHAPTER TWENTY-EIGHT

VIKA STILL FELT A little shaky in the knees from the adrenaline comedown as she and Sky rode the lift up to the Gardners' flat. If Sky wasn't able to make any headway on suspects using the Chapin will, there at least had to be *something* in the papers clutched under her arm that the constabulary had missed.

Hopefully something that pointed at any suspect other than Hal.

Sky was also jittery beside her and checked the screen of his mini-holo for the third or fourth time since they'd left the constabulary.

"What is it?" she asked.

"Nothing."

As the doors opened into the foyer, Vika heard Hal's voice.

"Where is the damn boy?" he was saying. "Foster!"

Sky leapt out of the lift. "Here, sir."

"You're late!" Hal said. "I don't pay you to faff about, do I? No, I pay you to work. You should have been back from lunch fifteen minutes ago."

"I know, sir," Sky said. "I assure you—"

"It's my fault, Hal," Vika said, rushing forward. She supposed she didn't really care if Sky was in trouble, but she didn't want him fired, not when she needed his help. "I needed him to help me with some shopping bags. I didn't mean to keep him past his time."

"Oh." Hal seemed unsure of how to handle this information. "Well. That's a different matter then. Come with me, we have work to do."

Sky flashed her a brief smile of gratitude and followed Hal toward his office, but she felt unsettled. Why hadn't he told her he would be in trouble for going over his lunch break? It hadn't even occurred to her, and he hadn't once mentioned it. Maybe he was afraid she was heartless enough to actually go through with her threat and tell Hal about what had happened at Greenbriar and cost him his job. But somehow, remembering how comfortably they had sat together under that tree eating sandwiches, she didn't think so. Of course, it could just be the belly full of good food that had made him seem so content in that moment.

That gave her an idea. Vika went upstairs to her bedroom, locking the door behind her and throwing herself onto the freshly made bed with the Chapin file. But before she opened it, as her fingers were itching to do, she pressed the call button and gave instructions to one of the servants.

When Sky left for the night, the concierge would hand him a bag on his way out. Dinner from the restaurant down the street for him to deliver to her family. She didn't know why she hadn't thought to do this before. She also had them include a few days' worth of lunches for him for his trouble. It eased a little of the discomfort she felt in her stomach at getting him into trouble.

With that done, she spent the next several hours reading the constabulary's investigation file and taking notes on anything that seemed especially noteworthy. There wasn't as much as she'd hoped. She declined hails from Miranda and Nova and ordered up dinner from the kitchen as the sky outside of the windows flared with the setting of the sun and then began to darken. The constabulary's best lead was the Philomeni man who had traveled aboard the

Leander and then disappeared once he reached Alastor. But how could she find him if the authorities couldn't? She could hardly travel to Alastor herself and just start asking around, hoping to bump into him.

Vika kept paging through the file, growing more and more hopeless as she met walls of vague information and dead-ends in the investigation. But then her gaze snagged on a familiar name.

Knox Vega.

Knox was a regular of hers at Nicky's. He spent hours at the bar, mostly slumped over on a stool in the corner, searching his pockets for bits he knew were long gone, begging a drink or a bit of change off of other patrons until the bar muscle would throw him out. An irritating but harmless drunk like the kind every bar had a few of, his nose perpetually red and his mind soaked in confusion from years of hitting the bottle too hard.

The name came up in the middle of an eyewitness statement from the night of the explosion. A salvage craft that had seen the explosion from a distance was heading toward it to look for survivors—supposedly, though more likely he was hoping to snag the choicest bits of salvage from a fresh catastrophe—and witnessed another craft fleeing the area.

> Witness reports that the craft was familiar to him and belongs to fellow stream salvager Knox Vega. States certainty of identification at ninety plus percent. Vega was interviewed and provided evidence he was planet-side at the time of explosion, so likely misidentification. Identity of craft needs verification.

Vika had known Knox was a stream salvager, although she was never able to figure out when he actually went searching for debris since he seemed to live on his barstool. Still, he must have worked occasionally since he drank through dozens of bits most days. Could it really have been him another salvager saw fleeing the area where the *Leander* exploded? It was something to go on, at least.

The next morning, Vika woke early and headed downstairs. Mira and Hal were having breakfast on one of the balconies as they often did. Vika was usually still sleeping at this hour, having come in late from some party or outing with her friends.

"Good morning, my dear!" Mira said. "Would you like to join us? We can have another plate made for you."

"No, I'm fine," she said. "I've decided to go home to Philomenus for the day to visit my parents."

"Oh, that's a lovely idea," Mira said. "I'm sure they've been missing you."

"Have Grant take you to the dock," Hal said. "I'll arrange a transport to be waiting for you."

"Isn't it his day off?" Vika asked. The last thing she wanted was to get in that car, even though the mechanics who'd examined it hadn't found anything out of place.

Hal smiled and patted her arm. "Yes, but he's hasn't worked the last two days while the car was being looked at, so he owes me some hours, and I don't like the idea of you taking some hired car off the street. I insist."

Vika would have argued, but she was worried Grant would pay for it later if she did. So instead she apologized to him as she slid into the car, and he waved her sorries away and took her to one of the private docks that ringed Central City. Waiting for her on the launching pad was the transport Hal had hired for her. Vika had only ever taken the atmospheric ferry between the planets, but a private spacecraft, as she soon discovered, was a whole different matter. It was a sleek, shiny thing with a pointed nose that seemed like a totally different species from the clumsy, lumbering beast of the ferry. A smiling attendant in a smart red suit was waiting at the stairs with a glass of sparkling water and a warm towel that smelled of mint for her to clean her hands and face with, as though she had so much sweat and stress to wash off from her short journey in the back of a fine chauffeured car. But she took both happily and buckled herself into the plush seat in the belly of the craft. The attendant brought her a variety of snacks and reading materials to choose from, and when she said she was ready to leave, the pilot launched the craft into the air just moments later.

She was just tucking in to a butter pastry stuffed with cheese and riverberry jam when the attendant told her they were landing. The trip to Philomenus had taken less than half the time in this needle-nosed craft than it did in the ferry. As they descended and the atmo-haze clouded the view from the ports, Vika's heart began to feel heavy. The fairy tale, at least for a while, was over.

The attendant and pilot said goodbye and assured her they would be waiting for her whenever she was ready to make her return trip to Ploutos. Luckily Hal had also thought to hire her a car since the long walk to the tram stop would have been less than ideal in her spindly heels. Why hadn't she thought to wear something more sensible? On Ploutos, this simple skirt and blouse had seemed like a casual, low-key outfit. Here on Philomenus, it was ridiculous.

There were few privately owned cars on Philomenus, so heads turned as they drove down the streets, people hoping to catch a glimpse behind the glass. Vika remembered doing that as a child whenever a car passed, always secretly convinced it was some star of the Ploutosian drama feeds hidden behind there, though she never had a good theory as to why a famous actor would be driving around her backwater planet. It was a strange feeling being the one on the inside for once, the fancy person separated from her dirty world by dark glass, utterly untouched by it.

She left the hired car idling on the street outside of Nicky's and stepped into the bar. Immediately she felt the air in the place shift as people took notice of her, like a ripple that started at the door and expanded outward. It gave her a weird kind of thrill up the back of her neck that she wasn't sure if she liked or not. She'd always felt like the drinkers in here had thought of her as less than them since they were the ones barking orders she scurried to fulfill. Now the difference between her and them was much starker—spelled out in the faint click of her satin shoes on the floor and the sway of her custom-tailored skirt—and for once she was the one on top.

"Well, look at what the cat dragged in," Stella said as she approached the bar, giving her an evaluating look up and down. "All right, Vika?"

"Good day to you, Stella," she said. "I'm well, thank you."

Stella and a couple of nearby regulars burst into laughter.

"*Ooh*, milady is well, is she?" Stella asked, affecting the new Ploutosian-style accent Vika had adopted. When she'd first come to stay with the Gardners, she'd taken pains to stop using Philomeni slang and to speak more properly—not dropping her g's and half-swallowing words the way she'd grown up doing—because she knew how much it made her stand out and she dreaded people judging her as just some bit of Philomeni gutter trash. Only now, with Stella holding up this mirror to her, did she realize how far her way of speaking had swung in the other direction and how utterly phony she must sound. "And for what reason does Her Majesty Princess Vika grace us with her presence today?"

Vika tilted her chin up just a fraction farther, to show Stella that her teasing didn't bother her. "I'm looking for Knox, as a matter of fact. Have you seen him lately?"

Stella nodded toward the barstool in the corner that Knox normally occupied but which was now empty. "Not for a few days. Nicky finally got fed up and banned him. I think he's drinking down at the Thorn and Crown now."

"Thanks," Vika said.

"Anytime, princess. Come back and visit again soon."

Trying not to show it, Vika hurried back out to the car.

"Take me to the Thorn and Crown," she said to the driver as she slid into the back seat.

He looked at her through the rearview mirror. "You sure, miss?"

"Yes."

"Let me advise you against that. That place an't—"

"I know what it is," she said. She might look—and apparently sound—like a Ploutosian lady now, but she wasn't. She'd grown up right here on these streets and she knew the Thorn and Crown was an informal hub for the Philomeni Liberation Front. She'd never been afraid of them before and she wasn't going to start fearing them now just because she looked like the enemy. In fact, her heart was pounding with something like excitement. If Knox was connected with the PLF—and hardly anyone drank in the Thorn and Crown unless they were—that might mean the *Leander* bombing really was just a random, isolated terrorist attack and she had no reason to worry someone was coming for Chapin heirs.

"Drop me just here," Vika said a few blocks away from the tavern. She might not be scared, but there was no reason to call extra attention to herself by rolling up in a hired car. The driver pulled the car up to the curb and she stepped out. "I'll be back."

She started walking in the direction of the tavern and was less than a block away when she heard her name.

"Miss Hale?"

She turned and stared, astonished.

"What are you doing here?" she asked Sky, who was standing farther up the pavement, looking as shocked as she felt.

"I might ask you the same thing," he said, recovering from his paralysis and stepping toward her. "Although I realize now that's a foolish question. You're obviously in town visiting your family."

"Yes," she said, lying. She nodded at the tavern. "But I'm also looking for someone."

Sky's eyes widened ever so slightly. "In there?"

"Yes, he was an old regular of mine at Nicky's, and supposedly he drinks here now." She lowered her voice, leaning in to Sky so he would be able to hear her. "I found his name in the constabulary file. A witness reported seeing his salvager fleeing the area just after the *Leander* exploded."

"Oh my." He blinked. "And the constabulary . . . never followed up on that lead?"

"They did, but supposedly he had an alibi to prove he was on the ground at that time."

"Well then it must have been mistaken identity, right?" Sky said. "Why even bother talking to the man?"

"Because I want to know for myself," she said, turning to head for the tavern.

He caught her around the wrist. "Wait. What if it's not safe?"

"Oh please, I'm not scared of Knox Vega or the PLF, either," she said. "I'm not some fancy Ploutosian lady, remember? I'm just another girl from the wrong side of the stream. Come with me if you're worried, but I'm going."

He followed her to the Thorn and Crown, trying to convince her not to go in the whole way, but she was deaf to his protests. A couple of mercs were stationed outside the doors, by the window where the kitchen usually served free soup to hungry Philomenis but which was boarded up for some reason. They gave her curious looks but didn't try to stop her as she stepped inside, Sky at her heels. As her eyes adjusted to the dimness of the tavern, she scanned the faces of the customers. It didn't take long. Unlike Nicky's, which was always packed at this hour, the place was nearly empty.

She sighed. "I don't see him."

"Terribly unfortunate," Sky replied. "I suppose we should just go and—"

She walked up to the bar and signaled for the barkeep. The man gave her a suspicious look as he approached, taking her in from head to toe.

"Help you?" he asked.

"I'm looking for Knox," she said. "He been round here today?"

"Not sure I know who you mean."

She leveled a look at him. "If I'm right, he's been camped out here practically night and day this week. Small guy, big brown coat, drinks the cheapest grock you've got on tap til the doors close. Works salvage in the stream."

"Oh." The bartender glanced at Sky. "Right, that guy. An't seen him."

Why was this man lying to her? Was it just instinct since she didn't look like someone who belonged? Heaven knows she'd lied to her fair share of mercs for no reason other than because they were mercs. In any case, Knox wasn't here, so there was no point in staying any longer. She thanked him for his help and turned to go.

"Well, that was a waste of time," she said as she and Sky exited the Thorn and Crown. Should she just go back to Ploutos? Without being able to find Knox, this mission was a bust. But no, so many people had seen her at Nicky's that word would soon get around to her family that she'd been in town. Maybe her mum and Lavinia wouldn't care, but it would break her da's heart if he found out she'd been so close and hadn't come to see him. She dreaded having to explain to him what she'd been up to for the past few weeks, but the idea of him putting his arms around her and telling her it was all going to be okay made it seem bearable.

"Come on, I'll accompany you back to your car," Sky said. "What were you hoping to discover here?"

She shrugged as they walked. "I don't know. Maybe Knox's alibi was just a cover and he saw something that night he didn't tell the constabulary. But if it was a case of mistaken identity, I'll never find the actual salvager who was there."

"Whoever it was, it's unlikely they know anything useful anyway," Sky said. "I think your initial instinct to focus on the recipients of the will is the right one. The constabulary is so focused on their theory that the PLF bombed the *Leander* that I doubt they've . . ."

Sky continued to speak, but Vika was no longer hearing him, because a familiar face had just turned the corner farther up the street. It was a girl, a few cycles younger than Vika, with fair skin and blond hair, and Vika couldn't remember where she knew her from but an alarm was blaring inside of her head all the same. Then it hit her. She knew exactly where she'd seen the girl before: hauling

Knox out of Nicky's, bracing his weight with her shoulder, lecturing him in the tone of the long-suffering, her slight frame and pointed chin a perfect replica of his own.

That girl was Knox Vega's daughter.

"Hey!" Vika called out. "Hey, you!"

"Vika, what—" Sky followed her eye line to the girl up the street, who had frozen in her tracks.

"Stop there!" Vika said. She took off running, or as close to running as she could manage in her heels, hearing Sky's footfalls a beat behind hers.

The girl looked around her, as though searching for an escape route, but she didn't move. Vika had almost reached her when Sky caught her hand, pulling her to a stop.

"Miss Hale, I don't think this young lady—"

Vika threw up a hand to silence him and turned to the girl. "Hi there," she said. "I know you, don't I? You're Knox Vega's daughter?"

The wide-eyed girl glanced at Sky and then back at her. ". . . Yes?"

"Do you know where he is right now?" she asked. "I've got a couple questions for him. He an't in trouble or anything."

The girl shook her head. "I'm sorry, I don't. He's kind of . . . unreliable, my da."

"I get it. He's a stream salvager, right?"

The girl nodded.

"When does he usually work?" Vika asked. "Daytime? Nighttime?"

The girl shrugged, no longer meeting Vika's gaze. "Depends."

Vika looked at her closely. She was young, it was true, but probably older than Vika had been when she started working to help put food on her family's table. Her trousers were stained with black smudges that could be grease, and she had a small compass clipped to one belt loop.

Vika narrowed her eyes at the girl. "You know, it's funny. There were times when I was working at Nicky's when Knox would be camped out on a barstool from opening til we were locking the doors. How did he make enough money to keep drinking when he never seemed to go salvaging at all?"

The girl tensed.

"It was you, wasn't it?" Vika asked, suddenly sure she was right. "You were the one flying away from the *Leander* that night."

CHAPTER TWENTY-NINE

LEO DIDN'T KNOW WHAT TO DO. The collision had already happened, so it was too late to prevent it. He just had to wait for it to be over and hope the two halves of his life slamming into each other wouldn't leave too much damage behind.

"I an't got a clue what you're talking about," Ariel said. "I've got to go."

Vika caught her around the arm as she turned to leave. "Oh, I think you do. And you're going to tell me what you know."

Ariel's eyes flared, and Leo braced for another impact.

"Ariel!"

The cry came from across the street. A woman whose name he still didn't know, despite her being the PLF member who had given him clothing and his disguise during his first day on Philomenus, ran up to them. She was clutching her baby in one arm and holding her toddling daughter by the hand. "Ariel, they've come for me!"

Ariel broke out of Vika's grasp to go to her. "I thought you were in a safe house."

"I was, but they found me somehow," she said, her voice edging on hysterical. "We were coming home from the market and they were already in the flat. We just ran. We an't got anywhere to go. If they find me—"

Leo knew very well what the mercs would do if they found her. Rank-and-file members of the PLF had been taken off the street by mercs on flimsy or nonexistent pretenses ever since the explosion on the *Leander,* and many hadn't been seen since, disappearing into the detention center or being taken to Ploutos. The woman who made the fake ident cards for the organization would be a valuable get for them.

"They're not going to find you, Liane," Ariel said, taking the woman by the shoulders to steady her. "The plan was always to get you away from here til the heat cooled down. We'll just have to move up our timeline. Come on."

Ariel turned to go, but Vika stepped in front of her. "Wait! I have questions for you."

"I'm not answering your questions, lady," Ariel said, her voice made of steel. "Now move or I will move you."

Leo put a hand on Vika's elbow. "Perhaps we should let her go. You don't want any part of whatever's happening here."

"No way! I an't letting her out of my sight." She looked at him with a hint of true desperation in her eyes as she added more softly, "This is all we have, and I won't lose it."

"Get out of my way, toser," Ariel said, "or I swear I'll—"

"There are two mercs a couple of blocks away," Vika interrupted. "How fast do you think they can get here if I start screaming?"

For a moment the two girls stared each other down, and Leo held his breath. He'd never known either of them to back down.

Liane's daughter whimpered. Ariel looked at the little girl and then at him. "Fine," she said. "But at least move fast. We've got to get off the streets."

"Fine," Vika said, and Leo knew there was no point in arguing. He would just have to follow along and hope they'd all emerge in one piece.

Ariel took the lead, hurrying the group down back alleyways and shortcuts she'd mapped through the Philomeni maze of streets over the years, deftly avoiding high-traffic areas and spots the mercs often patrolled.

"Where are we going?" Vika asked.

"She's got to get off-world" was all Ariel said.

The baby began to stir, and Liane had to drop the little girl's hand in order to quiet it. The girl was exhausted and stumbling over her feet, so Leo scooped her up and let her ride on his back. Liane met his eye and gave him a smile of gratitude, and he felt like he'd repaid a tiny portion of his debt to the PLF.

At one point, they were forced to cross one of the busier streets. As they emerged from an alley, they spotted a cluster of mercs on the corner who were coming out of a shop they had probably just shaken down. Ariel stopped in her tracks and pretended to look at some of the secondhand clothes hanging in the window.

"Look at this," she said. "What do you think?"

Vika immediately caught on. "I think that would look great on you!" she said with convincing enthusiasm.

Leo watched the mercs from the corner of his eye as he pretended to peruse the wares in the window. Two of them were paying them no mind, but a third was squinting at the group. He elbowed his buddy, saying something to him in a low voice. That merc turned to look at them more closely, his eyes widening when they landed on Ariel.

"Fecking hell," Ariel muttered, half a second before the man—who, judging from his closely set eyes and sharp nose, had to be Ariel's nemesis Ratface—pointed and yelled, "Hey!"

Ariel grabbed Liane's hand and took off running in the opposite direction, Vika and Leo on her heels.

"Friend of yours?" Vika asked as they thundered down the street.

"Just stay close!" Ariel said.

With the sound of heavy boots pounding behind them, Ariel led them into a narrow alley with pathways between buildings shooting out from it on all sides. But instead of taking one of those, she pushed open the door to one of the buildings, an abandoned office of some kind. She opened a second door to reveal a stairwell with a dark alcove beneath it. She pushed them into the alcove, cloaking them in the shadows.

"Stay here," she said. "Wait three minutes and then head for the docks, got it?"

"Without you?" Liane asked, her voice high and thin.

"I'm going to go back out there and let them spot me," Ariel said. "As long as they're chasing me, they won't think to look for my skiff. I'll lose them and meet you there. Don't worry, even with a broken leg I'd be faster than Ratface."

Leo grabbed her wrist. "I think that's a spectacularly bad plan."

"Maybe, but it's the best one I've got," she said, pulling her arm free. "See you soon."

"Ariel!" Leo hissed after her, but she was already gone. All he could do now was follow her instructions.

The five of them huddled together in the darkness under the stairs, counting the seconds, ears straining for any sound that might tell them what was going on outside. Leo bobbed up and down gently to try to keep the little girl on his back calm, while Liane was on the verge of tears and attempting to breathe through it. Vika put a hand on her shoulder.

"Hey," she whispered. "It's going to be okay."

"They'll put me in jail," Liane said. "They'll take my children away and put them in an orphanage."

"That's not going to happen," Leo reassured her, even though he knew there was nothing he could do to stop it.

When at least three minutes had passed, they came out from under the stairs and crept out of the building. There were no mercs in sight, and the alley was empty and silent.

"Where are we going?" Vika asked.

Luckily Liane knew, because Leo wasn't sure how he would explain his knowledge of where Ariel and her father warehoused their ship. They made their way through the streets, trying to find a balance between moving quickly and not attracting attention. Mercifully, the baby was now sleeping soundly in Liane's arms and the girl seemed content on Leo's back, even though his arms were beginning to ache from holding her.

They reached the warehouse at the docks, and Leo pretended not to know exactly where the ship was parked as Liane searched in vain for it among the other salvagers and junked transports that littered the space. It was straining his nerves, knowing that every second could mean mercs bursting through the doors.

"Have we tried over here yet?" he finally asked, steering the group in the direction of the northwest corner of the hangar. "Does anything look familiar?"

"Oh, there it is," Liane sobbed as she rushed up to the ancient skiff. "Thank the stars."

"Now we wait, I suppose," Leo said, trying not to imagine the other possibilities. Ariel already apprehended, being dragged off to detention, Liane stranded on Philomenus to suffer the same fate, her children parentless, himself and Vika caught up in all of it.

"Do you think the girl's okay?" Vika asked him softly.

"I hope so," he said, dizzy at the other possibilities. "She seems . . . pretty tough."

"It's possible this was not my best idea ever," Vika said. "I should have left well enough alone when you told me to."

He tried to smile, for her benefit. "What else did we have to do today?"

They all jumped at the sudden clang of a door crashing open, followed by footsteps pounding concrete. Ariel, red-faced and sweating, came running toward them. She raised her hand and tossed something in the air at Leo; he instinctively reached up and caught it. Keys.

"Get in!" she said. "They're not far behind me."

He reached up to stick the key in the lock beside the sliding door that led into the interior of the skiff, but his hands were shaking and clumsy. Vika withstood his fumbling for about two seconds before she grabbed the keys from him and pushed him aside, unlocking the door and throwing it open just as Ariel reached them.

Leo gave Liane his hand as she climbed aboard and then handed her daughter up to her. Ariel offered her hand to Vika.

"I hope you're still determined not to let me out of your sight," she said to Vika, "because you're a part of this now."

"I guess I am," Vika said, climbing aboard.

"Why did you bring her here?" Ariel whispered furiously when the two of them were the only ones left standing in the hangar.

"I didn't!" he said. "I'll explain later."

"This is bad."

"I know."

"Well, it's too late to do anything about it now," she said. "Get in."

Leo climbed aboard to join the others in the cargo area while Ariel clambered in after him, securing the door behind them. Once the door was bolted into place, she kicked aside a bin full of tools and engine parts and reached for a small metal ring in the floor. Grunting, she lifted up what turned out to be a large panel that was acting as a lid to a small cavity in the skiff's floor.

"In you go," she said to Liane. Liane nodded and lay down in the narrow space, her baby clutched to her chest and her daughter nestled in tightly beside her. Ariel gently lowered the panel back over them, hiding them from sight. Then she lifted a second panel, revealing another cavity about a foot away from the first. She turned to Leo and Vika. "Okay, your turn."

"What?" Vika said. "We're not fugitives."

"This skiff is only registered for one occupant working the stream at a time," Ariel said. "If they scan me and see more than one person aboard, they'll take me in. These compartments are lined with an isotopic alloy that confuses the sensors, so get in. Now."

Leo frowned; he hadn't heard of this before, so he supposed it was lucky Ariel hadn't been scanned when she'd been returning to Philomenus with his unconscious body. But there was no time to think of that now, because he was too occupied with the fact that Ariel was asking him to share a *very* small space with Vika.

He looked over at Vika. The corners of her mouth were pinched tightly.

"I'll get out," he told Ariel. "Just leave me here and I'll make my way back to town."

"Don't be stupid," Ariel said, giving him a *look*. "You'll get caught. We all will."

"It's fine!" Vika said, stepping into the compartment. "Just get in and let's get out of here before they find us."

She lay down and Leo shot Ariel a miserable look before climbing in after her. He took pains to touch her as little as possible as he arranged his body beside hers, pressing his back into the side of the compartment until the metal girders dug into his skin to give her more room. But still she was mere centimeters from him and when Ariel lowered the panel and plunged them into darkness, she seemed even closer. He could actually feel the warmth radiating from her skin, could feel the way the air shifted around him as she breathed.

"Hold on!" came Ariel's muffled voice from the direction of the cockpit. The engine roared to life, and moments later they were lifting off the ground, metal grinding and vibrating around Leo as the wheels retracted into the ship. Without warning, Ariel punched the gas, launching them forward and to the left. Vika yelped as the g-force knocked into them, making her roll back against him. The force didn't let up, pushing her tighter against him, sandwiching him more firmly between her and metal at his back, pressing the air out of his lungs, but he managed to unpin one arm enough to get it around her waist. It felt safer that way, like he might be able to protect her if they suddenly changed directions, although logically he knew he wasn't nearly strong enough to hold her in place if it was him against physics. He tried not to notice the warmth of her body or the smell of her soap or any of the other sensations that crowded against him in the dark.

Once they broke atmo, the pressure lessened and he pulled his arm away.

"I'm sorry about this," he whispered.

He felt her shift, and soon he could just make out her face in the near-darkness as she turned to face him. "It's none of your doing. I could have stopped at any point but I'm too damn stubborn."

And he had just gone along for the ride, as usual, so afraid of doing the wrong thing that he did nothing at all.

"I guess things have gotten pretty bad while I've been gone, huh?" she said.

"Yes."

"Maybe . . . we can fix that," she said. "If we find out the truth."

A lock of her hair was brushing against his neck and causing an infuriating, ticklish itch on his skin, and one of her knees was pressed into his thigh. He wanted to close the small gap between them so badly he thought he might die of it.

Instead he moved his leg away from hers.

"I hope so," he said, and they lay there together in the dark and the silence while Leo tried not to feel her breathing.

Eventually, he heard movement above him, and then Ariel was lifting the panel that covered them, cool air rushing into the compartment that had grown warm and stuffy with recycled oxygen. "Okay," she said. "I think it's safe to come out now."

They climbed out of the cavity and then helped Liane and her children out of theirs. Ariel returned to the pilot's seat, and Leo could see that they were deep in the stream, Ploutos looming large in front of them.

Ariel glanced at Vika over her shoulder while Liane strapped herself and her daughter into the passenger's seat. "Can I trust you to keep your mouth shut about what you're going to see?"

"I don't care about your business," Vika replied. "I just want my questions answered. Nothing else concerns me."

Leo gave Ariel a tiny nod. "You can trust us. I promise."

"Okay, then," she said. "Guess I an't got much of a choice any-way."

As she maneuvered through the stream slowly and deliberately, as though trolling for debris to collect, Ariel reached for her comm, which was emitting constant low-volume chatter from the other ships in the stream. She dialed into a new frequency, one that was totally silent.

"Sprinter to Outpost Six, come in," she said.

There was a moment of silence and then a voice crackled back, "Receiving you loud and clear, Sprinter."

"Outpost, I'm on my way to you with an express package," Ariel said.

"Roger that, Sprinter. Safe flying."

As the skiff approached Ploutos, Ariel killed all the running lights inside and outside the craft and set a course away from the Plou-tosian space ports and toward a more isolated part of the planet. Leo had always known, of course, that she smuggled people across the stream for the PLF, just one link in a chain that got people who needed to leave Philomenus off-world when there was no other way for them to escape. But he'd never seen her in action before. She was so cool under pressure, so decisive. He had never been those things, and he was slightly in awe of her.

Eventually, they touched down at a small building surrounded by woods. Ariel helped Liane and her children out of the craft, leading them to the building where someone outlined by the lighted win-dow behind them was waiting. This was where Ariel's job ended; she had gotten Liane from Philomenus to Ploutos. The next link in the chain would get her somewhere else, where she and her kids could start a new life, hopefully a better one.

"I knew this kind of thing happened," Vika said as she and Leo waited for Ariel to return, "but I can't say I ever expected to be part of it."

"No, me neither."

She turned to look at him. "I'm glad you were here. I would have been a lot more scared if I'd been alone."

His throat went dry and he had to swallow before he could say, "I'm glad, too."

Ariel returned, hauling herself up into the pilot's seat. She turned to look at Vika. "Want to ask me your questions now? It's a long ride back, and I don't know what might be waiting for us on Philomenus."

"So it was you the eyewitness saw near the *Leander* that night?" Vika asked.

Ariel nodded. "Yeah, I was there. My father is so out of his mind most of the time that he has no idea I use the ship when he's out drinking. Usually I'm just salvaging debris so the two of us don't starve."

"And you didn't go to the authorities about the explosion because—"

"Cause the authorities an't people I trust with anything," she said. "And obviously I'm involved with some things I'd rather they didn't know about, so I didn't want anyone looking at me too close. But honestly, I just happened to be nearby when that spaceliner blew. I didn't have anything to do with the bomb, and neither did anyone else in the PLF."

Vika glanced at Sky and then back at Ariel. "How can you be sure?"

"Cause," Ariel said, "they're *my people*. I would know."

With all of Vika's questions answered, Ariel helped them back into the hidden compartments and they took off. When they got back to Philomenus, Ariel landed the craft at another warehouse in a different part of town. She couldn't go back to her old hangar bay, at least not until the heat was off. Vika thanked her for her help and then began the walk back toward town.

Once Vika's back was turned, Leo squeezed Ariel's hand. "Talk to you soon," he whispered, and then hurried after Vika.

"So," he said as he caught up with her, "do you believe her?"

"I don't see how I couldn't after all of that." Vika stopped and tore the heels from her feet, hurling them into the empty field of dry grass. "Another dead bloody end!"

"Well, the more dead-ends we hit, the closer we must be to finding something useful, right?"

She kept walking toward town, barefooted now. "Are you a weirdly optimistic person and I've just never noticed before?"

"Hardly. I just . . ." He sighed. "You seem to be taking this hard, and I suppose I just want to make you feel better."

She looked at him sideways. "Why? I've never exactly been nice to you."

"That's not true."

She raised an eyebrow at him.

"There've been *moments*," he said. "You bought me lunch the other day."

"Ah yes, I'm practically a saint," she said. "I am sorry, you know. If I've been unfair to you."

He shook his head. "When everyone wants something from you, it can be hard to trust people. I understand that."

"I think you're just a glutton for punishment," she said. "Why else would you stay in a job where you're treated so poorly?"

"Ah, spotted that, have you?"

"It's hard to miss," she said. "The Hal I first met was such a kind, openhearted man. But now . . ."

"He's changed?" Leo asked it like a question, but he knew it wasn't. The man he now worked for bore little resemblance to the Hal of his childhood memories, who used to give him piggyback rides along the corridors and let Leo act as his assistant as he went around fixing things, trailing at his heels like an eager puppy. Maybe he had just been too young to know the real Hal, the person who was more complex than just a kindly father figure, or maybe the money really was eating away at Hal's soul.

Vika nodded. "It hurts me to say, but I think it's all gone to his head. Or maybe, I don't know, it just released something that was always inside of him. In fact, I'm starting to worry that . . ."

He waited for her to finish, but she was biting her lip, like she didn't want to let the words out. "That what?"

She shook her head. "Nothing. Never mind."

"You can tell me," he said.

"No, because if I say it, I can't ever unsay it, and I couldn't bear to be wrong," she said. "But the way he talks to you sometimes . . . it makes me feel sick."

"Well." He smiled. "That's something at least."

She rolled her eyes good-naturedly. "Yes, you should take my nausea as a great compliment."

"I do."

"I guess I just don't understand why you put up with it," she said.

He shrugged. "It's a job. It pays me well enough to live and it's dependable work."

"But you're so smart," she said. "You could get another job."

"Maybe I prefer the devil I know."

She frowned. "I don't believe you. What's the real reason?"

He looked at her, her cheeks flushed and sweat beading at her hairline, her dress stained from the greasy interior of Ariel's skiff, her hair mussed around her face, and all he could think about was what it would feel like to kiss her.

"I don't think you'd believe me if I told you," he said. "But I have my reasons."

"Good ones?"

He nodded. "Very good ones."

CHAPTER THIRTY

ANOTHER NIGHT, ANOTHER PARTY. She was headed back to the symphony for the first time since her initial night on Ploutos, but thinking back to the girl she'd been that evening, she already felt like an entirely different creature. She'd been so scared of fitting in, so giddy with excitement, the contradictory emotions swirling around inside of her and fizzing up within her like bubbles in a champagne flute. She had imagined herself dressing up and going out every night and never tiring of it, but now she was faintly bored at the prospect of another night discussing the same dull topics with the same rather dull people. Was she really so spoiled already that she required increasingly elaborate entertainment to please her? Or was this discontent simmering in her belly something else entirely?

She wondered if Mr. Keid would be there and couldn't decide if the spiking of her pulse whenever she thought of him was excitement or anxiety. The day after the party at the botanical gardens, he'd had four dozen roses delivered to her, along with an invitation to dinner that weekend. Mira had clapped and squeezed her shoulders, and Vika had tried to smile. She'd sent Mr. Keid a message saying she was visiting her family but could they have dinner the next weekend, and he'd agreed. Now that date was fast approaching, and the roses were beginning to wilt at the edges where they sat on her vanity, their sickly sweet fragrance tinged with the scent of rot.

Vika was less fastidious about her dressing than usual, so she was ready to go sooner than she expected. Mira and Hal would still be getting ready, so she stole down to the kitchen, hoping to grab a snack while the cook was off duty. Otherwise he'd insist on preparing her something and she didn't feel like being waited on. In her gown and bare feet, she snuck inside the kitchen and opened the door to the massive refrigerator that was always fully stocked and clearly labeled. She rooted around, coming out with a container of riverberries and a hunk of Demetriosi cheese.

She was hunting for a knife when she heard raised voices nearby. She recognized the deepest tone as Hal; the kitchen was in the working part of the house, just down the corridor from his office. She opened the kitchen door a crack.

"—have it to them by tomorrow morning," he was saying. "I don't care how long it takes you. I pay you more than enough to justify one night's overtime with no complaints."

"Yes, sir," she heard Sky reply. "Of course. I'll have it ready for you by the time you return."

"You might thank me for providing you with such a good job in the first place," Hal continued, "and be grateful for it."

"I am, sir."

Vika tried to imagine how she would have reacted if Nicky had ever said such a thing to her. She had depended on that job to help keep food on her family's table, so she would have tried to hold her tongue. But knowing her temper, she suspected she would have dumped a pitcher of grock over his head before she let him condescend to her that way.

But Sky was so patient and, well, *kind* that he didn't even seem to mind the indignity. She probably would have been disgusted with his attitude only months ago, thinking him weak and perhaps a bit pathetic, but she had believed him when he said he had a good reason to stay in this job. That made his forbearance seem almost admirable. There was a quiet kind of steadiness in him that intrigued her, maybe because it was so unlike anything she'd ever known in herself.

Which was why she wasn't just going to let this happen. She dropped her snack and rushed out into the hallway.

"Hal!" she called, opening the door to his office. "Oh, there you are. You're not dressed yet!"

"No," Hal said. Sky was sitting in a chair while Hal was perched on the edge of his desk, hanging over him like a big black cloud. "Mr. Foster and I have had some business to attend to."

She gave Hal her most charming smile and threaded her arm through his, drawing him away from Sky. "Well, you'd better hurry or the old lady won't be happy!"

He smiled. "I believe you're right, my dear. I'll head upstairs. Foster, back to work."

"Yes, sir."

Hal headed toward the foyer, and Vika hung back.

"I'm sorry about that," she said to Sky.

He smiled at her, although the expression looked to have cracks around the edges. "I appreciate the rescue."

"Are you all right?" she asked, troubled by the sadness she thought she could feel radiating off of him. "Truly?"

He nodded. "I'll be fine. Enjoy your evening, Miss Hale."

She found herself reluctant to just leave him there. Probably, she reasoned, because the idea of the symphony didn't exactly seem enjoyable to her right then. But she knew that was ridiculous, so she wished Sky a good night and went to collect her shoes and bag.

She and the Gardners were once against guests of Evelyn Lyons and took their seats in her box by the stage. No sign of Mr. Keid, and Vika was happy to discover that Archer was also one of Ms. Lyons's guests. The evening was looking up as he took the seat beside hers when the music began to play.

Archer leaned over and whispered in her ear, "You look stunning, as usual."

She tried to smile. He couldn't know how hungry she was becoming to receive some morsel of compliment or praise for anything other than the way she looked. "Thank you."

"Ah, Archer." Hal had stood, ready to join the parade of men moving from box to box. "I have some instructions regarding the estate that my assistant will be sending over to you shortly."

"Excellent, sir," Archer said. "I will see to it first thing."

Hal patted his shoulder. "Good lad."

When he was gone, Archer turned back to her. "I'm glad Mr. Gardner is keeping that assistant of his busy. Gives him less time to proposition you, I imagine."

"Oh, that." Vika waved her hand. "It was nothing, really. He's not so bad."

"I can hardly blame him anyway." Archer reached out and gently repositioned one of the jewels in her hair to make it more secure. "You are . . ."

Vika held her breath.

". . . so beautiful."

She exhaled slowly.

The Lyonses' box began to empty as soon as the lights came up for the interval, people joining the stream headed to the lobby for drinks and gossip. Vika and Archer were sitting in the far corner of the box, so it was nearly empty by the time Vika stood to follow.

Archer's hand encircled her wrist. "Vika, wait."

She turned back to him, expecting that he had noticed something she'd dropped or needed to tie his shoe before following her from the box. But his face was suddenly so serious, every hint of his mischievous smile gone, that anxious butterflies instantly came to life in her stomach.

"I've wanted to say these words to you for so long," he said. "And I am sure they will come as no surprise to you because I have been so obviously entranced with you since the day we met, but I didn't feel I was able to declare myself before. I will never be worthy of you, but as a lowly associate solicitor I couldn't even dare to hope.

But I have spoken to Ms. Lyons and she says I will be promoted by the summer."

Vika frowned. Her brain, suddenly so slow and stupid, was not keeping pace with his words. "I . . . I don't understand . . ."

He smiled. "Of course you don't. I'm babbling like a fool, but then that's what you do to me. Viktoria Hale, I am most profoundly, desperately in love with you."

All of the air left Vika's lungs in a whoosh, like she was in a spacecraft that had just hit atmo, g-force slamming her sideways. "You . . . you're what?"

He was still holding her hand, and he used it to draw her down into the seat next to him. "You can hardly be surprised since I've made no secret of it. And you've given me so much reason to hope."

"Archer—" Bloody hell, the butterflies in her stomach were lurching around inside her now. Not so long ago this would have made her happy. If she had told the girl sitting on the roof of her TH with the handsome, charming young solicitor from Ploutos that he would one day be declaring his love for her, she would have been thrilled.

"I know I'm no Mr. Keid," he continued, "but I'll be the youngest senior solicitor Lassiter and Lyons has ever had, and I'll be able to provide you with a comfortable life. And I don't intend to stop there. One day that firm, this box, all of it, will be mine, I promise you." He drew her hand up to his lips, pressing a kiss to her knuckles. "And more importantly, I love you and I always will. We're cut from the same cloth, you and I. No one has ever understood me like you do. Please, Viktoria, make me the happiest man on this planet and say you'll marry me."

She was frozen. She knew she should be happy. Archer could be the perfect solution to all of her problems. He might not be as rich as Mr. Keid, but she actually *liked* him. She didn't think she was in love with him, but there were times when the brush of his fingers or his gaze meeting hers made her heart beat faster and she wondered. If nothing else she enjoyed spending time with him, and maybe that could blossom into real love in time.

She shook herself. Since when was *love* her primary concern, anyway? Archer could give her a good life. Not an extravagant one, perhaps, not like the way she lived with the Gardners or would if she were Mrs. Keid, but she would never have to worry about the power going out in the middle of winter or having enough food on the table. She wouldn't be able to bring her family to Ploutos on a solicitor's salary, but there should be enough for her to send money home and perhaps help them move out of the THs in time.

The question was, was that enough for her?

"Oh, Archer." She slipped her hand out of his. "I'm very fond of you. There are so many times I might have gone crazy if it weren't for you and your friendship."

His face fell. "But?"

"I'm sorry." She felt sick to her stomach. "I . . . I can't accept your proposal."

He sighed. "I don't suppose begging would help my cause? It would be embarrassing but I'd be happy to do it if it might make a difference."

She shook her head.

"I understand," he said, standing. "I'm not grand enough for you. You're like me, ambitious, and I respect that. I daresay it's part of why I love you."

Her mouth dropped open. "That's not it—"

He gave her a sharp, almost conspiratorial smile. "No, of course it isn't. If you'll excuse me, I believe a drink is in order."

He left her alone in the box, and she sat there, heart pounding as though she'd run a kilometer. That's not it, she'd told him, feeling affronted. But of course she was lying, wasn't she? She liked Archer much better than Mr. Keid, so it had to be the fact that he was barely clinging to the edge of Ploutosian high society, not much more than a glorified servant, that kept her from accepting his proposal.

She wanted someone richer, not just someone . . . else.

Right?

* * *

The rest of the performance seemed to stretch on for hours. Vika
did her best to keep her attention focused on the orchestra, hoping her apparent absorption in the music would keep anyone from
talking to her. It mostly worked, except she could feel Archer's gaze,
heavy with what she supposed must be longing, on her throughout
the night from the seat he had switched to at the other end of the
box. As soon as the musicians took their bows, she leaned over to
Hal and asked if they could go straight home, pleading a terrible
headache.

Once they arrived back at the penthouse, Hal called out for Sky
and headed for the office. Vika heard them talking as a maid took
her coat, and she hoped Hal wouldn't find some fault with Sky's
work so he could just go home in peace. She gave Mira a kiss and
headed upstairs to nurse her nonexistent headache. But it felt like
the walls of her bedroom were closing in on her, more claustropho-
bic than the tiny rooms of her TH had ever been. So many thoughts
crowded her head, suffocating her. How had she ended up here? A
few months ago she'd just been a simple girl, a barmaid on a nothing
little planet, idly dreaming of a better life she never really expected
to have. Her days had been easy. Well, not easy. They had been full
of struggle, but there were no *decisions* to make. Her circumstances
made all her decisions for her, so she never really had anything to
lose by making the wrong choice. As doubts about turning down
Archer's proposal nagged at her, she realized what a strange sort of
gift that had been.

If only she'd never met Rigel Chapin, never let the damn Shadow
Man buy her that freeze cream when she was a little girl. Who was
he to turn her life upside down this way? Her whole life revolved
around him and yet he was still a total stranger to her.

Vika wasn't aware of making the decision until she was opening
the door to the stairwell that led down to the lower level of the penthouse. Mira and Hal hadn't touched it since Mr. Chapin died, and
she was suddenly perversely curious about it. Maybe it would help

her make some sense of the man who had thrown her life into such chaos, give her some idea why he had chosen her.

She descended the stairs feeling like a burglar, waiting for lights to come on and sirens to wail, but of course there were none. The air felt still and stagnant, and even the moonlight coming in through the windows seemed a little dimmer, filtered through the ghosts that lived down here.

She wasn't sure what she was expecting, but it was a perfectly normal flat, if decidedly less elegant than the one two levels above, with lower ceilings and less grand fixtures. Much of the furniture was covered, but that which did show was shabbier than she would have imagined, as though it had been fine once but then been lived in so long that it had begun to break down and fray. She wandered through the rooms, occasionally running her fingers over the top of a chair or the spine of a book, trying to imagine the man who had lived here in this collection of rooms for twenty cycles. Why had he retreated from the brighter levels above him, driving away everyone who should have loved him? What kind of person collected one of the largest fortunes in the quadrant but didn't seem to spend it and had no one to leave it to other than an estranged son, a couple of servants, and a handful of charities? Part of her had hated Rigel Chapin for so long for turning her into a thing to be bought and sold and given away, but looking at this sad collection of rooms, she began to wonder if she should feel sorry for him instead.

She reached the last room in the flat, one which she knew she'd been subconsciously avoiding. There was no trace of any child in these rooms, no toys or picture books or brightly colored things. Mira spoke to her only rarely about her would-be fiancé, usually when she was a little tipsy and emotional, tears welling instantly in her eyes when she said his name. According to her, Leo had been sensitive and kind and terribly held down by his father, but Vika couldn't imagine Mira having a bad opinion of anyone, and she knew how much a person could change when they left home. Since he'd died, Vika had spared only a handful of thoughts for the man she would have married, mostly forgetting about him. Maybe if she learned anything more about who he'd been, she wouldn't be able to do that so easily, which was why she'd avoided his bedroom.

But with so much uncertainty in her life, the idea of taking a peek at the one path that was definitely closed to her now was becoming oddly irresistible. What might her life had been if the *Leander* had docked safely on Ploutos?

She slowly pushed open the door and stared in confusion at what she found.

"Sky?" she said.

He shot up from the chair he'd been slumped in, head buried in his hands. "Miss Hale!"

"What are you doing here?"

He looked around the room. "I, uh . . . I just needed a moment. To collect myself. I'm not entirely sure how I ended up down here."

"Hal?" she asked.

"Yes, he's not exactly pleased with me right now." He frowned at her. "What brings you down here?"

"I guess I was just curious," she said. "Is that morbid?"

"Perhaps." His smile was gently teasing. "But I think it's understandable."

"This was my fiancé's room," she said, looking around. It was more . . . sterile than she had expected. Leo Chapin, she knew, had been sent away to school when he was young, but, as with the rest of the flat, there were very few signs a little boy had ever lived here. Only a bookshelf full of adolescent novels and the telescope that stood beside the window marked this as anything other than a guest bedroom. She picked up one of the novels from the shelf, examining the cover as though it might give her some insight. "I don't really know anything about who he was."

"I don't know if you'll be able to glean much from this room," Sky said, sitting on the sofa by the window.

She sat beside him. "I think you're right. Was Hal very harsh with you?"

He looked down, picking at a fraying seam in the upholstery. "He's under a lot of stress. How was your evening?"

She sighed, considering how to answer that. "Confusing. I feel like I've been confused about one thing or another for months now."

"I know what you mean."

"I just don't understand it," she burst out suddenly. "Why would he pick me? Of all the girls to choose from, why would Mr. Chapin choose me for his son and turn my whole life on its head?"

Sky shifted to face her, running his eyes over her, like he was contemplating the question, looking for the answer in her features. "I have a theory."

"What?" she asked. "He thought I'd make a suitable ornament on the arm of his son who could give him strong, healthy little heirs and was too poor and desperate to turn down his insane scheme?"

Sky's smile was faint. "No doubt that was part of the calculation, but I suspect it was something else entirely that made you his choice. From everything I've gathered about the man, Mr. Chapin thought his son was weak. You, Viktoria Hale"—he looked her right in the eyes—"are strong. *That* is why he picked you."

The breath she took was unexpectedly deep, like it was her first inhalation of air after being just on the edge of suffocating.

"Strong . . ." she whispered. It sounded like a compliment when Sky said it, looking at her like that, but why would Mr. Chapin care about her strength? From what she could see, Mr. Chapin had cared for nothing but his fortune. That was when she understood. "Oh, I see. Strong like uncompromising, you mean. Like *ruthless.*"

"Maybe that's what he'd hoped for," Sky said. "That you could keep his soft, feckless son in line, stop him from squandering his inheritance and ruining the family name and business."

Vika's stomach began to roil, and she stood, pacing away from Sky.

"But if that's what he wanted, I think he made a mistake," he continued.

"Did he?" It was bad enough that Mr. Chapin thought—rightly, as it turned out—that she could be bought. But him wanting to buy her for her hardness and selfishness, the worst parts of her, was even worse. She thought she might be sick. "I am those things, aren't I? He had me tested and monitored most of my life to be sure of it, and he must have been sure to pick me."

"No." Sky stood and caught her by the shoulders, halting the momentum she was building up. "He didn't know you. *I* know you. You're tough and shrewd and heavens help you a true pain in the ass sometimes, but you've had to be those things to survive. And underneath all of that, you're also kinder and more caring than I think you know. So Mr. Chapin would have been disappointed with you, but Leo . . ." He swallowed. "Leo would have been lucky."

Vika felt weak and shaky, and she barely had the strength to lift her eyes up to his. "Do you really think so?" she whispered.

He slowly raised one hand so that his fingers hovered just over her cheek, so close she swore she could feel the warmth from them on her skin. She held her breath.

"I do," he said.

He was so close and his eyes were so soft and he sounded so sincere. She wanted to lean her cheek into his hand and feel his fingers curl around her jaw, and maybe that was why she found herself backing away from him.

"I should go," she said. But she paused at the door, because she was already saving his words somewhere inside of her to bring out and examine again later, like a letter to be reread until it's thin and tattered around the edges. She glanced back at him. "Thank you. For saying that."

One corner of his mouth turned up. "Thank you for letting me."

CHAPTER THIRTY-ONE

AS HE LEFT CHAPIN TOWER, Leo felt as though his insides had been given a good shake and now nothing was quite where it should be. He had tried to keep his composure in front of Vika, because why would an assistant being abused by his boss be that upsetting or uncommon, but his treatment from Hal was tearing him up inside. Each rebuke was like a knife to his heart, making him doubt his own memories of the person he had once loved so much. They turned him into that little boy again, quaking with fear at disappointing the only man he wanted to please, knowing deep down in his bones that he would never be right, never be enough. When Hal had shouted at him and told him to get out of his sight, he had meant to take the lift down to the lobby and head back to Philomenus, but instead he'd found himself running down the stairs into his old home, taking refuge in his childhood bedroom the way he had so many times growing up. Powerless and utterly unsure of what to do, he had been more miserable in that moment than he could ever remember being.

But then she'd been there, his own misery reflected back at him in her eyes, and he'd felt so close to her. She felt it, too, he was sure.

It made him want to *hope*, as he hadn't since the days they'd spent alone together at Greenbriar House.

But hope, he knew from bitter experience, was dangerous.

When he got back to TH 76, he discovered Ariel and Mr. Hale sitting together on the front stoop, their faces lit by a flickering streetlamp as they chatted.

"Oh, Sky," Mr. Hale said, hastily stubbing out a dakha cig when he spotted him. "Your kind sister here offered me one for turning a blind eye to her staying in your flat a few weeks ago, and I could hardly say no without seeming rude, could I? Don't tell the missus, eh?"

"Never," Leo reassured him. Mrs. Hale was a fearsome thing at the best of times.

"What kept you?" Ariel asked. "I've been waiting for ages."

"I had to work late," Leo said. "Vika sends her love, Mr. Hale."

The man beamed. "She's well?"

"Very well," Leo said. "Other than missing you, of course, sir."

Mr. Hale stood, pocketing what was left of the cig, and clapped a hand on Leo's shoulder. "It's damn lucky for me that she rented you that room before she left. I know she's all grown so I don't want to be a bother to her, but I believe I'd go crazy not knowing how she was doing over there on that planet. It makes me feel better just knowing you're there, looking out for her. You're heavens-sent, my boy."

Leo's throat got suddenly tight. "Thank you, sir. But I don't think your daughter needs anyone to protect her."

Mr. Hale laughed. "You're probably right. Maybe it's Ploutos that needs protecting from her. Your day off soon, isn't it? Join me for a drink?"

Leo nodded. "It would be my pleasure."

After Mr. Hale had gone inside, Ariel said, "He's a nice man."

"The nicest."

"Hard to believe he raised a daughter who is so . . . forceful? Assertive?"

"You obviously haven't met her mother."

Ariel shivered. "Nor do I wish to."

She followed him inside, up the four flights of stairs to his small studio flat, which consisted of a single bed next to a window that looked out into the blanket of fog, a one-burner cooktop and refrigerator, and a rickety bureau where he stored his few items of clothing. He set his ancient teakettle to boil on the cooktop, while Ariel sat on his only chair, the one pulled up to the plank of wood attached to the wall that served as his desk and dining table. She picked up the slip of paper that was on it.

"You okay?" she asked, holding up the past-due rent notice. "Need some help?"

"I'm just a little behind. I'm taking care of it," he said. "Remember when I told you money didn't matter?"

She snorted. "Yeah."

"That was *profoundly* stupid of me," he said. "I appreciate your self-discipline in not immediately punching me in the face."

She smiled. "It was pretty hard. So, any luck with the investigation?"

"Definitely none of that," he said, "but I have made a bit of progress. One of the shell companies my father left money to is tied to a propaganda operation on Korybas. There's a movement there to make scientific disclosure of technologies used on the planet mandatory—which would require my father to give up his business there or reveal the trade secrets behind his reactor process—so that appears to be nothing more than a business move. The other two shells are better constructed, though. I'm having a hard time figuring out who's behind them."

"Well, that's better than nothing, at least."

"Barely." The kettle screamed and he reached to take it off of the burner, so distracted by his thoughts that he forgot to use a tea towel to protect his hand. He grabbed the bare metal handle and hissed as it sizzled against his hand, dropping the thing with a clang. "Dammit!"

Ariel jumped to her feet. "Here," she said, taking his hand and thrusting it into the sink. She turned on the cold tap.

He looked at the angry red skin underneath the water. "I'm sorry, Ariel," he said softly. "I'm trying to clear the PLF, I really am. But I just keep hitting dead end after dead end."

"Don't you worry about that," she said. "We can take care of ourselves."

"But I *do* worry about it," he said. "I see the food lines and the clinics being closed and the mercs on every corner. Every day I worry that you're going to be hauled off to detention. And I feel like I could fix it if I could just prove that the PLF didn't plant that bomb on the *Leander.*"

She gave him a sweet, sad smile that made her look ten cycles older than she actually was. "Oh, Leo. That wouldn't fix it." She turned off the tap and examined his hand. "I think you'll live. So, what's your next step?"

He shrugged and, using a tea towel this time, poured out two cups of tea, black for Ariel and with milk for him. "I keep trying. I can't abandon the PLF after all they've done for me, and I can't leave Mira in danger."

"And Vika?"

"Her, either."

She gave him a look. "That *so* an't what I meant."

"Nothing's changed," he said, although he felt his face heating as he remembered how she'd looked up at him with big, soft eyes as he held his hand just a hair's breadth from her face. "She made her feelings clear, and I respect that."

"But I thought—"

He shook his head as he scooped a precious spoonful of sugar into Ariel's tea, knowing her sweet tooth. "I can't start thinking that way. It's too hard. I'm here for Mira and the PLF, and if Vika doesn't completely despise me in the meantime, well, that's simply a pleasant bonus."

"And she hasn't said anything about me? Told anyone about me and my . . . cargo?"

"No, of course not." He sipped his tea, realized the milk he'd added to it had curdled, and dumped it into the sink. What a waste. "If only I could get ahold of the Gardners' will. I'm sure Vika was right and the perpetrator stands to gain financially. I've learned everything I can from the Chapin will but I still can't get my hands on Hal's."

"He won't let you look at it?" she asked.

He shook his head. "He doesn't trust me. I've tried every excuse I can think of to get a glimpse of it, but he's dodged them all. I've tried to finagle it out of Lassiter and Lyons with no success, and Hal's holo has a biometric lock on it."

"Is that all? We should go talk to Maia," Ariel said. "She does tech stuff for the PLF. I bet she'll know a way to hack that holo. I'll find out where she's hiding and take you in the morning."

Leo gazed at her in wonder. Had she really just solved his problem in ten seconds flat? "What would I do without you?"

She laughed. "Die, probably, since you're basically as helpless as a little baby."

He pulled her close and kissed the top of her head. "My hero."

Leo walked toward Chapin Tower feeling lighter on his feet than he had for weeks, like gravity had a less solid hold on him than usual. It had taken several hours that morning, starting well before the sun had risen, to track down the PLF's hacker, Maia. Like most of the upper leadership of the Philomeni Liberation Front, she was deep in hiding, knowing the mercs would instantly scoop her up and disappear her if they got half a chance. They'd finally found her staying in the attic of a shop whose owner owed the PLF a favor. She was sleeping on a cot under the eaves with little more than the clothes on her back and a bag full of her most indispensable gadgets.

"Oh, I've got exactly what you need," she'd said when they explained the problem of getting into Hal's holo. "It's a device that'll let you pull a fingerprint off of practically any surface and recreate it to fool a biosensor."

"That's amazing, Maia," Ariel had said. "This might be just what we've been looking for to clear the PLF of the bombing."

"I an't got it with me, though," Maia had added. "It's in my workshop."

Leo had kept watch while Ariel shimmied into Maia's workshop through a back window, rummaging until she found the device Maia had described in painstaking detail: a rectangle of metal, a little smaller than the palm of Ariel's hand, with a glass plate on top and a long, thin opening along the bottom.

It was now hidden in the pocket of Leo's coat, lightly bumping his thigh with each step he took toward Chapin Tower. Soon he would have the information he needed to unmask the person targeting the Chapin heirs. Soon Mira and Vika would be safe, the PLF would be cleared, and he would be free to leave the twin planets and start his new life.

As he was headed inside the doors of Chapin Tower, someone else was heading out. He didn't see the dark-haired young man until it was too late, and they collided.

"Oh, terribly sorry," Leo said, patting his pocket to make sure the device was still secure inside.

The other man, who looked familiar, gave him a strangely bright smile. "Oh no, it's all my fault."

When the lift doors opened into the Gardners' penthouse, Leo was surprised to find Vika there, as though she were waiting for him. She had pressed herself flat against the wall and was peering around the corner into the foyer. She spun at the sound of the doors sliding open, her eyes wide.

"Get out of here," she hissed, waving him away.

"What?"

She rushed to his side and pushed him back into the lift carriage.

Distantly, he heard the sound of Hal's voice raised in anger and then something smashing.

"Tell him you were sick or something," she said. "He's been raging for half an hour. You don't want to walk into it."

"What happened?" he asked.

"I have no idea, but you should leave."

"I can't just go," he said. "I finally know how to—"

"Foster?" came Hal's voice, closer now.

"Go!" Vika said, but Leo pushed past her.

"Yes, sir, I'm here," he said.

Hal appeared at the top of the stairs, his face full of thunder and a pale-faced Mira at his heels.

When he spoke, his voice was deadly, stonily calm. "I would like to speak with you. And you, too, Viktoria."

CHAPTER THIRTY-TWO

VIKA FOLLOWED HAL, MIRA, and Sky into the sitting room, feeling like she was being marched to the gallows. She didn't know why; neither she nor Sky had done anything wrong. But the air was heavy, like the minute before a thunderstorm.

"Have a seat, my dears," Hal said gently to her and Mira, gesturing to the sofa clad in rose-colored silk. "I wanted you to be here for this, Viktoria, because a wrong has been done to you, and I want you to see it righted."

"A wrong?" Vika asked, bewildered, as she sat beside Mira.

Hal turned to face Sky, the two of them standing on opposite sides of the fireplace, staring each other down.

"Well, Foster," Hal said. "What do you have to say for yourself?"

"Hal—" Mira began to protest.

"You will let me handle this, darling," Hal interrupted sharply. "I assume you know what this is about, Foster?"

Sky glanced at her, his forehead crinkled in confusion, and then back at Hal. "I'm afraid I'm at quite a loss, sir."

"You thought to prey upon this girl," Hal said, advancing on him a step. "To use her for your own gain."

Vika's stomach dropped like a stone.

Sky didn't back down as Hal moved closer to him, though Vika could practically see his toes curling inside his shoes, gripping the floor to keep from retreating. "I did not."

"No use denying it now; your whole operation has become clear to me! You heard of our good fortune and the part Miss Hale here played in the Chapin will, and you thought, ah! I will ingratiate my-self with those Gardners, those simpletons who know nothing of the way the world works," Hal said, "and then I'll cash in. But you underestimated our Miss Hale, didn't you?"

Sky broke Hal's glare to look at her. "No, sir, I don't believe I did."

"Please," Vika said. She tried to get to her feet, but Mira's viselike grip on her hand stopped her. "Please, Hal, don't do this."

"This girl here knows what she's worth," Hal continued as though she hadn't spoken, "and she knows what she wants. She's not go-ing to throw herself away on some no-account assistant when she could have her pick of the finest, wealthiest men on Ploutos. No less a man than Miles Keid has already asked me for his blessing to pursue her, so why would she possibly entertain you? And thus she foiled your plan to squeeze money out of us. What do you have to say to that?"

They were practically the same words she'd said herself, the same ones she'd been thinking in horror as Sky Foster leaned toward her that night at Greenbriar, his arms around her and a lingering smile fading from his face. In Hal's sneering voice, the words sounded more toxic than she'd realized. Her head was pounding and the taste of bile was bitter at the back of her throat.

But Sky suddenly looked . . . calm. The young man who was al-ways tripping over his words and trying to disappear into the furni-ture was standing straight and tall. For once, he didn't look scared.

"My feelings for Miss Hale have nothing to do with her position here," he said, his unwavering gaze meeting Hal's. "They couldn't, since they began before she came to this place, before you had ever met her. I stayed here in this job, despite its difficulties, in large part so I could be near her. Since she rejected me, I haven't renewed my advances with a word or a look, but my feelings for her haven't changed"—he looked at her—"except that now they are deeper and better-founded."

Tears burned at the backs of her eyes, and she clutched Mira's hand.

Because . . . she *believed* him.

Sky continued, his eyes soft and deep, like sinking into warm water. "I may be just a poor assistant and unworthy of her in so many ways, but that doesn't mean my feelings are anything to be ashamed of. I . . ." He took a deep breath, a diver poised on a cliff. "I love her. I have no expectation of fortune or of her ever loving me back, but nothing can change the way I feel about her. Nothing you say, Mr. Gardner, can take that away from me."

Tears were rolling down her cheeks now, but she couldn't wipe or blink them away. Couldn't tear her eyes from his. It felt like a bridge between them, and the small smile he gave her sent so much warmth and strength across the bridge to her that it warmed her down to her toes.

"A very pretty speech," Hal said. "But even if it's true and this wasn't some scheme to extort money from us, you're a damned fool. This is a sensible, pragmatic girl who knows what's important in life: money. That's what she wants, and that's what she'll have."

Was this how Hal saw her? A heartless mercenary who was only interested in wealth, just like the person he had become? Well, how could he not? She had acted like that person for months. But had she truly become it?

Sky snapped his attention back to Hal. "You slander her. She's a better person than that. Than you."

"You're fired," Hal said. "I want you out of here at once."

"Hal, no!" Mira said.

Hal shoved a nearby chair, sending it toppling over. "Dammit, don't tell me what do, woman! I won't have it."

Mira's mouth snapped closed, her grip on Vika's hand going slack as she sank farther into the sofa, like she was trying to disappear.

"Now clear out, Foster," Hal said in a low, menacing voice, "and don't you dare come back."

"Gladly," Sky said. He went straight to Mira, who had begun to weep silently. He took her hand and pressed her knuckles to his lips. "Mrs. Gardner, thank you for your unending kindness and care. You are the very best of women and"—he seemed to choke up and cleared his throat—"and I feel very blessed to have known you. I hope you know you deserve all of the very best." Mira was too overcome with tears to respond, and Sky turned to Vika, bowing. "Miss Hale. I truly apologize for any discomfort this conversation has caused you, and I hope you know I meant every word I've said."

Then he turned and headed for the foyer and the lift that would take him out of Chapin Tower forever, and Vika staggered to her feet.

"How could you do this?" she demanded of Hal, but before he could answer, she ran out of the room after Sky.

"Wait!" she called, catching up to him in the foyer as he was pressing the call button on the lift. He looked up at her as she slid to a halt beside him. "Wait, Sky, I'm . . . I'm so sorry."

"Don't be," he said. "You didn't do anything wrong."

"But I *did*. Stars, this is all my fault," she said, tears clouding her vision again. "The only mistake you ever made was in falling for such a shallow, selfish girl, and I'm sorry for that. Please say you forgive me."

The lift doors slid open with a soft ding. He looked like he was going to say something but thought better of it, instead taking her hand and bringing it to his lips. He didn't give her the formal touch of the lips to the knuckles considered acceptable on Ploutos, but instead pressed a lingering kiss to her palm, his breath hot against her skin and the ends of his hair brushing her fingertips.

"Goodbye, Vika," he said softly, and then he was gone, and she could do nothing but stand there, numb, staring at the spot where he had been.

"Good riddance," Hal said from behind her. "There now, my girl, you've been righted."

She turned and found Hal and a wan Mira coming into the foyer, and her despair dried up, consumed by the fire of her rage.

"You," she said, advancing on Hal, "are a monster." She'd tried so hard to believe that Hal was still a good man, that he wasn't capable of the worst she'd suspected of him, but she couldn't anymore.

Hal stared at her. "Excuse me?"

"You heard me," she said. "If this is what money does to a person, then I don't want any after all. Your money has made you a miserable old miser, and you don't deserve the man you just lost."

"You'd compare me to that penniless boy?"

"No," she said. "He's worth a hundred of you."

Hal went red in the face. "Now careful, Viktoria. I understand emotions are high at the moment and I'm willing to be forgiving, but don't trespass too far on my kindness."

"Your kindness?" She gaped at him, and in that moment her decision was made. She headed for the stairs. "I have to leave here. I have to—I have to go home."

"Oh, Viktoria, no!" Mira said.

Hal caught her by the wrist. "Think about what you do now, my dear. Stay and we'll put this incident behind us. All's forgiven. But don't expect to ever come back if you leave now, and don't think we'll be settling any money on you."

Vika was stuck, one foot on the stairs, one still on the marble. She thought of her father, thin and confused, the weight of the world bowing his shoulders. Her mother, shrunken and embittered by hardship. The pullout mattress and her sister's ice-cold feet against hers in the night. Without Mr. Gardner's money, all her hopes of changing her fate and that of her family would be gone. There'd be no marriage to Miles Keid or any other rich man, no dowry or inheritance, no path out of her old life of work and deprivation and a perpetual thick gray haze blocking out the sun.

But she couldn't become—couldn't stay—the girl that Mr. Gardner thought she was. The one Mr. Chapin had thought she would be. The one who would choose this angry, fearful man and his billions over the kind and generous one who had just walked out of this flat.

The Ploutosian game was to use or be used and she had thought that it was better to be the user, but now she realized . . . she didn't want to play.

She would beg for her family's forgiveness every day, but she couldn't sacrifice a version of herself she actually liked and respected—one she thought must exist somewhere because Sky saw it—in order to better their lives. It was a prize with too many strings attached, and she was . . .

Her vision suddenly seemed to clear, and she took what felt like her first full breath of air in months.

She was worth more than that.

"I'll be in gone fifteen minutes," she said and headed up the stairs to pack the few belongings that were actually her own.

CHAPTER THIRTY-THREE

LEO EXPERIENCED ABOUT THREE minutes of breathless euphoria at finally standing up to Hal and confessing his love to Vika, feeling the trembling in her hand as he pressed his lips to her skin.

But by the time he was walking out of Chapin Tower, the doubts and fears began crowding in. His chest was on fire and he rubbed his collarbone to try to soothe the ache. What had he just done? In the heat of the moment, he'd burned all of his bridges without considering the costs. Hal would certainly never let him near Chapin Tower again, so how would he ever find out who had sabotaged the *Leander* and the Gardners' airship? Maia's bloody hacking tool was still in his pocket, where it was of no use to anyone. If only he'd taken one second to think before he stormed out of there, he could have at least given it to Vika to use. His recklessness had now put Mira and Vika in danger, and there was nothing he could do to protect them. For once he had acted on his instincts, and he'd made a mess of everything.

So . . . now what? All of his reasons to stay on the twin planets were gone. But could he really just abandon Mira and Vika without knowing they would be safe? Could he really leave everything here to go live some anonymous life on Alastor?

Heavens above, was he the biggest fool who had ever lived?

He rode the ferry home to Philomenus in a kind of a daze and barely even saw Mr. Hale as he passed him on the street.

"Sky!" the man said in greeting. "You're home early."

"Good morning, sir," Leo said.

Mr. Hale cocked a head at him. "Are you okay, son?"

Leo felt as though he was hearing the other man's voice through a fog. "Yes, fine, thank you."

He kept walking, fumbling his way into TH 76, taking the stairs up to the fourth floor but then passing his landing without pausing. He couldn't breathe. He kept heading up to the roof, his head full of Vika. The first smile she'd ever given him, as the two of them sat on the ledge looking out over the gray. He threw open the door to the roof, gulping in a huge lungful of air. What had he done? How had he made such a terrible mistake?

He stood at the edge of the roof, taking deep breaths until a little of the panic ebbed away. It wasn't pretty, exactly, up here, but it was peaceful. As a child his sanctuary had always been underground, fleeing to the basement of Chapin Tower to hide out in Mira and Hal's apartment. Vika's had been this roof, being wrapped up in the soft, dense haze that hid the rest of the world and turned everything blurry. He'd spent countless nights up here since he'd met her, and he thought it had made him understand her a little better.

He tried to imagine what he would do next. He pictured himself turning over the key to his little flat back to Mr. Hale, hugging Ariel goodbye, boarding some passenger liner back to Alastor. He had friends on that planet, people he'd known for years even though they felt distant and indistinct to him now. They would help him find a job, and eventually he would finish his schooling. He wouldn't be the son of a billionaire anymore, but he was learning how to live without a bottomless pool of money at his disposal. He would be fine.

And eventually he would forget Vika. Well, not forget her, but the thought of her wouldn't be like a red-hot knife to his heart. He would meet someone else someday, fall in love with someone who actually loved him back, and he would realize that his feelings for Vika hadn't been what he'd thought, hadn't even been real, had just . . .

The hinges on the roof door squealed, and he turned.

She was standing there, her face clean and pale, wearing a worn gray dress that looked nothing like her Ploutosian finery. She was staring at him with the same stunned expression he knew was on his own face.

"What are you doing here?" he whispered.

She swallowed. "What do you think?"

He was about to tell her he had no idea what to think, but then suddenly he realized. What she'd done.

And *why* she must have done it.

He couldn't stop himself. He was rushing toward her and she was rushing toward him, and then they collided, arms tangling around each other, his face pressed into her sweet-smelling hair, her fingers curling into his shirt. He kissed her, or maybe she kissed him, but it didn't really matter either way because they were kissing each other, and her lips were so soft and her breath so hot and hair so silky between his fingers that the feel of her crowded out every other thought. The place in his chest where his heart sat, normally heavy and aching, seemed to have dissolved and spread a tingling warmth through his whole body, and he vaguely wondered if this might be what a heart attack felt like because surely a person wasn't meant to survive feeling like this for long.

He rested his forehead against hers, both of them breathing heavily, their breaths mingling in the centimeters between them.

"Vika," he said, running the sides of his thumbs over her jaw. "I love you."

The sound she made was something like a laugh and a sob and a hiccup at once. "I . . . I think I love you, too."

"You do?" he asked.

She nodded.

"Are you . . . are you sure?"

She laughed. "Pretty sure."

"You may have to keep assuring me of that for a while before it sinks in," he said. "But I meant it about leaving. I couldn't ask you to do that."

She pulled away, just enough to look into his eyes. "You didn't."

He kissed her forehead, her eyebrow, the hollow beneath her ear, and then they just stood together in the haze, holding each other tight, and the center of gravity in Leo's world shifted until it merged with the girl in his arms.

CHAPTER THIRTY-FOUR

VIKA LAY IN BED, staring listlessly out of the window at the outer wall of the neighboring TH, while the flat bustled round her.

"Where's my fecking jumper?" Lavinia was saying, rummaging through the pile of laundry that had overflowed the basket in the corner. "Mum, it an't here."

"Don't say 'an't.' Vika, you seen your sister's jumper?"

"No," Vika said.

"I'm gonna be late!" Lavinia said.

"Maybe cause no one's done the laundry in weeks," her mum said, hurrying to the stove when the pot atop it began to bubble over, hissing as the water hit the red-hot burner. "The least you could do is help out round here a bit more since you're not even working, Vika."

"Actually the *least* you could have done would be to stay on Ploutos," Lavinia said, "or at least bring back some of that fat bank balance you accumulated with you after you left—"

"I spent the whole day yesterday helping Da sort out the office downstairs," Vika said, "and I wasn't going to take any of the Gardners' dirty money."

"Nothing stopped you before." Lavinia gave up on the laundry and grabbed a jumper out of Vika's dresser drawer, pulling it on and heading out.

"She's not wrong," her mum said. "When I think of what you threw away—"

Vika hauled herself out of bed. This particular lecture had been on repeat in the days since she'd come back home, and she could practically recite it word for word.

"I'm going out," she said, grabbing her coat from the peg by the door.

"Pull a comb through your hair first," her mum said. "You're not even dressed—"

"I don't care!" Vika closed the door between them. But she didn't head out, she headed up. She took the stairs two at a time, skipping the one that sagged, and knocked on Sky's fourth-floor door. "It's me."

"Come in!" he called.

He was sitting at the small desk against the wall, reading through a document she'd bet all of the sixteen bits she had to her name was the Chapin will. She threw herself down onto his unmade bed, burying her face in his pillow, which smelled warm and familiar, half-hoping to suffocate herself.

"They hate me," she said, the words muffled.

"No, they don't."

"They do! And I can't even blame them."

The mattress dipped below her, rolling her toward his weight as he lay down beside her on the narrow bed. She turned her head to look at him, and he brushed the hair out of her eyes.

"I could have given them a better life," she said softly. "If I'd just stayed and married Miles Keid or some other rich society person, I could have helped everyone."

"Except yourself," he said. "Your life, and the things you want for it, have value, too."

"I know," she said. That had seemed so clear to her when she'd decided to leave the Gardners', but the power of the realization had faded when she'd returned to the harsh reality of life on Philomenus and seen how her family had continued to struggle in her absence. "So, you don't think I'm selfish?"

He pressed a soft kiss to the tip of her nose. "It's possible I'm biased, but I think leaving was the most selfless thing I've ever seen a person do."

She drew him back to her, kissing him for real. This, she knew now, was what it was supposed to feel like. Seeing his expression change that day on the roof as he'd realized she'd left the Gardners for him had been the moment she knew she was crazy about him. She'd believed it when she packed up her few possessions and left the penthouse for the last time, had probably suspected it somewhere down deep inside of her for much longer than that, but til she felt the way her heart melted when he smiled at her in total wonderment that day she hadn't been *sure*. And then he'd kissed her, and it turned out kissing someone you loved was a whole different experience from kissing a near-stranger you didn't particularly like.

Now she couldn't stop doing it. He touched her so gently—like he didn't entirely trust she wouldn't disappear between his fingers like a puff of smoke—that it sometimes made her want to cry.

"Sorry," she whispered into the sliver of space between their lips. "I haven't brushed my teeth yet."

He smiled. "I'll persevere."

She rolled onto her back, pulling him over her. It felt safe but also scary, like exciting scary, and that was a combination she'd never imagined before but discovered she liked very much. He whispered her name between kisses, his hand drifting under the hem of her shirt, his fingers warm on her ribs. She scratched her nails lightly up his back and into his hair, and he shivered, which made them both giggle. He moved his lips to her neck, and she sighed.

"Sky . . ."

He stilled, and then sat up, his brow furrowed.

"What is it?" she asked.

"I . . ." He looked at her, frozen. "Nothing."

"Are you sure?" she asked, running a hand down his forearm. It didn't look like nothing. It looked like he might be sick.

"Yes. It's only that . . ." He pressed a hand to his sternum. "There's something I should tell you."

She lifted her eyebrows and waited as he seemed to search for the words.

There was a knock at the door. "It's me!" a voice called.

"A-Ariel's coming over," he said, jumping up from the bed. "That's what I wanted to tell you."

Vika sat up and straightened her shirt as Sky opened the door for Knox Vega's daughter. The visit wasn't a total surprise; the night before, they had decided to approach the girl with a proposition. As a member of the PLF, chances were she'd be just as interested in learning the true identity of the *Leander* bomber as they were. Vika did wonder how Sky had been able to track her down so quickly, though.

"You wanted to see me?" the girl asked, arms crossed over her chest.

"Yes, thank you for coming." Sky waved her inside and offered her the lone chair in the room. "I expect you didn't think you would be hearing from us again."

"Can't say I did," she replied. "But since I an't been arrested yet, I guess I can probably trust you. What's this all about?"

Sky sat down on the bed beside Vika. "We have a proposal for you. We don't believe the Philomeni Liberation Front had anything to do with the bombing of the *Leander*."

"Then we agree."

"We think someone was targeting Leo Chapin specifically," Vika said. "There was also an explosion on an airship carrying the people who inherited the Chapin fortune after Leo died. It's believed to have been a mechanical issue, but—"

"But what are the odds?" Ariel said.

"Exactly."

"You want to clear the name of the PLF," Sky continued, "and we want to find out who's targeting Chapin heirs. We have a certain degree of access, or we did, and you're the only person we know who's knowledgeable about spacecraft."

"Okay . . ."

"We want you to go to Ploutos," Vika said.

"The Gardners' airship is in a mechanics' bay right now," Sky said. "Mr. Gardner believes it's being repaired, but I gave them instructions weeks ago not to touch it, so it should be in the same condition it was in immediately after the explosion. Assuming they still think I work for Hal, I should be able to get you in to examine it."

"We're hoping you might be able to find something that could help us identify the person who sabotaged it," Vika added.

"Okay," Ariel said. "And what's in it for me?"

Sky just stared at her for a moment in apparent confusion. "Well, Miss Vega . . . this is a first step to prove the PLF wasn't responsible for—"

"There's a reward," Vika interrupted. "The Gardners are offering a hundred thousand bits for the *Leander* bomber's identity."

Ariel's serious expression suddenly cracked into a smile and she kicked Sky's leg. "I was just teasing you, but now I'm definitely in."

The three of them worked out all the details and when the girl was gone, Vika sighed and leaned back against the wall. "What if this doesn't work?"

Sky took her hand and looked down at their interlaced fingers. "It will."

She smiled, suddenly so absurdly happy—despite all of the difficulties they faced—that he was there. She'd never been a very grateful person before, always feeling like she was the victim of the coltane crash or the mercs or just malign fate, but she felt so lucky that he had walked into her TH all those months ago.

"Thank you," she said. "For understanding why I couldn't let this whole business go. I don't think I could have done this without you."

"Of course," he said. "If Mira's in danger, we have to do whatever we can to help her."

"You don't really think it could be Hal, do you?" she asked, dropping her voice even though there was no one to overhear them. Just saying the words out loud still felt like a betrayal. The first time she'd done it, she'd only been able to whisper her suspicions into Sky's ear when it was dark and quiet and they were surrounded by the blanket of haze on the roof.

He flipped her hand over, tracing his thumb along the lines of her palm. "I want to believe that it couldn't be. But I don't know."

"Maybe Ariel will find a mechanical issue with the airship after all," she said. "Maybe you and I are just suffering from raging paranoia and everything is fine."

"I would be thrilled to be proven so wrong," he said. "But if we aren't and Ariel doesn't find any evidence of who might have sabotaged the craft, our next step has to be getting our hands on Hal's new will. It will obviously be harder to get access to Hal's holo now that neither of us is welcome in the penthouse, but I'm sure we can devise some scheme to get me up there."

"And get yourself arrested for trespassing," Vika said, "and then beaten up by some hardened gangster criminals in jail? That doesn't seem like a good plan to me."

He smiled at her so sweetly that she felt the warmth of it down to her toes. "I don't know how many gangsters there are in the typical Ploutosian jail. Besides, I'm much tougher than I look."

"Oh, really?" She jabbed him in the ribs with her elbow and a shockingly high-pitched yelp exploded out of him.

He recoiled from her. "Stay away!"

"I thought you could take it?" She lunged at him, her fingers going for the sensitive spots on his sides that she'd inadvertently discovered the other night.

"No!" he pleaded, trying and failing to fend off her attacks. "The hardened criminals aren't going to tickle me, so you're proving nothing!"

She tackled him, laughing as he squealed and squirmed under her attack, til she took pity on him and just kissed him.

* * *

A short time later, Leo headed out to get some food from the nearby market. Vika's reentry to Philomeni life hadn't exactly gone smoothly, with her sister resenting her for being back and her mother resenting her for having left, so she was spending a good portion of her days in his flat, which meant he needed to shop twice as often. It seemed to him a small price to pay for the tremendous upside of having her inexplicably near him, smiling at him, touching him. The image of her casually lying on his bed, her hair spread across his pillow so that it would smell like her when he lay down to sleep that night, did things to him that he couldn't quite describe.

"Hey!"

He nearly jumped out of his skin—doing further damage to his masculine image, which was already wounded by Vika's ruthless tickling fingers—when Ariel popped out from an alleyway. "Hell's teeth, you nearly gave me a heart attack."

"Just what do you think you're doing?" she demanded of him.

He frowned. "I was just going for some bread and—"

"Not that." She rolled her eyes and dragged him into the sad little park across the street, sitting him down on the bench like a parent putting their naughty child in a corner. "With Vika, I mean. Why haven't you told her yet, you dummy?"

He sighed. "It's not that easy."

"Oh, right," she said, dropping onto the bench beside him. "You two get married, the Chapin fortune reverts to you, you live happily ever after all rich and smug and disgustingly in love. Seems real complicated."

"All right, assuming your ridiculous version of events is accurate," he said, "I can't put that kind of target on her back. Right now she's *safe*. And whoever's going after the Chapin heirs doesn't know that I am one, which gives me a chance of actually discovering their identity before they can strike again. I can't tell Vika who I am until I know it won't put her at risk."

Ariel gave him a penetrating look, and he struggled to maintain eye contact. She might have been small, but she was also the fiercest person he knew and that stare was more than a little intimidating.

"Bullshit," she finally said.

"Excuse me?"

"That's not the real reason you haven't told her. At least not all of it."

He threw up his hands. "You're right, okay? It's not. The truth is I'm terrified to tell her who I really am. Just contemplating it makes me nauseous. I've almost done it twice now, but then I just freeze up."

Her expression softened. "How come?"

"Because . . ." He closed his eyes against the sudden rush of grief he felt even imagining it. "Because what if she can't forgive me for lying to her? I could hardly blame her, but it would kill me. Now that I know what it's like to have her . . . to have her not hate me."

"She wouldn't hate you," Ariel said.

"She might," he replied. "And it's more than that. What if she just . . . doesn't love me enough? She might have left the Gardners for me, but the will says we have to get *married*. Not only is neither of us ready for that, but I can't tell her I'm Leo Chapin unless I know that she actually *wants* to marry me. Because otherwise I'm putting her in the exact same position she was in before, of feeling like she's selling herself for money. I can't do that to her. I'd rather stay dead."

"But you can't keep living this lie just cause you're scared," Ariel said, folding her legs up under her so she could turn to face him. "At some point you have to make a *choice,* Leo. You've got to stop being dead and start choosing the life you actually want. Want to renounce your fortune and go back to Alastor and live an anonymous life free of the legacy of your father? Do that. You want to stay here and live an honest life with Vika? Tell her. You'll never know for sure how she'll react, but she deserves the truth at least. And you deserve to be who you actually are and to inherit the fortune that's rightfully yours."

"Maybe I don't even want it," he said, thinking of Hal's kindly face pulled into a sneer. "With all the misery I've seen money cause . . ."

"I say this with love and as someone who has been poor a lot longer than you, okay? That's idiotic," she replied. "Money's a tool, not good or bad. Think of the good someone like you could do with a tool that powerful."

He swallowed. "I don't want to lose her. It was bad enough thinking I was losing her when she wasn't even mine, but now . . ."

She wrapped her arms around his neck, pulling him close. "I know. But you're perfectly lovable, Leo Chapin, and at some point you're going to have to give her the chance."

CHAPTER THIRTY-FIVE

ARIEL WAS READY TO leave for Ploutos the next day, disguised as a mechanic. Sky had hailed the repair bay to tell them she was coming to take a look at the Gardners' airship on the couple's behalf, hoping no one there was aware that he no longer worked for Hal. But the man on the other end of the line had been supremely unconcerned and agreed to give Ariel complete access to the ship. They could only hope he wouldn't look too closely at the very small, very young-looking mechanic who arrived at his door.

Vika accompanied Sky as he went to the hangar with Ariel to see her off. He had tried to tell her she didn't need to bother to come with him, but Vika had insisted. She waited til the last moment, when Ariel was climbing inside the cockpit of the skiff, to step forward.

"Wait," she said. "I'm coming with you."

Ariel blinked. "You are?"

"*What?*" Sky demanded.

Vika had anticipated this and took his hand. "We need Hal's will. We both know it, and I have an idea how to get it that doesn't involve you getting arrested for trespassing."

Realization dawned on Sky's face. "Archer?"

She nodded.

"No," he said. "I don't like this. It's dangerous."

"It'll be fine! Ariel will get us to the planet, we'll both go gather our information, and we'll be back before you know it." He shook his head, but she stopped him before he could object. "The more times we cross the stream, the more danger of getting caught. So let's just kill these two birds with one stone."

"She does have a point," Ariel interjected from the cockpit door.

Sky rolled his eyes at her. "You're the most reckless person I know, so I don't know why you think I might listen to you," he said with surprising familiarity. He turned back to Vika. "Please don't do this. We'll find another way."

"This is our best chance," Vika said, sliding open the door to the skiff's cargo bay. "Now you have to let us go, or Ariel's going to be late to the repair bay and that may raise alarm bells."

"As though that's not exactly the way you wanted it," Sky said. "I don't like this."

Vika smiled. "You've mentioned that already."

"And yet you're unmoved."

"It's going to be okay," Ariel said as she climbed into the cockpit. "I'm a professional."

"You're actually not," Sky replied. "And it's illegal."

"Do you have enough spare bits lying round for a ferry ticket?" Vika asked.

"No."

"Then this is how it has to be." She put her hands on his face, gazing into his unhappy, dark eyes. "Don't worry so much. We'll be back in a couple of hours."

"Won't you just let me break into Chapin Tower?" he asked. "That honestly worries me less."

"No." She kissed him and climbed into the skiff. "I'll see you soon."

"Be careful!" Sky called over the revving of the engines. "Take care of yourselves!"

Vika shut the cargo bay door and exhaled the breath she'd been holding.

"So how scared are you really?" Ariel asked from the pilot's seat as she flipped switches and turned dials, preparing for liftoff.

"I'm . . . not thrilled about it," Vika said. She looked out of the port window at Sky, who stood miserably to the side watching them, and gave him one last wave. She really hoped she hadn't been lying to him when she said everything was going to be all right.

"You put on a pretty good front."

Vika went to stand beside the pilot's seat. "This doesn't scare you at all? Breaking the law like this?"

Ariel smiled as the engine sounds increased in pitch and volume. "Every time. I've just had longer to work on my game face."

"I don't know if that makes me feel better or worse," Vika said. "Help me into the hiding compartment?"

"Huh?"

Vika frowned at her. "The compartment lined with the ionized alloy. So the sensors don't see that there are more people inside here than you're permitted for?"

"Oh." Ariel waved a hand. "I made all that up."

"You *what?*"

The girl laughed. "Yeah, I just didn't want you pestering me with a bunch of questions while I was trying to fly. Now sit down."

Vika buckled herself in to the passenger's seat, and Ariel lifted off. As they shot up through the haze, Vika remembered the hour she had spent in that dark, cramped compartment, Sky's body warm at her back even though he was excessively careful not to touch her, the slight shifting of the hair at the base of her neck every time he exhaled. She had noticed then for the first time how he smelled, like something clean and a little sweet that must have been his soap, which had felt like a surprisingly intimate thing to learn about him. But mostly she'd been surprised by how quickly she'd felt comfortable being in such close proximity to him, and she'd spent the trip cycling between enjoying the closeness and worrying that he would somehow *sense* her enjoying it. She wasn't sure if she was annoyed or grateful about Ariel's ploy.

Soon they broke atmo, and Ariel maneuvered them expertly through the stream, slowing the skiff down to a crawl and pausing to scavenge debris on the rare occasion a Ploutosian patrol came within range. Unauthorized travel off of Philomenus was illegal but it was also expensive, which meant it was so rare that Ploutosian law enforcement didn't spend a lot of resources trying to stop it. It was one way the poverty that Ploutos kept the citizens of Philomenus in actually worked in the PLF's favor. As long as she got on and off the planets undetected, there wasn't much chance of discovery for Ariel.

"So, Sky," Ariel said after a long time of them riding silently together. "You two are pretty close, huh?"

Vika narrowed her eyes at her. "Are you sure you only put us in that compartment to avoid my questions?"

Ariel smiled but kept her eyes forward. "He just seems like a good guy, is all."

"He's the best, actually."

"Think you'll marry him?"

Vika let out a shocked laugh. "I'm only eighteen, you know."

"But can you imagine it? Spending your life with him?"

Vika thought about it. Not long ago, despite her age, she was spending a good part of her day thinking about getting married. But when she pictured her life as a wife, it was all about the security and comfort it would provide for herself and her family. She had imagined choosing her own place to live and being entirely in charge of her own existence instead of being ordered about by her mum or Stella or the ghost of Rigel Chapin. She had pictured herself telling her parents and Lavinia that she was bringing them to Ploutos, the looks on their faces as she showed them the fine house she'd bought them in a sunny spot on the outskirts of Central City, where her father could retire and rest and Lavinia could continue her schooling and her mum could hire a maid to boss about. Rarely had her husband entered her thoughts when she contemplated her married life, cept when it was to worry about what all of those dreams would cost her.

If she imagined marrying Sky, though, the picture was entirely different. She wouldn't be gaining a fortune and moving to a new planet. She'd be moving four stories up from where she already lived, trading her family's cramped flat for Sky's tiny studio. They'd both find new jobs, and eventually, maybe, they'd be able to save enough money to move to a two-or three-room flat in a different building, somewhere where she wouldn't have to run into her mum every day on the stairs.

And she'd be with someone she actually liked. Someone she *loved*. She would have stood up and told the world that this person—this nervous, generous, deeply kind person—was the one she wanted as her partner for life, navigating the world with her, having her back. And the thought of that . . . she didn't expect the rush of happiness she felt go through her body at just imagining it. She'd always thought money was security, but she'd never felt as safe in the months she'd been a rich heiress as she did just thinking about Sky being by her side forever.

Ariel suddenly laughed. "I'll take that dopey look on your face and the last two minutes of total silence as a yes."

Ariel landed the skiff at the PLF outpost on Ploutos without incident, easily dodging the scant patrol ships that circled the planet. A man there took them to the nearest bi-rail station where they went their separate ways, Ariel to the repair bay north of town while Vika headed into the heart of Central City. She had secretly hailed Lassiter and Lyons earlier that day, trying to trick the receptionist into giving her Archer's home address, but the woman hadn't budged. She couldn't very well walk into his office and start asking him questions; word would no doubt get back to Hal. So Vika bought herself a cup of tea and settled onto a bench in the park across the street from the office building, her eyes trained on the glass doors.

Eventually she spotted Archer leaving the building for the day.

She got up, tossing her long-empty cup, and followed him down the sidewalk from a safe distance. She trailed him down into the bi-rail station on the corner and then onto a train heading west. They made stop after stop and the train began to empty, til there were so few people left that she was sure he would spot her. She rucked the collar of her coat up a little higher, trying to obscure some of her face.

Finally, Archer exited the train, and she jumped out after him. When they emerged from the station, she realized they were at the very outskirts of the city. Instead of wide boulevards lined with trees, the streets here were narrow and the buildings packed in tightly together, housing thousands of workers who were better off than Philomenis but had about as much chance of ever living the life of Ploutosian high society. The landscapers and sanitation workers who kept Ploutos beautiful were imported from Philomenus, but this is where the receptionists and security guards and waiters who kept it running lived.

Archer disappeared into one of the buildings, and Vika checked the call buttons posted outside. SHERATAN: 803. The door had a biometric scan to allow entry, so she waited for someone else to come out and then slipped in through the open door as it started to close behind them. A rumbling lift took her up to the eighth floor, chugging all the way in a manner that made her worry it might snap loose and plummet to the ground at any moment. She stepped out of it gratefully and headed down the dim hallway til she found 803 and knocked.

Steps approached the door and then the sentry camera blinked on. She smiled in what she hoped was a winning way, but still it took a long, tense moment for the door to open.

"Viktoria?" Archer frowned at her as he cracked the door just a few centimeters. "What are you doing here?"

"I just wanted to see you," she said. "I hope you don't mind."

"Um, no, of course not," he said. "Allow me to take you to dinner? I'll just retrieve my coat."

"Oh, we don't have to do that," she said. She wanted him at home, where he felt comfortable and where he, presumably, had access to his work files. "How about you make me a cup of coffee?"

"Right." He didn't open the door any farther at first, but how could he keep her standing in the hallway without looking rude? "Yes, of course. Come in."

She stepped inside, surprised at what she found. Archer moved in such affluent circles that she had somehow always assumed that he, well, belonged there. She realized now what a stupid assumption that had been, especially for her of all people. Archer's studio was larger and better appointed than Sky's, but it felt almost smaller since it was so crammed with things. Books and stacks of papers and strange odds and ends that didn't seem to make any sense, like two empty silver candlesticks and a couple of paintings in gold gilt frames that were just leaning against a wall. Whatever hopes he had for his future prospects at Lassiter and Lyons, it was clear just how much Archer was clinging to the edge of high society, his fingernails dug into it even harder than hers had been.

It was a good thing she hadn't married him for his money.

"I do apologize for the mess," Archer said, kicking some dirty clothes under his bed hurriedly. He flashed her the blinding smile that had once made her feel warm and confused. "I would have had the maid visit if I knew I was going to be having such charming company."

"You're right, it was terribly rude of me to just drop in on you like this," she said. He moved a stack of books off of one of the chairs at his small dining table and held it out for her. "It just feels as though we haven't talked in so long."

He abruptly turned away from her, going to the kitchenette on the opposite wall to start a pot of coffee. "I suppose you're right."

Stupid. The last time they'd spoken, of course, was when he'd told her he was in love with her and she'd rejected him. Reminding him of that was probably not the best way to get him to do her a favor. Unless . . . hell's teeth, she hated herself for even thinking it. Hadn't she finished with *use or be used* when she left the Gardners? But then she thought of Mira bleeding amidst the wreckage of the airship and heard the words coming out of her mouth.

"The thing is," she said, "I . . . miss you. I know that things didn't work out quite the way you'd hoped—they didn't work out the way I'd hoped, either—but I don't want to lose you from my life."

That, at least, was basically true. She did miss Archer. She'd always liked him.

He smiled at her as he brought her a cup of coffee. "Oh, I suppose I can forgive you the grievous sin of not being madly in love with me." He sat down opposite her. "I've missed you, too, Viktoria."

She needed to get him talking about work, so that she could steer the conversation toward Hal's will, but she couldn't just come out and ask about it without seeming suspicious. "So, how have you been?"

"Oh, can't complain, yourself?" he asked.

She nodded. Heavens, she hated small talk. "I'm well. It's been nice to be home, see my family again."

"I would imagine."

Lord, Archer had never been this hard to talk to before. It felt like pulling teeth. She was about to comment on the weather of all things, just to have something to say, when she noticed the collection of photographs and paintings on the narrow bookshelf beside her. She stood and began to examine them, relieved to have something else to focus on.

"These are lovely," she said, resisting the urge to brush her fingers over the thick swipes of beige paint on one picture: a man, his features abstract and fractured, looking out of a window. "Did you paint them?"

"Yes."

Beside the painting was a photograph in a silver frame: a small, dark-haired boy of six or seven cycles sitting on a man's lap, his face out of the frame but his hand resting on the boy's head.

"Aww," she said. "Is that little baby Archer?"

He laughed. "I'm afraid so. My father's name day."

"You were so cute!" she said. "And these paintings are beautiful. You're very talented."

"If only art paid the bills," he said.

At last! "How *is* work?" she asked.

"Busy," he said. "I'm not sure if you're aware since it happened around the same time you left, but Hal let his assistant go. Instead of hiring a new one, he just has *me* doing most of that work for him now, all for free, of course. So I'm managing the Chapin estate, helping Hal dissolve his charitable foundation because it was costing him too much money, redrafting his will, and even managing his household staff and outside contractors for this huge anniversary party he's throwing tomorrow. It's ridiculous, really, but you know we're all about client care at Lassiter and Lyons! Or so I keep being told."

"How someone so rich can also be so cheap is beyond me." Her heart was beating faster and she tried to breathe slowly to control it. "I thought Hal already wrote his will?"

Archer laughed. "He did, but it had *you* in it. Whatever you said to him when you left must have really done a number on him, because he called me up immediately wanting to remove you. We should be finished with the new, Viktoria-free document in a day or two. Do me a favor and wait a little while before you reconcile with him? I don't have the energy to draft a third will for him until at least next month."

Vika tried to smile. "I promise. So who did he replace me with? Some other needy Philomeni waif he can play house with? I would dearly love to see that thing."

"I wish I could show you," he said, "but that damned attorney-client privilege."

She reached out and squeezed his forearm. "Oh, come on! I won't tell anyone you showed me. Who would I even tell? Now that I'm out of Ploutosian society, I need to get my gossip fix somehow."

He was smiling but shook his head. "I really can't."

She batted her eyes at him. "Archer . . ."

He laughed. "That won't work on me. Remember, you and I are cut from the same cloth. I know your tricks too well."

Damn. She'd felt so certain she could get the will out of him somehow, blithely sure of her power to charm it from him. But if she kept pressing, he might get suspicious and tell Hal she'd been snooping round.

And now that she and Sky were going to have to break into the penthouse to get their hands on the will, she couldn't afford to make Hal any more paranoid than he already was.

"My trip was a total failure," she told Ariel when they met back up at the bi-rail station. "Any luck on yours?"

"Well, it definitely wasn't a mechanical issue that brought that ship down," Ariel said. "When you glance at it, it looks like the engine was damaged by routine corrosion, but I found traces of hydroxazine residue. Someone must have stuck a chunk of it to the engine, knowing it would blow as soon as it got hot enough and leave little trace."

"How long would that take?" Vika asked.

She shrugged. "Depends, but I'd say no more than fifty or sixty klicks."

"That means it must have been placed during the party," Vika said. "If it had been sabotaged earlier than that, the ship wouldn't have made it out to the country house in the first place. Would you have to be knowledgeable about aircraft design to do it?"

Ariel shook her head. "Not at all. Anybody with a couple of minutes on their hands could get it done."

Vika rubbed her head. "So one of the guests . . ."

"Or staff," Ariel said. "I'm guessing there were a bunch of waiters and caterers and cleaners there that night, right? I bet anyone could have slipped in with them and you wouldn't have known they didn't belong."

"You're right. So this doesn't narrow the suspect pool at all."

"I'm sorry," Ariel said. "I wish I could have been more help."

Vika sighed. "At least we know now that someone really *did* sabotage the Gardners' ship. It's nice to have confirmation that Sky and I aren't crazy."

"Well, I'm not convinced about you yet," Ariel said, "but Sky seems to have his head on straight."

Someone from the PLF arrived and gave them a ride back to the rural outpost where Ariel's skiff was docked, and soon they were headed back to Philomenus.

"Thank you for helping today," Vika said as they slowly trawled the stream, pretending to be scavenging space garbage. "I don't know if I said that before."

"I wasn't exactly doing you a favor," Ariel replied. "I've got my own reasons, so there an't no need to thank me."

"Still. Let me buy you some dinner or something when we land? For your troubles."

Ariel shook her head. "I should be getting straight home."

Vika recognized that tone of voice. "Your da?"

"Yeah, if I an't there to remind him, he forgets to eat."

"So you take care of him?"

"Sort of." Ariel glanced at her from the corner of her eye. "I mean most of the time I want to kill him, but I guess I do my best to keep him from actually killing himself."

Vika looked at the girl beside her. Ariel was only a few cycles younger than she was but older than Vika had been when her da went through his troubles and Vika started feeling she had to take care of him instead of the other way round.

"That's a lot of pressure," she said. "For someone your age."

Ariel huffed out a little laugh. "I don't know that I've ever exactly felt my age. I'm guessing you understand that. Ooh, look." Ariel had spotted a chunk of metal floating a couple hundred meters from them. As they got closer, Vika could tell it had once been part of a satellite. Ariel hit a button on the control panel in front of her, and something began to vibrate and whir beneath them. "I *was* just trying to keep the patrols from noticing us, but this is a nice little bonus. I an't found a single piece this big in weeks."

"You been working the stream for long?" Vika asked as Ariel expertly scooped up the chunk of satellite with a tool of magnetized webbing that extended from the belly of the craft. She reeled the tool back in, depositing the debris in the hold of the skiff.

"I used to come out here with my da all the time when I was little, just to spend time with him, you know. But then my mum left and he said goodbye to whatever soberness he'd been clinging to." She steered them back toward Philomenus, picking up the speed. "We were doing a salvaging run one night when he passed out cold, just slipped right out of this seat and onto the fecking floor. I thought he was dead. I had to pilot us back Philomenus and land it myself based on what I remembered seeing him do. Pretty lucky we made it down in one piece. After that, I learned how to fly for real and started doing runs myself."

"Hell's teeth," Vika said, staring at the girl whose impassive face didn't reveal a sliver of emotion at the story. Ariel really *had* perfected her game face. "How old were you?"

"Twelve."

Vika shook her head. "Lord. I started working young, too, but at least I didn't have to worry about dying if I messed up a pour."

And at least her da, thin and nervous and forgetful as he still was, had recovered from the worst of his troubles instead of still being stuck right in the middle of them. If she and Ariel had been different kinds of people, less the prickly by-products of life on an unforgiving planet than they were, she might have been tempted to take the younger girl into her arms, to try to reassure her the way *she* had always wanted to be reassured that things would get better, somehow. One thing was for sure, she was going to give her da a good long hug as soon as she got home.

THIS WAS IT. SO many months of planning, so many sleepless nights, so many thousands of bits he'd painstakingly saved over years of working for that bastard, spent. But now, finally, all the pieces were coming together. There wouldn't be any lucky near-miss this time.

When the smoke cleared, it would all finally be *his*.

CHAPTER THIRTY-SIX

ALL THE RELIEF LEO felt when Vika and Ariel returned safely from their trip to Ploutos drained away when Vika told him that the Gardners were nearly done with their new will. If the attacker had stood to gain from one of the previous wills, they would want to strike before they were taken out of line for the money. That could mean just a matter of days.

"We have to get into the penthouse," Leo said, trying to suppress the wave of panic that washed through him. He saw a flash of Mira crumpled at the bottom of the airship, bleeding and broken. Imagined what hadn't happened but easily might have if he and Hal had left Greenbriar just a few minutes later: himself running for the craft, too far away to do anything, as the flames reached the fuel tank and blew. "Right? We need to see Hal's will *now*, or . . . or it may be too late."

"I have an idea for that," Vika said. She told him about the party Archer had mentioned to her, a giant bash to celebrate the Gardners' fortieth wedding anniversary. The next evening there would be dozens of staff and contractors in and out of the flat, providing the best cover they could hope for.

"Ariel?" Leo asked. "Are you up for a bit more lawbreaking?"

She didn't hesitate. "Always."

The next night, the three of them donned all-black, typical clothing for caterers, waiters, and other support staff. Ariel smuggled them across the stream in her skiff, and they rode the train into Central City with all the other workers heading in to man lavish Ploutosian parties.

"I've never been to a fancy shindig like this before," Ariel said as the train whizzed toward the center of town, "even as a servant. Think there'll be a chance to snag some food?"

Vika sighed. "I do miss the food."

When they reached Chapin Tower, Vika headed for the back entrance she had always used while living there, but Leo tugged on her hand.

"Not there," he said. "The concierge will be checking invitations and ident cards."

"How are we supposed to get in then?"

Leo led them around the corner to the main entrance of the building, the one through which men and women in suits carrying briefcases streamed in and out. They passed through scanners that ensured they carried no weapons, but otherwise there was no security to check the constant parade of people. Leo led them to the bank of two dozen lifts that serviced the high-rise. One, removed a little from the others and partially obscured by a large planter, said PRIVATE above it in looping gold letters.

"This was old Mr. Chapin's. He had a lift solely for his own use installed in every building he ever owned, even the ones he never visited," Leo explained. Vika looked confused and Ariel was simply staring at him like he was the dumbest person she'd ever encountered. "I . . . I saw the code for it once. In some of Hal's papers."

Beside the call button was a keypad. As soon as Leo entered the ten-digit code that had been drilled into him during childhood, the call button lit up and he was able to summon the lift.

"Wow," Vika said. "It's lucky you remembered it. I had no idea this lift even existed."

Neither did Hal, thankfully. Leo exchanged a brief look with Ariel; her puckered lips said *Just tell her already* and his furrowed brow said *Not the time.*

They rode the lift up to the bottom level of the penthouse, the one the Gardners didn't use. The doors opened into the dim corridor outside of his father's bedroom. Leo had never been allowed in his father's bedroom, and it had always held a combination of fear and fascination for him as a child. Still, it was the one room he hadn't visited on the few occasions in the past months when he'd found himself wandering this old home of his, like the specter he was, floating over the floors and running his fingertips so lightly over the furniture and objects that he didn't even disturb the fine layer of dust that had settled over them all. Whatever ghosts were in that room, he didn't want to meet them.

The only stairs that led up to the main level of the penthouse that hadn't been sealed off were on the opposite end of the flat. Leo headed that way, the girls following close behind in the dim light of the moon that came through the windows. As they crossed through the main sitting room, Ariel suddenly stopped.

"Is that him?" she asked.

Leo followed her gaze. She was looking at the large portrait over the fireplace. His father's icy blue eyes, peering out from under slightly wild eyebrows, looked down at him. Even now, he looked disappointed.

"That's him," he said.

"He looks kind of scary," she said.

Leo swallowed. "He was. From what I've heard."

Vika took a step closer to the portrait, scrutinizing the other figure in it, the fair boy with the round face and unformed features standing at his father's side. Leo had been five cycles when this portrait was painted; he remembered the long hours of standing there, his father's hand like lead on his shoulder, the artist telling him to keep still.

"Poor Leo," Vika said as she looked at the unhappy little boy.

Behind Vika's back, Ariel reached out to him and gave his hand a brief squeeze.

Leo cleared his throat. "We'd better get moving."

The stairs opened into a corridor in one of the back corners of the penthouse. Unfortunately, it was on the opposite end from where Hal's office was, so they'd have to make their way through the gauntlet of the party without being noticed.

"Hey!" a voice said as they entered the hallway. Leo jumped and turned to find a woman dressed in blacks like them, but with the bearing and attitude of a manager, approaching them. "What do you think you're doing?"

"Just, uh"—Leo glanced around—"looking for a washroom."

The woman narrowed her eyes at him. "All three of you?"

Leo saw Ariel wince, as though his terrible attempt at a lie gave her actual pain.

"Um . . ." he said, wishing he'd let her or Vika come up with the excuse instead.

The manager rolled her eyes. "Get back to work."

"Yes, ma'am," Leo said, and the three of them scurried away.

Soon they had reached the ballroom, which they would need to cross in order to reach Hal's office. They paused in a darkened doorway just out of sight in order to plan their passage. Luckily the lights inside the ballroom were low, the dance floor lit with thousands of candles in extravagant freestanding candelabras and floating in the air on tiny hovering platforms. A table piled high with colorfully wrapped gifts was placed in front of the windows, and Leo spotted Mira and Hal among the dancers on the floor.

"Ariel, you walk in front since no one here will recognize you," Leo said. "Vika and I will stay behind you, and you can block us."

"I'm not sure the laws of physics will actually allow that," Ariel said, "but I'll do my best."

Ariel took a deep breath and then stepped into the ballroom, and Leo and Vika followed closely behind. Ariel was shorter and slimmer than both of them, but they did their best to keep her between them and the guests at the party who would be able to recognize them. They made their way around the ballroom like this, sticking close to the walls, heads down, doing little to draw attention to themselves. Every time Leo glimpsed up, he caught sight of someone he knew either from his previous life or from this one: Evelyn Lyons, Georgiana Howell, Chief Constable Lich. Vika flinched beside him as Miranda Harkness went sailing past on a cloud of perfume, dancing in the arms of a man who was not her husband.

Finally, what felt like ten cycles later, they had made it across the ballroom.

"I guess it's lucky Ploutosians are used to pretending servants are invisible," Vika said as they reached the arched entryway that led back to the main parlor. "Otherwise—" She suddenly froze and then spun, turning her back on the parlor. "Fecking hell. There's Archer."

Leo glanced into the room. It took him a second to place the person he'd briefly seen Vika chatting and dancing with at the Gardners' last party, a handsome young man with an easy smile that showed his straight white teeth, laughing a shade too hard at a joke made by another, older man. He looked . . . not quite the way Leo had imagined he would from talking to him on the phone several times. Brighter, somehow, and certainly friendlier. There was something else about him, too, that tugged at some memory in Leo's mind, but he couldn't quite put his finger on it.

But there was no time to worry about that. Vika wouldn't be able to just stroll past her friend with tiny Ariel as a cover and expect not to be noticed. Leo spotted a discarded tray of empty champagne flutes on a side table and scooped it up, handing it to Vika. She held the tray on her palm, lifting it into the air so that the empty glasses obscured her face.

"All your years of barmaid training are finally going to serve you," he said.

She gave him a tense smile. "Remind me to write Nicky a thank-you note."

"Ready?" Ariel asked, and when Vika nodded, she stepped into the parlor. They followed, making their way around the perimeter of the room, Vika with her tray held high. Leo could hear the faint tinkling of the glasses as her hand shook, and from the corner of his eye he watched Archer Sheratan until, at last, they had reached the corridor on the opposite side of the room.

Out of sight once again, the three of them rushed to Hal's office. Leo put a hand on the knob and found it locked.

"What do you think are the odds that Hal changed the code after he fired you?" Vika asked.

"Low," Leo said. Hal was not the most technologically savvy person. "But there's only one way to find out." He entered the old code and, just above the noise of banging pots and pans and shouted instructions coming from the kitchen, he heard the metallic whirr of the locking mechanism disengaging and pushed the door open.

"Ariel, go back to the parlor and keep watch, okay?" he said. "Let us know if Hal starts heading this way."

"You got it."

Vika snagged Ariel's sleeve as she turned to go and handed her the tray of empty glasses. "Take this, but switch it out for a fresh one as soon as you can. The surest way to attract attention as a waiter is not to be working."

Ariel shook her head. "Lord, these people are terrible."

She headed back to the party, and Vika locked the office door after her while Leo went straight for the holo, bringing up the display in the air above the desk. As usual, it prompted him for a fingerprint. He took the device they'd gotten from Maia out of his pocket.

"We need to find a print," he said. "You've got the powder?"

Vika nodded and produced a packet from her own pocket, while Leo dug through a drawer looking for a roll of tape. Inside the packet was a few grams of talcum powder. She carefully sprinkled the stuff over the surface of the desk, blowing the excess aside until she discovered a spot where Hal had pressed his entire hand down on the surface of the glass, the way he often did when he was leveraging himself out of his chair.

"Here," she said, pointing out a perfect impression of Hal's index finger. Leo pressed the piece of tape against the imprint in the powder, peeling away a perfect replica of Hal's fingerprint.

"Let's hope this thing works," he said and put the tape over the small scanner on the top of Maia's device. He pressed the button to activate it, and a bright purple light swept down the piece of tape. The device got warm, and then hot, in his hand, and he put it down on the desk as it clicked and whirred. Each second that ticked by seemed to last an hour, and Leo tried to remind himself that Ariel was keeping watch, that she would let them know if Hal was coming. Assuming she hadn't already been discovered herself. Hell's teeth, what if he had just led the two people he cared most about into disaster, what if this didn't work or they were caught or—

Suddenly the device went quiet, and a small slip of something that looked like plastic was spit out of the slit at its base. It was a perfect printout of Hal's fingerprint on razor-thin silicone. Leo stuck it to his own finger and held it above the biometric sensor on the holo.

"Here it goes," he said and pressed his finger to the sensor.

Moments later, the holo display lit up.

Vika exhaled. "Thank heavens."

Leo hurriedly explored the files on the holo, quickly zeroing in on a folder than contained all the drafts of Hal's will. There were actually six, dated from only days after the Gardners had received the fortune through earlier that week. Leo pulled up two: the one Hal had completed just before the airship crash and the new one that would go into effect soon. Vika leaned over his shoulder to read along with him.

"They've taken me out, all right," she said as she skimmed the words of the new will. "No mention of me at all."

In the earlier version Leo was looking at, Vika was to receive a hundred thousand bits when Hal and Mira died. He had known this, of course, but actually seeing the amount she'd thrown away on account of him, written out in black-and-white, was enough to make his head spin. The other recipients were mostly names Leo remembered from when he was assisting Hal. A few distant relatives and friends and then a slew of charities, none of which were included in his father's original will.

"*What?*" Vika suddenly exclaimed.

Leo glanced over his shoulder at her. She was staring, openmouthed, at the screen. "What is it?"

"It's Archer," she said. "Look, they replaced me with Archer!"

She pointed at one paragraph of the will, and he lined it up on the screen with the version he was reading. The texts were identical, except "Viktoria Hale" had been replaced with "Archer Sheratan." Leo pictured the big, self-satisfied smile of the man he'd just seen and . . .

And then he remembered exactly where he'd seen that smile before.

"The day I was fired," he said, "I bumped into him on the street outside of the building. I knew I recognized him but I couldn't place him at the time."

Vika's eyes widened. "Oh, stars above. That son of a bitch!" She balled her hands into fists like she was preparing to punch someone, but then her face crumpled and she opened her fingers to cover her face. "Oh, I'm such an idiot."

"What is it?" he asked.

She dropped her hands to look at him. "I told him. About the night you tried to kiss me. He was . . . he was the only real friend I had at the time and I was angry and confused. And he ran *straight* to Hal and told him all about it in order to get you fired."

"Why would he do that?"

"Don't you see? So that he could take your place," Vika said. "Become Hal's right-hand man. He's been cozying up to Hal, and probably undermining you, ever since the beginning."

Leo sank down into Hal's desk chair. He'd always assumed Vika had told Hal what had happened between them the night of Mira's name day party. As concerning as this revelation was, he was also a little relieved to know she hadn't been the one to give him up.

"Do you think that was his plan all along?" Leo asked. "To ingratiate himself with the Gardners and convince them to put him in their will?"

She nodded. "It's what I would have done in his position, so I'm sure of it."

There was a sudden pounding at the office door, and the two of them jumped. There was nowhere to run, with just the one entrance and a window that opened onto one hundred and twenty floors of open air. They were trapped.

"Let me in!" Ariel hissed from the other side of the door, and Leo sagged in relief.

Vika unlocked the door and Ariel threw it open, dragging another person inside after her, a young man dressed in rather shabby blacks who didn't seem to mind Ariel's manhandling.

Leo frowned as he recognized the other man's face from the countless times they'd spoken across the bar at the Thorn and Crown. "Merak?"

CHAPTER THIRTY-SEVEN

"HEY, SKY," THE YOUNG man dressed as a waiter said, Ariel's fingers still bunched in his shirt. "How's it doing?"

Vika looked over at Sky, whose confusion was written all over his features.

"What are you doing here?" he asked.

"Tell him," Ariel said.

The waiter—Merak, apparently—shrugged. "Me and some of the guys from the Thorn and Crown were hired to come work this party. What are you doing here?"

Vika's head began to spin. Why would someone hire the employees of a random Philomeni tavern to work a luxury party on Ploutos? There were dozens of agencies that specialized in providing workers for this kind of thing, highly trained staff who knew how to tell a salad fork from a dessert fork and which vintage of Demetriosi wine paired best with—

And then she realized. The Thorn and Crown *wasn't* a random Philomeni tavern. It was a PLF stronghold. And she was suddenly sure that each and every waiter in the building tonight who had been hired from the Thorn and Crown was a member of the Philomeni Liberation Front.

"What are you going to do?" she whispered, rage stealing her breath. "What are you planning for tonight?"

The young man looked at her in befuddlement. "Just serving drinks and stuff, the usual."

They'd killed Leo Chapin, thrown her life into turmoil, blown her out of the sky, and now they were coming for Mira.

"I don't believe you!" Vika said, lunging for him, her mind a white-hot blank as her instincts told her she had to stop this man.

But Sky caught her round her waist, swinging her away from the waiter. "Wait! Merak, you're not here for the PLF, are you?"

"What? No!"

"Liar!" Vika said. Sky's arms were like a band of iron round her waist, keeping her in place, but her blood was hammering through her.

Ariel put her hands on the man's shoulders. "Swear it, Merak. Swear to me this isn't some kind of op."

"No way!" he said. "It's just a waitering gig. We were hired by some rich guy's assistant to work the party, and it was good money."

Vika's rage flickered and then went out, like the power failing on Philomenus. Of course. Anger and panic had momentarily short-circuited her brain, but it *couldn't* be the PLF behind it all. They had no stake in who inherited the Chapin fortune, no ability to sabotage the Gardners' airship. Which meant . . .

Ariel turned to her and Sky, her eyes lit up with all the fire that had just left Vika. "They're being set up. Something's going to happen tonight, and whoever's behind it wants the PLF to take the blame. *Again.*"

"Archer," Vika said, feeling the floor tilt beneath her. "He told me he was helping with the arrangements for this party. He must have been the one who hired you. We know Hal wouldn't have deigned to do it himself."

"Archer's in the will now," Sky said. "If the Gardners die . . ."

Vika clutched her stomach as a wave of nausea rolled over her. "Oh stars. But . . . but he *can't* be the one behind it all! Hal's only just put him in the will. He didn't stand to gain anything when the *Leander* exploded or when the airship crashed."

Sky frowned. "You're right." He went round to the holo and pulled the documents back up. "The only entities who benefited from the *Leander* explosion that we haven't been able to identify yet are the Ploutosian Defense Fund, the Sagittarius Aid Society and—"

"Sagittarius?" Ariel said. "That was the name of one of the beneficiaries?"

Vika nodded. "It's a shell corporation. We haven't been able to find out who's really behind it."

Ariel fisted her hands into her hair and looked like she was torn between laughing and screaming. "Sagittarius? Hello?"

"What?" Sky said.

"Sagittarius is a constellation in the form of an ancient bowman," she said.

Sky went pale. "You mean an archer?"

She nodded. "Sound familiar?"

"Fecking hell," Vika breathed. *Archer.* The kind toser stranger who had comforted her when she'd fled to the roof of her building. Her charming, ambitious friend who was the only person on this planet she'd really understood, cause his hungriness for something better was the same as hers. The earnest, wide-eyed young man who'd told her he loved her and wanted her to be his wife.

"Bloody hell, we should have thought to consult a space pilot months ago," Sky was saying. "As soon as Archer found out the Gardners were about to replace the Chapin will with their own, which would remove Sagittarius from the equation, he tried to kill them in the airship accident."

Vika sank down into one of the chairs, but that wasn't low enough. She kept folding in on herself til her head was resting on her knees, each realization making her want to shrink even further. The dismissive way Archer had spoken to her at Mira's name day party, when he'd thought she'd be no more use to him, and how apologetic he had been afterward. How he'd comforted her on the roof the very first time they met by assuring her that she didn't have to marry Leo Chapin, that she could just walk away. Maybe if she'd put her foot down that day and refused to let herself be bought and sold like no more than a piece of furniture, the *Leander* would still be sailing and Leo would be disinherited but alive and well.

"Oh no," she said. *"No."*

Sky knelt beside her, drawing her face up with a gentle hand on her cheek. "What is it?"

Another memory was crashing over her, Archer's face looking so earnest as he told her he loved her and wanted to marry her. The guilt she'd felt at turning him down and breaking his heart.

"After the airship," she said. "When the Gardners put me in their will. Archer asked me to marry him."

"Bastard," Ariel said.

So much was churning through her gut that Vika felt like she would be sick. Betrayal, guilt for ever having suspected Hal of being behind this evil, worry for Mira, the stunning realization that she couldn't trust her own instincts about people, and the fact that yet another man had tried to cash her in as a chip in order to gain a fortune. It rose like bile in her throat, and she had to swallow once, twice, to keep it all down.

"When that didn't work," she whispered, "he used the information I gave him to get you fired and to get himself closer to the Gardners so that Hal would put him in their will."

"How did he end up in old Mr. Chapin's will in the first place?" Ariel asked.

"No idea but there's no time for that," Sky said. "We have to get the Gardners and everyone else out of here. Whatever he's planning, he's going to do it tonight and pin it on the PLF. We're all in danger."

The four of them rushed out of the office. Since Merak was the only one who was actually supposed to be at the party, he was tasked with finding Archer and keeping him from doing anything. Sky and Vika were going to look for the Gardners and explain to them what was happening, while Ariel was going to find the catering manager and make up some excuse for why they needed to start evacuating the penthouse. But as soon as they reached the parlor, they discovered that all of the guests, instead of milling about and mingling, were making their way into the ballroom. The current was so strong that it was pointless to fight against it, so they let themselves be pulled inside along with the crowds, hoping the people they were searching for would be inside as well.

The crowd of guests was gathering round the large table by the windows, the one filled with presents wrapped in brightly colored paper. The Gardners stood beside it, and as the guests looked on, they started to open one of the boxes.

"Mira!" Vika called, but her voice was lost in the din.

"Hey!" Merak said. "There!"

Vika followed where he was pointing. Archer was at the back of the ballroom, and instead of pressing forward like everyone else, he was heading for the door in the opposite direction. He glanced back, and their eyes met. For the first time, she truly saw him, and he saw her right back. They stared at each other for one brief moment and then both burst into action, Archer grabbing the attention of one of the security guards standing nearby, and Vika trying to get to the table of presents she was now *sure* contained a bomb.

"Sky, the presents!" she said.

He lunged toward the table but hands were suddenly on him from behind, and then on Vika as well, security guards seizing them.

"Get out!" Vika started shouting to the people round her, but then a hand came clapping down over her mouth. Her arms were pinned to her sides, and when she tried to kick, she was lifted off of her feet.

Meanwhile, even with two men trying to drag him back, Sky had wrestled his way to the front of the crowd. As he emerged from the group of guests, red-faced and dragging the security guards behind him, Mira gasped and almost dropped the present in her hand.

"Sky, what are you doing here?" she said.

"Mira!" He managed to get one arm free and grabbed her hand. "You have to get out here!"

"Take this man away!" Hal snapped. "Hail the constabulary and tell them we have a trespasser."

"No, you have to listen to me!" Sky said. The strength that had propelled him forward was giving out, and the guards began to drag him away. "You have to believe me, Mira, you're in danger!"

"Nonsense," Hal said.

"Oh, Sky," Mira said sadly. "Please don't do this."

As the guards hauled Sky backward, Hal turned to his goggling guests. "Everyone, please excuse the dramatics. Just a little trouble-making from a disgruntled ex-employee," he said. He retrieved a gift from the table and handed it to Mira. "Here you are, my love. Back to business."

"Stop fighting, girl," the guard holding Vika said as he dragged her toward the foyer. He was too strong, and she couldn't break free or cry out. Closer to the Gardners, Sky was struggling so violently with the guards holding him that she was afraid he would break his own arms. But no one was listening to Sky's warnings and Mira was unwrapping another gift and Vika didn't know what to do—

This was it. Time to make a choice, Ariel had said. Time to stop living in stasis, so sure that whatever he would do was wrong that he never did anything at all.

Time seemed to slow to a crawl around him. He looked over at Vika, struggling against the guard who held her in his arms. Flushed and panicked, and so, so beautiful, in the way that a person can only be in the moment before you're sure you're going to lose them.

Mira was still watching him, the shadow of a frown on her face, while Hal tried to get her to unwrap the cream-colored package with the bright red bow that was in front of them. Her eyes met his, but he couldn't run, couldn't grab her and drag her away from the table of presents.

There was only one thing he could think to do, one thing that might cut through all the noise enough for her to truly hear him and believe what he was saying, and for once in his life he didn't hesitate.

He clamped his teeth down on the hand of the guard who had covered his mouth. The man's grip loosened for just a moment, but that was all Leo needed.

"Mimi, it's me!" he yelled. "Run!"

Sky's shout sliced through the commotion, the sound of his voice so anguished that it cut through Vika like a knife. And there was something else—

Mira suddenly seized Hal, heaving him away from the gift table, the cream-colored package tumbling from his hands.

As it hit the floor, the gift detonated.

A fireball billowed out from the package, shattering the massive windows that looked out over the city. The explosion was so loud that it momentarily blocked out everything else, and everyone round her was frozen cept for Sky. He broke the grasp of the stunned security guards holding him and mowed through the cowering crowds to reach Mira and Hal, who had been blown off their feet. Smoke from the flaming remnants of the gift table rolled thick and black into the air, and people were screaming and running in all directions, some bleeding and burnt, a crush of bodies at the doors trying to get out while others were rooted into place, too stunned to move.

Vika slowly realized she was on the ground, not sure if she'd fallen or been pushed in the stampede, unsure of when the guard holding her had let her go. Her ears were ringing and she could feel hot tears sliding down her face. Not far from her, Mira had her arms round Sky, sobbing as she rocked him in her arms.

"Oh my boy, my boy," she kept saying. She took his face in her hands, pushing the hair out of his eyes. "It's really you? Heavens above, it's a miracle."

Mimi.

He'd called her Mimi.

Mira and Hal were safe. No one in the ballroom was dead. Archer Sheratan wouldn't get far.

But Leo felt the world crumbling around him, because Vika was staring at him with the worst kind of betrayal in her eyes, tears streaming down her cheeks.

Mimi.

Mimi.

Mimi.

Mira was still clutching Sky, crying over him, and Hal was staring at him in disbelief.

Cause Sky wasn't Sky.

Sky was Leo Chapin.

Suddenly Ariel was there at her side, trying to help her up off the ground. "Vika? Hey, are you hurt?"

"He's Leo Chapin," she whispered. "He's . . . he's . . ."

Ariel took her hand, pulling her to her feet. "It's going to be okay."

Merak and a couple more men dressed in black, no doubt his co-workers from the Thorn and Crown, dragged Archer back into the ballroom, which was now crawling with security guards. Through the open window, which howled with wind, Vika could hear sirens on the street below. Merak pushed Archer into the center of the room.

"Here's your bomber," he said. "Caught him trying to get away."

Suddenly Sky—Leo—whoever—was jumping to his feet and lunging at Archer.

"Leo, no!" Mira cried, and Archer's eyes went wide just before Leo fell on him, fists flying. They both went crashing to the floor.

"You son of a bitch!" Leo caught Archer in the jaw with a solid punch.

Archer was spitting and hollering obscenities as they wrestled. Vika couldn't make out most of it, but then—

"Damn you, you got everything"—he spat—"that should have been mine . . ."

Shock was descending over Vika's senses like the atmo-haze on Philomenus, but those words cut through like a spotlight, and suddenly things that had never made sense began to fall into place in her mind. How so young a man, barely out of law school, got such an important job at a prestigious law firm and was put to work on one of the biggest estates in the quadrant. Why Archer—stars, how had she not realized this at the time—had a photograph of himself with his father on his bookshelf when he had supposedly never known his father. Why Rigel Chapin would leave him money in his will but disguise it using a shell corporation so that no one would ever know. The eyes in the portrait beneath their feet and in the face of the man who'd tried to kill her the same cool shade of blue.

Archer had to be Rigel Chapin's son, too. An illegitimate child he had helped get a good job and left some crumbs to in his will but would never acknowledge.

"Fecking hell," Vika whispered. "They're brothers."

"What?" Ariel demanded, overhearing her. Her eyes widened with the same realization. She ran toward the fighters, pushing her way through the guards who were trying to separate them. "Leo, stop!" she said, grabbing his arm as he reared back for another punch. "He's your brother!"

He froze, looking up at Ariel in bewilderment, and the guards swooped in and seized them both, pulling them apart.

Soon the room was swarming with the constabulary. They cuffed Archer and led him out, while others fanned out to take the statements of everyone who'd been present. Vika sat by herself at one end of the room, someone's discarded coat draped over her shoulders. She kept her eyes down on the floor as she told the officer her story, only occasionally finding the strength to look across the room to where Mira and Hal were sitting with . . . him.

Mira was overcome, crying and sometimes laughing and never, never taking her hands off of him, so overjoyed that he was alive. Vika could see Hal trying to smile, trying to be happy, but the expression would falter as he realized his worst fear was coming true: the money was slipping away from him. He looked over at her, their eyes meeting for the briefest instant, and she looked away.

Ariel sat down beside her once the officer had left and handed her a glass of water.

"Are you going to talk to him?" she asked. "Maybe he has an explanation."

"You knew, didn't you?" Vika asked instead of answering her question. "You've always known."

Ariel sighed and nodded. "I was there when the *Leander* blew. I rescued him from the void."

Vika stood, dropping the coat. "Thanks for telling me the truth."

She crossed the room slowly, her joints feeling loose and watery beneath her. *He* scrambled to his feet as she approached.

"Vika," he said. "Please, let me explain—"

But she walked right past him, putting her arms round Mira.

"I'm so glad you're safe," she said. She glanced at Hal, then at him. "I'm leaving now."

She turned and walked away from them, finally done with it, done with it all.

CHAPTER THIRTY-EIGHT

LATER

"YOU DON'T HAVE TO do this, Mira. I renounced my inheritance for a reason," Leo said as the two of them walked into the Bank of Ploutos. The week before he'd told a judge he wouldn't abide by the terms of his father's will, forfeiting his claim on the Chapin fortune, and he had felt good about the decision. But as soon as the hearing had ended, Mira had told him she was turning the money over to him anyway.

"I know, my boy," she said, patting his arm, "but I'm giving it back to you for a reason as well. So respect your elders and stop arguing with me."

The process didn't take long. Their identification was checked, some papers were signed, some surprised looks were given to them, and then the fortune was transferred out of Mira's bank account and into Leo's. Most of it, anyway. Leo had insisted that she keep several million bits for herself. It was important to him that she would always be taken care of, and he wouldn't budge on that. As the transfer took place, Leo felt a little queasy, thinking of everything that wealth had come to represent to him. The way it had corroded Hal's good nature, the decadence of Ploutosian citizens while the people of Philomenus struggled to even put food on the table, the evil he'd seen done in pursuit of more money than one person could ever spend in their lifetime. How money had poisoned his relationship with Vika from the very start.

But he also heard Ariel in his head, calling him an idiot. Reminding him that money wasn't inherently bad. Prodding him to think of all the good that could be done with it, how many soup kitchens and clinics it could open, how much it could change the lives of the people he had lived among for so many months.

He kept thinking about that as he and Mira left the bank, strolling arm in arm down the sidewalk to a small restaurant by the park, and as a waiter laid a meal in front of him that he couldn't even remember ordering.

"Mimi," he said suddenly. "I have an idea."

She glanced up at him as she speared a tomato from her salad. "Yes, my dear?"

He took a deep breath. "I want to spend all of my money."

They ended up sitting at that restaurant table for almost four hours, coming up with the plan, sketching it out on napkins. First, Leo would give up the patent on his father's hydrino fission technology. He'd put it into the public domain so that any planet could build one for themselves and provide their citizens with abundant, free energy. But he would take a more active interest in Philomenus. It seemed like the least he could do, considering how his father had paved the way for the exploitation of that planet and given the love he had for so many people who lived on it. He would finance the building of a hydrino reactor there himself, freeing the planet from its dependence on dirty coltane that worsened the atmo-haze. He'd hire all the laid-off miners, and more besides, to work the new reactor and rebuild the limping power grid, and he'd pay them a good wage. He'd work with the Philomeni Liberation Front to get their soup kitchens and clinics, which had been shut down by the merc crackdown on the planet, back up and running with ample budgets to do their work. He'd pour millions more into the planet to build new homes and schools and vital infrastructure, like a spaceport of its own so that the people could legally import goods or afford to leave the planet if they chose to. When the people of Philomenus were no longer at the economic mercy of Ploutos, its grip on them would loosen. Eventually Philomenus would get its independence back.

"I did say I would pay the PLF back with interest," Leo said as they surveyed their napkins, Mira on her second round of dessert while he sipped his third cup of tea. "I hope this will fulfill that promise."

"I think it's a beautiful idea, darling," Mira said. "But are you absolutely sure you want to do this?"

"I'm sure," he said without hesitation. "I imagine it will be a much harder and messier process than it sounds and it may take the rest of my life, but I've never been more sure of anything."

"In that case," she said, "I believe this will be a lot of fun! It may not be exactly what your father expected when he spoke of the Chapin legacy, but it's so much better. *You* are so much better. I couldn't be more proud of you, Leo."

He dropped his eyes to the table, momentarily overwhelmed by her words. It wasn't approval from the parent he had always longed to receive it from, but perhaps this was better as well.

"I was also thinking," he said carefully, looking down at his tea as he gave it a stir. "I could give Hal a job overseeing some of the construction of the new reactor. A good job. It would mean he'd need to live on Philomenus."

Mira's face clouded over. She and Hal hadn't spoken, he knew, since the day she'd decided to give Leo his inheritance back. Legally the money was hers to do with as she pleased, but they'd had a screaming row when she'd told Hal her decision, and apparently their relationship had been on a knife's edge for years. The excitement of the money and their new life had papered over the cracks for a while, but that was over now.

"I think . . . that would be good," she said at length, and Leo nodded. Because of the love he still had for the man who had been so important to him as a child, he would make sure Hal made a good living and had a comfortable life. But he wanted that life to be far away from Mira's and his own.

"I'm going to need your help with all of this," he said. "I can't do it by myself."

"If only there was someone else with an intimate knowledge of Philomeni problems and a good head for money who could help as well," Mira said, glancing up at him over the rim of her coffee cup as she took a sip.

The feeling of missing Vika suddenly struck him like a rogue wave, choking his eyes and ears and lungs with stinging salt water. It was like this sometimes. He could go hours, maybe even a whole day, and the thought of her would only give him a dull stab of grief, but then other times it would knock him right off his feet.

"Oh, I'm sorry," Mira said, laying a warm, worn hand over his. "Have you spoken with her at all?"

"I've tried," he said. "She doesn't want to talk to me, and it seems the least I can do is respect her wishes."

Vika was in the cramped office at Nicky's, doing the figures for the month, when the juice suddenly sputtered out. A cry went out through the bar, but Vika grinned cause she wasn't out there dealing with frustrated drinkers who couldn't wait two minutes for the generator to switch on. She leaned back in the squeaky office chair to wait for the lights to come back so she could continue with the books. Numbers made sense to her and, unlike people, they didn't talk back.

Two days after the disastrous anniversary party at the Gardners', she'd walked into this office and demanded that Nicky give her this job. He hated doing the books and he was terrible at it, so he should just let her. She'd expected a fight from him, but he'd been happy to turn over his calculator and take his place back behind the bar. He hadn't known it then, but she'd learned a little something about business during her time on Ploutos, and she was going to change everything for him.

The first thing she'd learned: money makes money. She'd heard Hal say this more times than she could count. Why should he put so many bits into the Leo Chapin Foundation when he could be using that money to generate more bits of his own? If the bar wasn't always strapped by what cash they had on hand, they could make smarter decisions. Nicky was buying kegs of grock for a hundred bits as he needed them cause that was all he could afford, but if he had more cash, he'd be able to buy a hundred kegs at once for only ninety bits apiece. That meant a 10 percent increase on the all-important profit margin she'd learned so much about from hours of pretending to be interested in Mr. Keid. All he needed was someone who could bankroll the operation, and luckily Vika had just the someone in mind. In only a matter of weeks, she had streamlined the bar's inventory system, upped their average ticket by adding a few simple food options to the menu, and increased their overall margin by 14 percent. Nicky's was thriving cause of her, and she was earning a good wage without having to cater to the drunken whims of a single patron.

The lights came back on as the generator kicked in, and Vika glanced at the clock on the wall. Quitting time. She gathered her things and locked the office door behind her.

"You off?" Stella asked from behind the bar as she poured a glass of grock.

"Yeah," Vika said. "Remember to do a full count of the inventory before you cash out, okay? I know it an't fun, but it's important."

"No worries, I'll make this one do it." Stella nodded at the flustered new hire who was sweating as he tried to deal with the press at the bar.

Vika laughed. "See you tomorrow."

When she got home, she found that Ariel had already lit their oil lamp and a handful of candles. Their new flat, in a TH just down the road from 76, was the same size as the one Vika had lived in with her family, but with just the two of them, it felt practically palatial. Vika had the bedroom in the back all to herself, including a real bed she could stretch across in all directions, and Ariel, when she slept at all, had a bed in the front room that they'd hung curtains round to give her some privacy. Ariel had bought a couple of strings of twinkle lights and tacked them up over the windows, which gave the place a pretty, homey glow, at least when the electricity was working. Still, even in the dark and with the air growing hot and muggy without the fan to push it round, just being in this flat made Vika happy cause it was *hers.*

Ariel was sitting on the couch, a bowl of pasta in her lap. "There's more in the fridge if you want some," she said.

"Oh, great, thank you." Vika served herself a bowl. "You working tonight?"

Ariel shook her head. "Just going to visit my da."

"How's he doing?" Vika asked as she sat on the sofa beside her.

"He's all dried out," Ariel said, "so here's hoping he stays that way."

"Oh, before I forget." Vika grabbed a packet of bills from her bag and handed them over. "Here's your cut for the month."

Ariel put the money in her own bag. You wouldn't know it from the state of their flat, or Ariel's same old grease-stained trousers and worn leather boots, but the girl was a lady of means now. The reward for the capture of Leo Chapin's killer had been a hundred thousand bits, and Mira had decided that the person who'd saved Leo Chapin's life was close enough. Ariel had been overwhelmed, the money more frightening to her than anything else. She'd immediately handed half of it off to the PLF, her only condition being that they use some of it to open a rehab clinic to help her da and other people struggling like him. And she'd agreed to become an investor in Nicky's, letting Vika use some of her money to run the bar and collecting a percentage of the profits. Otherwise, she didn't seem to know what to do with her new wealth. She'd even stayed in her makeshift home in the machine parts factory til Vika asked her if she wanted to move in here with her, and she continued to salvage in the stream, even though she insisted that was just so she could keep her skiff for smuggling without arousing any suspicions. At least Vika didn't have to worry that money would change Ariel into some hard-hearted miser.

"I, um, got a new feed screen from Sullivan Street today," Ariel said. "Want to watch something?"

Vika's face lit up. "Good for you! It's about time you did something nice for yourself."

Ariel blushed and shook her head. "I don't know. I got a good deal on it."

"Well, let's see it!"

Ariel pulled the screen out of her bag, propping it up on the table and tuning in to a Ploutosian drama feed.

"It's a lucky thing it came with a full battery since these blackouts are getting ridiculous," Ariel said, slurping up a noodle. "I can't wait til they get that new hydrino reactor up and running."

Vika looked askance at her. "Don't."

"What?" she asked, the picture of wide-eyed innocence. "I just—"

"I know what you just, and I'm saying don't."

Vika focused on the characters on the screen and the pasta in her bowl and definitely not on thinking about Leo Chapin.

Once she'd finished her dinner, Ariel left to go visit her da. Vika was doing the washing up when there was a knock at the door. She frowned but figured it was her own da coming round for a visit, like he often did, cause otherwise she and Ariel rarely had visitors.

Maybe the last face she expected to see when she opened the door was Mira's, as bright and kind as ever. Vika's mouth dropped open and she threw herself into the woman's arms.

"Oh, Mira, I'm so happy to see you!" she said. "How are you?"

Mira gave her a squeeze and a kiss to the cheek. "I'm very well, my girl, how are you? Tell me everything."

"I'm good, come in!" Vika went to the stove to boil some water for tea while Mira sat down at their small table. "I have a new job that I'm really good at, if I do say so myself, so I actually sort of *enjoy* it. Never thought I'd say that about work."

"And you've moved," Mira said.

"Yeah, Ariel and I are living here together. Being an entire planet away from my family was too far and being in the same flat with them was way, *way* too close, but this is a good middle ground." Vika poured two cups and sat in the chair opposite Mira. "It feels . . . nice. Being in control of my own life for once, you know, making all my own decisions. Being independent."

Mira sipped her tea. "I know *exactly* what you mean."

"Oh, right." Vika winced. "I heard you and Hal split. I'm so sorry."

Mira waved the words away. "Don't be. I'm an independent lady now, too!"

Vika smiled and held out her cup. Mira clinked it with the rim of her own.

"So what brings you here?" Vika asked. "Not that I an't thrilled to see you, but I figure you must have a reason to come all this way."

"I wanted to give you something." She drew a small collection of papers out of her bag and handed them over. "I respect your decisions, Vika darling, I always have. But I think you have to have all the information in order to make the best ones."

"What is this?" Vika scanned the top of the first page. It was the transcript of some kind of legal hearing. "Oh fecking hell, Mira, I don't want to read this! I'm done with all this Chapin stuff."

"I know, I know. Just please take a look at the bit I marked."

Vika flipped through the pages til she found the section Mira had highlighted.

HJAK: Let me be clear. You wish to renounce the inheritance your father left for you in his will?

LC: That's right, Your Honor. My entire life my father tried to control me, because my own decisions were never good enough for him. Never strong or decisive or clever enough. I don't want to give him that power over me even in death.

HJAK: This is a significant decision, son. Are you entirely sure?

LC: I am. Even if I wanted that fortune, it would require me to hurt someone I love in order to claim it and I wouldn't–couldn't–do that to her. My father treated her like she was an object to be used in the power struggle between us, but she's not a thing. She's . . . she's an incredible person who deserves to be treated that way by everyone she ever comes into contact with. I've already hurt her in ways I can never atone for, but at least I can refuse to re-victimize her. So no, I have no intention of honoring the wishes of my father, who put her in this position in the first place. No amount of money is worth hurting the girl I love that way.

Vika couldn't read any further cause her vision was too blurry with tears. She could hear his voice in her head, so measured and kind, but also filled with more conviction and certainty than she'd ever heard in it in real life.

"He lied to me," she whispered. "About so many things."

Mira laid a hand over hers. "I know, and I understand if you can't forgive him for that. But he never lied about how he felt about you. I just thought you should know."

The building wasn't particularly noteworthy. It looked like any large office building that could be found in a dozen towns outside of Central City, gray stone facade with rows of windows. Except this building was several kilometers from the nearest town and it was ringed with thin, lighted towers every hundred meters that powered the invisible electric barriers that ensured that those held inside stayed inside.

Leo passed through several levels of security before he reached the visitation room. He'd set off on the journey to this place several times, always turning back before he reached it, but that morning he'd woken up and known it was time.

He hadn't told anyone he was coming, and he saw the uncertainty on Archer Sheratan's face as a guard ushered him into the holding room on the opposite side of the plastecene. Clearly he hadn't expected any visitors. His frown of confusion didn't immediately melt away when he saw that it was Leo waiting to talk with him. Now that Leo's hair and eyes were back to their natural color and he didn't have heavy-framed glasses perched on his nose, Archer probably didn't recognize him.

But a moment later he did, and all the blood drained from his face. He sank onto the stool in front of him like his knees had stopped working, and Leo could sympathize since his own pulse was racing through his veins.

Leo hit the two buttons on the wall beside him, one that opened up an intercom between him and the inner room where Archer sat and the other that created an inaudible sound interference that kept their conversation private.

"Hello," he said. All of his attempts to plan out this conversation in advance had failed him. Mostly he wanted to scream at this monster Archer Sheratan for all the death and destruction his selfish mission had caused. But there was also a small, sad part of him that wanted to embrace the other young man—the only family he had left—and to apologize that he'd been saddled with such a wretched father. To tell him how much he'd always wanted a brother.

So, "hello" it was.

Archer didn't seem to know what to say, either. Many tense moments passed before he said, "I . . . didn't expect to see you here."

"I wasn't sure I'd come," Leo admitted, looking into the familiar blue eyes of the young man in his prison whites. Eyes the same color as his own. He studied Archer's face, looking for other pieces he could recognize, trying to adjust his understanding of his life in order to find a place for this person to fit into it.

Archer seemed less interested in looking back at him. Maybe

because he'd spent his whole life seeing Leo, perfectly aware of the brother he had just the way the whole world was aware of Leo, the Chapin heir, the only son.

Instead Archer studied his nails with deliberate nonchalance. "Well, ask me your questions then. I assume that's why you're here."

Leo had a million. What Archer had hoped to accomplish, how he had done it, *why*. More than anything, why. But the question that came out of his mouth was the one he'd never had the bravery to even think to himself in all these weeks, although it had always been lurking there just beneath the surface, the vague and uncomfortable feeling of it making him pace his flat at night.

"Did . . ." Leo's voice hitched. "Did he love you?"

Archer was everything he wasn't, all the things his father had so desperately wanted in a son. Someone confident and decisive. Ambitious and charming and bold.

Ruthless.

Archer dropped his head. Whatever question he'd been expecting, it wasn't that. But his voice was steady when he looked up and said, "Yes. He loved me."

The way he said it, so sure, was like a white-hot dagger to Leo's heart.

"He taught me to read. He bought me a bicycle and taught me how to ride it," Archer continued, and Leo wondered if he knew how much it hurt to hear, if that was why he was saying these things. "After my mother died, I thought I would go to live with him, but he visited me and brought me gifts and made sure I went to the best schools. He said I was just like him. That he was proud of me."

Leo tried to swallow the hard, tight ball lodged in his throat before it could choke him.

"But you were still the one he chose," Archer continued, fixing a gaze that was as straight and piercing as an arrow on Leo. "Always you and never me because of his fortune and his legacy and his bloody fecking *name*. Because he loved those things more than he loved either of us. So I suppose we were both losers in the end, weren't we?"

For a moment, understanding passed between them, and they were both just their father's sons, molded by the same cruel hands into two very different shapes.

"I guess we were," Leo said, and he thought perhaps now he'd be able to put his father's ghost to rest.

Ariel couldn't take it anymore. Months of watching both of them pine for the other but unwilling to make the first move. It was the stupidest behavior she'd ever seen.

And apparently, as usual, it was down to her to fix it.

It was easy to do. She asked Seren to shut down the Thorn and Crown for a few hours, and he couldn't ever say no to her anymore. Leo was on Philomenus to see the progress being made on the hydrino reactor construction, and Ariel invited him to meet her for lunch. She convinced Vika to do the same. Now all she had to do was wait and it would happen, like two drifting moons pulled into the orbit of something larger than themselves.

Vika arrived first, and she frowned when she saw the empty tavern. "Where is everyone?"

Ariel shrugged. "Business is slow, I guess."

But Vika wasn't as stupid as her recent behavior suggested, and she didn't buy the weak explanation for a moment. "What are you doing?"

"Nothing!" Ariel said, fighting to hide her smile. "Come sit down."

Before Vika could, the doorway darkened as a familiar figure stepped inside. Vika turned, and for a long time the two of them just stared at each other. The air was thick and electric, time seeming to bend round them. Ariel wondered if they even remembered she was there.

Then, slowly, Leo stepped forward. His eyes were drinking Vika in like he had been lost in a desert and she was the only thing that could quench his thirst, but at the same time he looked terrified.

He extended his hand to her, and Ariel saw the faintest tremor in his fingers.

"Hello," he said. "I'm Leo Chapin."

Vika took him in, the dusty-colored hair and blue eyes, the straighter set of his shoulders, the desperate expression he was trying so hard to contain. A faint frown creased her brow, and Ariel honestly didn't know if she would punch him or kiss him, or maybe both. Ariel held her breath, waiting to see what Vika would do.

Then she reached across the distance between them and took his hand. "Vika Hale."

Leo's face broke into a tremulous smile. His fingers curled round her hand and he breathed, "It's very nice to meet you, Vika."

Vika nodded, her own expression serious but her hand still resting in Leo's. "I look forward to getting to know you, Leo."

Ariel exhaled, cause she knew, seeing the way they looked at each other in that moment, that those two were as inevitable as gravity.

ACKNOWLEDGMENTS

PUTTING A NOVEL INTO the world requires a group effort, and there are many people who were instrumental in getting this one out there.

First of all, I can't say thank you enough to my frankly superhuman agent, Jim McCarthy. His unwavering support and savviness have made all the difference for me in this business, and I feel so safe knowing he always has my back. Plus, the rumors are true: he really is the nicest guy in publishing.

In addition, I'm tremendously grateful to my wonderful editor, Jennie Conway, for believing in this book and seeing its potential at a time when I honestly didn't think anyone would. The entire team at Wednesday Books—including but not limited to Rivka Holler, Sarah Bonamino, Kerri Resnick, Sara Goodman, and Eileen Rothschild—has been amazing, both in the incredible work they do and also in supporting me and this book.

Profound thanks also go to my writing family: the people of Wordsmith Workshops and especially my indispensable better half, Beth Revis. The friendship, encouragement, inspiration, and gossip you've all provided me over the past six years have meant the world to me, and I'm grateful every day to have you guys in my life. I'm genuinely not sure how I would have coped with drafting this behemoth during the first months of lockdown without you to cheer me on/bully me to continue. I adore you all, and I can't wait to start our cult.

And finally to my family for always believing in me, supporting me, and encouraging me to dream big. I cannot adequately express my gratitude in words. I love you guys more than anything.

And thank *you* for reading!